THE SECRET THIEF

NINA LANE

SNOW QUEEN
PUBLISHING

The Secret Thief

Published by Snow Queen Publishing

Cover photography: Sara Eirew
Cover design: RBA Designs

ISBN: 978-1-7360527-4-7

For my family

Fairy tales are more than true:
not because they tell us that dragons exist,
but because they tell us that dragons can be beaten.

—Neil Gaiman
(based on a sentiment by G.K. Chesterton)

PROLOGUE

*T*he jagged, rocky coastline spills into the ocean as if it's
breaking apart. Trees stud the cliffs sweeping downward to the water's edge, the striated patterns of the slate
bedrock crafted through centuries of pounding waves and rough
weather. Gray-black clouds bruise the sky, throwing shadows
over the sea.

I hike through the wet grass, navigating around rocks. My
breath comes in fast puffs of white. I've only been in Maine for
seven days, having arrived near the end of September, but
already I feel winter approaching.

After crossing a sedge-covered path, I stop at the base of a
sharply graded hill. A crumbling stone wall climbs up the hill and
across the edge of the cliff. Just beyond it, the Castille Lighthouse
sits overlooking the ocean like an eagle in an aerie.

The conical tower, dating to 1843, is made of white stone and
topped with an octagonal iron lantern. I can easily imagine the
light appearing on a dark horizon, a harbinger to weary sailors of
firm ground; hot, comforting food, and tranquil sleep.

A two-story keeper's cottage hugs the side of the tower,
making the structure resemble an oddly shaped teapot. A modern

addition is attached to the western side of the cottage, probably an expansion of the living quarters.

I've heard a man lives in the lighthouse, a caretaker of the grounds and the nautical history display. Likely a grizzled old fisherman who's lived in Castille his whole life and enjoys chatting about his youthful days lobstering on the open seas.

A cold morning wind rustles across the valley, plastering my thin suede trench coat to my body. Shivering, I hitch my satchel strap higher on my shoulder and push my hands into my pockets. The coat and my heeled leather boots have served me well during cool Southern California days, but soon enough I'll have to exchange them for a fleece-lined parka and insulated snow boots.

I trudge up the hill, my head bent. My boots slip on the damp, mossy rocks and grass. The sharp wind loosens my ponytail and lashes strands of damp red hair around my face.

Finally I reach the crest, which flattens into a grassy plateau stretching toward the cliff's edge. My heart hammers. Clearly I've underestimated both my utter lack of fitness and the steep grade of the hill.

As I catch my breath, I peer at the lighthouse close-up. The surrounding grounds are tidy and well-kept, with a half-moon flagstone terrace and flower boxes. A smaller building housing a nautical history exhibit is set a distance from the lighthouse.

The stone wall borders the cliff like a rim on a dinner plate. The rough-hewn granite rocks, stacked like firewood and weathered from the sea, have been there since the lighthouse was built.

According to the locksmith who'd installed deadbolts in the doors of my inherited old house, no one knows how the stone wall came to be the keeper of secrets.

But it is. For decades, the notches between the stones have held countless scraps of paper—everything from index cards to thick pieces of vellum to old receipts—on which visitors have scrawled secrets.

Some might be innocuous enough: *I stole a piece of my kid's*

Halloween candy. I only dated him because I liked his dog. I don't recycle. Others are likely more sinister in tone: *I want to leave my husband. I'm in love with my best friend's wife. I lost my scholarship and can't tell my parents.*

Everyone leaves secrets in the wall, the locksmith had told me. Townspeople, tourists, visitors from neighboring towns.

Now, as a new resident of Castille, I suppose I should carry out the ritual myself.

But what secret to leave? I'm not sure I have any left. All of my secrets have been exposed and thrown around with malicious gossip.

I had an affair with a married man.

I destroyed my career.

I'm scared my life is ruined.

I don't recognize myself anymore.

I sit on a wooden bench and pull my organizer and a pen from my satchel.

What is a secret, really? Something meant to be kept unknown from others. But how many people need to know before it's no longer a secret? Is it only a secret if we keep it entirely to ourselves, not divulging it to anyone or anything? Not even a pile of old rocks?

I open the planner to the note pages in the back and scribble the only secret I can think of, then tear the sheet of paper out. Feeling a bit silly, I walk to the edge of the cliff. I fold the paper into a tiny square and kneel to shove it deep between two boulders in the wall.

I straighten and stand. I don't feel much different, not as if I'm suddenly unburdened or lighter. But maybe as my secret disintegrates into the old stones, it will have less hold on me. Maybe it will even change.

As I turn back toward the path, I glance up at the lighthouse tower. Behind the smoky glass surrounding the tower on all sides, the indistinct figure of a man stands.

Though his image is blurred, his stance is wide and secure, his arms appearing crossed over his chest. He's still as a rock. I can't see his face, but I have a strange, sudden sense that he's watching me.

My heart thumps. A shiver races down my spine. I grab my satchel from the bench and hurry away, almost running down the path in my haste to escape.

Fiamma.

She opens like a canvas sail in his mind. A bird spreading wings of red and gold. Razor-sharp feathers, golden talons. Fierce, untrusting, wild.

Fucking perfect.

She's an outsider. She's wearing a thin trench coat and stylish leather boots that are no match for the coastal Maine weather. Her profile is sharp—straight nose, firm jaw, long, slender throat. The wind whips her shoulder-length hair around her face. It's dark red, the color of rust, copper, the powdered dust of burnt sienna.

Fiamma.

She's the first spark in years. The one who will set his world on fire.

CHAPTER 1

*O*nce upon a time, I learned that beauty and happiness exist alongside blood and death. I learned that good often fails, people will shape-shift into a lie, and desire can be predatory and dangerous. I learned there is often a happy ending…but not always and not for everyone.

My uncle was the wizard who honed these truths for me on the sharp edges of fairy tales. Seated in his worn leather chair, his deep-set eyes squinting behind his glasses, he brought unreal worlds to life and populated them with ogres, talking horses, and water sprites who live in enchanted forests and atop glass mountains.

In such lands, rose gardens are spiked with thorns, curses fly like arrows, and the forbidden becomes unbearably tempting. Mothers are dead or absent, stepmothers are evil, and girls run away to escape the twisted lust of their fathers or the unwanted advances of would-be suitors. And because the veil between everyday life and the realm of magic is thin enough to be transparent, these runaway girls transform into cats, bears, and donkeys, enveloping themselves in animal skins to hide.

For months, I've wished that, like Preziosa, Allerleirauh,

Maria, Catskin, running away will somehow transform me into someone, or some*thing*, else entirely.

Unfortunately, thirty-three years of life have also taught me I can't rely on spells or curses to right the wrongs I've done and that have been done to me.

I also don't live in a fairy tale. My father died when I was four, my mother is the wicked queen, I've never met an animal that talked, and the last rose garden I tried to cultivate had gotten infested with aphids.

But oh, how I miss Uncle Max's tales of wonder with a ferocity that still takes my breath away. He succumbed to cancer a year ago, a battle valiantly fought and lost. The only comfort I've found in his death is that he's not here to witness my spectacular downfall from an esteemed UCLA art history professor into a vilified whore exiled from her job and home.

I've landed—or rather, shipwrecked—here, in this small town on the Maine coast where the only things of value I have are the old house my uncle left for me and a nest egg that won't last long.

I slip my keys into my purse and walk toward the turn-of-the-century Seagull Inn, which also houses the most acclaimed restaurant in town. A covered porch sprawls around the perimeter of the Georgian mansion, and towers jut up at various angles.

As I enter the restaurant, my body closes in on itself like an oyster, tightening and snapping shut. All day, my brain has refused to focus on anything except a strategy for defense. Excuses, explanations, and apologies roll and pitch in my head, none of them anchoring.

The stark fact is: I have no strategy for defense, not about this. I never have.

"Eve Perrin," I tell the host at the front counter. "I have a six o'clock reservation for two."

"Sure. Please follow me."

Picking up two menus, he leads me through the dining room

to a table by the window. Floral paintings adorn the papered walls, flowers bloom from vases, and mismatched china plates decorate the calico-draped tables. Well-dressed couples and families enjoy their meals and conversation.

After declining the host's offer of a drink, I go to the restroom to freshen up. I've armored myself in a white tailored blouse and gray tweed suit—the skin of a conservative, well-behaved daughter—with a pencil skirt that falls to my knees in a smooth line. My suede pumps match my coat, and I've pulled my shoulder-length reddish hair into a tight chignon that intensifies my cheekbones and the lines of my face. If nothing else, I look like a plainer version of my mother, which means she'll be forced to acknowledge I'm still her daughter.

Much as she might wish otherwise.

I return to my table, sitting down just as a prickle of awareness skates over my spine.

My mother enters the room. Her blonde hair is swept into a flawless French twist, and her slim figure is encased in a powder-blue linen sheath and matching cashmere sweater. Cosmetics enhance her porcelain skin and features. She looks like a fashion model, a wealthy wife, a philanthropist.

She is none of those things. She's a neurosurgeon, one of the top in her field of neuro-oncology and the head of the Stanford Neurology Department. She has a mile-long list of publications, awards, academic appointments, and fellowships, and she's earned every one of them through both brilliance and intensively hard work.

As she approaches, my chest fills with a tangle of emotions—love, pride, envy, desperation, anger. I rise, and our right hands extend simultaneously. She turns her face so I can brush my lips across her smooth cheek.

"I don't have a great deal of time." She sets her Prada bag on an empty chair and takes her seat. "I have a consultation at

Boston Medical Center tomorrow morning, and I need to review the patient's files."

I suppress the urge to remind her she'd been the one to suggest we have dinner. Three months ago—the last time we'd communicated—she'd told me she would be in Boston for a few days en route to Berlin, and she would come to Castille to meet me.

Even if it had been a request rather than an order, I'm in no position to refuse. She knows that, too. She knows everything.

"God." She glances around, her mouth twisting with distaste. "It's like a Victorian duchess threw up in here."

One of the women at the next table glances at us. I give her a weak smile of apology.

"It's supposed to be the best restaurant in town," I tell my mother.

"That's not saying much, is it?" She instructs a nearby server to bring her a glass of pinot grigio, then slips her sweater from her shoulders.

"I've taken a position on the board of directors of the Association of Neurosurgery." She opens her menu. "So I'm giving the keynote speech at the congress."

I deflect the pointed undercurrent of her announcement—the one reminding me she's the brightest star in her field at the exact moment I've flamed out in mine.

"That's great," I say mildly. "Congratulations."

She lifts a shoulder and levels her green gaze on me. "So you're settled in Max's house? Have you found a job yet?"

"Yes and no."

"You'd better get started." She places a pair of Tom Ford reading glasses on her nose and skims the menu. "You can't exactly live on your savings."

As if that's news to me.

Though I've been frugal with my finances over the years, my

nest egg has been depleted by legal fees and fines. I'd never intended to tap into my investments, but I'd had no choice. I'd used some of the money Max had left me to pay for my cross-country move, and what's left won't last long. I need a job, or I'll soon be broke.

Juliette studies me over the tops of her glasses. "How long do you intend to stay in this town?"

"I don't know. At least I have a place to live, thanks to Max."

At least I'll be close to him in spirit there.

I don't bother telling my mother that. She'd always found Max, and his interests, rather ridiculous. Her quixotic, absent-minded uncle who lived in a world of gingerbread houses and enchanted forests where he couldn't be bothered with the practical things in life.

That was one reason why, after Max's death, Juliette had auctioned off the vast collection of fairy tale books, paintings, illustrations, and manuscripts he'd spent almost his entire life compiling.

As usual, I'd been unable to stop her. Now the collection is gone, sold through Sotheby's to the highest private bidder. Just one more thing I've lost.

Silence falls between me and my mother until the server stops beside our table. After we place our orders, Juliette takes a sip of wine.

"Awful." She makes a face and pushes the glass away. "I suppose a ridiculous little town like this is a perfect place for you to hide."

My chest tightens. I dislike the idea that I've been reduced to *hiding*, but it's the painful truth. I've run away, and now I'm hiding in the hopes people will finally leave me alone. That *he* will leave me alone.

"Have you spoken to Graham recently?" Juliette asks.

"Yes. He said he'd let me know if he hears of any art history job openings."

"I still don't know why he bothered coming to your defense. I hope you appreciate him sticking his neck out for you."

"Of course I do."

"If you'd been one of my students, I'd have dropped you faster than you can blink."

"You did anyway, didn't you?" I'm unable to keep the caustic note from my voice.

Juliette studies me, her lips thinning in the way I recognize all too well. I've seen it enough times over the years. One would think I'd be immune to my mother's disapproval by now, but the opposite has happened.

As I worked my way through undergrad and graduate school, I'd become more and more vulnerable to her barbs and judgment. After receiving my PhD in the History of Art from Yale, I'd scored a coveted assistant professorship at UCLA. That, I'd believed at the time, was certain to impress even Juliette Perrin, renowned and seminal neurosurgeon.

I still don't know if it had impressed her, though. Five years later, my career is on life support, and I'm boiling with shame over my spectacular recklessness and stupidity. Facing my brilliant, contemptuous mother is part of my penance.

"I've heard people are curious about you and Graham." Her eyes are like pieces of sea glass. "Most advisors would wash their hands of a student who behaved as idiotically as you did."

The slight doesn't affect me as much as the thought of Graham, who advised and guided me through six years of PhD research and writing, taking heat for having been the one person in the world to defend me. I grip the paper napkin in my lap.

"There has never been anything untoward between me and Graham."

Juliette rolls her eyes slightly. "And you think your word is enough for me to believe you? What about Graham's wife?"

"Mary knows perfectly well Graham and I are friends and colleagues only," I reply coldly. "Even if *you* don't trust my word,

Graham is honorable to the core. He would never betray his wife."

"I'm sure that's what people said about…what was his name again?"

Bitch. She knows his name perfectly well. Everyone does. He's the one who was so badly wronged by an obsessed female professor twenty years his junior.

I suddenly wish I'd ordered a glass of wine…no, whiskey.

Juliette tilts her head toward me, the silence so portentous I have no choice but to fill it with the response she demands.

"David." His name cuts my tongue with bitterness.

"Oh, yes." Juliette arches a brow. "I suppose people believe that a woman who chooses to have an affair with a married man is stupid enough to repeat her mistakes."

I clench my teeth. A familiar tightening of my jaw warns me of impending tears, but I can control those. I've spent a lot of time battling back tears, refusing to give my adversaries evidence that they'd broken me.

"I didn't know he was married." I keep my voice low, but the words are glass crushing in my mouth.

How many times have I said that to myself? To others? It became my lifeline, the only thing I could cling to when my world crashed down around me.

The server stops by our table and deposits salads in front of us, his expression impassive.

"For God's sake, Eve," Juliette snaps. "You can tell yourself that as much as you like, but you're stupider than I thought if you believe it. How could you not have known your *lover* was married?"

My body goes numb, only a burn of embarrassment rising as the server glances at me and departs. I've asked myself that question countless times too. My only answer had been *"naïveté,"* which still rings hollow in my head.

"I just…didn't."

Or did I?

I'd been prudent with boyfriends throughout my twenties, choosing young men who were studious and practical about their lives. Juliette had never married my physician father, and he'd died in a car accident when I was four. My memories of him are faint at best. By contrast, I've spent my whole life in my mother's shadow, trying to earn her approval. That reward is not to be won by having rich, passionate relationships that expose all of one's vulnerabilities.

Still, even with a lack of romantic experience, I should have been astute enough to read David's clues—if he'd given me any.

"I didn't know," I repeat, more to myself than to Juliette.

"Liar." The word snaps out of her like breaking ice. "What were you trying to prove? Do you know how many people coveted the position you held? You were on the path to a well-regarded career. Instead you ruin your life by fucking around with a married man...who had *children*, for the love of Christ. Don't you dare shirk blame by claiming you didn't know he was married."

But I didn't know. Did I?

Shit. I stare down at my plate, fighting the sharp sting behind my eyes. I can't stop it, the barrage of images, the incessant rehashing of the two months during which I'd let the handsome older professor into my life, my bed.

"He had an apartment." My breath hitches. "His own, right in Westwood Village. There was no sign that...no ring or even a line where a ring would have been. He didn't have any personal social media sites, and there was nothing in his official biographies about a wife or family. I used his cell phone numerous times, and there was nothing on it that led me to believe he was lying to me. We...we went out..."

"Right, and I'm certain you stayed in a lot too." Juliette curls her lip. "You lived in Los Angeles, you idiotic girl. You could have gone out every night of the week and not run into anyone either of you knew. But more often he suggested you both snuggle up in your apartment, didn't he? He knocked on your door with a bottle of wine and a smile. Next thing you knew, you were letting him do whatever he wanted to you."

Her assessment is not far from the truth. Back then, I'd seen David as a welcome respite at the end of a painful journey.

A year ago, in the midst of watching Uncle Max disintegrate under relentless chemo treatments, I'd been exhausted by weekly trips to San Francisco to visit him combined with the pressures of my tenure-track position. I was a young professor, still needing to prove myself to my esteemed colleagues and the department's students. I couldn't let anything slide.

Juliette had orchestrated the medical side of the situation from afar—calling upon her colleagues, sending in troops of specialists to review Max's case. She'd viewed his illness with the same clinical detachment as she did her neurosurgery patients, but I've no doubt that her influence bought him more time than he'd otherwise have had.

Max had had an endless stream of visitors—friends, students, colleagues. But no other family. Only Juliette ensuring no medical stone was left unturned, and only me to deal with the messy practicalities of everything else.

Two days after Max told me he was stopping chemo, I'd been sitting in a campus coffeehouse, trying to focus on work through my grief. I'd looked up from my laptop to find a silver-haired, handsome man two tables away watching me with an intent, almost predatory air. That look broke through the shell in which I'd been living, resonated through the deep, dark well inside me.

He moved to sit at my table, his hand extended, his smooth voice rolling over me as he introduced himself as a professor of corporate finance at the School of Management. Only later when I'd looked up his faculty profile—after I'd accepted his offer of lunch the following day—did I discover the level of his esteem as a professor, investment consultant, and author.

Yes, I was impressed by his credentials and by him. Even more, I was flattered by his interest in me, an assistant art history professor who was just starting to make her mark. Our affair was a welcome escape from the pain of losing my uncle, a buffer against the shock of realizing I had no one left in the world except my mother, and that there was so little I could do in the face of her power.

I did have control over what I did with David, however. With him, I regained a sense of security, of grounding. He was suave and polished, a man who'd attained the pinnacle of success in his field. He knew so much about politics, the stock market, mutual funds, art investments. He was a highly skilled lover who assured me I was doing everything right, both in and out of the bedroom. I was lulled into a welcome security and physical satisfaction, not realizing until it was too late that I was also being deceived, misled, lied to…

…or was I?

Had I really missed any sign that he was married? A secretive phone call, a brief look on his face as he typed out a text? Had I not wondered why he sometimes cancelled our dates, claiming work as an excuse?

But why wouldn't I have believed him? He had so many students, papers, meetings, lectures. Of course he was swamped with work.

And when he made time for me? All I thought about was how good it felt to be with someone who liked being with me, with no weighty expectations or demands, no need to think about anything but pleasure.

"Face it, Eve." Juliette drops her fork and reaches for her sweater. "Any intelligent woman would have figured it out. Instead you chose to stay and demean yourself for him. If you had been the only one affected, then fine. Do as you please and face the consequences. But you never gave one thought to how your actions would affect others, did you? Not even after your humiliating comeuppance."

I push my plate away. "Why did you come here? So you could lecture me about being stupid and naïve?"

"To tell you to get to work salvaging your career." Her voice rises. "You'll always be the woman who fucked around with a married man and paid the price, but you can rise above your reputation if you do something about it. I will not have you sitting around this shithole town, wasting your education and the opportunities you were given. So figure it out. Write a paper, apply for professorships, attend conferences. By the time you leave here, the whole mess will have died down and you might still stand a chance of having a decent career."

Her lips compress. "Despite your naked slut pictures that will live in infamy on the internet."

The people at the tables around us have gone oddly quiet. My heart hammers. Panic spreads through my veins, burns my face.

Naked slut pictures. Jesus Christ. What if—

Juliette stands, pinning me with her gaze like a butterfly to a mounting board. "If you ever again do something to tarnish my reputation, or Graham's for that matter, *or* that of your former colleagues, I will wash my hands of you for good. Perhaps I should have already done that. Try and stay out of the gutter, Eve."

She strides away, electricity crackling in her wake. The people around us turn back to their dinners, conversation humming. I take a deep breath and force the anger down deep where it will fester and burn like it always does.

I am Eve Perrin, gifted art historian and scholar who was offered graduate scholarships to Yale and Princeton and had her pick of three prestigious professorships before she'd been awarded her doctoral degree. I've lectured at international universities, I have publications in every major art history journal, and I've consulted with museum curators all over the world. I'm a goddamned prodigy.

Rather…I *was.*

I still can be again. A tiny gleam of determination flares. Everything inside me is battered and bruised—my heart, my soul, my ego, my trust—but my intellect is still intact. Though I haven't pursued anything scholarly or academic in over a year, I'm still an art historian. Still good.

Reaching for my coat, I catch the eye of an older man seated at the opposite table. A sick feeling rises to my throat at the look in his eyes, a mixture of intrigue and sly hunger. Like he thinks he knows exactly what kind of woman I am. The kind men like to use.

I pay the bill quickly with my overloaded credit card, then grab my coat and purse. Hurrying from the room as fast as I can, I wish I could run and run and keep running.

CHAPTER 2

*U*ncle Max's fairy tales gave me an early romantic view of old buildings—houses where sweet, pretty girls live before being cast into daring adventures; castles populated by kings and queens; forest cottages owned by woodcutters and cobblers. I love stories in which houses are almost another character. Manderley, the Burrow, Villa Villekulla, Miss Havisham's mansion, the Gingerbread House.

When I was born, Uncle Max had willed to me the house he'd owned in Castille and a collection of two dozen rare books and paintings. Over the subsequent thirty-three years, his collection grew into the vast library that my mother auctioned off after his death, and I assumed he'd sold the house fourteen years ago when he moved to San Francisco.

So when I'd discovered he'd still owned the old Colonial house, a deep, tender nostalgia struck me. My uncle's old home, where the walls resonate with his presence and the air whispers about magic spells and golden eggs, now belongs to me.

I had never seen the house. Growing up, my mother refused to let me visit "the backwoods of Maine," so I only saw Max during the months he spent in San Francisco. But after the catastrophe with David left me jobless and unable to afford the rent on my LA apartment, Max's house became a beacon pulling me to Castille.

I imagined it as a sheltering haven where I could put myself back together, find my strength again, start fresh. Maybe I'd even give the property a name, like *Eve's Nest* or *Fairy Hollow*.

So I arrived—emotionally ready, but in reality completely unprepared for the state of the place. Situated at the end of a narrow drive just outside of Castille, the decrepit house is bordered by an expanse of public woodlands on one side and an ancient shed on the other. If it were restored properly, the house would be beautiful—a grand white Colonial with a gambrel roof and symmetrical windows perforating the façade.

But Uncle Max's former house is the opposite of *restored*. The paint is peeling, the floorboards are warped and creaky, drafts slither through the cracked windows, and I still haven't cleaned all the mildew and cobwebs. In the ten days that I've been here, I've heard a rustling in the walls that I've been attempting to attribute to ghosts rather than living rodents.

I had a contractor come out to get the lights, water, and heat working, such as they are, but the bill made me wary of hiring professionals to do much of anything else.

Which is why I find myself staring at an ancient toilet, which is hissing and gurgling as if it has indigestion. I take the lid off and peer into the entrails. Rusty pumps and levers, greenish-brown water, a slimy-looking inflatable thing.

Now what?

I swipe the screen on my phone to display the "How to fix a toilet" website I've pulled up.

Inspect the float—must be the slimy thing—*and inlet valve.*

Wincing only a little, I stick my hand into the gross water and lift the lever holding the "inlet valve." The website says the running water should stop. It does not.

I adjust the "float arm" with a screwdriver, but the toilet

continues to rumble and gurgle. I experience a brief but intense longing for Chuck, the maintenance guy from my LA apartment who, in my estimation, was Dumbledore's equal when it came to fixing pretty much anything with sorcery.

After another unsuccessful few steps, the website informs me I need to replace the "ballcock." As if I haven't had enough of ball-cockage in recent months.

I turn on the sink taps and rinse my hands in the freezing water before descending the wooden staircase to the first floor.

I don't love facing a mountain of repair work, but I'm grateful for the house. Even though it creaks and groans like an old ship rolling over the sea, the rickety Colonial is my new home.

Even more, it's the one thing in the world that's actually *mine*. One of the few things I have left.

Aside from clothes and my favorite tea sets, I'd sold most of my belongings before moving since I didn't want to pay the cost of shipping. That turned out to be a wise decision considering the bills I've already had to pay. The house still has a few pieces of old wooden furniture—table, dressers, night stands, cabinets—which are fine for my needs right now.

I take my organizer off one of the dozen or so cardboard boxes stacked in the living room. The boxes contain the fairy tale books and paintings Uncle Max had willed to me. Though the collection my mother auctioned was much bigger, at least I still have something to represent my uncle's passion for fairy tales.

Eventually, I'll organize the books on the built-in shelves of the living room and choose paint colors based on the aesthetics of the artwork.

But first things first. *Find a job.*

And: *Buy a ballcock.*

Well, *figure out what a ballcock is.*

After spending so much time in the ivory tower of academia, it's past time for me to start handling the practical things in life.

I sketch out a *To Do* list in my planner, then head outside into the gray morning.

The woods bordering the house scent the air with pine and the mossy smell of undergrowth. I've always loved forests—Uncle Max and I spent many happy hours traipsing among the California redwoods—and the woodlands are like a gate keeping the world away.

A sudden animalistic growl breaks my thoughts. A large mixed-breed dog that looks to be part German Shepherd stands at the corner of the house, ears flattened back and teeth bared. Yellow eyes fixed on me.

Fear quickens my heart. I can't tell if he's wearing a collar or not. He barks, deep and sudden. I back toward my car, reaching slowly for my phone in case I need to call for help.

Before I can take it out, he barks again and races off in the opposite direction. Relieved, I get into the car. I'll find out about the humane society or animal control in town.

I drive to Lantern Street, the main road cutting through downtown. Settled in the seventeenth century, Castille wears its past in the old homes and churches bordering narrow, tree-lined streets, the signs marking historic sites, the festivals and farmers markets. The brick buildings of Ford's College sit in the center of town, a visual reminder of Uncle Max's twenty-five year position there as a literature professor.

There are far worse places I could hide. Lined with cafes, restaurants, a historic inn, gift shops, and art galleries, downtown Castille has a quiet charm that I can certainly use right now.

I'm safe here too. No one—David and his arsenal of lawyers, his vindictive wife, the administration, the reporters—knows I moved to small-town Maine. Even if it wouldn't take much to find me, they don't have a reason to anymore. They defeated me already, and they know it.

But there is a way to come back from defeat. I just need to figure out how.

Since I don't have internet, and the cell service at Ramshackle Manor is spotty at best, I stop at the library to use one of their computers. After sending a message about the growling dog to the humane society, I print out copies of my curriculum vitae and make a list of possible job openings in town.

The college art library, an architectural firm, the high school. Anything to keep me in the art history field so I can find a way back to my career. Given what happened, it won't be easy, but all I need is a chance to prove myself.

Heartened by the possibilities, I leave the library and walk to a modern art gallery. A woman with a narrow, Picassoesque face glances up from a sleek computer.

After introducing myself, I extend my CV. "I recently moved to Castille and am looking for an arts-related job. I have a PhD in Art History with a specialty in nineteenth-century European art, but I've taught classes on everything from ancient Greek to American art. I'd love to find out if you have any openings."

She scans my qualifications without expression. "One moment, please, Dr. Perrin."

After rising from the desk, she walks back to where a tall, slender man is directing the installation of an abstract painting. She hands him my CV and gestures toward me. The man glances in my direction. They converse.

Something about their interaction unsettles me. Raised eyebrows, narrow glances, a sudden laugh. The woman grabs my papers from the man and strides back to me.

"I'm sorry." She extends the papers. "We're not looking to hire anyone."

Well, then, what the fuck was that about? They hadn't had time to do an internet search on me.

I smile tightly and take my papers back. "Thanks for checking."

Straightening my shoulders, I walk to another gallery specializing in nineteenth and twentieth century East Coast artists. The owner, a woman with a streak of blond cutting through her gray hair, introduces herself as Sarah Ellington.

"Impressive credentials," she says after perusing my CV. "We could use another person on the floor. Can I get back to you tomorrow?"

"Yes, of course. Thanks so much."

We exchange goodbyes, and I leave with a heightened sense of hope. Access to local art and artists could lead me to a new subject for a paper or presentation. Something that will put me back on the damned map—because I'm an astute, perceptive scholar, not because I'd spread my legs for a married business professor.

Shame, old and fetid, surges through me.

Oh, Uncle Max. I wish you were here but I'm also glad you're not. Does that make me the terrible person so many people think I am?

I push those thoughts aside. First, I cover all the art galleries, receiving "no, thank yous" at three of them, and an "I'll give your resume to the owner," at two more.

Next, I stop at a French Provencal design and antique shop, where two elegantly dressed older women—nametags reading Vivian and Lucy—are organizing a display of silver jewelry.

"How may we help you today?" Vivian asks pleasantly.

"I see you have a Charles Calderon painting." I gesture to a landscape of Venice situated on the wall behind them. "His use of color and light is lovely. I believe it was inspired by his trips to Turkey."

"Why, yes." Vivian smiles at me. "Are you interested in nine-teenth-century French art?"

"I've studied it quite a bit. My name is Eve Perrin." I extend my CV. "I'm an art historian currently living in Castille. If you're looking for either a buyer or consultant, I'd love to help you."

"How nice to meet you, Eve." Vivian scans my credentials. "We're always looking to partner with experts."

Lucy, who is scrolling on her phone, nudges her colleague in the side. "Can I speak to you privately?"

Though Vivian throws her a vaguely irritated look, she nods. "Excuse us a minute, please, Eve."

They walk a short distance away and begin consulting over my resume. Lucy shows Vivian something on her phone. My stomach knots with unease again. I've been on guard ever since that mess with David went down, but I hadn't expected to be ostracized in a small Maine town.

"I'm sorry." Vivian returns, her expression bland as she hands me my papers. "We're not looking for anyone at the moment."

They glance at each other, lips pursed. A sudden "you're not welcome here" force radiates from both of them. I stuff my CV back into my satchel and walk back outside.

As I return to Lantern Street, I catch sight of the Seagull Inn and Restaurant. The other night, a few people clearly overheard parts of my conversation with Juliette—or rather, her tongue-lashing of me—but that couldn't have anything to do with this odd treatment.

Could it?

In Los Angeles, no one cares about other people's conversations. Well, they might listen and smirk, maybe store the info away to include in their next screenplay, but then they go about their business because everyone has their own lurid story to tell. More than likely, a lurid sex story involving restraints, if not restraining orders.

You're not in LA anymore, Eve.

No, but this isn't Mayberry either. Aunt Bea isn't running around spreading gossip about the new girl in town with the slutty past.

Is she?

Shit.

I sink down on a bench. There's no way I can hide from my past. News stories and pictures of me are accessible on the internet with a little digging, but I'd hoped that people clear across the country from LA wouldn't care enough to bother searching for my name.

But if Juliette's caustic lecture had filtered into certain corners of town, and people were then curious enough to look me up... well, they'd find out renowned business professor David Landry had accused me of stalking him.

That he'd taken out a restraining order against me. That I'd been fired from a prominent, tenure-track position at UCLA. That there were *naked slut pictures* of me plastered on internet sites.

Even if all that had taken place on the moon, people would find it salaciously gossip-worthy, no matter where they live.

I close my eyes. I can't let this thwart my efforts. I need a damned job. I need to jumpstart my career again. I need people to believe *me*, not the stories. Not what they can read on the internet.

I have nowhere else to go.

Tomorrow I'll start fresh with the chair of the Art History department at Ford's College. I'd made the appointment with him last week. Though the Ford's professors will know all about the scandal—everyone in art history does—maybe I can deflect the speculation first. Own the story. Hope people will respect me for being upfront.

I have to try. I have no other choice.

Deflecting a stab of loneliness, I start back to my car. Countless fairy tale heroines transform themselves, shedding the tattered clothes of their former lives and becoming the women they were meant to be all along.

If only I could do the same thing.

In the dusk, the sky shimmers gray-blue like a marble. I visit a hardware store to get whatever I need for the Toilet of Antiquity.

The white-haired proprietor gives me a lecture about plumbing assemblies. I dutifully make notes in my organizer, noting that a "ballcock" is the mechanism for filling the water tank. I leave with a bag full of contraptions, one of which I hope I can properly install.

On my way back to my car, I stop in front of a bookstore café called Jabberwocky whose window display showcases books about monsters, puzzles, and alternate worlds. *Harry Potter and the Goblet of Fire*, *The Eleventh Hour*, the *Mirror Mirror* series, *The Maze Runner*, *The Garden of Abdul Gasazi*, *Where the Wild Things Are*.

I pull open the door and step into a cozy space that smells like coffee and chocolate. Wooden shelves stuffed with books sit beside a café area of round tables, and a fire in a stone fireplace warms the room.

Pleased at having found what looks like a town gem, I peruse the bookshelves. A tall, husky man with a neatly trimmed gray beard, in his mid-fifties, is studying the fiction section. He glances in my direction when I take *A Tree Grows in Brooklyn* off the shelf.

"Old favorite." I gesture to the book. "I haven't read it in years."

"My number one old favorite is *As I Lay Dying*." He turns his attention back to the shelves. "Hemingway was a master."

"Er, William Faulkner wrote *As I Lay Dying*."

He gives me a sideways smirk. "Faulkner's *Of Human Bondage* is also exceptional."

"That was Somerset Maugham."

His eyes narrow. "Stendhal's *Madame Bovary*."

I shake my head, smiling. "Flaubert's *Madame Bovary*."

"James Fenimore Cooper. *House of the Seven Gables*."

"Nathaniel Hawthorne."

"*A Wrinkle in Time* by E.L. Konigsburg."

"Madeline L'Engle."

"*Pride and Prejudice.*" He furrows his brow. "Charlotte Brontë."

"Seriously? Jane Austen."

"*The Master and the Margarita.* Dostoevsky."

"Bulgakov."

"What are you, a bluestocking?" He peers at me, a smile curving his lips.

I grin at the old-fashioned term. "Just a quiet girl who used to spend all her time at the library."

He arches an eyebrow and taps his finger on a book spine. "Reading Bulgakov and Flaubert?"

"*Harry Potter* and *Sweet Valley High*, but I've picked up a few things over the years."

He gives a wry *"young people today"* chuckle and turns back to studying the books.

Feeling better at having had an amusing encounter with at least one person in this town, I make my way through the labyrinth of shelves to the front counter. A crossword puzzle book on a spinning rack display catches my eye. When I was a girl, I'd loved doing crossword puzzles.

I set the book on the counter alongside *A Tree Grows in Brooklyn*.

"Anything else for you?" A young man in his early twenties with a nametag reading *Alex* punches a few keys on the cash register.

"I'll have a coffee." I study the chalkboard menu behind the café counter. "Café latte, please. For here."

"Ma, café latte for here," Alex calls to a blonde woman in her forties who is putting cookies into the cold case.

"Coming up." The woman waves me toward the counter. "Two percent okay?"

"Sure." I pay for the books and hitch myself onto a stool. "You wouldn't happen to be hiring by any chance, would you?"

"Sorry." She turns on the machine to steam the milk. "We're a family operation, just me, Ned, and Alex when he doesn't have classes at Ford's. In the summer we sometimes hire another college kid or two, but we're heading into our slow time of year."

She sets the coffee in front of me. "Did you try over at Seagull Inn? They sometimes start looking for holiday hires right about now."

"I'll look into it," I reply evasively. As if I'll ever set foot in the inn or restaurant again. "I'm Eve, by the way. Just moved here about ten days ago."

"Welcome to Castille, Eve." She extends her hand for a shake. "I'm Carol. What prompted your move?"

"I inherited my uncle's house over on Sparrow Lane," I explain. "So does the job market pick up around here over the holidays?"

She shrugs. "Depends. We used to get more people in town for winter, but tourism has dropped off a lot lately. What kind of job are you looking for?"

"Anything I can get," I admit.

"There's usually jobs over at the Hillman ski resort," Alex calls from the cash register area. "When winter sports pick up, at least. Snowmobiling, ice fishing, snow-shoeing."

Given that I know nothing about winter sports, except that they're cold and involve things like blades and poles, I'm pretty sure I wouldn't be at the top of a hire list. Then again, beggars can't be choosers.

"I'll keep that in mind," I say. "Thanks for the tip. And the coffee."

I pick up my books, slide off the stool, and head toward the door. Buttoning my coat, I push it open. Just as I step outside, my body comes up against something rock-solid and strong.

I stumble backward, my heel tilting off-balance. My bag of books falls to the sidewalk. Two large hands close around my arms, steadying me. Though the touch is one of mere polite assistance, my reaction is totally disproportionate as my heart crashes against my ribs and shock floods my veins.

"Easy." His voice is deep and all-encompassing, like the roots of an oak tree spreading beneath the earth.

Easy? The word sounds odd, incongruous to my life. Nothing has been easy of late.

I struggle to regain my composure and pull away from his grip. Aside from a few brief handshakes, I haven't touched, or been touched, by a man in close to a year. I've smothered all my desire and physical urges, blaming them for instigating my downfall. If I hadn't been attracted to David, if I hadn't let him do what he did, none of it would have happened.

Now I don't know what to make of my reaction to a stranger. Even with a foot of space between us, my pulse is racing and my skin is hot.

Trembling, I reach for the books I've dropped. He bends at the same time and picks them up before I do. He straightens and hands them to me. Our fingers brush, sending a shiver clear up my arm.

"Are you all right?" he asks.

I nod. He's big, well over six feet tall, his presence blocking the street, his shoulders broad and his chest wide beneath a charcoal button-down shirt. I force my gaze from his shirt front up to his face.

A hot sensation breaks open inside me, melting the ice lodged inside my chest. Gray eyes, the color of a granite wall, regard me from beneath thick black eyebrows. His features are strong and bold, the angles of his cheekbones sloping down to a square jaw dusted with stubble and a well-shaped mouth. His dark hair, long enough to brush the back of his collar, is messy in an unintentional way, as if he's been dragging his hand through it.

The rest of the world fades into black and white, all color distilling into the gray of his eyes.

A sense of unreality washes over me, as if I've seen him

before, but through a dream blistered with eroticism, the kind I used to wake from hot and aching.

He steps away, then stops. His gaze arrows in on my face with a perception that is shockingly intimate, as if he can penetrate right down to my core. That look arcs into me like a shooting star, exploding heat through my blood.

What the...?

I can't move, can't break my gaze from his. Sudden tension laces through his body, tightening his shoulders.

""I...I need to go," I stammer.

"Wait." He moves forward, closing his hand around my wrist.

I should be alarmed, but his grip is warm and tight, his fingers resting against the pulse beating wildly under my skin. Rather than controlling, his hold is steadying, the way an anchor keeps a boat from drifting. I catch his scent—all things I like. Salt and citrus, autumn leaves, the faintly bitter smell of ink.

"What's your name?" Urgency threads his voice, like he not only wants to know my name, he *has* to know. Is compelled to know.

"Eve." *Why am I telling him?*

"Eve." He says my name as if he's tasting it, rolling the letters across his tongue, over the surface of his teeth, before swallowing them whole.

I have the sudden sense he can do the same to me, like Red Riding Hood and the wolf.

I drag in a breath and twist my arm from his grip. The loss of contact, the sudden cold, reminds me who I am and why I'm here.

"I have to go," I repeat.

He backs away, one hand up as if he doesn't want to scare me. Not that he could. I'm afraid of men who wear tailored suits, of lawyers, consultants, administrators, board members. He doesn't seem like any of those things. With his dark, messy hair and whiskered face, his storm-gray eyes, he's like a force of nature, untamed and unkempt.

Move, Eve. Walk back to the car. But moving would require breaking eye contact, dissolving the hot sensation melting inside me, letting the cold back in.

My God. I've forgotten what it feels like to *feel*.

I tighten my grip on the books. "Who are you?"

His mouth compresses, a shutter coming down over his gray eyes. "No one you want to know."

Stepping back, he breaks the spell holding us together. He walks away, his long stride taking him to the end of the block in seconds. He turns a corner and is gone.

I pull in a breath. A surreal feeling washes over me, as if I'd imagined that whole encounter. Dreamed it up from some deep part of me that still longs to be touched.

I look back at the corner. The air shimmers, almost as if his absence has left a hole in the atmosphere. My skin still tingles from his tight grip.

Oh, don't, Eve. That path led you to destruction.

I've changed, grown up, faced the punishment of my mistakes. I can't get all wistful about a random encounter with a stranger, no matter how captivating he is and how unreal the sense that I've seen him before.

Not to mention, he all but warned me away.

In stories, nothing good ever comes from failing to heed an overt warning, no matter how great the temptation.

Don't go into the woods. Don't unlock the door. Stay away from the castle. Don't open the box.

Above all, don't even look at the beautiful, tantalizing apple.

CHAPTER 3

I'm aroused.

Three hours after my encounter with the stranger, my blood is still hot. It's a strange feeling, almost foreign. I haven't experienced sexual feelings in months. My memories of sex with David are all discolored with guilt and humiliation.

Even before him, I hadn't been intimate with a man in ages. I'd once enjoyed sex with a few undergrad and grad school boyfriends, but as a new professor at UCLA, I'd been so involved with work, research, and keeping up with my tenure-track position that I hadn't had the time or the interest in dating. And during the year-long downward spiral of Max's diagnosis and death, I'd fought just to keep my balance.

Which was part of the reason I'd crashed into the affair with David. I'd lost my footing, and he'd been in the right place at the right time to catch me. It had been such welcome relief to focus on something else besides Max's brutal illness, my mother's tyranny, the pressures of work, my own exhaustion. It had been so nice to have a man focus on *me*. To lose myself in physical desire. I found myself craving the intimacy, his touch, his reassurances that *everything will be all right*.

For him, I guess *everything* turned out just fine. For me, not so much. But in some cobwebbed part of my mind, I remember that being sexual can feel *good*.

I rest my head on the pillow, looking at the ceiling where moonlight slants through the uncurtained bedroom windows. The house creaks and rumbles comfortingly around me.

I think of *him* again—his hand gripping my wrist, the intensity of his eyes. Apparently my body still knows how to react to a man I find compelling because my nipples are hard, and a warm pulsing spreads through my core.

When was the last time I masturbated? Is one brief encounter with a hot stranger—less than three minutes—enough to spark my sexual urges back to life? If my tingling skin and throbbing blood are anything to judge by, then…*oh, yes.*

I touch my breasts through my cotton nightgown. Heat courses down between my legs.

What does he look like naked? A solid, muscular chest, maybe patterned with a dusting of dark hair, smooth shoulders and thick biceps. Long legs corded with muscles and tendons. A ladder-like abdomen, traceable ridges guiding the eye downward to a heavy, thick cock.

I grasp my nightgown and pull it up over my hips. Despite the chilly air, my naked skin is warm to the touch. Suppressing a twinge of embarrassment, I push the covers aside and open my thighs. I dip a tentative finger into my folds, drawing in a sharp breath when I discover I'm wet. *Ready.* Like he's already primed me.

A hot flush rises to my face. I close my eyes and ignore whatever misgivings I have about this. I've been slut-shamed and sexually demeaned enough in recent months. Those vile echoes will not be allowed in the privacy of my own bedroom.

I slide my nightgown higher, exposing my breasts to the cold air. I've forgotten how sensitive my nipples are. Just the light brush of my fingers over them sends currents of heat into my veins. I stroke my hands over my belly and back up to my breasts, cupping and squeezing them. Though my breasts aren't particularly large, in the midst of the scandal I'd taken to wearing boxy jackets and shirts that hid all my curves and concealed my femininity.

Here, now, I don't have to hide anymore. And damned if the touch of my own hands doesn't feel exquisite—light, cool, arousing. I skim my palms across my hips and down to my thighs, taking my time and reacquainting myself with the feel of my own body.

Would he like my body?

The question emerges through the warm haze of lust descending over me. Would he like the fact that my breasts might fit perfectly in his big hands, my nipples peaking at one touch of his fingers? Would he admire my legs—not long, but well-shaped and toned—and the soft curves of my hips and belly?

Would he like *me*?

I stretch one arm over my head and slide my other hand between my legs. I imagine him looking at me, gray eyes burning like storm clouds, muscles tense and coiled with lust. His erection sways as he pushes my thighs apart and positions himself between them. He slides into me, a slow easy penetration, setting my nerves on fire. His breath is hot on my skin. He pulls back and starts to fuck me.

Shivers rain down my spine, little pulses of electricity popping and cracking. A moan rushes through my lungs. I rub my clit harder and slide one finger into my body. Though the penetration pales in comparison to what *he* would feel like, I'm so aroused by *being aroused* again that my excitement ratchets up quickly.

Raw images fill my mind—his fingers digging into my bare thighs; his sweaty chest moving above me, muscles shifting smooth as cream under his taut skin. My body bouncing and jostling underneath him, cries of pleasure streaming from my lips. Time dissolving, pain disappearing, thought evaporating, everything else conquered by the power of sheer physical pleasure.

He pulls out of me, leaving me momentarily bereft before making a sharp gesture that is an unmistakable command. I turn and get onto my hands and knees, my heart pounding and my head swimming with lust and urgency. He opens me with his fingers before easing into me again, such a full, intense pressure that I gasp and stiffen in resistance.

He stops, spreading one hand over my lower back. Our breath rasps through the hot air. He slides his other hand between my legs and strokes, an expert, precise manipulation that loosens the tension in my spine. I fist the bedcovers and push my hips backward in invitation. He pushes forward, filling me.

Oh my God.

Sweat trickles between my breasts. I pump my hips upward, working my fingers faster and faster. Delicious pressure wraps around me like bright red ribbons.

In my mind's eye, he's thrusting hard now, rhythmically, his grip tight on my hips. My whole body sways and jerks with the force of his strokes. I lower my upper body to the bed and squeeze my eyes shut. My nipples chafe deliciously against the sheets, and my thighs tremble with strain. I open my legs wider, aching to feel him in every part of me. I'll be sore in the morning, but I want him to keep going, deeper and harder, to fuck me until the world shatters and everything else ceases to exist.

Explosions burst through me, a fireworks display of color and sensation. The instant my rapture peaks, I see him pull his cock out of me and grasp the shaft, stroking and stroking...until a deep groan rumbles through his chest and he comes. His gorgeous body shudders and jerks as he crests the wave.

I rub my clit gently until the final sensations ebb from my

blood. Panting and sweaty, I collapse back against the pillows. As my eyes drift closed, I can almost feel the evidence of him—his seed dampening my skin, the ache inside me, the bruises forming on my thighs.

As if he stripped me bare, opened me up, and turned me into someone new.

CHAPTER 4

*T*he toilet hisses at me. I ignore the insult—wish I'd honed that skill earlier—and reach into a web of ancient cobwebs to turn the shut-off valve. The October morning sun streams through the bathroom window, shining an unwelcome light on the moldy caulk around the toilet base.

I flush the toilet to drain the tank and gingerly grasp the slimy flapper attached to a rusted chain. After employing pliers to wrench it off, I take the new flapper and secure it to the side pegs.

So far, so good.

Studying the website on my phone, I follow the instructions to attach the chain. Then I turn the water back on, watching anxiously as I flush the toilet and wait for the tank to fill. I fully expect the hissing to start up again, but it doesn't.

The toilet is silent.

I flush again. The tank refills and then politely shuts up.

I'll be damned. I fixed the toilet.

Only when my phone buzzes do I realize I'm just standing there grinning to myself. It's an email from Sarah, the owner of the East Coast artists gallery. *Eve, thanks for stopping by yesterday. Sorry we're not hiring now but we'll keep your info on file.*

Not a surprise. Also not my last option either.

Feeling rather badass—I had a spectacular orgasmic fantasy last night, and I fixed a broken toilet this morning, so get the hell outta my way—I head downstairs to make a cup of tea with honey.

As the fragrant Earl Grey steeps, I make a list in my organizer of all the things that need immediate repair: wobbly staircase banister and doorknobs, leaky faucets, loose floorboard in the foyer. Hopefully I can get it all done before winter hits.

Winter. If I were still living in Los Angeles, I'd imagine a Maine winter and a ramshackle house as a thoroughly romantic combination. Wood-burning fire, cozy quilts, hot chocolate and all that. In my present circumstances, however, I envision myself waking up with icicles on my eyelashes and my teeth rattling.

Which means that despite my *can-do* attitude toward repairs, I am going to have to hire a professional to make sure the roof and heater will get me through winter.

My stomach knots. I have no idea what to do if I can't find a job. Asking Juliette for money has never been an option. She'd made it clear when I turned eighteen that I was on my own, and I've always been driven by the need to prove to her that I can do it. Caving now and asking her for money would just add ammunition to the arsenal she already has.

I pack my satchel for the day, then take a shower and search through my wardrobe of high-quality clothes I'd purposely selected to command respect among my colleagues and students. Hopefully the professional styles will still work. I dress in a navy pencil skirt and pale blue, button-down blouse, adding silver stud earrings, my watch, and a chain necklace.

I walk out to my car. My heart stutters at the sight of the big, German Shepherd mix hovering near the woodlands. He watches me warily, ears perked. I hesitate, not wanting to do anything to spook him.

For a moment, we look at each other. His body is guarded,

cautious, like he's ready to spring into self-defense if attacked. Weirdly, I understand his demeanor. I'd felt that way myself for months. I still do.

The dog barks once, then retreats, turning to trot off into the woods.

I press a hand to my chest and hurry to my car. If the dog is lost, it doesn't make much sense that he'd keep returning to Uncle Max's house. The humane society hasn't responded to my email yet, so I'll try calling them this afternoon.

I drive to Ford's College and find the building housing the art history department. I've always loved college campuses. I love the students shuffling from class to class with their ratty backpacks, take-out coffees, and dangling ear buds. I love the big lecture halls and smaller discussion rooms, the whiteboards and projectors. I love that the air hums with knowledge, curiosity, boredom, and ambition all at the same time.

But when it felt like an entire university population had turned against me, the campus became my battleground. Even now, my shoulders tighten as I approach the art history office, my whole body alert to potential whispers and laughter.

The chairperson, Dennis Peterson, greets me cordially and invites me into his office. After an exchange of pleasantries about the town, I get straight to the point.

"I'm sure you've heard stories about what happened out at UCLA," I say.

He responds with an uncomfortable laugh, which tells me right away that he knows all about it. He's probably seen the goddamned pictures. I steel my spine and keep going.

"I fully admit to having made mistakes, but I'm not the person I was made out to be." A flush begins to scorch my neck. "A private situation unfortunately became public, which led to my termination."

Dennis clears his throat. "Uh, you don't have to explain, Dr. Perrin. Eve."

"Yes, I do. I know everyone has heard the rumors, but the truth is a different story. I'm not a stalker, and I didn't do the things I was accused of. I'm telling you this because regardless of what happened, I'm still a scholar and an art historian. I love research and teaching, and I miss them both. I'd like to get involved with the art history department here, if at all possible…"

Dennis holds up a hand to stop my words. My flush deepens. If I sound desperate, it's because I *am*.

"Dr…Eve, unfortunately our staff is full and none of our professors are scheduled for leave or sabbaticals. But I'd be happy to keep your CV and contact info on file."

Though it's the response I was expecting, disappointment stabs me hard. I nod and pick up my satchel. "I'd appreciate that."

I'm not about to reduce myself to groveling—at least, not yet. I thank Dennis again, and he walks me to the door.

As I leave the office, I hear the receptionist ask him, *"Isn't she the woman who…"*

Bitterness swells in my throat. Will I ever peel away the disgrace still clinging to me like a black, oily film? No doubt the speculation here is the same as it was in LA. *What was she thinking? Did she really do that? Crazy bitch.*

I return to Lantern Street and walk to the Castille Art Museum, a quaint brick building with white shutters. In the foyer, a greeter's desk is covered with museum flyers and local brochures.

"Hello, there." A woman in her sixties approaches, her face open and friendly. "Come on in. Have you been here before?"

"No, but I'd like to see the exhibits. I just moved to Castille."

"Welcome." She takes a museum plan off the desk and hands it to me. "We don't get too many new residents these days. I'm Miriam Walker, education coordinator."

"Eve Perrin."

I'm starting to get wary of even introducing myself, but

thankfully my name doesn't appear to register with Miriam in any significant way.

"Come in, Eve." She waves me into the galleries. "I have to staff the front desk, but I can give you a quick tour."

We enter the exhibition spaces. One room documents Castille's history with photographs and artifacts, and the main collection contains paintings and sculptures by artists who'd had a connection to the area.

I pause in front of a portrait in the main gallery. A young, fresh-faced woman sits at a piano in a darkened room, looking with frank directness at the viewer. A spray of flowers on the piano top adds a splash of pink, and a glowing light falls over the woman like a warm caress.

The plaque beside the painting is engraved with the title: *Portrait of Allegra King, by Andrew Wyeth, 1987.*

My interest flares.

"Allegra King." I look at Miriam. "My uncle used to be a professor at Ford's. I think he mentioned her a few times."

It's a purposeful understatement since I don't want to give Max's secrets away. He'd more than just "mentioned" Allegra. He had been deeply in love with her.

"I wouldn't be surprised." Miriam studies the painting. "Allegra is married to William King, who was a three-term mayor of Castille. He owns a finance company in town, and her father had made his money in ship-building. Her family used to be quite prominent in Castille, but they've all either passed or moved away. She's the only one left."

"She's very beautiful." I nod toward the painting.

"Yes. She's always been renowned for both her beauty and all the good she's done for Castille. She really loved this town. Still does, I imagine."

"Does she still live here?"

"More or less." Miriam shakes her head with a slight frown. "The Kings have an estate on Bird Lane, just outside of town.

Allegra and William live there for most of the year, but unfortunately she's become a shut-in after suffering health issues. She's still young too, only in her fifties. But she never visits town anymore, and her husband has taken charge of all her affairs. Terribly sad, really."

A weight descends over my heart. Had Max known that about Allegra? He'd have been devastated to know of her suffering, even if they hadn't seen each other in over fourteen years, if not longer.

"Do you have any other paintings of her?" I ask.

"No, just the one. If you're interested in Wyeth or other local artists, however, we do let people look at our storage area and archives for research."

"I'd like that." I hesitate for a second before taking the plunge. "I'm an art historian, so this is all within my field. If you're looking to hire a curator or consultant, I'd love to be considered."

"Hmm." Her lips purse. "Our budget is always tight, but let me contact the museum director. Can I get back to you?"

"Of course. Thank you."

Miriam glances at her watch. "I need to staff the front desk, but feel free to look around. I'll let you know as soon as I talk to the director."

She hurries back to the foyer. Heartened by both her welcoming attitude and the lack of an immediate rejection, I study the paintings and artifacts relating to Castille's history. Several other visitors arrive, and an elderly man leads a group of schoolchildren on a tour.

My phone buzzes with a call. I take it out of my satchel and swipe the screen. Graham. Relief and pleasure lights inside me. My PhD advisor had been the one person in the world who believed *me* instead of David and all the nasty rumors.

Moving to a quiet, isolated corner of the gallery, I answer the call. "Graham."

"Hello, Eve. Thought I'd call and see how you're settling in."

The warmth of his greeting brings an unexpected tightness to my throat. How welcoming to hear a friendly voice.

"Oh, just fine," I manage to say. "I even fixed a toilet that predates the Civil War, so I might have a new career as a plumber in my future."

He chuckles. "You could probably make more money as a plumber rather than an art historian, but it would be a terrible waste of your talent. How's the job search going?"

The tightness forms into an outright lump. *Jesus, Eve. Don't cry.*

"I have a few possibilities." I try to keep my voice light. "Nothing yet, but I'm waiting to hear back from a few art gallery owners."

"What about Ford's?"

"They're not hiring or looking for lecturers at the moment, but they're keeping my CV on file."

"I'll give them a call, put in a good word for you."

I bite my lip, torn between gratitude and the worry that Graham's intervention will lead to more speculation about me and him.

If Juliette had heard rumblings about something untoward going on between me and Graham, then what if he—or worse, his wife—had heard it too? I don't want to contribute to such gossip. In fact, I'll shut it down however I can.

"No, don't. You've done enough for me, Graham. I'll find a job on my own."

It might be slinging burgers or cleaning floors, but I'll find one.

He sighs. "Ah, I hate that this happened to you. I wish there was more I could do to help."

Tears sting my eyes. "I'll be fine."

"I know. You're too strong to let this mess break you."

What if it already has?

Before I do start crying, I switch the conversation to Graham and ask about his classes and his family. Talking with him eases some of my frustration, and I end the call with a renewed sense of hope.

Job searching is never easy, whether you're a high-school student or a corporate shark. And at least I have a place to live and excellent qualifications, so already I'm ahead of the game.

I continue admiring the artwork. Maybe I will write a paper about one of the paintings or artists. As I walk toward a nautical history display, I catch sight of a dark-haired man sitting on a bench beside an antique ship's wheel.

I stop in my tracks. It's the man from yesterday, the one whom I'd fantasized about with utter abandon.

A flush rises to my cheeks, and my breath shortens. I can't move, my attention locking to him like a magnet. His dark head is bent over a notepad, and he's writing with a pencil, his hand working swiftly across the page. The movement is almost hypnotic, like watching a flock of birds soaring over the sky.

My gaze travels over his arms, past the sleeves of his chambray shirt rolled up to reveal the corded muscles of his forearms. Then down across the faded areas of his jeans, stretched at the knee and hugging his long legs. His scuffed black boots. The breadth of his shoulders and chest, which I'd imagined naked and sweaty—

My mind suddenly fills with a memory of a broad-shouldered man standing behind the smoky glass of the lighthouse tower.

Oh my God. So much for thinking the lighthouse keeper is a grizzled old lobster fisherman.

He glances up. Our gazes meet. With a quick intake of breath, I step back, struck by the sudden sense that he can read my mind. That he knows every detail of my raw fantasy.

Energy crackles between us. My knees weaken as I remember his warm, strong grip on my wrist, his fingers resting against my throbbing pulse.

"That's just so *weird.*" A young girl's chattering voice breaks my attention.

The school group bustles noisily into the room, the tour guide and teacher attempting to rein in their enthusiasm.

A surge of self-preservation jolts me into movement. I hurry to the front of the museum, trying to suppress the attraction still simmering inside me, trying to avoid looking back at the man who gave me an incredible orgasm last night—even if he doesn't know it.

I stop in the main gallery, where Miriam is talking to Lucy, the woman from the Provencal Art and Antiques shop yesterday who'd clearly discovered the stories about me. My teeth clench. Surely she wouldn't…

Both women glance at me. Lucy smiles tightly.

Oh, yes, she would.

What the hell? Am I in the middle of some nightmarish Stephen King novel where gossip becomes a living creature slithering through town and striking people down? Is this really how small towns operate? Or was I too hopeful to think I could have a new start here? That the scandal and naked pictures of me wouldn't have *this* kind of rippling, caustic effect?

Any pleasure or hope I'd felt vanishes, dissolving like black smoke.

"Don't tell me," I say to Miriam. "You're not hiring anyone at this time."

A crease appears between her eyebrows. "I'm sorry, but it seems as if there's a bit of an…issue."

Well, that's one way of putting it.

Although I want to say something bitchy—what, I have no idea—I force myself to remain polite.

"All right," I say. "I appreciate your time."

Straightening my shoulders, I walk past them and out the front door. The crisp autumn air does nothing to cool my hot face or quell the shame and embarrassment flooding my veins. *Again.*

I return to my car, throwing my satchel into the passenger

seat. I try to push the key into the ignition, but my hand is shaking too hard. I drop the keys onto my lap and grip the steering wheel.

Fuck. Fuck fuck fuck *fuck*.

The curses fire like bullets through my brain.

Goddamn you, David, for being a lying, cheating, manipulative bastard.

Goddamn you, Juliette, for being so brilliant, so judgmental, so terrible.

Goddamn you, cancer, for existing.

Goddamn you, Max, for dying.

Goddamn my colleagues and students, the board of regents, the chancellor, the police, every single person who believed a powerful older man over a junior female professor and who thought her voice was worth nothing.

Goddamn you, Eve, for being such a stupid, trusting wretch.

A sob chokes me. Tears flood my eyes. I rest my forehead on the steering wheel and start to cry. I'd once thought I'd used up all my tears, but no. They spring up from the dark well inside me, running down my cheeks in hot, salty trails.

All the anger and pain that I've suppressed boils up into painful, wrenching sobs. I squeeze my eyes shut, trembling and crying for what feels like an eternity. My chest hurts. My throat hurts. My heart hurts.

A knocking sound, knuckles on glass, suddenly filters through my sobbing. I manage to suppress another rising outbreak of tears and lift my head, wiping my face on my sleeve. I stare in blurry shock at the man standing outside my car, right next to the driver's side window.

The man from the bookstore, the museum, my pornographic vision.

He indicates that I should roll down the window.

What the...?

My defensive instincts kick into gear, overpowering my pain.

Orgasmic fantasy or not, this man is a stranger. In LA, I would never roll down the window for anyone except a legitimate police officer.

But this isn't LA—even if the scandal did follow me here—and it's mid-morning with plenty of nearby businesses open. Two couples stroll on the other side of the street, and a heavy-set, bald man is leaning against a lamppost, checking his phone.

I roll the window down a crack.

"Yes?" Though I try to keep my voice cool, a hiccuping sob breaks through.

He leans down to peer at me, a crease appearing between his dark eyebrows. God, he has an incredible face—thick-lashed eyes, cut-glass cheekbones sloping down to a strong, whisker-dusted jaw, and a mouth that looks as if it was made to do dirty things to a woman.

I half-expect him to say something like *"You okay?"* even though it's abundantly clear that I am anything *but* okay.

Instead he says, "Eve Perrin."

Of course he knows my last name. Everyone around here does by now, thanks to the small-town gossip mill that spits out rumors like watermelon seeds.

"That's me." I hiccup again and fumble in my satchel for a tissue. "What do you want?"

"I overheard your conversations in the museum."

Great. I should just wear a microphone and save everyone in this godforsaken town the trouble of eavesdropping. Irritated, I scrounge deeper into my bag. I don't have a fucking tissue.

The guy pulls a folded handkerchief from his pocket and pushes it through the window crack to me. I grab it and blow my nose. The soft, clean cotton has a pleasant smell of citrus and spice. Not that I care.

"You're looking for a job," he says.

Even with his chivalrous handkerchief gesture, I'm no longer interested in being polite. "So what's it to you?"

"I'll help you."

I throw him a wary look. "How?"

He straightens, resting his hands on his hips. The movement draws my eyes unwillingly to the way his shirt stretches across his chest and shoulders. His voice is a deep rumble of temptation.

"Come with me, Eve."

ome with me, Eve.

Serpent. Garden of Eden. Tree of good and evil.

Come with me, Eve, and eat this delicious fruit. That hadn't ended well for her. Or humanity.

A long moment passes, broken only by the sound of my occasional hiccuping sob. He just stands there, immovable as a mountain, his booted feet planted apart and the wind rumpling up his thick dark hair.

My intellect tells me to refuse. To toss him the snotty handkerchief, close the window, and drive away without a backward glance. But my intellect has not made the best decisions lately.

I can help you.

What the hell? It's not as if anyone else can. And sadly, I don't seem to be able to help myself—at least not where a job is concerned.

"Where are we going?" I finally ask.

He tilts his head toward an old blue pickup parked nearby. "Follow me."

So he's not trying to lure me into his truck. That makes the decision easier. I fish my keys out of my lap to start the car. After waiting for him to get to his truck, I ease my car behind him. He drives down Lantern Street and onto the narrow, two-laned road heading out of Castille and east toward the ocean.

Coastal grasslands spread out like blankets on either side, sloping toward the ocean at the cliff's edge. A small circular parking lot, occupied by three cars, sits a short distance from the plateau. I pull into an empty space and get out of the car.

He climbs out of his truck and approaches me.

I peer up at him. "You're the lighthouse keeper, aren't you?"

He nods.

"How long have you lived here?"

"Fifteen years."

He looks like he's around thirty-eight, which means he's been here since his early twenties. Seems to be an odd career choice for a young man.

"What's your name?" I ask.

"Flynn."

"Flynn." I say his name aloud without thinking. Smooth and velvety, with no rough edges. Melting in my mouth like a hot buttered biscuit.

Without giving me further information, he starts toward the winding pathway. I follow, his handkerchief still crumpled in my fist. Several people hike along the coastal trail, and an older couple stands near the secrets wall, peering out at the ocean through binoculars.

"So you actually live here?" I ask as we pass the nautical display building.

"In the cottage." He points to the lighthouse at the top of the slope. "The exhibit is open to the public, but the lighthouse and keeper's cottage are both private. No visitors allowed."

We ascend the slope to the large, modern addition attached to the back of the cottage. The addition is made of the same stone material as the cottage, so it melds very well with the original structure.

He unlocks the door and pushes it open, moving aside to let me precede him. Though his chivalry softens me a little, I don't immediately step forward. Aside from developing a guard as thick as leather over the months, my basic survival instinct warns me not to enter a closed room with a man I don't know.

He extends the keyring to me in a silent offering.

I take it, unable to prevent a hollow laugh. "This is supposed to reassure me?"

"Get your phone out," he says. "The signal should be fine up here. Go ahead and call someone you know, tell them where you are."

Who would I even call? I take my phone out of my bag anyway and step into the room.

Boxes and crates fill the large space, which is lined with wooden shelves. An old desk and a straight-backed chair sit near a window overlooking the plateau and the woods farther inland. Another leather chair and a sofa are positioned against the opposite wall.

There's no other furniture, just dozens of cardboard boxes, wooden crates, storage containers that look as if they contain file folders. Stacks of archival boxes sit near the desk, and a drop cloth covers a vertical shelving unit on the opposite wall.

Okay. It's a storage room, not a creeper's dungeon.

I don't move past my one-foot entry into the room. A strange familiarity hovers in the air, as if I've been here before. Which I definitely haven't.

"And?" I ask.

"Open one of the boxes." He points toward them.

"Which one?"

He shrugs. "Doesn't matter."

I take a few cautious steps into the room and turn to a nearby box. A few numbers are scrawled in black pen on the side. I tug at the flaps and open the box to reveal a stack of old books.

I lift out the first one, an old, thick cloth-bound hardcover imprinted with a gold floral motif around the title. At the top of the design, a winged fairy hovers over a crescent moon.

I stare at the cover. I can't move, but my heart is suddenly racing.

The Fairy Tales of the Countess d'Aulnoy. Translated by J.R. Planche.

A thousand emotions bubble up inside me with the power of a storm. I grip the book tighter and force myself to look at Flynn. He's still standing in the doorway, his arms crossed and his expression shuttered.

"This…" My mouth goes dry. "My uncle owned this book."

He nods. I take out more books. My hands are shaking. *Norse Fairy Tales by G.W. Dasent. Edmund Dulac's Fairy Book. The Sleeping Beauty in the Wood.*

Uncle Max's beloved personal collection. The one my mother had sold through an auction. The one I'd thought was gone forever.

Love and grief well up inside me, tightening my throat. I turn away, painfully aware of Flynn watching me and not wanting him to witness yet another breakdown.

"How…" My breath catches. "How did you get all of this?"

"Sotheby's New York."

"*You* were the anonymous bidder." I turn back to him, a fresh wave of shock hitting me. "Wait a minute. Do you know I'm related to Max Dearborne?"

He inclines his head. "You're his niece."

"How did you know?"

"That's why I asked your name outside the bookstore." He uncrosses his arms. "Max spoke of you often. Last I heard you were an undergrad art history major at Stanford."

Something fragile breaks open inside me, splintering my heart with hope, fear, curiosity, anticipation. "You knew him. How?"

"We were friends." A hint of warmth enters his voice,

contrasting his impassivity. "But he took another job and moved to San Francisco about a year after I came to Castille. He said he wanted to be closer to you."

Tears fill my eyes again, but this time from happiness rather than anger. "I can't believe it. His colleagues from Ford's literature department all retired or moved, so I didn't think there was anyone still in Castille who knew him. Were you his student?"

"No." He pushes away from the doorjamb and approaches a stack of boxes. "I didn't know until the auction how extensive your uncle's collection had become."

Swallowing past the lump in my throat, I gaze down at the Dulac fairy tale book. "He spent his life building this collection. He'd always intended for it to be used by anyone who was interested in fairy tales. He let students and professors into his house in San Francisco all the time to research, talk, or just read. One woman even did the bulk of her PhD research using the books in his library."

"How did it end up at Sotheby's?"

Oh, Uncle Max. Wonderful, brilliant, disorganized Uncle Max who could read Grimm's fairy tales in the original German, but who didn't know a legal document from an appliance manual.

"My mother sold it." Old guilt claws through me. "Max had always wanted the collection to end up in a museum or library, but he didn't make specific donation plans. He spent most of his time immersed in books and research, kind of living in another world.

"Aside from a basic will, he'd never had much legal paperwork drawn up. So after he died, my mother inherited most of his stuff and could do whatever she wanted with it. When Sotheby's said the collection was valuable enough to sell, my mother didn't hesitate to auction it off."

But my uncle's entire life's work had ended up back in Castille, purchased by a man who'd once been friends with him.

If the collection had to be sold at all, surely it couldn't have met a better fate than this.

"Why did you buy it?" I ask.

Flynn doesn't respond. He turns to face me, a sudden remoteness infusing his eyes. "I asked you here because I heard you need a job. You're having trouble finding one."

Okay, he's not going to answer my question.

My face heats. He must know what everyone else does about me. But discovering that he and Max were friends, that he *bought Max's entire collection*, worsens my embarrassment, as if my salacious story has stained something pure.

"That's true," I admit.

"And as impressive as this collection is, it's something of a mess."

I can't help chuckling. "My uncle had many wonderful qualities, but an efficient, systematic approach to life was not one of them. His collection has always been a haphazard mess. He said he'd never be able to find anything if it were organized."

Max's gruff voice echoes in my head. *"Evie, I can find anything I need in thirty seconds or less!"*

A rush of tender fondness fills me. For years Max had divided his time between Castille and San Francisco, and part of his collection was stored in his old San Francisco Victorian house. I'd loved visiting him in his cluttered library when I was a child—books piled on every available surface, paintings amassed on the walls, shelves stuffed with manuscripts, lithographs, bundles of old letters. It had been a treasure trove, albeit a chaotic one.

"That's the job," Flynn says. "I'll hire you to organize and catalog the entire collection."

I stare at him. "Are you serious?"

His mouth twitches. "Well, I'm not funny."

"But why…" My voice trails off.

"Look." Flynn straightens, his arms coming up to cross his broad chest again. "The collection is a mess. I don't have the time or the expertise to catalog it. You appear to have both, and you need a job. That's my offer. Do you want it or not?"

"Yes!" I press a hand to my racing heart. "Of course I want it. I'm just...well, you're kind of shocking the hell out of me here."

He regards me from beneath a hooded gaze. "I'll pay you well, but I have certain conditions."

"What kind of conditions?" *Dungeon-like conditions? Original sin conditions?*

"I require that you sign a contract agreeing not to disclose anything about the job or me. You are not allowed to ask why. Your questions can only relate to the collection. When you're working, you're to stay confined to this room only, except if you need to use the bathroom. You're not to go into any other part of the lighthouse, especially the tower. Do you understand?"

Christ. What's his deal?

Though my skin prickles with apprehension, I nod. Organizing Max's collection, being surrounded by the books, manuscripts, and paintings that meant so much to him, is a pull too powerful to withstand. Even if Flynn the Lighthouse Keeper inspires an utter cacophony of emotions in me, from lustful attraction to curiosity and a touch of fear.

"What..." I flick my tongue out to lick my dry lips. "What will you be doing when I'm working?"

His eyes narrow. "No questions."

My stomach twists. Secrets were what almost destroyed me. And as much as I long for this job, I also need to protect myself.

"I'm sorry, but I'm going to need some kind of assurance that you're not Bluebeard, hiding dead bodies up in the forbidden tower."

"Wait here." He crosses to the door leading to the keeper's cottage.

When he's gone, I take a few more books from the box. Just touching the tattered covers and fragile pages floods me with memories of Max's house, the ever-present scents of coffee and

Russian tea cookies, the sound of pages turning, voices low in conversation, dust motes swimming lazily in a sunbeam.

The door clicks open. Flynn strides across the room and extends a worn dark blue book without a dust jacket. The cover is embellished with a gold image of a witch on a broomstick and a cloud-dusted full moon.

I open it to the title page: *Andrew Lang's Blue Fairy Book*. A single notecard rests between the pages, scrawled in a distinctive pointy penmanship.

Flynn,

"To keep alive isn't enough. To live, you must have sunshine and freedom and a little flower to love."

(Hans Christian Andersen, The Butterfly)

—Max

Tears sting my eyes. I swallow hard and close the book. "Did he…did he give you the whole set of Lang books?"

"All twelve. Right before he left Castille."

I hand the book back, comforted by the knowledge that Max thought so highly of Flynn that he'd gifted him the entire set of fairy tale books. *Does that mean my uncle also knew Flynn's secrets?*

"Will you agree to the conditions?" Flynn tucks the book underneath his arm, his inscrutable gaze on me.

My desire to organize Max's collection far outweighs my dislike of secrets. And obviously my uncle trusted Flynn, so—

"Yes."

"Good." He pushes back his cuff to glance at his watch. In an era of relentless technology, he wears an old-fashioned watch with a plain analog face, Roman numerals, and a worn leather strap. "You can start on Monday. Be here at eight."

He strides back outside, making a gesture indicating I should follow him. I place the other fairy tale books back into the box, giving the volumes a lingering pat before hurrying after my strange new boss.

A man who appears to have a thousand secrets.

CHAPTER 6

I have a job.

In the next couple of days following my visit to the lighthouse, my emotions swing between disbelief and outright giddiness. Maybe I haven't been shipwrecked here after all. Maybe the lighthouse is still calling to weary sailors, saving them from the relentless battle of the sea. Maybe it's beckoning me to safety as well.

Mysterious keeper notwithstanding.

How in the world did the lighthouse come to be inhabited by such a strange man? Why did he buy Max's collection? What's he hiding?

Maybe nothing at all. Maybe he's just a loner type who fiercely guards his privacy. Given that my privacy has been ripped to shreds, I can respect the urge to lock it down, not let anyone in. Ever.

In spite of the peculiar job conditions and the reticence of my new employer, and the fact that the job hasn't started yet, I'm already breathing so much easier. I'm half-tempted to call Juliette and tell her the news (*guess what, Cruella?*) but I suppress the urge.

She'll say something caustic that would burn right through my pride, and I refuse to let her do that.

So Lighthouse Guy is a super-hot, eccentric loner who wants to be left alone. Given the opportunity he just gave me, I'm more than happy to comply with his demands. He could have left this damsel in distress to fend for herself, but he didn't.

I have a job.

Not just any job either—one in which I'll be able to take care of my uncle's beloved collection, the one I'd thought was gone forever. The task is both emotionally priceless and perfectly aligned with my expertise. The Max Dearborne collection is of great value and deserves to be properly inventoried.

And through a stranger's generosity and a marvelous twist of fate, I get to be the one to do it. I can both honor my uncle and satisfy the art historian in me who has always wanted to ensure the collection is cataloged and preserved to archival standards.

Putting Max's collection in order is a step toward putting my life—and *myself*—back in order. I can't wait to get started.

The Friday before my first day of work, I give the kitchen a thorough cleaning while an electrician checks out the house's wiring and fuse box.

After scrubbing all the cabinets, I toss the sponge into the sink and take the whistling kettle off the stove. I measure a few tablespoons of loose-leaf orange pekoe tea into an elegant, hand painted ceramic teapot and add boiling water.

The tea set with matching cups and spoons had been a gift from Graham's wife, Mary, when I received my doctorate. For me, tea has become a ritual that keeps me somewhat stable. Even when a shitstorm had spun around me, I could find a few moments of peace in brewing and drinking a perfect cup of tea.

"Okay, miss." The electrician, a gray-haired, bespectacled man, stomps up the basement stairs. "You're good to go with the fuse box. You might want to take a look at rewiring the place if the lights keep blinking."

"I was planning to just blame the ghosts." I pour the tea into a cup.

He grins, setting his toolbox down. "You staying here long?"

"Through winter, probably."

"Then you'll need to get your HVAC system checked out too." He takes a pad from his pocket and starts writing up the bill. "Had your windows and locks checked?"

"I had the locks changed and deadbolts installed when I moved in, but I haven't had the windows checked yet."

"You got an alarm system?"

"Not yet."

He frowns. "And you're out here by the forest alone?"

A shiver runs down my spine, which is odd. I've never been afraid of forests. Quite the contrary. My hikes among the redwoods aside, *the forest* is where fairy tale heroines—Snow White, the Goose Girl, Donkeyskin—find safety and shelter. It's where they defeat wicked witches, discover magical helpers, get lost and find their way again.

"I've heard Castille is pretty safe."

"Oh, sure, in town, yeah." He tears the bill off the pad and hands it to me. "But with the economy going south, there've been some bad seeds, you know? Over in Benton, they had some issues with low-income housing, some folks got kicked out, couldn't afford another place, and ended up camping out in the woods."

He gestures to the woodlands spreading out acres past my house. "Caused some trouble, police had to run them out. I mean, yeah, the trails are great and fine during the day, but use common sense, you know? Look into getting an alarm system."

"I will," I promise. "Thanks for the advice."

"Give me a call, I'll get you some names." He picks up his toolbox and heads for the door.

After he's gone, I click the deadbolt and look at the bill, the total of which is a lot scarier than rumors about the dark woods. Chest tightening, I take out my checkbook and credit card statement to calculate how long the money I have will last. Minus this bill.

A knock comes at the front door. I open it and greet a delivery man holding a large box and a thick manila envelope. As I sign for both, I notice the box's return address of a company called *Cynet Corporation*.

The delivery man leaves with a cheerful wave. I start to close the door when I catch sight of the large mutt stalking alongside the edge of the woodlands.

Though my heart kicks into gear, I grab the bowl of kibble I'd set beside the door for exactly this occasion. I set the bowl on the porch and retreat back into the house, closing the door behind me.

The humane society had responded that no one has reported a lost dog matching his description, but that I should either call animal control or bring him in if he keeps showing up.

I have no intention of trying to catch him, but I'm also a little worried that animal control might take him to the pound. And I'm not sure why—maybe because I can relate to his guarded stance and the suspicious glint in his eyes—but I don't want him to end up at the pound.

Plus, given the electrician's warnings about the woods, it might not be a bad thing to have a large dog prowling around the house.

A crunching noise sounds faintly through the door. I peer out the front window, pleased to see the dog has accepted my offer and is gobbling down the kibble. Maybe if he associates me with food, he'll stop growling.

I return to the kitchen and open the delivered box. Inside, carefully packaged in foam and bubble wrap, is a sleek, very expensive-looking laptop computer.

What the...

I scrounge around for a note, and find one typed onto the packing slip.

Eve, this is your work computer. It's preloaded with a collections management software program. Bring it with you. Knock at the workroom door. —F

"Yes, sir," I mutter, gently lifting the computer from the box.

Since he didn't say I couldn't also use it at home, I review the manual and study the software. The laptop is smooth and powerful, easily the most high-end computer I've ever used. Between the hardware and the professional database, it's clear that Lighthouse Guy takes this cataloging job seriously. Good. So do I.

The envelope feels like it contains a sheaf of documents. Warily, I open it and pull out the infamous contract. He was serious about this too.

I skim the clauses and turn to the signature page. He's already signed it, a barely legible scrawl with the name Flynn Alverton typed underneath.

Alverton.

I grab my phone. Though the signal is weak, I pull up a search engine and type in his full name. Guilt pinches my nerves. I constantly hope no one will do this to me, but I'm also always resigned to the fact that *of course they will.*

The search, however, yields nothing for anyone of that name. Not even a different person. He's not listed on the website for the town of Castille as the current lighthouse keeper, he doesn't have any social media accounts, and his name isn't on any websites. In this day and age, the lack of a digital footprint is like he doesn't even exist.

Leave it alone, Eve.

I don't want people prying into my life. I have no right to pry into Flynn's. Especially considering he's the only person who not only offered me a job, but doesn't seem to hold my past against me.

Maybe he doesn't know about my past. It's not likely—it seems like everyone here knows about me—but Flynn is obviously a bit different.

Doesn't matter either way, as long as I do the job well and prove he's done the right thing by hiring me.

As I'm putting my phone away, a text from Graham pops up: *FYI*, followed by a link to a news article in a Los Angeles paper. The short article claims that a former UCLA student, anonymous due to fears of retaliation, is accusing business professor David Landry of "systematic sexual harassment." David has, of course, denied the charges.

I put my phone in my bag, not sure how to feel about that. Karma is a bitch, for sure. Yet knowing David has been preying on his students…could I have done anything else to expose him as the manipulative, lying creep that he is?

My stomach knots. I've gone over this a million times. I'd argued and fought tooth and nail, and I'd ended up fired, my voice silenced. I couldn't have done anything more.

But the limits of David's destructive force clearly haven't yet been reached. He's capable of *more*. Of that I have no doubt. And knowing he's out there, a monster against whom I have no weapons…that's the most terrifying thought of all.

CHAPTER 7

J refuse to let my lingering fears about David ruin the excitement of my new job. On Monday morning, I'm up at six, jittery with nerves. Though the initial part of the job involves unpacking dusty boxes, I dress in a pleated A-line skirt and gray blouse. I've never *not* dressed professionally for work, and this situation is no different.

Since I'm still pinching pennies, I make a peanut-butter sandwich and fill a baggie with saltine crackers. I toss them into a brown paper bag along with an apple and a thermos of tea. Satchel, computer, signed contract...and I'm off to the lighthouse.

The sight of the building, so picturesque perched on the cliff above the ocean and silhouetted against the foggy sky, makes me feel a bit sick.

Please let this work out. I need this job more than anything.

Flynn's truck is the only one in the lot. I gather my belongings and approach the side door leading to the workroom. Before I can knock, the door swings open.

Oh.

His sheer physical impact hits me with renewed force. Damp,

messy hair, gray eyes like steel, his muscular body clad in a plain blue T-shirt and faded jeans that fit his lean hips and long legs to perfection.

"Good morning." His voice slides over my skin like a caress. "I appreciate punctuality. Come in."

"Thank you." I slip past him into the room. My nose twitches. Salt and citrus. Sea and earth. "Where would you like me to start?"

"I'll leave everything to your expertise." His gaze moves over me, lingering on my loosely knotted red hair before sliding down to my tailored blouse and skirt. Heat flashes in his eyes, a reaction that intensifies my own warmth. So I hadn't imagined the urgent way he'd looked at me outside the bookstore.

Did he fantasize about me too?

The question whispers at the back of my mind, intensifying the burn.

He rests his hand on the worn wooden desk. Long, blunt fingers and square fingernails. His skin is slightly chapped at the knuckles, his fingers smudged with black ink. A sudden image emerges of his hand on my bare skin—sliding over my waist, the indentation of my hip, and down farther, his stained fingers curving to grip my inner thigh.

A hot shiver races down my spine, arousal collecting between my legs. I let out my breath slowly, welcoming the resurgence of feelings I've suppressed for so many months, a slow dissolve of the ice in my veins.

"...the contract?" His query slices through the haze descending over me.

The contract. Well, that cools the burn. I bring my focus back to the fact that I'm here to work, not get all hot and bothered.

Hopefully, he doesn't plan to hang out here while I'm working. I'd have a hard time getting anything done with him distracting me just by *existing*.

I take the signed sheaf of papers from my satchel and hand them to him, then retrieve my organizer and a gel pen.

"I'll have a copy for you tomorrow." Flynn leafs through the contract and points to an outlet on the wall. "You can plug the computer in there. Bathroom is right next door. You can leave at four."

I open my organizer to a fresh note page and click the gel pen. "Okay, I'm ready."

"Ready for what?"

"To take notes."

A puzzled frown appears on his face. "Notes?"

"About the collection." I wave my pen toward the boxes. "How you want me to organize everything. I'll make an outline of the plan."

"There's no plan."

"No plan? How can you not have a plan?"

"That's why I hired you," he says shortly. "You come up with the plan."

He starts across the room to the adjoining door that leads to the cottage. I blink with surprise.

"Wait a minute."

He stops and faces me.

"That's it?" I shake my head. "You're just giving me free rein?"

"This is your field, so yes."

"But don't you want things organized in a certain way?"

"No. I want them entered into the database and shelved." He gestures to the bare wooden shelves. "There's no internet up here, so you can't pull info from online catalogs. You'll need to input the data manually. Add descriptions yourself. If you want to move the paintings from the rack, go ahead. Do whatever you want."

"What about keeping a time card?"

"Your hours are eight to four. That's the time card."

"Do I have a lunch hour? Breaks?"

"Whenever you want." Impatience flickers across his expression. "Anything else?"

When do I get paid?

I don't want to irritate him further by asking that, so I shake my head. "No."

"Good." He starts toward the cottage again.

"Wait."

He expels a noise of frustration. "What?"

"What if I have a question?" I ask. "Can I text you or something?"

"I don't have a phone. If you have a question, write it down. I'll answer it in the morning."

I guess that means the only contact he plans to have with me is when he lets me in. I don't know whether that's a relief or a disappointment.

"Okay." I indicate my organizer. "I'll keep a list of questions in here."

He strides through the door, closing it behind him with a sharp click.

All righty then.

His presence lingers like a ghost. I force my mind to the task at hand. The instant I open a nearby box, anticipation curls through me like a Christmas present ribbon. I take out a slender volume titled *Fairy Tales by Hans Andersen*, illustrated by Arthur Rackham.

I open the book to my favorite story, *The Snow Queen*. I have always loved the devoted friendship between the girl Gerda and the boy Kay. At the story's beginning, a wicked sprite creates a magic mirror that distorts the world for anyone who looks into it. The beautiful becomes ugly, and the good becomes evil.

When the mirror breaks, one shard pierces Kay's eye and the other freezes his heart to ice. His soul shrivels, turning him against his beloved Gerda. He is forced under the spell of the icy Snow Queen, who carries him off to her palace and kisses him until he forgets everything about home. But Gerda, impelled by a powerful love, sets out to find him. Scared and alone, she does not stop until she rescues Kay from the Snow Queen's palace.

The two children return home together, both changed for their ordeal yet still innocent and more devoted to each other than ever. *"And they both sat there, grown up yet still children at heart, and it was summer—warm, glorious summer."*

I gaze at a Rackham illustration of golden-haired Gerda, a large book spread open on her lap, and dark-haired Kay sitting in a shingled rooftop garden flourishing with rose vines. The buildings and spires of Amsterdam stretch out in the background, but the two children are deep in conversation, lost in their own world.

And just like that, I'm a scholar again, an art historian who loves the authors and artists whose creativity blossoms through history. I set up the laptop on the desk, arrange the surface with a notepad, pencils, and sticky notes, and get to work.

The hours melt away. I compile bullet point lists and an outline of my cataloging plan. I immerse myself in pictures of moon maidens, golden swans, sharp-toothed leviathans. I study publication dates, tables of contents, ISBNs, countries of origin. I examine access points, hierarchies, search fields. I write descriptions and make notes.

At noon, I pull on my coat, taking my lunch bag and crossword puzzle book outside. I sit on the bench overlooking the cliff to eat and work on a particularly challenging puzzle.

The air is salty, cold, and fresh. The secrets wall snakes up the hill to the cliff's edge. Bits of paper stud the crevices of the granite stones, my own secret still hidden deep among them. Birds crest overhead, and waves splash against the rocks.

For the first time, I'm glad I'm not in the smoggy, sunburned haze of Los Angeles.

I toss my lunch trash into the recycling bin and return to the bench to spend the last fifteen minutes of my break working on the crossword puzzle. I'd forgotten how engrossing and meditative a crossword can be. *Doctor Faustus novelist, part of an oven, Eureka!*

A shadow falls across the half-filled grid of the puzzle. I glance up, shading my eyes against the sun, and absorb the sight of Flynn—jeans, work boots, flannel shirt, navy parka. Messy hair so artfully tousled that male models probably pay a fortune in styling products to achieve the same look.

On an aesthetic level, it's not right to hide such masculine beauty away from the world. It's like keeping a Michelangelo sculpture locked in a storage closet.

"Hi." My voice comes out a bit breathless.

"Hello." He gives me a short nod.

"It's such a beautiful day that I came out here to eat lunch," I explain, in case he thinks I'm slacking off on the job.

"Good idea."

He's close enough that I catch a delicious whiff of spice and citrus, carried on the wind. I still have the handkerchief he lent me the other day. Even though I washed it, his scent still clings to the cotton.

Do you know about what happened to me? Anxiety tightens my belly. Even though I barely know him, I don't want him to think badly of me because of the rumors.

"When you came after me last week," I say slowly, "did you know...I mean, had you heard..." Cheeks heating, I can't finish my sentence.

He studies me, tension lining his jaw. "You had an affair with a married professor and were fired from UCLA."

I shouldn't be shocked all over again. If the whole town knows, there's no reason he wouldn't, but a fresh surge of disbelief, and regret, fills me. I must have thought—*hoped*—that loner lighthouse guy would be the one person in town who knows only what I choose to tell him. Not what everyone else also knows.

"I might be the local recluse, but I still need to buy groceries and go to the hardware store," he says.

"Well, that whole mess is the reason I ended up here. The reason I had a hard time finding a job too." I gesture to the workroom. "So you can see why I owe you a lot for hiring me."

"I owed your uncle a lot." He shrugs and peers at the crossword book open on my lap. "But I hired you because you're qualified. Not because I wanted to pay a debt. Or because I felt sorry for you."

"Regardless of why, thank you."

He nods again and indicates the book. "You like puzzles."

"I guess so." I skim the list of clues. "I used to do crosswords when I was a kid. It's like a little mystery, figuring out the clues and secrets of the grid. I found this book over at Jabberwocky and thought I'd give it a try." I tap my pencil on five down. "Become rusty. Seven letters."

"*Oxidate.*"

I lift an eyebrow and write the word. "Impressive. Historical accounting, including the *I* in *oxidate*. Wait, I got it. *Memoir.* Fanatics, seven letters."

"*Zealots.*"

"Nice." I write the word on the grid and gesture to the seat beside me. "Sit down. We'll have this done in no time."

"I gotta go." He looks at his watch. "Did you leave the door unlocked so you can get back inside?"

"Yes. Where are…"

He turns away to stride down the pathway to the parking lot.

"…you going?" I finish to the empty terrace.

Even if he'd heard me, I wouldn't have expected an answer. In fairy tales, questions don't usually have the desired response anyway.

Mirror, Mirror on the wall, who is the fairest one of all? Can your name be Rumpelstiltskin? Do you love me, Beauty?

Though my life is no fairy tale, it's still better not to ask any questions at all. I watch Flynn until he rounds the bend and disappears from sight.

I want to know him.

The wish, the new *secret*, forms in my mind like watercolors flowing together. Given his reclusiveness, I can't imagine it will ever come true, but it's nice to feel curiosity again, to think about something else besides my own struggles.

I close the crossword book and return to cataloging my uncle's books and paintings.

By the time four o'clock rolls around, my eyes are peppery with fatigue and my neck hurts, but I'm filled with an exhilaration I haven't experienced in longer than I care to remember. I'm *good* at this, and I love everything about it.

A tiny flame of warmth lights in my heart. I might even be happy again.

After organizing my workspace for the following day, I pack up my things and leave through the side door.

White-capped ocean waves shift and roll, splashing rhythmically against the rocks. The hiking trail stretches alongside the coast for as far as the eye can see.

A perfect place for a run—yet another thing I haven't done in a long time. I used to work out regularly at the gym and run the UCLA track, but I'd lost the motivation to keep myself in shape when my life circled the drain like dirty bathwater.

Tomorrow I'll pack running gear so I can change and go for a jog after work, get the stiffness out of my limbs. I start back to the parking lot. A prickling sensation courses down my spine.

I stop and turn slowly, lifting my gaze to the lantern room at the top of the tower. Again he stands behind the glass—a big, shadowy presence like an overlord looking down upon his kingdom. But this time, I know *who* he is and the powerful effect he has on me.

I look up at him. Strange energy courses between us even from such a distance. *What does he do up there in the tower?*

Despite my natural curiosity, there's a strange freedom in knowing he's forbidden. I can enjoy thinking about him, speculating about him, fantasizing about him, but without any emotional complications or fear about what he might be hiding. Lord knows I've had enough of that to last me a while.

I walk to the half-filled parking lot. A heavy-set, bald man getting into a blue sedan looks vaguely familiar. For some reason, unease hits me. I pull out my keys and get into my car.

Castille is a small town. Of course I'll see many of the same people in passing. I shouldn't be so easily spooked. Still, I lock the car doors quickly and waste no time leaving the parking lot.

CHAPTER 8

My first week of work falls into a welcome routine. I arrive at the lighthouse at eight sharp, and Flynn opens the workroom door before I even knock, as if he's been waiting for me. After I set my things on the desk, he answers whatever questions I've written in my organizer.

(What do you want me to do with books that need repairs? Make a list and set them aside. What about digitization? Finish the cataloging first. Do you want bibliographic as well as content descriptions? Yes.)

While he's still in the room, I indulge in a few minutes of privately unabashed gawking because every morning he looks so tempting—rumpled and rough around the edges like an abstract painting, but unbearably tangible at the same time. I'm seized with the urge to drag my fingers through his hair to discover if it's as thick and coarse as it looks, to rub my palm over his sand-papery jaw, to feel all the hard muscles so evident under his T-shirt.

I start to enjoy my hidden little fantasies, the thawing of my blood. My interaction with Flynn is so limited that I'm no longer worried that he'll discern my attraction to him. Especially considering that he barely glances at me.

Every morning, there's a *look*, though. Sometimes I think I'm imagining it—the flash of heat, the electric crackle, the darkening of his gray eyes—but other times I swear I feel it right down to my bones. Then he turns away, and the moment disappears.

When the cottage door clicks behind him, I focus on work, immersing myself for the rest of the day in stories of frog kings, resourceful princesses, powerful giants. I unpack boxes, study the books, input information into the database. I cross items off my bullet point lists one by one.

I take a break at noon for my peanut-butter sandwich lunch and tea in a thermos. Aside from going into the cottage to use the bathroom, which is small but surprisingly elegant with a polished stone floor and gleaming fixtures, and sitting outside for lunch, I don't leave the workroom. The ocean rumbles and birds call through the windows.

At four, I change into track pants and a sweatshirt, leave my belongings in my car, and head out for a jog along the trail curving beside the coastline like a string of yarn. I've gotten out of shape in the past year, and at first my body protests the exertion. But the cold, damp air is delicious against my face, my heart beats heavily, and adrenaline floods my veins.

I don't get very far on my first run, but I push myself a little harder the next day, and harder still the next. Though remembering I used to run five miles at a time while now I can't even manage one is rather discouraging, I like the soreness of my muscles, the strain and effort, the ache in my lungs.

I like touching myself again too. I still have to smother shame about my sexual instincts, but relearning my body's responsiveness feels good. In the shower—rubbing frothy soap over my nipples, down across my belly, working up a lather between my legs. Getting ready—smoothing lotion into my skin, brushing my hair, applying makeup. Dressing—adjusting my breasts in the cups of my bra, sliding my panties over my hips, rolling stockings up my legs.

Alone in bed at night, I work my fingers against my sex, pushing my lower body up into the increasing pressure of urgency. Raw, uninhibited images of *him*, of *us*, flash behind my closed eyelids.

Flynn stretched out on the bed in a white T-shirt riding up to reveal the ridges of his abdomen, naked from the waist down with his thick cock sticking straight up like an invitation. He beckons me toward him with a crook of his finger. His smoky dark eyes gleam with lust.

And me, sliding my cotton panties off before climbing onto the bed and straddling his powerful thighs. Bracing my hands on his chest, spreading my legs, positioning myself. Easing down… slowly, so slowly…feeling him penetrate me, my body already slick and ready for him. A twinge of pain as he stretches me fully, his cock hitting that exquisite spot so deep inside me.

His hands gripping my hips. His rough command. *"Move."*

I move…no, I writhe, squirm, bounce, curling my fingers into his chest, working myself up and down on his shaft, everything distilling into the sensation of our bodies slamming together. Groans and hoarse growls of encouragement fill the air. I splay over him, whimpering with need, my tender nipples rubbing against his chest, his mouth hot on my temple.

In my mind, he comes first, shooting so powerfully inside me that the vibrations send me over the edge. With a cry of pleasure, I shudder and convulse with bliss. I collapse on top of him, our sweat-slick bodies heaving together.

It's the moment when he comes—hard and heavy, a growl tearing from his throat—that I bring myself to orgasm, one finger thrust into my body and my other hand frantically massaging my clit. I moan aloud, arching upward, the intense sensations stealing my breath.

Then I lie back against the pillows for a long time, absorbing the lingering pulses and being thankful that I haven't, in fact, lost my sexual desire. I'm still a woman capable of erotic pleasure, still allowed to revel in fantasies and to love having orgasms.

After David, I'd been so ashamed of everything I'd done, of how needy I'd been both in bed and out of it. I hadn't even wanted to look at myself in the mirror, humiliated by the idea that people were imagining salacious things about me. Maybe now I can finally let my shame die.

If there's a nagging realization that masturbating alone every night isn't the same as being touched by a man who loves me... well, I can ignore that. I'm just grateful to be rediscovering the pieces of myself that had been so badly broken.

Maybe one day I'll even be whole again.

CHAPTER 9

The silvery, mid-October dusk falls as I struggle through my after-work jog. Panting, I come to a halt at the bend in the trail. An icy ocean mist prickles my face like needles. My breath rasps through my throat, and my leg muscles ache.

I remind myself that I've only been exercising for a week. I can't expect to run a mile yet, much less two.

I straighten and eye a large boulder jutting over the cliff at a curve. The boulder appears to be about three miles from the lighthouse. I'm nowhere near it, but one day soon I'll run all the way there without needing to stop.

Sea air sweeps across the rocky promontory. I trudge up the hill to the cliff's plateau. The lighthouse windows are all dark.

Where is he?

He's kind of like a crossword puzzle in and of himself, a grid of clues leading to the complete theme. *A building on the coast, ten letters. Espionage objective, seven letters. Seductively attractive, four letters. Lacking transparency, six letters.*

Not nearly as solvable as the *New York Times* puzzles. And those suckers are tough.

I return home to shower and change, deciding to head over to the Jabberwocky Bookstore. A couple of hours reading or working on a crossword by the fireplace is a lot more appealing than trying to fix another old toilet.

I drive downtown and walk to the bookstore, reaching the front door just as a tall man in an expensive cashmere coat approaches. He grabs the door handle, stepping aside to hold it open.

"Beg your pardon," he says.

"No problem. Thanks." I start past him when his voice stops me.

"I'm sorry, miss. I haven't seen you in town before."

I pause and eye him cautiously. "I just moved here about three weeks ago."

He's in his early thirties, blond hair, brown eyes, noble features like those you'd see on the face of a Roman emperor.

"That explains it." He extends a hand. "I pride myself on knowing everyone who lives here, but if you're new, we haven't been acquainted yet. Jeremy King."

I shake his hand. Wary curiosity rises to my chest. "Are you any relation to Allegra King?"

"She's my mother." He studies me with growing interest. "Why do you ask?"

How much should I tell him? How much does he know about Max?

"I've heard a lot about her," I finally say. "I'm Eve Perrin."

"Pleasure to meet you, Eve Perrin." He gestures to the interior of Jabberwocky. "I'm getting a coffee before heading to a city council meeting. Can I buy you one?"

I hesitate, not wanting to give him the impression that I'm available.

Except...*am I available?*

My crazy-hot reaction to Flynn is evidence that I still have sexual urges and interests, even if intellectually I know I could never get involved with him. Aside from the fact that he's my boss, he has a clear *Keep Out* sign in front of both him and his lighthouse. And my self-preservation instincts won't let me get taken in by a man who is anything less than totally straightforward and honest.

"Okay," I say to Jeremy, who's still holding the door open and waiting patiently. "Thanks."

We enter the café, order coffees, and sit in a couple of chairs near the fireplace. Though my reading plans have gone awry, it's still a warm, pleasant ending to my day.

"So what are you doing here, Eve?" Jeremy leans forward. "We don't get many new residents in Castille anymore. People are more apt to move away, head to Portland or Boston."

"Long story, but my uncle used to be a literature professor over at Ford's. Max Dearborne."

Something flickers in his eyes that I don't recognize. Surprise? Dislike?

"You knew him."

"I knew *of* him," he corrects. "The fairy tale expert."

"I'm living in his place over on Sparrow Lane."

Jeremy arches an eyebrow with faint distaste. "That old place? I'm surprised it's still standing."

I experience a rush of indignation on the house's behalf. "It's actually a historic house. It just needs some work, that's all."

"Is that why you moved here?" He sips his coffee, studying me over the rim of the cup. "To restore the house?"

"Sort of." It seems he hasn't heard about me yet. He will, of course, if he doesn't look me up on the internet first. But I'm not going to dredge up my past and try to explain myself to him. I don't want to do that with anyone anymore.

"I've heard a lot about your parents." I pick up my coffee from a nearby table. "I saw your mother's portrait over at the museum. Your family is a big deal around here."

"Yeah." His mouth twists with both pride and resignation. "Tough act to follow sometimes, especially when you're an only child. Everyone expected me to follow in Dad's footsteps and become a politician."

"But you didn't?"

"No. I wasn't interested in politics. I've always been involved with Castille and want to help however I can, but from the private sector."

"So what do you do?"

"I work for my father's financial management company, King Financial. Our office is over on Greenbrier Street." He sets his cup down, glancing at me with interest. "What about you? What do you do besides restore old houses?"

"Actually, my restoration expertise so far extends to fixing an old toilet," I say wryly. "But other than that, I'm an art historian."

"Really? My mother used to collect Victorian art." He chuckles and shakes his head. "Can't say my father and I ever loved it, but she sure did. Are you working over at Ford's?"

"No, I'm doing some…consulting work at the moment."

It's as close to the truth as I can get, given that I've agreed not to divulge any details about my new job.

"Interesting." Jeremy glances at his phone. "I'd love to hear more, but I'm afraid I have to join my father over at the city council meeting. Much as I'd rather stay here with you, it's a meeting I can't miss."

I let myself be flattered by the *stay here with you* comment. "What's going on at the meeting?"

"Debate about the lighthouse." A crease lines his forehead. "You'll hear about it sooner or later. Big town controversy at the moment."

"Why?"

"I'm hoping to sell it."

My heart does a sudden, strange drop. "Sell the lighthouse? You can do that?"

"I hope so." He smiles faintly. "Given that we own it."

"You *own* the lighthouse?"

He cocks his head. "Well, my mother's estate does. My father and I are working out the details of a trust involving the building itself and about fifteen acres of land. My mother's family has owned it ever since the lighthouse went out of commission in the 1970s. The Castille Forestry Department leases it to preserve as a tourist attraction, but with the town's economy in decline, we don't think it's worth it to keep anymore. It's on a prime piece of coastal land, and developers have been interested in it for years."

"So you want to sell it to them?" I tighten my hand on the coffee cup. "Why?"

"To build a hotel resort and golf course." He shakes his head with a chuckle. "I know, makes me sound like the evil town villain, right? Destroy an old relic for the sake of money. Unfortunately, the fact is that Castille may look pretty, but underneath the façade, we've been struggling for a long time. Enrollment is down at local schools, Ford's College is having a tough time recruiting students, and no one is even bothering to try opening a business anymore. Young people are moving to cities for more opportunities, and older people are retiring and moving to warmer climates. The main things Castille has going for it are history, small-town charm, and tourism…so attracting people with an all-inclusive resort would do wonders to save our economy."

"Do you have to destroy the lighthouse to do that?"

Jeremy shrugs. "If we sell the land, it's not up to me. And we're not talking about a monstrosity or eyesore here. My father would never allow that. The Oracle Development Corporation has plans for an elegant, Georgian style building that will blend in with the coastline. I'd make them contractually obligated to ensure the construction has a limited impact on the environment."

"How do the town residents feel about it?"

"I'd say they're divided fifty-fifty right now." He rises to his feet and picks up his coffee. "Hopefully that will be closer to seventy-thirty, if not more, after the meeting. The big issue coming up in a few weeks is that the council has to approve a change in the zoning law before we can close the deal. That's why we need to convince them it's the right thing to do."

I almost wish him luck, then stop. I'm not at all sure I want him to be *lucky* about selling the lighthouse.

"It was nice meeting you," I say instead.

"You too." He pauses, a touch of nervousness entering his eyes. "Would you like to have dinner sometime, Eve?"

Surprise ripples through me. For a moment, I can't respond. A man hasn't asked me out since…David.

"Dinner?" I repeat lamely.

"With me." He smiles.

"I…" Uncomfortable heat crawls up the back of my neck.

Oh, come on, Eve. You're not fifteen years old. Dinner with a nice man is…dinner with a nice man. And God knows it feels good to have someone be nice to me for a change.

I haven't given any thought to what I might do if a new romantic opportunity presents itself in Castille, but I've also told myself that David has done enough damage to my life. I won't let him destroy the possibility of a future relationship—or, at the very least, one date.

I glance at Jeremy's left hand. No ring. No evidence of a ring tan line either, not that that means anything.

"I'd like that," I finally say. "Thanks for asking me."

We agree on next Saturday, and he inputs my number into his phone. After he's gone, I suppress the worry that he might cancel after discovering my sordid story. I'm not naïve enough to think he *won't* look me up on the internet. Maybe he's even doing that right now as he goes to the city council meeting.

But if he does cancel…well, there's plenty of repair work at Ramshackle Manor to keep me busy next Saturday night.

"More coffee, Eve?" Carol stops beside me with the coffeepot.

"Thanks." I extend my cup.

"I see you met Jeremy King," she remarks, a little too casually.

My stomach twists. More gossip? Just what I need.

"He was telling me about his idea to sell the lighthouse." I take a sip of the fresh coffee. "I didn't know that was even an issue."

"Oh, it's an issue all right." Carol straightens, her lips pursing. "It'd be a shame to see the lighthouse torn down, but honestly I can see the other side. A resort could really help put Castille back on the map, and Jeremy wouldn't do anything detrimental to the town. He and his family have deep roots here, so his heart is in the right place."

"What about the lighthouse keeper?" I ask carefully.

"You mean the loon?" Alex approaches with a wet rag starts wiping down the tables.

"Flynn isn't a loon." Carol throws her son a chastising frown.

"Yeah, he is." Alex rolls his eyes. "And it's so annoying because all the girls around here are always, like, *oh, he's so hot*, which is stupid because they say they want to *get to know* a guy, and yet no one really *knows* anything about Flynn."

"He's a bit private." Carol looks at me, her eyebrows raised. "He doesn't say much, but you'll definitely hear people talk about him. He's something of a legend around here."

"*So* stupid." Alex flicks the rag over a coffee stain. "The headless horseman is a *legend*. Flynn is just strange."

Hoping they can give me more info, I ask, "So what does he do?"

"He takes care of the lighthouse, the history display, and the secrets wall." Carol shrugs. "Technically he's employed by the Forestry Department, but I hear he doesn't take a paycheck. Apparently Allegra King let him move in years ago and he's never left."

My interest spikes. "He's friends with Allegra?"

"I don't know that Flynn is *friends* with anyone," Carol says. "But Allegra has allowed him to live in the lighthouse all these years, and she wouldn't do that for just anyone."

"Even if he's a total weirdo." Alex circles his finger near his ear.

Carol gives him a scolding poke on the arm. "He's a lovely young man, just a quiet loner type."

"That's what they say about serial killers." Alex straightens and wads the rag into a ball. "Did anyone ever think of that?"

"Ignore him," Carol tells me with a long-suffering sigh. "He watches too much *Forensic Files*."

"What does Flynn have to say about the possibility of the lighthouse being sold?" I ask.

"He's not happy about it, but there's not much he can do." Carol starts back to the counter with the coffeepot. "Not much anyone can do, for that matter. We'll have to live with whatever Jeremy and his father decide."

"Does Allegra have a say?" I bring my coffee cup to the counter. I'm asking too many questions. It's time for me to leave before Carol and Alex start wondering about my interest.

"No one knows." Carol sets the pot back on the coffee machine. "If it's true that Jeremy and his father have taken over her affairs due to her illness, then I guess not."

I gather my things together and thank them both. Leaving the bookstore, I'm even more confused and curious than I was before.

When I get home, I park beside the porch. Beady yellow eyes blink at me in the darkness. Cautiously, I get out of the car. The dog remains standing near the fence. I pick up the empty dog food bowl and unlock the front door.

I fill the bowl from the bag I'd left in the foyer and set it on the porch. This time, the dog approaches while I'm still standing there. His tail even wags a little as he lowers his head to the food.

I refill another bowl with water, then wait beside him. When he's finished eating, I give his big furry head a tentative pat. He doesn't respond with tail-wagging affection, but he doesn't growl either. After licking his chops, he bounds down the stairs and into the woods.

At least it's progress. It will probably be a heck of a lot easier earning the trust of a stray dog than that of a guarded lighthouse keeper.

I start back into the house. Wind whistles through the woodlands, stirring and crunching the dried autumn leaves. I peer toward the darkened tree-line. Branches fork out like skeletal arms. Shadows drift behind the pines, mutating into large, shapeless forms like phantoms.

Sudden fear ripples over my skin. My blood grows cold. I hurry inside. Heart pounding, I shut and bolt the door.

I take a few deep breaths and tell myself not to be so easily frightened. I'm safe here. Except for Graham and my mother, no one from my former life knows where I am.

Still, I need to be careful. Tomorrow I'll call around for estimates about an alarm system.

CHAPTER 10

The following Monday, I expect Flynn to give me a review of my work performance so far, but we only have our brief morning interaction before he disappears. The second week begins much the same as the first—a productive workday broken by lunch, followed by a jog along the coast.

And the incessant wondering about Flynn. *What in the heck does he do all day?* Sometimes I see him outside through the window. He's either heading toward the parking lot, carrying a duffle bag or a backpack, or doing work around the grounds.

Aside from that, I neither see nor hear him, which certainly makes for a quiet working environment. I receive several estimates for alarm system installation, but the prices are just too far out of my range. Deadbolts will have to suffice until I can replenish my funds.

I spend Wednesday morning unpacking a number of French fairy tales and inputting their data into the system. Close to lunchtime, I discover a cardboard folder bound with a tattered red ribbon at the bottom of one box. I pull the ribbon off and open the folder.

A colored drawing of a half-naked young woman, her face

shadowed by a red hood, leaps off the page in vivid, shocking detail. The wolf, who in the original *Red Riding Hood* tale lures her into his bed before killing her, is a half-man, half-creature lounging in a wooden bed.

His dirty fangs are bared, and there's a lewd bulge at his groin beneath the bedcovers. In Red Riding Hood's hand, concealed by the folds of her cloak, is a sharp silver knife.

Recognition sparks in me, though I don't know why. I don't think I've ever seen this drawing before, though the art historian in me is struck by the sheer expertise of the image—elegant lines, precise detail, clearly the work of a trained artist. At the bottom, there's a signature, faint but legible. *Maria Wood. 1858.*

How odd. There's an Italian fairy tale called *Fair Maria Wood* about a daughter who has to fight the incestuous advances of her father after her mother's death. She escapes him by wearing a dress made of wood and throwing herself into a river.

The wood keeps her afloat, and upon reaching another kingdom, she indentures herself as a servant to a young man who falls in love with her. She eventually loves him in return, and though the ending is a happy one, the story falls into the tradition of fairy tales in which young women are forced to flee twisted sexual advances.

So why would an artist take on the pseudonym of Maria Wood? And why do I feel like there's something about this drawing I should know?

I set the book aside. My mind burns, imprinted with the disturbing, graphic image. But there's a spark too, one of potential discovery.

I take out my phone and search both popular and scholarly websites for something, anything, about a nineteenth-century artist named Maria Wood. The internet yields nothing.

The nineteenth century is my field. I've written books and papers about the Pre-Raphaelites, Victorian imagery in its social context, French visual culture, art and literature, Van Gogh and astronomy. I know the prominent fairy tale artists—Walter Crane, Arthur Rackham, Anne Anderson, Jessie Wilcox Smith—but not only have I never heard of Maria Wood, I've never seen any paintings or drawings like hers before.

Or have I?

I fish my phone out of my bag and call Graham. After an exchange of pleasantries and updates, he asks, "Hey, did you get that link I sent you about David Landry and the sexual harassment accusation? Seems another student of his has come forward with a similar complaint."

"Good for them. I don't doubt for a minute that it's true." I tighten my fingers on the phone, suppressing a quiver of fear. "Unfortunately, I also know David. He'll find a way out of it. At least I don't have to deal with him anymore."

"I'm sorry you ever had to. But maybe your story is what prompted these other women to come forward."

Given all that I lost, it's not much comfort, but I'm glad that people are being made aware of David's horrific behavior. Maybe this will stop him from manipulating and hurting someone else.

"Enough about him," Graham declares. "Let's talk about you. Any luck with the job search?"

My stomach clenches. Graham is the last person in the world I would ever lie to, but omitting information isn't the same as actually lying. And my work for Flynn does fall under the "consulting" header.

"I'm doing some consulting and cataloging for a private collector," I explain. "I wanted to ask you about an illustration I found."

I describe Maria Wood's drawing, then ask, "Have you ever heard of her?"

"No, but artistic pseudonyms were relatively common in the Victorian era," he says. "Though it was usually a woman using a male pseudonym. I'll do some digging and ask around."

I thank him and end the call, glancing at the clock. Almost

noon. I take out my sandwich and open a thermos of peppermint tea. It's overcast and drizzly today, so I stay inside. To avoid staining any of Max's books, I work on a crossword puzzle while I eat my peanut-butter sandwich and saltines.

The handle on the cottage door clicks and turns.

My heart jumps. Aside from our morning interactions, Flynn hasn't come into the workroom during the day. But now he stops in front of the desk, his sharp gaze slipping over me and the desk's surface.

He's still in his jeans and T-shirt from this morning, but he's also wearing a gray hoodie with a small, faded *USA Hockey* logo on the left side. And he's all stormy blue and smoky gray at the same time, sea and sky, a force of nature, a—

"I need a book about the Russian story of the Firebird," he says.

I blink, not sure I heard that correctly. "Um…"

"Do you have one?"

"I know Uncle Max had a number of Firebird books, but I'm afraid I haven't come across any yet."

He gives a swift nod. "Look for them. Tell me when you find one."

"Yes, sir."

Faint amusement rises to his eyes. "You don't need to call me *sir*."

"Well, you do tend to inspire…er, obedience." I wince inwardly. *Why did I say that?*

He arches an eyebrow. "Obedience?"

Okay, not the best choice of words.

"Just doing my job." I pick up a gel pen and start to write *Find Firebird stories* in my organizer, but the pen is out of ink. I mutter under my breath and fish around for a pencil to finish the sentence. "Will there be anything else?"

"No." He studies me, his nostrils flaring slightly. "What's that smell?"

Oh, dear. Is he one of those people who has a sensitivity to certain scents?

"Maybe it's my lotion?" I suggest.

He furrows his brow, as if I just spoke a different language. "Lotion?"

"For my skin." I gesture to my arms. "I use an apple-lavender scented body cream after my shower in the morning."

He shifts his eyes from my face down to my neck, all the way to my arms bared by my short-sleeved blouse. A slight flush crests his cheekbones, as if he's imagining me smoothing lotion into my skin.

What if he knew how much I enjoy applying it? Sliding my hands over my breasts, my palms slick with rich, thick cream, drops of water still dripping down my thighs...

Eve!

"If it's too strong, I'll stop using it," I assure him.

"No." He jerks his gaze back to my face and clears his throat. "You don't need to...uh, stop using it. But that's not what it is."

He picks up the thermos from my desk and sniffs. "Peppermint."

"Oh." I'm mildly disappointed that he wasn't so attuned to me he caught my scent. "I usually have tea at two o'clock, but my old thermos doesn't keep it hot that long. So I've been having tea with my lunch."

Flynn sets the thermos down and frowns. He points to the remnants of my PB&J and saltines. "What's that?"

"My lunch, of course."

A line appears between his eyebrows. "You're eating peanut butter and crackers? Why?"

His words are clipped. Though I'm not sure why he's interrogating me about my culinary choices, I remind myself he's my boss. Employees have to indulge their boss's eccentric ways sometimes, but his irrational annoyance scrapes my nerves.

"You did tell me I'm allowed to set my own breaks and lunch

hour," I remind him. "And frankly, there are labor laws about employees being able to eat and—"

"I mean, why a peanut-butter sandwich?" A scowl creases his face. "Why don't you bring something more substantial?"

"I like peanut butter."

"Every day?"

"Well, no, but…"

"But what?" His tone is hard, almost angry, and I have the unpleasant sense he'll interrogate me with increasing force until he's certain he knows the truth.

"I don't…" Fresh warmth rises to my face again, but this time from the embarrassment of admission. "I can't afford much right now."

Flynn's expression turns from a scowl into a thunderstorm. "You don't have enough money to *eat*?"

Bristling, I lean back in my chair. "Of course I do. Peanut butter is a perfectly healthy option."

"Why didn't you tell me you need money?"

"Why else would I need a job?" I reply stiffly. "And I don't *need* money…well, we all do, of course, but I'm not living in poverty." *Not yet anyway.* "I'm just being fiscally careful at the moment."

"Stay here." Flynn stalks out the door.

Where else would I go? I still have four hours of work left.

Shrugging off his apparent peanut-butter aversion, I pick up a box cutter to open a box. I've been inputting book data into the system as I open each box, but now I'll have to change my strategy and keep unpacking until I find the *Firebird* books.

The cottage door slams open again. Flynn stomps in like an irritated bear.

"Come here," he snaps.

Do this. Do that. Stay. Come.

"I'm not a dog," I mutter, though I drop the box cutter and approach him.

He smirks. "I know. Dogs don't use body lotion."

I can't help chuckling. "You're the strangest boss I've ever had."

"Funny. You're the only employee I've ever had. Come on."

I follow him out of the workroom. We're halfway down the corridor before I realize we're actually going *into* the cottage. The only rooms I've seen are the bathroom and the separate building containing artifacts of the lighthouse's history. The cottage and tower are both his private living quarters.

Flynn steps aside. Though I can't be certain, I think I hear him inhale deeply as I precede him into the kitchen.

I stop, taken aback by the room's charm. The wooden floor gleams with age, a weathered table sits near a window overlooking the cliff's plateau, and the walls are lined with blue cabinets that speak to the house's nautical history. The countertops and appliances are all polished and modern, but somehow both old and new mesh in a way that suits the building perfectly.

"This is lovely," I remark.

Flynn shoots me a narrow glance. "You sound surprised."

"With you being all scruffy and mysterious up here, I didn't know what to expect. Did you do the renovations yourself? Sorry, sorry. No questions."

"The answer is yes." He spreads a hand to the stove and refrigerator. "I'm amending clause three of the contract. You're no longer allowed to bring food into the workroom. Peanut butter, in particular, is banned. Instead, you'll use the kitchen and whatever food is here. You can bring your tea and make it here too. There's a teakettle around somewhere. Eat at the table instead of your desk."

"Thank you, but I'd really prefer bringing my own food."

He frowns. "You'll eat what's here, Eve. Is that understood?"

Frustration shoves at my chest. Given what I endured through the investigation, being *told what to do* scrapes my nerves raw. But Flynn's dictates don't inspire the same kind of impotent fury that other people's have.

Maybe because—stomping and glowering aside—he appears to want to make things a little better for me. I wouldn't go so far as to say he *cares*, but he certainly *notices*.

"All right," I concede. "I'll eat lunch in the kitchen. I just hope you don't only have Spam."

His mouth twitches. "I promise you'll have more than Spam. More than peanut butter too."

He starts back down the corridor. I follow, unable to help being pleased at the idea of taking breaks in such a warm, homey kitchen.

We return to the workroom. Flynn stops by the door and reaches into his sweatshirt pocket, producing a thin envelope. He extends it to me.

"What is this?" I take the envelope.

"Advance on your first two weeks' pay."

I take a check out of the envelope, shocked by the size of the number. "I can't accept this."

"You can, and you will," he replies shortly.

"Oh my *God*." I choke out a laugh. "Do you seriously think ordering me around will get you what you want?"

"It usually does." He crosses his arms over his chest and levels me with a stern look. "I'm your employer. I decide what I'm going to pay you. You will accept it."

"I don't need your pity." I press my lips together. "I intend to work hard both to earn a paycheck and for personal reasons, but I won't take charity."

I fully expect him to argue and lay down the law again, but instead he regards me with a curious intensity. Then he nods.

"Advance on your first *month's* pay," he concedes.

"Done." I slip the check back into the envelope. "Thank you."

I wait for him to turn and leave, but he doesn't move, his gaze still on me. Penetrating. Deep.

I clear my throat. "Will there be anything else?"

"Yes." He uncrosses his arms and steps toward me. His presence fills me with heat.

"Okay." My voice trembles a bit. I take a step back and come up against the wall.

He stops a scant few inches away and places his hand on the wall behind me. For a heart-stopping instant, I realize this is the closest we've ever been. My whole body tingles.

He leans forward to look me in the eye. He's so close I only need to reach out slightly to rest my hand on his chest. So close that he only needs to lower his head just a little to...

"I have a new contract clause." His iron-gray eyes are serious, his whiskered jaw set.

Really? I blow out a breath of exasperation. "What is it, *sir?*"

"You are required to use apple-lavender body lotion before coming to work."

Then he straightens and leaves, closing the door behind him.

CHAPTER 11

*J*ust a few hours after work, I'm on my knees in bed, my face buried in the pillow and my hand working between my spread legs. I've given up all pretense of decency or inhibition. As usual, I come blissfully hard, shuddering and quaking, a gasp catching in my throat.

But afterward, as I sink onto the bed and catch my breath, a strange hollowness opens inside me. Not because I spend every night masturbating alone—although that might get wearisome soon—but because the man making me *feel* all these delicious sensations again is so forbidden.

I can't start imagining what the *reality* of him would be like. Aside from the fact that he's my boss and he has an irritating, dictatorial temperament, he's far too reclusive. And with any luck, I won't be in town for long. Even if I did plan to stay in Castille, I wouldn't get involved with the secretive lighthouse keeper. A man's secrets and lies destroyed me once. I won't risk it again.

Not to mention, a volcano of rumors would likely erupt if scandalous Eve Perrin were to hook up with the town's resident loner.

With a sigh, I roll onto my back, skimming a hand over my breasts. I hate knowing I'll let other people's opinions dictate what I do, but I have no choice. People's opinions skewered me once. I won't give them the opportunity to do it again.

Besides, no one seems to know much about Flynn. He could be anything. A criminal, a mobster, a killer.

While not impossible, I can't make myself believe he has a black heart beneath his stoic exterior. My instincts failed me miserably with David, but they're not wrong about Flynn.

He's strange, yes, but not dangerous. He was once friends with Uncle Max. He bought Max's collection and wants to look at books about the Firebird. He'd noticed how upset I was that day at the museum, and he'd come after me to offer me a job instead of just walking away.

I refuse to believe that the man who'd both rescued me and earned the trust of my beloved uncle is someone to be feared. It would be wise to keep a distance between us, but I'm not afraid of him.

Just the opposite, in fact. I'm developing an unfortunate and intense crush on the mysterious lighthouse keeper.

The next morning after my shower, I smooth apple-lavender cream over my calves and thighs. The daily ritual has a heightened significance now that I know Flynn likes my scent.

I tell myself this is all good for me—this return to feeling attractive, to liking my body again, even doing a little something because I know it's appealing to a man.

I finish getting ready and walk out to my car, pausing at the strange sense of being watched. Skin prickling, I turn to see the dog looking at me from the side of the house.

Relieved, I ask, "You hover around here a lot, don't you? You're like a ghost."

He barks.

"Ghost, huh?" I toss my satchel in the car and pick up his food dish. "Okay, then."

I refill his food and water. He's waiting on the porch when I come back out. He nudges his head against my hand before starting to eat.

Seems I have a pet now. Or an animal companion, at least.

I drive to the lighthouse, where Flynn greets me at the door looking so ridiculously edible that my fantasy of last night blooms in my mind with renewed force. I skim my gaze over his worn jeans and unzipped gray hoodie. A faded blue T-shirt clings to his muscles.

God. What would he think if he knew what went on in my imagination?

"Good morning." I set my belongings on the desk and pick up my organizer. "No sign of the Firebird books yet, but I'll keep looking."

"Good. Any questions?"

"No. I'm going to work on the Hans Christian Andersen tales today." I sit down. Several unopened packages of clickable gel pens are on the desk. "Are these for me?"

"Yes." Flynn rests his hands on his hips. "Isn't that the brand you use?"

"Yes, but…you bought me some pens?"

He shrugs. "Just office supplies. I noticed your pen ran out of ink yesterday. I figured you could use more."

"Oh. Thank you."

He turns and leaves. I open the package and take out a pen. They're all blue ink, the color I always use.

It's a little silly to be so pleased by a gift of new pens, but given Flynn's self-imposed distance from…well, the *world*, I appreciate that he noticed such a small thing. Not to mention, it's been a long time since someone has done something nice for me.

I organize my workspace. No lunch today, per my new orders

to eat in the kitchen. I did bring my tea set and a selection of gourmet teas, all packaged tidily in a woven basket. My mid-afternoon break will be much nicer with a properly brewed cup of tea.

I start unpacking boxes, keeping an eye out for *Firebird* stories or a history and criticism of the tale, as well as any other illustrations by Maria Wood.

Her name simmers at the back of my mind. Why do I feel like I should know something about her? That I've seen her intense, dramatic style before?

Though my internet phone search about her yielded no results, I write a text to Graham:

I'm going to start writing about the Maria Wood Red Riding Hood drawing, so I can include the paper with my applications. An artist no one seems to have heard of— vengeful, feminist, breaking taboos—it will be quite provocative.

I send the text. Excitement flickers inside me. If I can bring to light the discovery of an unknown female artist who shattered social norms and artistic traditions…if that doesn't pull attention away from my miserable affair and back to my scholarly work, nothing will.

Close to noon, my stomach rumbles in a plea for lunch. I pick up my tea set and crossword book before heading to the door. After Flynn's dictates and his contract, I'm still a little apprehensive about crossing the threshold into the cottage.

Everything is quiet. I walk to the kitchen, peering around the corner to make sure my boss isn't looming anywhere nearby. The room is empty, a few shards of sunlight gleaming on the hardwood floor, appliances all bright and clean, and the weathered table looking pleasantly inviting by the big window.

I leave the tea set on the counter and open the refrigerator. My jaw almost drops. The fridge is filled with food. Leafy greens, organic chicken, gourmet cheeses, farm-fresh eggs. The cupboards are likewise well-stocked with rice, pasta, canned goods, fruit, crusty loaves of bread.

Well, geez. No wonder he wants me to eat here, if he has this much food.

Unless he bought it all for me?

No. I dismiss the thought with a shake of my head. That would be silly.

Still, it's lovely to have my choice of such delicious food, and none of it peanut butter. I select a shiny apple—ripe, deep red, as if he'd chosen only the best—and rummage in the fridge for thick slices of turkey and cheese. I make a sandwich and eat my lunch at the table while working on a crossword puzzle.

Beneath the distant sound of the ocean waves, faint music filters through the heating vents. I tilt my head to listen. It's coming from a different part of the lighthouse. Elvis, "Can't Help Falling in Love."

He listens to Elvis. I tuck that bit of knowledge away. The graceful melody and lovely lyrics float in the air, eliciting a longing I'm unwilling to examine too closely. Instead I enjoy the odd companionship of listening to the same music as Flynn while I finish my lunch and he…does whatever he does.

After cleaning my dishes, I return to work. I unpack another box, which contains a collection called *Russian Fairy Tales*, compiled by Alexander Afanasyev, and two single-story picture books. *The Tale of Tsarevich Ivan, the Firebird, and the Grey Wolf*, and *Russian Tales: The Firebird*.

Success! I set the books on my desk to give to Flynn tomorrow morning when I see him again. Maybe he's also a scholar of fairy tales, though why would he want to keep that a secret? But it would certainly explain how he and Uncle Max became friends.

At two, I return to the kitchen and put the shiny silver kettle on the stove before setting out my teapot and cup. As I wait for the water to boil, I gaze out the window, which overlooks the ocean and the secrets wall. The sky and ocean are charcoal-gray, and a cold drizzle has been falling all morning.

The kettle whistles. I swish boiling water around the teapot to warm it, then add the tea leaves and water. A pleasant, fragrant steam rises.

"What is that?" Flynn's deep voice suddenly fills the room behind me.

"Jesus." I startle, pressing a hand to my leaping heart. "For a big guy, you have the tread of a cat."

I turn to face him. He's standing in the doorway leading to what looks like a dining room, everything about him as tempting as ever.

It would be nice, for a change, to look at him and just see *my boss*, not *my gorgeous, hunky, hot-as-hell boss who invades my fantasies every night and makes me come so hard I see stars.*

"It's tea." I fight back a heated flush. "Darjeeling Sungma, to be precise. What are you doing here?"

"I live here," he replies dryly.

"Yeah, but you're always skulking off to do something mysterious. Oh, wait a second! I found something for you."

I hurry back to the workroom and grab the Firebird books off my desk, then return to the kitchen.

"I was going to give these to you tomorrow. This collection has a version of the story, and the other two are illustrated. This one was illustrated by Ivan Bilibin, who earned quite a bit of renown in the late nineteenth century for his fairy tale collections."

I open the book and leaf through the pages. "There are a lot of different influences in his work. He studied ethnography, Japanese prints, and had a strong interest in Russian village architecture. All of that is reflected in these drawings. But you probably know that already."

I close the book, consternation rising in me. I'm lecturing a man who probably knows more about fairy tale artists than I do.

"I didn't know any of that." Flynn takes the books with a nod. "Thanks for telling me. And for finding these."

"No problem."

I expect him to turn and leave, as per his usual exit strategy. He doesn't. I check the teapot, giving the steeping leaves a quick stir. If he stays, maybe I can learn a little more about him.

"Would you like a cup of tea?" I ask. "This is a really nice black tea, smooth and flavorful."

He lifts an eyebrow. "You're a tea connoisseur."

"Not really, but I like it a lot." I indicate the teapot. "This was a gift from the wife of my PhD advisor. She believed strongly in the power of a good cup of tea, and I realized soon that she was right. Tea doesn't make everything better, but sometimes it helps soften the rough edges."

"You think I have rough edges that need softening?" Amusement laces his voice as he sets the books on the counter.

"Don't we all?" I take a second teacup from the basket and remove the filter from the pot. After pouring the tea, I set the two cups on the table along with the sugar bowl and creamer. Flynn waits for me to sit down before he takes the chair opposite me, his presence making the table seem even smaller than it is.

I pick up the creamer. "Do you take milk and sugar?"

"I have no idea. Make mine the same as yours."

I add cream and sugar to each cup and slide his closer to him, nodding toward a spoon. "You have to stir it yourself. It's bad luck to stir someone else's tea."

"Why's that?"

"Just a superstition. If you stir someone else's tea, it means you're stirring up trouble for them."

"I didn't know tea was associated with superstitions." He stirs his own tea, then takes a swallow. "You have tea every day?"

"Right at two." I sip my tea, appreciating the hints of spice and sweetness.

We both fall silent, the air between us perfumed with aromatic steam. Rain spills down the window. Despite our fraught history, it's not awkward, only surprisingly pleasant.

I study him surreptitiously, the aesthetic side of me appreciating, as always, his strong features and thick-lashed eyes. But now I also notice the brackets of tension around his mouth and the frustration shadowing his eyes.

Who has loved you in life? Do you love anyone?

He shifts his gaze from the window to me. A current passes between us, something almost warm and tangible. As usual, a thousand questions pop into my mind, but for now, I don't want to ask them, don't want to pry into any part of him that he doesn't want to give me freely.

Instead I ask, "Do you happen to know anything about an artist named Maria Wood?"

He shakes his head. "Why?"

"I found a drawing of hers in the collection. *Red Riding Hood*, but a pretty disturbing image, kind of monstrous and sexual at the same time. She's holding a knife, implying that she'll kill the wolf before he has a chance to hurt her. I know I've never seen it before, but I feel like I've seen something *like* it before, if that makes sense. You've never heard of her?"

"No."

"I'm sure Uncle Max never mentioned her either." I shrug and sip the tea. "I was just wondering. I'm going to write a paper about her. I need to get my art history career back, hopefully with another university professor position, but first I have to remind my colleagues I'm still a good scholar. Maria Wood will be a great start. I've never written about a fairy tale artist before."

Flynn studies me, his expression as impenetrable as ever. "What's your favorite fairy tale?"

"*The Snow Queen* by Hans Christian Andersen." I smile. "Did you know about Max's class assignment?"

"No."

"On the first day of every class, he had his students write an essay about their favorite fairy tale and explain why. He said it gave a great deal of insight into their hopes, values, and dreams. Like it was their essence."

Though I can't be certain, curiosity appears to gleam in Flynn's smoky eyes.

"So what does *The Snow Queen* say about you?" he asks.

I look out the window. A sweet, painful ache nudges my soul.

"I'm not sure," I admit. "I love so much about it. Gerda and Kay's fierce loyalty. The way she makes her way into the world with such bravery and determination. She doesn't give up on Kay, even when he's cruel to her. She knows he's not truly malicious. She faces all her fears and goes to the end of the earth to save him. She helps him see the good in the world again. She melts the ice in his heart."

"What does he do for her?"

"He loves her. He trusts her infinitely. If the situation were reversed, he'd risk everything to save her. They both know it. How many people are lucky enough to have that kind of devotion?"

Heavy silence falls. Self-consciousness seizes me. I risk a glance at him. My heartbeat increases.

For the first time, his defenses are down. The bleak look in his eyes, the lines of tension creasing his brow, give me a brief glimpse into...*him*. A man who has feelings and emotions like the rest of us, much as he tries to conceal them.

He meets my gaze. Just like that, his implacable shield slams back into place. Blocking any hint of vulnerability.

My heart is still thumping hard. I lower my head to sip my tea.

"I also like stories that have a magic object," I continue in an effort to diffuse the sudden tension. "A spindle, a glass slipper, a feather, a golden apple, a spinning wheel, a mirror. The idea that we're surrounded at all times by magic is a powerful concept. Even if it doesn't always work in your favor."

"Indeed."

A combination of amusement and exasperation rises in me. He gives new meaning to the term *strong, silent type.*

"What's your favorite fairy tale?" I ask.

"Don't have one." He drains his cup before shoving to his feet. "Thanks for the tea."

He starts toward the cottage door. After my little soul-baring about *The Snow Queen*, I'm not about to let him off the hook quite that easily.

"Everyone has a favorite fairy tale," I call after him. "Is it the *Firebird?*"

"No." He opens the door.

"*Snow White?*"

"No."

"*Cinderella.*"

He glances over his shoulder. "Guess again."

"Ah ha! You do have a favorite one." I narrow my gaze at him. "I'm going to figure out what it is."

"You are, huh?"

"Your favorite fairy tale must be *Beauty and the Beast.*" I roll my eyes and indicate the lighthouse. "Mysterious creature locked in a tower? Surely you can relate."

He frowns. "*Your* favorite fairy tale should be *Goldilocks and the Three Bears.*"

"Why's that?"

"A nosy girl who can't mind her own business?" He pulls open the door. "Surely you can relate."

He leaves, shutting the door behind him.

A laugh bursts out of me.

What's that feeling bubbling underneath my heart? It's light and fluffy, like a marshmallow, a cotton puff, a baby chick.

I'm charmed.

CHAPTER 12

*A*fter work, I stop at the usual curve on the trail, my breath wheezing out in puffs of white. The damned boulder looks a thousand miles away. I rest my hands on my hips and peer back at the lighthouse. Aside from the boulder, I have no other way of marking my progress.

I search the ground and pick up a smooth white stone, nestling it in the roots of a grass plant well off the trail. On Monday, I'll see if I can pass it without stopping.

As I start back to the lighthouse, my phone buzzes. I pull it from the pocket of my track pants and swipe the screen.

Juliette. I suppress a groan. Relentless as she is, she'll keep calling until I answer. I accept the call.

"Have you found a job yet?" she asks after a brief exchange of pleasantries.

"Actually, yes." Much as I long...no, *ache* to tell her about Max's collection *("I found it again, Cruella.")*, Flynn's contract is embedded in my brain. Not even for the satisfaction of finally having one up on my mother will I jeopardize my job.

"I'm doing some consulting work," I say.

"For whom?"

"Various people. How's your new position on the board?"

She *tsks* with impatience. "Will this *consulting work* do anything at all to revive your career? Have you been networking? You have to put yourself out there, Eve, because God knows no one will come to you."

I breathe in the view of the vast ocean, the rippling whitecaps, the endless sky. All the forces that are far more powerful than even my mother.

"I'm looking into several possibilities."

"Where?"

"Duke has an interim nineteenth-century position opening next fall. Northwestern is looking for guest lecturers in an undergrad seminar for the spring semester."

"You have a next to nothing shot at working at Duke or Northwestern," Juliette says sharply, "especially considering the eager, fresh-faced doctoral students who will be applying. You need to start somewhere smaller and network at conferences. What about a new publication?"

"I'm working on it."

"You'd better be," she snaps. "You might have screwed up your one shot at a prestigious tenure-track position, but you can fight your way back if you'd grow a damned backbone. I expect to hear more details the next time I call."

She ends the call before I can respond. I shove down the flare of anger, trying not to let her caustic words scald too badly.

Shoving the phone into my pocket, I trudge up the hill. As I reach the plateau, I look up at the tower. A light glows through the smoky glass. The sight eases the burn of my mother's call.

A memory washes over me of the day I first climbed up to the lighthouse and put my secret in the wall. That was almost a month ago, and I'm already finishing up my second week of work for Flynn. Strange how it feels like I've been here much longer than that, and yet I still know almost nothing about him.

But he's disarming me, that man up there. Peeling away the

thick leather armor I've worn for so many months. The armor that failed to protect me from a thousand slings and arrows.

He's also frustrating the heck out of me and irritating me with his dictates, but even those emotions are welcome after all my bleak, helpless despair.

He's making me feel good things again.

I run the rest of the way to the parking lot, wondering if he's watching me. Hoping that he is.

Saturday is my date with Jeremy King. Though I have misgivings about dating another man when I'm so attracted to Flynn, I'm not betraying him. Teatime, new pens, and scented lotion aside, he made it clear he plans to keep me at a distance. So I'm entitled to a normal date with a nice man. In fact, I'm looking forward to it.

I spend the morning at the library working on my paper about the *Little Red Riding Hood* drawing. I have both a newfound affinity and antipathy toward the story itself, the origins of which are rooted in a punishment for female sexuality.

She wears red, the color of blood and scandal. In the original story, after she undresses and gets into bed with the wolf, he devours and kills her. She doesn't escape, and no hunter saves her. The 1729 Charles Perrault published version of *Little Red Riding Hood* included a moral admonishing young women to stay away from wolves.

In her drawing, however, Maria Wood places the blame and punishment clearly where it belongs—on the evil, predatory wolf.

I write a solid rough draft, apply for three more professor positions, and message Graham with an update.

Despite my mother's admonishing call, things are finally going well for me. I need to keep it that way.

I've agreed to meet Jeremy at a downtown seafood restaurant for dinner. As the clock approaches six, the more nervous I become. Not only has it been ages since I've dated, I have no idea what Jeremy knows about me.

I dress conservatively in a plum-colored jersey knit dress and low-heeled pumps before heading downtown. Jeremy is waiting for me outside the restaurant, looking golden-boy handsome in a navy suit and tie. His smile at the sight of me elicits both relief and pleasure. If he knows about my sordid story yet, he doesn't appear to hold it against me.

"You look lovely." He takes my hand and brushes his lips across my cheek. "Thanks for agreeing to go out with me."

"Thanks for asking. I haven't had a date in quite a while."

"Then I'm honored to be your first in quite a while." He winks and pulls open the door.

After we're seated and have ordered cocktails, I decide to bring up the issue, or else I'll be wondering about it all evening.

"So you asked last time why I moved to Castille." I rub my finger over the handle of my fork. "Did you find out the real reason?"

A dull flush rises to his cheeks. "Uh...if you mean, did I look you up on the internet, the answer is yes. I was curious. You're a beautiful woman, and obviously I like you, so...well, yeah. I wanted to know more. Sorry if that was rude."

"I guess everyone does it these days, right?" I take a sip of water. "But not everything on the internet is true."

"I know." He pauses. "You don't have to tell me, if you don't want to."

"Everyone else around here already seems to know. But they don't know the truth."

He leans forward slightly. "Which is what?"

"I did have an affair and I was terminated," I admit, setting my glass down. "But I never stalked him, I didn't know he was married, and I didn't do any of the things he accused me of. In a nutshell, he was a powerful man, and I was naïve enough to believe whatever he told me. Not a mistake I'll make again."

Jeremy is silent, shifting his attention to the menu. My shoulders tense.

"We all make mistakes," he finally says. "I'm not one to judge. I figured you had your side of the story. Thanks for telling me."

"If you want to end the date here, I'll understand."

He looks at me, a smile tugging at his mouth. "I don't want to end the date, either here or anywhere else. I like to think I'm not stupid enough to believe the internet over an obviously accomplished woman who's being honest with me."

"Thank you." I return his smile, my tension easing. "I'd like it if we could talk about something else, though. You can imagine it's not my favorite subject."

"What is?"

"Art. Movies. Books. I'd like to know more about you. I assume you grew up in Castille?"

"Born and bred here. I'm pretty sure my first solid food was lobster."

We share a laugh as the waitress comes to take our order. As the evening passes, I'm increasingly glad I had the courage to say yes to the offer of a date.

Jeremy is a good conversationalist, warm and funny, and he's interested in everything *else* about me—my art history specialization, my travels abroad, my favorite books. He tells me about his own childhood growing up on the coast, taking his golden retriever out on a boat, trips to Canada, visiting the governor's mansion with his prominent parents.

"I preferred hanging out with Buster, but I didn't always have a choice." He gives me a rueful smile as he pushes his empty plate away. "Worst part was my mother made me wear a suit and a tie. Not a clip-on, either."

I suppress the urge to ask about his mother, instead saying, "By the way, how did the city council meeting go the other night?

Did you convince people that selling the lighthouse is a good idea?"

"Some, yeah." He picks up the wine bottle and refills our glasses. "I get why people are resisting, though. My buddies and I used to ride our bikes up to the lighthouse all the time. The first time I had a crush on a girl, I wrote her name on a piece of paper I'd torn out of my math notebook and stuffed it into the secrets wall. Hell, I had my first kiss up there on the cliff. That place has a lot of memories for me. If people think the idea of selling it is easy, they're wrong. But I'm doing it because I still believe it's the best thing we can do for this town."

"How does the rest of your family feel about it?"

"My father was the one who came up with the idea, which is actually the reason so many of the residents support it too. He hasn't been involved in local politics for a few years, but people still respect him and his opinions a great deal."

"What about your mother?"

He shakes his head, his mouth compressing. "She's not well, unfortunately, so she's not involved in the debate. There was a point last spring when we thought we were going to lose her. Had to deal with power of attorney, advance directives, all that stuff. She told us she didn't expect to leave the hospital."

"I'm so sorry."

"Thankfully she recovered. She's better now, but still…" His voice trails off. "She's always supported what I've wanted to do. My father's a little tougher, harder to please…" He shrugs, reaching into his pocket for his wallet. "Anyway, it's not a done deal yet."

"What about the lighthouse keeper?" The question escapes my mouth before I can stop it.

"Flynn." Jeremy's expression darkens. "He's been living there for way too long. Awhile back, I told my mother we should open up the tower and cottage for tourists…even asking a donation for entry would give us more income to help with the upkeep. But she refuses to kick him out. We can't evict him because he's technically employed by the Forestry Department. At least until their lease is up at the end of the year."

A bitter tone underscores his voice.

"Do you know him?" I ask.

"Not really. He's weird, likes being the mysterious guy on the cliff. Probably has a string of chicks up there." He winces a little. "Sorry. Didn't mean to be crude. Flynn just gets my back up."

I reach for my water glass, trying to ignore the knot tightening in my stomach. I haven't seen any evidence of "chicks" up at the lighthouse, but I've only been working there for two weeks. And for all I know, a woman might be the reason Flynn doesn't want me going into other parts of the cottage or tower. Maybe he does have a sex dungeon somewhere in the—

Eve. Don't get carried away.

Though I want to ask Jeremy more about his apparently antagonistic feelings toward Flynn, I don't want to arouse his suspicions. Even if I don't explicitly say anything about my cataloging job, showing an excessive interest in the lighthouse keeper could create gossip.

And God knows the last thing I need is more freaking *gossip*.

After dinner, Jeremy walks me to my car. I open the driver's side door and turn to face him.

He's standing close, just a few inches away, but his proximity doesn't spark any fear. It doesn't make me all hot and tingly either—which is my reaction to just the *thought* of Flynn, let alone his nearness—but that's also relief. Turns out I can still enjoy being on a date with a nice, handsome man without enduring a roller-coaster of emotions.

Another broken piece back in place.

Jeremy shifts closer, reaching behind me to rest his hand on the open car door. Unmistakable desire glitters in his blue eyes.

He's going to kiss me. I know it the instant before it happens.

My last kiss is burned indelibly into my mind—David's hands

on either side of my face, the musky smell of his aftershave filling my nose, his mouth pushing mine open. His erection pressed hard against my thigh because we'd woken too late for the morning sex he preferred. His whispered *I'll see you tonight,* his lips lingering against mine.

Three hours and twenty minutes later, the public discovery of our illicit affair burned across campus like a wildfire.

Jeremy is still looking at me, waiting for a signal, an invitation. My heart hammers. All I can do is not move, not push him away. He leans forward and kisses me. I return the kiss.

What had I expected? To be flooded with desire?

No. It's an entirely pleasant kiss—warm and gentle. I like the shape of his mouth, his restraint, even the rangy strength of his body, but the moment is devoid of heat, sizzling attraction, the melting sensation like syrup flowing through my veins…

"Ah, you feel good." He lifts his head, his eyes darkening, and puts his hand against my cheek. "And you kiss like a dream."

He lowers his head again. Without thinking, I put my hand on his chest and give him a slight push. He stops. Consternation floods his expression.

"I'm sorry, I…" He steps back, his hands going up. "I thought you were okay with it."

"I am. I mean, I…" I take a breath, trying to calm the racing of my heart. "I'm just a little gun-shy these days. Please don't take it personally. I really enjoyed our date, but I need to take things pretty slow."

He expels a sigh of relief. "I can do that. As long as you're not already kicking me to the curb."

"No. As long as you're not worried about being out with a woman who practically wears a scarlet *A*."

"Actually I kind of like that you have a *past*." Amusement gleams in his eyes. "I'm used to dating women who make it a point never to do anything wrong. Which is fine if you're a politician, but not a real person."

"I have the scars to prove I'm real." I fish my keys out of my purse and turn to the car. "Thanks again for the dinner, Jeremy."

"You're welcome, Eve." He walks around the car to the side-walk. "I hope to see you again."

I hope so too.

It's a natural response, one I want to say. But the words stick in my throat.

Instead I give him a wave before starting the car. I glance in the rearview mirror, seeing him watch me drive away.

I should date a man like him. After David, I didn't want to look at another man again, but if I'm going to be whole again, I need to restore the social piece of my life. Not to mention, Jeremy could divert my attention from the lighthouse keeper.

Jeremy is solid, grounded, honest. Everything about Flynn is a mystery and a fantasy. I'd gotten caught up in a fantasy with David, whose "mystery" had been a vicious lie, and I'd paid the price.

Never again.

CHAPTER 13

*O*n Sunday afternoon I go for a jog over the trails cutting through the woodlands beside my house. Despite the electrician's horror-movie warnings about "being careful," the atmosphere is cold but delightful—chattering birds, sunlight dripping through the pine trees, squirrels rustling in the underbrush. Snow White would love it here.

I cross a few narrow roads, nodding greetings at several passing walkers and joggers before circling back to Ramshackle Manor. Ghost is hovering at the side of the house, his yellow eyes wary.

"Hey, boy." I unlock the back door, leaving it open as I enter.

When I'm home, I've been opening the door when I see him outside in the hopes that he'll come in. In order to coax him into the car so I can take him to the vet for a check-up, I need to earn more of his trust. I continue to call the humane society and review the city website for reports about a lost dog matching his description, but none appear.

I mix leftover chicken soup with his kibble and place it on the floor. He takes a few tentative steps into the kitchen. We study each other. He trots to the bowl. After gobbling the food, he nudges his head against my hand.

"Yeah." I scratch him behind the ears. "I'm starting to like you too."

He runs out the open door and disappears into the woods. Maybe he's a wizard who shapeshifts in the forest. A magical helper.

I grab a bottle of water and go into the living room. The books Uncle Max left me are still piled in stacks on the floor. I leaf through one of the volumes, pausing on an illustration of *Sleeping Beauty*.

A black-and-white etching of the sleeping princess fills the page, her voluptuous body clad in a near-transparent gown, her face pale and lifeless. Beside her, the prince approaches, his eyes dark and his expression edged with lust.

My heart thumps. In the original tale from which *Sleeping Beauty* is derived, the princess is not roused awake by a kiss from the prince. No.

He takes one look at the sleeping princess, carries her to a bed, and rapes her as she lies in her comatose state. Then he leaves her. Charles Perrault and the Brothers Grimm later sanitized the story in favor of the famous kiss.

Has anyone ever illustrated the original story? Where have I seen the prince—

I grab my phone to call Graham. A woman replies, "Graham Baker's phone."

"Mary?" Warmth rises in me. In addition to Graham, Mary has always stood by her belief that I did nothing wrong. "It's Eve Perrin."

"Oh, hello, Eve. I didn't recognize your number." She gives a little laugh. "Not that I monitor Graham's phone."

"I'm glad you picked up. How have you been?"

We chat for a few minutes about her upcoming retirement

plans and a few new tea varieties she's discovered. She turns the phone over to Graham.

"I figured it out!" I tell him. "Where I've seen the Maria Wood illustrations before. She did an entire *book* of them. Maybe even more."

"Are you sure?"

"Yes, definitely. I saw one in Uncle Max's collection years ago. Before I went to college. I remember thinking they were so weird and disturbing, but I wasn't an art history major then, so I didn't look at them academically. Then I must have forgotten about them...until now. I can't believe I didn't remember. If I can find it, I'll have a ton of material for my paper. Maybe several papers. Maybe a book."

He chuckles. "I love hearing you so excited about this. Do you remember the title?"

"No, but it must have been a volume of fairy tales. I just hope it's still in his collection."

"Well, you'll have to *find* his collection first."

Shit.

My exultation pops like a needle-pricked balloon. I can't tell Graham that I have full access to Max's collection. I can't tell him much of anything.

"Yes." I swallow a knot of guilt. "Of course."

"Did you ever ask Max about it?"

"I don't think so. If I did, I don't remember what he said. I mean, I loved the storybooks back then, but I didn't have a critical eye for the drawings. The version of *Sleeping Beauty* was so awful, though, and I know Maria Wood was the one who illustrated it. Whoever she was, she subverted the fairy tales with this violent, disturbing imagery."

"It sounds like it could be extraordinary, if you can locate it."

"I'll try. In the meantime, I'm almost done with my *Red Riding Hood* rough draft."

"Send it to me when you're finished."

I thank him and end the call, suppressing the urge to hurry back to the lighthouse to begin my search. I'm sure Flynn wouldn't appreciate me showing up outside of work hours.

On Monday morning, I arrive at the workroom fifteen minutes before eight. Though I expect to wait for him, he opens the door right when I walk up.

"Oh, sorry." I pause. "I know I'm early. I can wait out here, if you want me to."

He frowns. "Why would I want that?"

"Because you seem very schedule-oriented."

"Come in, Eve." With a hint of impatience, he steps aside to let me in. "Any questions?"

"Not about the cataloging, no." I set my satchel on the desk. "But would you mind if I look for a particular book? While I'm doing my work, of course."

"What book?"

"I remembered Uncle Max had once owned a fairy tale collection illustrated by Maria Wood. At least I think it was illustrated by her. If I can find it, I'll have a much bigger scope of material to write about."

"Go ahead." He turns away. "And if you find any *Hansel and Gretel* stories, I need those too."

"Oh, I unpacked a few of those the other day." I hurry to the shelves to retrieve a few books. "Here's one that places the origins of the story during the medieval famine of the fourteenth century when it wasn't unheard of for parents to abandon their children. This book has the original Grimm Brothers version from 1812, and this one has incredible black-and-white illustrations by…"

Flynn has stopped right behind me to look over my shoulder. He's *close*. So close that his body heat warms my skin. So close that my arm is almost brushing against his side, and I can practically feel his breath stirring the tendrils of hair at my temple.

"By…?" His voice rumbles through his broad chest.

"By...um..." The artist's name has vanished from my now-blank mind. I flip to the front cover. "John Batten. He was a...a British illustrator and printmaker, part of the Art Nouveau movement."

Flynn makes a noise low in his throat, something between a *hmm* of interest and a murmur of appreciation. His breath escapes on an exhale.

Oh my God. Is he smelling me again?

I'm seized with the sudden urge to turn and breathe *him* in, to bury my face right up against his strong neck, press my lips to the hollow of his throat where his pulse beats...

"Thanks." He takes the books and steps away from me. "Appreciate the help."

A rush of colder air fills the void where he was standing. I return to my desk, attempting to gather my composure and wondering if that little interaction really happened or if it was again a product of my vivid imagination. My imagination *has* been working overtime lately.

"I'll leave you to work." Flynn starts toward the door.

"Hold on a sec." I unbuckle my satchel. "I brought you something."

I dig around and produce a fat little clay pig that fits into the palm of my hand. Two dimples appear on the pig's cheeks, and he's laughing at some unknown joke, his eyes scrunched up and ears perky.

Flynn eyes the pig dubiously. "What's that?"

"It's called a tea pet." I extend it toward him.

He takes it, his fingertips brushing my palm. The light touch ripples my entire arm with sensation. He examines the pig closely.

"Tea pets were started in China back during one dynasty or another," I explain. "Basically a long time ago. They bring good luck and good fortune, and they protect your tea collection. You just have to make sure you feed them regularly."

"Feed them?"

I smile at his confused expression. "Just pour a little tea over it, preferably the same type. I use Darjeeling for the pig."

Flynn shakes his head, as if he's still not following the conversation.

"It's for you," I clarify. "I've had it for a couple of years now, which is why it smells like Darjeeling. Tea pets absorb the color and scent of the tea."

"You're giving this to me?" A crease appears between his eyebrows.

"Yes."

"Why?"

"As a thank you for giving me the chance to work with Max's collection. And because we could all use a bit of good fortune. I can't say it actually worked for me, but maybe it will for you."

Silence falls. He turns the pig over in his hand.

Suddenly feeling rather silly, I sit at the computer. "It's just a superstition, like stirring someone else's tea. I don't know, I thought you might like it."

"I do." He closes his fist around the pig and clears his throat. "I mean, thank you."

"You're welcome. I hope it works."

"So do I."

I open my organizer to my *To Do* list and pick up a gel pen. Flynn is still standing there. I glance at him, my heart skipping as our gazes meet. Never before have I met a person so capable of concealing his thoughts, of not letting anyone see past the steel-gray of his eyes.

"Is there something else you need?" I ask.

"No." He gestures to my organizer. "Is that your plan?"

"Yes, I just wrote up a best practices way of approaching the cataloging, with subject headings, hierarchies, and bibliographic records." I turn the organizer toward him so he can see what I've written. "I'll use this as a framework for the paintings and lithographs. Those will have variances since they're different media. I'll create a separate index for the artwork, but you'll also be able to search it in the main database."

He doesn't respond.

I raise my eyebrows. "Is that okay?"

"Yeah, sure. It's fine." He takes a step back. "No questions?"

"Not right now, but I'll write them down as they come up."

He nods. "Good."

"Good." I turn my organizer back to me.

He hesitates, then turns and strides toward the door, closing it behind him with a sharp click. Only after he's gone does it hit me that he might actually have been looking for an excuse to *stay*.

Wouldn't that be something?

Right, Eve, and maybe he'll ask you to the movies next. Stop daydreaming.

Pushing him out of my mind, I organize my desk for the day's work. As I unpack and catalog books, I keep an eye out for both the Maria Wood book and more *Hansel and Gretel* tales.

At two, I head into the kitchen to make tea. Flynn shows up again right as I'm steeping the leaves. Without asking, I pour him a cup, adding cream and sugar the same way I take it. We sit at the table.

"*Hansel and Gretel* isn't your favorite fairy tale." I stir my tea and hand him the spoon.

He glances at me. "Why do you say that?"

"I don't think your favorite tale is about parents who abandon their children. Or about a brother and sister." I study him, trying to process the few things I know or sense about him. "I don't think it's *The Little Mermaid* or *The Brave Tin Soldier* either. A theme of dying for love doesn't seem quite your thing."

A smile tugs at his mouth, but doesn't reach his eyes. "You know what my *thing* is?"

"No, but my job is to decipher the meaning and secrets of

paintings, even if I don't know much about them to start. So you're kind of like my new thesis."

"I'm not interesting enough for a thesis." He drains his tea and sets the cup down. "Find another topic."

"Is your favorite fairy tale *Jack and the Beanstalk*?" I ask. "The giant does have a keen sense of smell. I'll bet he could smell apple-lavender body lotion from a mile away."

He blinks. A slight flush crests his cheekbones. He pushes to his feet.

"Get back to work, Eve."

"Yes, *sir*." I smile.

Even through his scowl, amusement sparks.

"Now." He strides to the door and leaves.

Though I'm enjoying the loosening of tension between us, I'm still aware of the contract. What if I push him too far with my questions and he stops joining me for tea? I finish my cup before returning to work.

My concern eases when he appears in the kitchen again the next day.

"Ceylon Kenilworth." I set a cup in front of him.

He swallows the tea and nods his approval like he always does. "What makes it Ceylon Kenilworth?"

"Ceylon is a black tea grown in Sri Lanka, known for being especially aromatic and strong. I think it's also used as a base for other teas like Earl Grey, but I like it as it is. Kenilworth is the estate where this tea was grown. Apparently the leaves are picked after the first monsoon, and then processed in cooler weather. That gives the tea its distinctive flavor."

He takes another sip. "Only a tea connoisseur would know such details."

"Do you like it?"

"Sure, but I can't tell anything about a distinctive flavor."

"That's because you haven't had a chance to compare different kinds of tea. I'll brew a few varieties next week and see if you can tell the difference."

"A tea tasting?" He looks dubious.

I grin at him. "Think you can handle it?"

"Sure." He tilts his head back and drains the cup. "Sounds like a par-*tea*."

I laugh, another burst of amusement that surprises me as much as the sudden lightness filling my chest. *When was the last time I laughed spontaneously, without thought or worry?*

Flynn's gaze is on me, and while he doesn't join in the laugh, a genuine warmth infuses his eyes.

"I'll plan it for next week." I rise to collect our tea things. "But I'll *tea* you here tomorrow?"

He takes his cup to the sink. "I'll be here, cu—"

His voice cuts off abruptly. He shoves his hands into his pockets and clears his throat.

"Uh, I'll be here." He ducks his head and leaves the kitchen.

I gaze at the closed door. I know instinctively what he was about to say. He was about to call me *cu-tea*.

I turn to the sink, unable to stop smiling.

To my distinct pleasure, Flynn shows up for tea the rest of the week. I even start making him a cup before he arrives in the kitchen, knowing he'll be there right at two. And he is.

We exchange a few words about the type of tea and where it's from (*Chinese oolong from the Guangdong province, Assam tea from India*), but since I don't want to scare him away, I avoid interrogating him about his likes and dislikes.

Poke a bear too many times with a stick, and he'll growl and lumber out of the cave. If he doesn't bite you first.

Like Ghost, I should take a gentler approach to keep Flynn coming back to the kitchen.

Though our morning interactions remain the same, I start to anticipate my weird little teatime with the lighthouse keeper. I'm aware of him more than ever—his lips closing around the rim of the cup, the worn leather watch strap fastened around his wrist, the corded muscles of his arms—but tranquility surrounds our unspoken break in the day. A peace in our togetherness.

It's an unexpected relief after having spent so much time in the past year fighting for myself. Arguing. Talking. God, the endless talking.

Answering questions. Giving statements. Delivering lectures in the burn of student judgment and barely suppressed laughter. Trying to explain my side of the story to everyone—my friends, the departmental chairperson, the university board, my lawyer, the police, my mother. It had been like talking to wall after wall.

Impenetrable though he is, Flynn isn't like a wall. He's a locked door. No wonder shutting doors is his preferred way of exiting a room. But maybe he's like all other doors and can be opened with one twist of the right key.

On Friday, I bring my crossword puzzle book along with my tea accessories. Flynn arrives, distracting me momentarily by taking off his gray hoodie and tossing it over the back of his chair. He's wearing a dark green Henley with the buttons unfastened, revealing the strong column of his throat and a tempting V of skin leading down to…

A few drops of boiling water hit my hand. "Ow."

"What happened?" Flynn is at my side in an instant, closing his fingers around my wrist.

A tremble courses through my body, my pulse ratcheting up.

"Nothing." Trying to regain my composure, I set the kettle down with a rueful grimace. "Just burned myself a little."

"Put some cold water on it." He guides me to the sink and puts my hand under the cold water. "You okay?"

"I'm fine, really."

But I will quite happily stand here for an hour with you holding my wrist and our bodies almost touching, and did I mention how much I love the warm, squishy feeling you elicit every time I'm close to you?

"Doesn't look bad." Flynn studies my hand, his eyebrows drawn together. "Keep your hand under the water. I'll pour the tea."

He releases me to pick up the kettle. "Uh, how do I pour it?"

With a smile, I direct him through warming the teapot, adding the right amount of tea, and setting it to steep. After he pours two cups, we sit at the table and settle into our now-usual silence.

I open the crossword book to a puzzle I've been working on and pick up a pencil. I feel Flynn studying the puzzle from the other side of the table.

"A witch doctor might be in one." I read the clue and tap my pencil on the grid. "Five letters, ends with an E."

"*Trance.*"

"Accessory on a chain, using the N. *Monocle.*" I write in the word. "Go pirating, six letters."

"*Maraud.*"

We keep going. *Auk, stamina, Brecht, allegory.* Though it doesn't qualify as a conversation, the activity diminishes the wall between us a bit more. As we figure out clues, I tuck away the little things I learn about Flynn. The man knows a lot, especially about history, sports, and literature, but he's not up on pop culture, TV shows, or musicals.

"*Pirates of Penzance*, for example, eight letters." I write the word for ten across. "Operetta."

"What's an operetta?"

"A short opera, usually with a kind of funny theme." I glance at him. "You've never seen *Pirates of Penzance?*"

"No, but I know that pirates *maraud.*" He gives me a smug look.

"Good point. Have you seen any Gilbert and Sullivan? *The Mikado? HMS Pinafore?*"

"I don't think so."

"What about Rodgers and Hammerstein?"

He slowly shakes his head. "No idea."

"They wrote *The Sound of Music*. When I was in middle school, we put on a stage production of it. I played one of the von Trapp children. Brigitta. My best friend Margie was Maria von Trapp, and we were always getting in trouble for giggling during rehearsals."

His eyes crinkle with amusement. "You ever had ambitions for Broadway?"

"Nah, I wasn't good enough." A bittersweet memory washes over me. "Uncle Max flew out to see the show, though. He gave me a bouquet of flowers afterward and asked me to autograph his program. I tried out for another show the following year but my mother wouldn't let me do it."

"Why not?"

"She wanted me to focus on my grades rather than stuff like theater." I shrug and close the crossword puzzle book. "Were you ever in a school play?"

He doesn't respond, but his body goes oddly still. He stares out the window at the grasslands. Regret hits me. I have the sudden sense I said something wrong.

"I was..." His throat works with a swallow. "I was in *Peter Pan* once. Two of us played the father...can't remember his name... and Captain Hook. We exchanged roles."

It's the most personal thing he's ever told me. The revelation rolls through me like a polished jewel. I have a sudden image of him as a tow-headed boy, brandishing a hook and a sword while darting around a cafeteria stage.

The picture brings up all the other things that go along with a school play—family, friends, teachers, a hometown. Surely he had all that, once upon a time. Didn't we all, to varying degrees of happiness?

A shutter descends over his expression, as if he's sorry he said anything. He scrapes his chair away from the table and stands. "Thanks for the tea."

And the door closes.

I rise to bring our tea things to the sink. His sweatshirt is crumpled on the floor behind his chair. I bend to pick it up, inhaling the scents of sea salt and fresh air clinging to the soft cotton.

When I hang the shirt over the chair again, my fingers brush against a bump in the front pocket. The size of…

I reach in and pull out the Darjeeling-scented, clay tea pet. For a moment, I look at the laughing pig, which had just been nestled deep inside Flynn's pocket. Kept there like a treasure.

I press my lips to the little pig and tuck it back into the pocket.

As I turn to wash the dishes, a vibration echoes in my blood, the striking of a chord. Like music starting.

CHAPTER 14

"I've been thinking," Juliette says over the phone.

So what else is new? I stare up at what looks like a growing water stain on the kitchen ceiling of Ramshackle Manor. There are a thousand other things I'd rather be doing on a Friday evening than talking to Juliette.

"What have you been thinking about, Mother?"

She tsks with impatience. I'd been fourteen, about to be shipped off to boarding school, when Juliette told me to start calling her *Juliette* instead of *Mom*. As usual, I'd done as she'd asked. Another sorry attempt to earn her approval.

"You need to go abroad," she says.

"What?"

"Get out of the States," she clarifies. "Your poor reputation may precede you, but institutions in other countries might be a bit more willing to forgive your stupidity. More likely, they don't know about it. So take a low-level job in a Budapest museum or something, give your CV some much-needed cache. An international position will at least be somewhat more impressive than you rattling around small-town Maine."

I roll my eyes. "And what makes you think I can afford to move to Budapest?"

"Your career is what," she snaps. "For God's sake, Eve. I put myself through medical school with scholarships, work, and minimal loans. Don't tell me you can't move for the sake of your pathetic career."

I won't tell you that. I won't tell you anything else either. Not about Max's collection or the lighthouse or Flynn. I have new secrets now, ones I can keep to myself.

"I'll think about it," I say instead, ending the call before she can start another rant.

I toss the phone on the kitchen table. Not for the first time, I wonder if I'd have cut her off long ago if she weren't the only person I have in the world. For a long time, I'd also had Uncle Max, the buffer to Juliette's harshness, but she'd still been my mother. The one who'd dictated everything I did—schools, lessons, travel. I hadn't known life without her until I was on my own at eighteen. Even then, she'd cast a long shadow. One I still haven't escaped.

Wanting to get out of the house, I drive to the Castille Art Museum, which closes at six. Miriam, the education coordinator, is staffing the front desk. She looks up with a smile that wavers when she realizes who just walked in.

Though I'm tempted to be frosty, an attitude won't get me anywhere. And it isn't as if I don't understand why she backed off her initial inquiries into hiring me. Scarlet letter *A* and all.

"Hello, Miriam." I stop at the desk. "Don't worry, I'm not going to ask you for a job."

She forces her smile wider. "I'm really sorry, Eve. I didn't intend to lead you on like that."

"It's okay, I get it. I'm here because I wanted to find out if your offer of looking through the museum's storage and archives still stands."

"Yes, of course." She rises to her feet and puts a *Back in 10 Min* sign on the desk. "Come with me. Are you doing specific research, or do you just want to look around?"

"A little of both."

I follow her down a rickety staircase to a concrete-walled basement. Wooden shelves fill the room, stacked with boxes, trays, and photograph storage cabinets. An adjoining room lined with books is marked with a *Library* sign.

"Just sign the ledger when you come and go." Miriam indicates an open book on a table. "You're welcome to have a look at anything or check out books from the library. I'm sorry, I need to get back to the front desk but I'll be upstairs if you have any questions."

"Great, thank you."

She heads back upstairs, leaving me alone in the quiet of the basement. I familiarize myself with the collection—the historic artifacts of Castille's past, the drawings, paintings, and sculptures by artists significant to the area. I examine the archives and check the computer for any holdings related to Maria Wood or fairy tales in general, but aside from a local artist's illustrations for *Cinderella*, there's nothing.

Then I look up information on the King family. There are a number of archival photographs and portraits dating back to the beginning of the nineteenth century. A storage box contains dozens of old photographs of William and Allegra King—on their wedding day, attending state functions, outside their home, at town events. William looks familiar, likely because I see his resemblance to his son. There are photos of Jeremy too, as a toddler and a young gap-toothed boy smiling at the camera. Castille's first family.

I study a formal photo of Allegra, resplendent in a silk gown. Pale skin, dark lipstick, coiffed hair. Has she been happy with William King? Does she know Max loved her until the day he died? Even through her marriage, did she love him in return?

After leaving the museum, I drive to Bird Lane, hoping for

some clue as to which house belongs to the Kings. As it turns out, there's only one house on Bird Lane, a Federal-style brick mansion set at the end of a long, curving drive and surrounded by manicured lawns. Floodlights illuminate the house in the evening darkness.

I park at the foot of the steps and eye the imposing façade. I don't know what I expect to say to her.

Gripping my handbag, I climb the steps and press the door-bell. Chimes echo from inside. The door opens to reveal a tall, broad-shouldered man in a gray suit and tie. In his mid-fifties, he has a thatch of graying hair and a neatly trimmed beard. It's the man I'd first encountered at the bookstore.

He studies me gravely and says, "Miss, you're interrupting my reading of Sophocles' *Metamorphosis*."

"Sir, I believe you mean Ovid's *Metamorphosis*."

He frowns. "So you're here to show me up in my own home, huh?"

I blink with surprise as it occurs to me this must be the legendary William King. I hadn't recognized him in the museum photos; both his beard and the intervening years have changed his appearance.

"Er...actually, I didn't realize who you are."

"Then you must not be from around here." He polishes his fingernails on his lapel. "I'm somewhat famous."

"Do people also know you have a somewhat dubious grasp of classic literature?"

"No, and don't you dare tell them." He inclines his head in a slight bow. "William King. What can I do for you?"

"Pleasure to meet you. I was wondering if I could see Allegra King."

A shadow falls across his face, aging him a good ten years. "My wife doesn't take visitors any longer."

"Ever?"

"Not since she took ill. Maybe even before that." His mouth

twists with regret, as if he's remembering a time when Allegra had scores of visitors. "Is there something I can help you with, Miss…?"

"Oh, I'm sorry. Eve." I extend my hand. "Eve Perrin."

"*Eve*." His bushy eyebrows lift as he engulfs my hand in his. "I've heard quite a bit about you. You're the young woman who's dating my son."

I smile weakly. "We had dinner once."

"Jeremy is quite taken with you." He regards me with more scrutiny. "Your uncle was a longtime resident of Castille, I believe?"

"Yes. Max Dearborne. He was a literature professor at Ford's." I swallow a rising sorrow. "Unfortunately, he passed away over a year ago."

"Oh." He frowns, as if processing that revelation. "I'm terribly sorry. Is his passing the reason you moved here?"

"Sort of." It doesn't sound like he's heard about my sordid past yet, not that he won't eventually. "I'm living in his house on Sparrow Lane. I'm also doing some research about a nineteenth-century artist who went by the name Maria Wood. I'd heard that Mrs. King collects Victorian art. I was hoping to find out if she knows anything about this particular artist."

"Unfortunately, I can't help you there." William steps back and closes the door halfway. "All the art and fancy stuff was my wife's domain, and she sold her collection years ago."

"Can I please leave my contact information for her?" I fish in my purse for a pen, catching sight of a door opening at the far end of the foyer.

"I'm sorry, Miss Perrin." William's voice firms, and he gives me a curt nod that's a sudden contrast to his earlier pleasantness. "My wife is unavailable, but thank you for stopping by."

Just as he closes the door, I glance past him. A slim, dark-haired woman with an air of fragility stands in the doorway at the end of the foyer. I glimpse her navy dress and silk scarf, and then, in that brief instant, our gazes lock.

The front door shuts. Though she was twenty feet away, and the whole interaction happened in less than a second, I swear I saw something in her eyes. *Recognition.*

Does she know who I am? Has she heard the rumors, or does she know me because of Max?

I walk slowly back to my car, struck by the sense that Allegra King is her own mystery.

"Eve?"

I turn. Jeremy King is coming around the side of the house, his blond hair shining in the floodlights. Consternation rises in me, as if I've been caught doing something I shouldn't.

"What are you doing here?" He stops in front of me, his eyebrows drawn together quizzically.

A few mental gymnastics assure me I can tell him the truth without giving anything away about Flynn.

"I wanted to know if I could see your mother," I explain. "I'm doing some art history research, and I thought I could talk to her about a nineteenth-century artist. But your father said she doesn't take visitors."

"No, not since she came back from the hospital." Jeremy shakes his head. "Long before that, even. She stopped wanting to see people when her heart condition was diagnosed. I think she fell into a depression."

"I'm sorry. I didn't mean to pry."

"That's all right." He puts his hands into the pockets of his khaki trousers. "So what artist are you researching?"

"A woman named Maria Wood, though that's likely a pseudonym. It's been tough finding any information on her."

"I'll ask Mother, if you'd like. Even though we don't have the art anymore, she might remember if she once owned anything by Maria Wood."

"I'd appreciate that. Thank you." I take my keys out of my purse. "Sorry again for intruding."

"No problem." He takes out his phone and glances at the screen. "Hey, can I buy you a quick dinner? I'm heading down to New York for the week later tonight, but I'm free for an hour or so."

Oh, dear.

I don't know how to respond. As attracted as I am to Flynn, I'm under no illusions that our strange relationship can or will ever be anything more. And if I do want to start dating again, Jeremy is a good choice—stable, smart, nice.

So why am I hesitating?

"I'm sorry, but I have some work to do." I offer him an apologetic smile.

"Just for an hour or so?" He swipes the screen of his phone. "There's a Mediterranean grill downtown that's usually pretty fast. I can meet you there in about half an hour. I'll grab my stuff first and see if I can ask my mother about the artist."

Though I dislike the hint of manipulation—if I say yes, he might give me more information about Maria Wood—I agree. It's not exactly a date, and he's going out of town, so I'll have time to figure out how to navigate this over the week.

After checking the address on my phone, I drive to the restaurant and request a table for two. Jeremy arrives a few minutes later.

"Sorry, but my mother had gone for a nap, so I didn't have a chance to ask her about the artist," he says, unfolding the cloth napkin. "But I'll talk to her as soon as I can."

"I'd appreciate that."

We turn our attention to the menus, and have a pleasant dinner of spicy grilled chicken and hummus.

"Why are you going to New York?" I ask.

"Dad's sending me down there to close a deal." He gives a rueful chuckle. "Actually I twisted his arm until he finally agreed to let me go. I'm thirty-one years old, and I still have to prove to him I can handle a business negotiation."

I smile with sympathy. "I get it, believe me. My mother is a neurosurgeon. She's always cast a very brilliant, blinding light."

"I wouldn't worry too much about that." Jeremy smiles back, holding my gaze. "You cast a pretty amazing light yourself."

Unease creeps through me. Before I can respond, a woman's voice calls my name.

I glance up as Carol from the Jabberwocky Bookstore approaches. "Hi, Carol."

"Good to see you." She stops, her gaze shifting from me to Jeremy and back again. "You too, Jeremy. How's your mother?"

"She's doing a little better, thanks."

"Your father's speech at the last council meeting was quite persuasive." She shakes her head with a laugh. "He hasn't lost his public speaking skills one iota."

"I'll tell him you said that."

"And Eve, did you find a job?" Carol turns to me. "My husband Ned has seen you jogging up at the lighthouse pretty often. He goes there to walk our dog."

"Yes, the trail is lovely."

"Did you ever inquire at the museum about work?"

Uncomfortable heat flushes my neck. "I did. I'm just doing some private consulting at the moment."

Jeremy glances at his watch. "I'm sorry, Carol, but I explained to Eve I need to get to the airport tonight. Say hello to Ned for me, will you?"

"Of course." Carol eyes us one more time, then strides away.

After paying the bill, Jeremy walks me to my car.

"Thanks for coming with me." Warmth flickers in his eyes. "I was hoping to see you before I leave."

"Thanks for the dinner." I search for my keys in my purse. "Have a safe trip."

I start to get into the car.

"Eve?"

I stop and turn to face him. He looks as if he's trying to figure out what to say.

"Not that it's my business." He rubs the back of his neck. "But Carol's not the first person who's mentioned they've seen you up at the lighthouse."

My spine tenses. "A lot of people use the trail."

"Yeah, uh…" He gives me an abashed smile. "Didn't mean to imply anything, but considering the time you've had of it, I thought you'd want to know."

"Have a nice trip," I say in a tight voice, then climb into my car before he can respond.

No, I think as I drive away from him. *I really didn't want to know that at all.*

CHAPTER 15

The kitchen sink at Ramshackle Manor is of the compression variety, I've learned. It also leaks like Niagara Falls, so I work for several hours on Sunday changing the washers. After that, I tighten several loose door handles, oil squeaky hinges, clean the stove exhaust filter, and install smoke and carbon monoxide detectors. It is immensely satisfying to cross each item off my *To Do* list.

I feed Ghost, then toss a stick to see if he'll fetch it. He does, though he doesn't bound back to drop it at my feet, and I'm not about to try and coax it out of his clenched teeth. But he lets me scratch his ears again. I reward him with a beef bone I picked up at the pet store.

For the rest of the evening, I plan the tea tasting I promised Flynn. I make a list of the teas I want to include and consider a visit to an out-of-town tea shop after work tomorrow.

It's not lost on me that Ghost and Flynn are alike. Their guardedness conceals something softer and even a bit tender. I've tamed Ghost with food, and maybe—just maybe—I'm also disarming Flynn with a properly brewed cup of tea. Why that's important to me is a question I'm not willing to examine too deeply.

I assure myself it's okay to enjoy being attracted to the lighthouse keeper. Though he's technically been my boss for three weeks, I'm not breaking any rules. It's kind of like having a crush on a movie star—he inspires all sorts of fantasies and dreams, but intellectually I know nothing will ever come of it.

But, oh how he makes me *feel*.

When he opens the workroom door on Monday morning, my whole body zings with excitement and anticipation. Despite his dark frown, the remoteness surrounding him like an aura, the clipped tone of his voice, I react to him as if he were stroking my hair and whispering sweet nothings in my ear.

"How was your weekend?" I set my satchel on the desk.

"Fine. Yours?"

"Great." I give him a once-over, looking for evidence of what he's been up to, but while he looks edible in his worn jeans and T-shirt, like a warm, rumpled bed I could nestle right into, his demeanor is as impassive as ever.

Does he ever smile? Every now and then I've caught a glimpse of amusement, a twitch of his mouth, but I've yet to see him fully smile.

"Any special instructions for today?" I turn on the computer and open my organizer.

"Stay away from Jeremy King."

I jerk my head up to stare at him. He's watching me with a narrowed gaze, his mouth set in a stern line.

"Um...*what?*" I can't get another word out.

"Stay away from him," Flynn repeats coldly. "He's not good for you."

Irritation breaks past my shock. "How would *you* know who is or isn't good for me? It's been an effort to get you to say anything to me the whole time I've been working here."

"I don't need to say anything to know the facts." His tone hardens. "I don't want you around him."

"You have no right to tell me that," I retort. "How did you know I went on a date with him anyway?"

His jaw tightens. "You think people around here don't notice when their favorite son has dinner with the new girl in town?"

Christ. I experience a sudden longing for the cold anonymity of a big city.

"I know people are talking about me." I scowl at him. "But I refuse to let gossip dictate what I can and can't do. And for your information, Jeremy knows about what happened to me, and it doesn't seem to bother him."

"That's not the point. You can't work for me *and* see him."

I focus on the computer, hitting the key to bring up the database software.

"My date with Jeremy has nothing to do with my work here," I reply stiffly. "I didn't, and won't, tell him anything about the job or the fact that you're my employer. You don't need to worry about breach of contract."

"This isn't about the damned contract." His voice is suddenly sharp.

He steps closer to me, his soapy, warm scent filling my nose. I hold my ground, not wanting him to see me weaken even though I'm melting inside at his nearness. Impassive though he is on the exterior, I can sense the energy coursing through him, his heavy strong heartbeat, the rush of his blood.

"How many times have you gone out with him?" He clenches and unclenches his hands.

"Once! Well, twice, but the second time was just a quickie...er, I mean a *quick dinner*."

God. I'm so flustered my whole body is hot.

"I don't want you around him *at all*," he repeats.

"Does your animosity have something to do with him wanting to sell the lighthouse?"

"I'm not answering questions." His gray eyes turn the color of metal. "I'm *telling* you to stay away from him."

"You don't have that right."

"I'm your boss."

"That doesn't mean you can make that demand." The words snap out of my mouth without thought. "And if you think you can threaten to fire me over this, then step back, mister, because I've been through the worst wrongful termination I can imagine. And even though my employer fucking *won* that battle, I still have plenty of fight left in me. I'll put on my gloves and get in the ring with you, if I have to."

Wow. Go, Eve.

I'm breathing fast, and my knees are quaking from my sudden fear he'll make me prove my bold statement. The air between us sparks with electricity. I force myself to stand firm, to look directly at him and—

Admiration flashes in his eyes, like a silver comet streaking across the sky. His stern expression doesn't change, but that brief glimpse of warmth eases the tension knotting my shoulders.

"I'm not going to fire you." His voice is measured and controlled. "But I will not have you seeing King."

"You don't like him, so that means I have to stay away from him?" I shake my head. "Sorry, no. He's one of the few people in this town who has been nice to me, and I enjoyed our date. I refuse to discount the possibility of Jeremy being my first real friend here."

Flynn clenches his jaw. "He wants to be more than your *friend*."

"I know." I put my hands on my hips and look him in the eye. "He even kissed me."

A vein throbs in his forehead. If I didn't know better, I'd think he was jealous.

But I do know better. He's mad because I'm refusing to do something he wants me to do. Despite, or maybe because of, his isolated lifestyle, Flynn is clearly a man accustomed to getting what he wants.

"He kissed you." The words grind out of his mouth like broken glass.

"Yes. And I kissed him back. Like our date, it was nice. *Nice* hasn't been the norm in my life lately."

"I could kiss you," Flynn retorts, his hands fisting. "But it wouldn't be *nice.*"

"Oh yeah?" My heart kicks into gear. "What would it be, then?"

His gaze settles on my mouth. "Hot."

"Prove it." The dare flies out of me, my brain failing to process the potential repercussions.

Before I can take another breath, he grabs my shoulders and pulls me against him. I freeze, stunned by the reality of a moment I'd imagined more times than I can count—the sensation of his body against mine. And God, he feels exactly the way I'd imagined, a solid wall of heat and muscle pulsing with life. Rock-hard arms that could wrap around me so tightly nothing would get past them.

He stares down at me, his steel eyes glinting with intent like iron striking stone. I can't move, can't breathe, can't think.

Then he crashes his mouth down on mine, an onslaught, a possession, a *claiming*. Hunger bursts through me, a desire so sharp and intense it destroys all my defenses in one fell swoop.

I moan, everything inside me weakening and aching for more. He slides a hand to my lower back, fitting our bodies together. I yield all the way to my bones, my curves softening against him, any thought of resistance dissolving in a haze of disbelief and craving.

I part my lips tentatively, let him inside. My head spins with the taste of him, something decadent and forbidden. Our tongues touch, breath mingling. Arousal floods me, swift and hard, as if all the fantasies in which I've indulged have primed me for this moment.

I bring my hands to his face, his stubble coarse against my palms, slide them down to the sides of his neck where his pulse throbs heavily. He's like the sea—mysterious, unpredictable, powerful. I could get lost in him, drown, let him sweep me away to a distant land where no one knows who I am and what I've done.

Time falls away. He grips my shoulders, pushing me up against the wall, our lips still clinging together. My blood sizzles. He plants his hands on either side of me, trapping me in the cage of his arms. I drag my hands over his chest, captivated by the sensation of his hard muscles through his T-shirt.

Emboldened by his intake of breath, I slip one hand under his shirt. Delight floods me. His abdomen is a ladder of tight ridges and warm, taut skin. I stroke upward, more eager than ever to feel his powerful chest against my breasts.

He mutters a curse, low and sharp. Trailing his lips to my neck, he cups my breast, his thumb rubbing my stiff nipple. Heat shoots to my core. He shoves his hips against me, pushing my legs apart with one knee.

He's hard. His erection pushes against the front of his jeans, prodding my thigh. A gasp catches in my throat. I'm already getting wet in response, in readiness. He takes my mouth again, open and hot.

Dizziness washes over me. He could lift my skirt, pull down my panties, and plunge into me right here, right now, finally giving me what I've craved since the day we met. Only he can fill the aching emptiness inside me, ease my desperate longing to be wanted for the right reasons, to be desired and lo—

He lifts his head, breaking our kiss and stepping away from me at the same time. Heavy breaths saw from his chest. A flush burns his skin.

I bring a shaking hand to my mouth, suddenly unsure if the

kiss just happened or if I'm like Alice in Wonderland, spinning downward, lost in my intricate imagination.

"That…" I drag in a breath, trying to grab on to my whirling thoughts. "That was both hot *and* nice."

He clenches his hands on my shoulders. His eyes darken to black.

"Get this straight, Eve." His voice is low and rough, his gaze pinning me down. "I'm not *nice*. I don't do things to *be* nice. I don't get involved. Ever. But I will be fucking damned if I let you start seeing that bastard King. Stay away from him."

He releases me and stalks across the room. A second later, the cottage door slams shut.

I grab the back of a chair to steady myself. My legs tremble as I stare at the closed door. A flame suddenly shoots to life inside me.

I yank open the door and follow him into the kitchen. He's standing at the window, his shoulders stiff and hands shoved into his pockets.

"Don't you fucking dare tell me that." I stalk toward him.

Control collects around him like a perfectly tailored suit.

"Kissing you was wrong." His tone is measured. "I shouldn't have done it. I apologize."

A sharp ache pushes at my chest. I turn away, blinking against an unexpected sting of tears.

Wrong.

A kiss that flooded me with light and promise. A kiss that reminded me in no uncertain terms that desire feels so damned good. A kiss I've been wanting, imagining, dreaming about…*wrong*.

Will anything I feel ever be *right* again?

"It wasn't wrong," I mumble.

"What?"

"I said…" I turn to look him in the eye. "It wasn't *wrong*. You think I haven't noticed the way you look at me? The way you stand too close and smell my hair? The way you can't stay away from the kitchen at two every afternoon because you know I'll be here? I'm not stupid, much as I've told myself otherwise recently. You don't want to spend time with me just because my Indian Darjeeling is so tasty."

Resistance laces his body, his eyes hardening. "I meant what I said about King. I also meant what I said about me."

"Right. If you didn't get *involved*, you'd never have followed me out of the museum and offered me a job. You sure as hell wouldn't care who I date."

His breath expels in a heavy rush. "Your association with Jeremy King could compromise your job here. It would be a breach of contract."

"Bullshit," I retort. "There is nothing in your stupid contract about who I can or can't associate with. And I've had enough people trying to order me around and control my life. I will *not* let you be one of them."

I whirl around and stride out of the kitchen. For once, it feels damned good to be the one shutting the door firmly behind me.

CHAPTER 16

*W*ith great force of will, I manage not to relive the kiss for the rest of the morning as I open boxes and analyze book data.

My body remembers, though. My nipples tingle and my core pulses. When I'm seated at the desk, I squeeze my thighs together to try and ease the lingering ache, suppressing the temptation to slide my skirt up and reach between my legs. It would take no effort at all—just a little tickle on the outside of my panties, and I'd come.

It wouldn't be against the rules, exactly. It's not like he put a "no masturbation while at work" clause in the stupid contract.

I give a little snort of laughter and type in a book's publication date. I mutter a curse and correct it. Despite my efforts, I'm making stupid mistakes today, typos and transposing letters and numbers.

Because Flynn Alverton kissed me. No, he *claimed* me in a deep possessive kiss that shook the ground beneath my feet. Why couldn't I have reacted that way to Jeremy's kiss? Why am I completely uninspired to fantasize about him, while images of

Flynn and me writhing in sensual bliss appear in my mind at any given moment?

I push away from the desk and try to work off my physical frustration by opening boxes and shelving books. After my rocky start in Castille, I've been happy with the way things are going—the job, learning my newfound fix-it skills, rediscovering myself, experiencing a pleasant date, bonding with a dog named Ghost.

Now hot-but-strange Flynn has thrown a wrench into my growing self-assurance. And instead of nursing my righteous anger over his dictate about Jeremy, I'm obsessing about my reaction to his kiss.

Stop it.

Over on the desk, my phone buzzes with a call. I swipe the screen to reveal an unfamiliar number bearing a Los Angeles area code. Though I've lost touch with almost everyone I used to know in LA, maybe a former friend is now calling to reconnect.

I answer the call. "Hello?"

"Eve."

Ice floods my veins. I can't speak. His voice is a nightmare of old memories—clipped and harsh, husky with lust, infused with a tenderness that turned out to be a lie. Everything was a lie.

"What…" I pull a breath into my tight lungs. "What do you want?"

"You did a good thing by moving as far away as you could get," David says. "But if you think you can still do some damage, you're wrong."

"What are you talking about?" I fumble to sit in my desk chair.

"You keeping your mouth shut," he snaps.

Fear, jagged and sharp, sinks into my skin. I know all too well how powerful this man is. He defeated me, stripped away all my defenses. I'd tried telling people the truth, but no one had believed me over him.

Why would I do anything now *except* keep my mouth shut?

"I'm…" My breath hitches, panic rising. "I haven't said anything to anyone."

"You'd better not," he says. "No one believed you then. They sure as hell won't now. But if you come forward again and tell people I slandered you and lied, I will destroy you worse than I already have. Got it?"

I can't push any words past my constricted throat. *How did he get my number?*

"You were nothing more than a passable fuck," he continues. "Unless you want more pictures of your tits and cunt made public, you stay in your little mousehole and keep quiet. If I hear anything out of you, you're done."

The call ends. I drop the phone. Every part of me is shaking.

He's supposed to be out of my life for good. I paid a catastrophic price for getting involved with him. Why would he suddenly think I'm going to say anything *now*, of all times? Especially right when I'm finally seeing some light again?

"What's wrong?"

I jerk my head up in surprise at the sound of Flynn's voice—deep and edged with contained wariness, a polar opposite to David's caustic tone. He's standing in front of the desk, his dark gaze on me.

I get quickly to my feet, trying to suppress my shivering. "I… nothing. I was just about to get back to work."

I hurry around the desk and busy myself opening another box.

"Eve."

Oh, how he says my name, like he's wrapping his voice around it, like he's wrapping his arms around me. I fight back tears and pull two fairy tale criticism books from the box.

"Just an unexpected call. Everything's fine."

He steps closer. His delicious scent, the presence of his strong body, make me want to crack wide open and confess everything. To give him my secrets so I won't have to bear their weight alone.

But I can't.

Not until now—right after our kiss—do I realize how horrified I am by the thought of Flynn knowing all the sordid details about me and David. What if he goes on to the internet and reads the news reports? He'll look at me differently then. Everyone does. I couldn't bear it if his hot glances change to disgust.

I hold up my hand. "You said I couldn't ask you any questions. Fine. You can't ask me any either."

He tightens his mouth, flexing his hands at his sides. "Something upset you. I want to know what it is."

I steel my spine, hating the thought of David encroaching on my work here, polluting the strange and fragile friendship I'm developing with Flynn.

"Well, you can't, all right?" I force an abrupt note into my voice. "It's my business, like whatever you do in the tower is your business. Now is there something else you wanted or can I get back to work?"

"Tell me, dammit."

"No." I whirl around to face him, sick to death of being told what to do. I'm tired of having every single element of my life wrenched out of my control. I'm tired of being threatened, of being afraid and alone. "You're not allowed to regret our kiss and then try and be there for me. You don't get *involved*, remember? Ever."

"I will get fucking involved if someone is scaring you." He stalks to the windows. "What happened?"

"Go away, Flynn." I walk back to the desk. "There's nothing you can do anyway."

Nothing anyone can do.

Silence fills the space behind me, broken only by what sounds like his teeth grinding together.

"I don't…" He pauses and pulls in a breath. "I don't regret our kiss. I regret not being able to stay away from you."

My heart thumps. Much as I've secretly longed for him, the

menacing call has slammed me with the knowledge that my past will never die. What if it somehow ends up hurting Flynn?

"Go away," I repeat dully.

"I'm not dropping this, Eve," he says through a clenched jaw. "No fucking way."

The door slams shut.

I press my hands to my eyes. Shame floods me alongside the fear I thought I'd finally conquered. A thirty-second call from David has revived it all—the sinking dread, the black fog suffocating my lungs, the icy cold terror of *what else* he could do.

Does he really have more explicit pictures of me?

Does he know where I am?

Though I'd had my phone number changed, it's easy enough to find that kind of information these days. It also wouldn't be a challenge for anyone to find out I've moved to Castille, but I've been counting on the fact that no one, least of all David, cares where I am now.

My only small consolation is that I'm no threat to him. I fully intend to stay in my "mousehole" and keep quiet. Yes, I want to jumpstart my career again, but David and his colleagues could give a shit about art history. Our paths will never cross again.

So what was that call about? It must have something to do with the two students now accusing him of sexual harassment, but I don't know any details of that situation. I don't want to know.

Or maybe someone said something to him about me. Maybe his wife received a call or a message. During the public blowout, she'd apparently been subjected to pranks by people pretending to be me.

I pick up my phone and call Graham. "Have you heard anything else about what's going on with David?"

"Only what I sent you." Concern laces his voice. "Why?"

"He called me."

"Oh, Eve." He sighs heavily. "I'm sorry. What did he say?"

"He told me to keep quiet, though it's not like I haven't told people everything already. I wanted to tell you since you're the only person who knows where I am."

"I haven't told anyone."

"I didn't think you had," I assure him quickly. "I just don't want you to take any more heat because of me."

"I'll let you know if I hear anything else, but try not to worry."

"I'll be fine. Give my love to Mary."

I end the call and sit back at the desk. Trying to put David's call behind me, I input book data into the computer database.

Threats aside, David has *zero* evidence I've tried to contact him or do anything else in the past year. All I've done is run away and hide.

Though I'm at work, I spend a bit of time trying to regain my balance by editing my Maria Wood *Red Riding Hood* paper. Even objectively, I know it's an excellent, sharp critical analysis, including both scholarly perceptiveness and a personal tone of both anger and empathy.

After all, no one knows better than me what it feels like to be the girl confronting a terrifying wolf.

CHAPTER 17

*A*fter work, I change clothes and hit the trail, running past the white stone markers I've hidden in plants off the trail. My legs ache and my heart is about to burst out of my chest, but the three-mile boulder is getting closer all the time. One day soon I'll reach it without stopping.

I keep jogging toward the second curve in the trail. My chest seizes. I come to a slow, gasping stop. Just catching my breath is painful.

Still...progress.

Satisfied, I turn and start back toward the hill to the cliff's plateau. The waves crash and spray over the rocks. A gleam of pale blue shows on the gray horizon.

A man wearing a hooded red sweatshirt jogs up the adjoining path from the direction of the woodlands.

Apprehension pinches my nerves. I've never felt unsafe out here, usually because there are other people walking or jogging, but today a quick glance around tells me the trail and hill are deserted. Fisting my hands, I edge to the side of the path. Hopefully he'll turn in the direction of the lighthouse.

No. He turns left and heads directly toward me.

More than likely he's just a harmless runner, but I lost any courage for *taking chances* a long time ago. Unfortunately, there's nowhere else I can go out here. I steel my spine and start to run again. I tell myself to avoid eye contact, to run past him as fast as I can.

He's getting closer. Is he slowing down?

Closer...

My sneakers slam against the dirt. My lungs tighten painfully. *Keep running, keep...*

He passes me in a rush of salty air, his gasps of exertion the only sound.

I keep going, glancing behind me once. He's heading toward the boulder, his footfalls rhythmic and steady.

Blowing out a relieved breath, I run toward the hill, ignoring the pain in my muscles and chest until I'm certain he's no longer in sight. Then I slow and struggle to catch my breath again.

Goddammit. I'm letting David's call get to me. I need to be careful, yes, but I lived in fear long enough during the investigation. And though my move to Castille had a rocky start, my job, routine, and research are giving me a new sense of security.

Not that that's affecting my common sense as, thanks to Flynn's advance on my paycheck, I've already made an appointment to have an alarm system installed at Ramshackle Manor.

"Miss Perrin."

I startle, half-expecting to see the hooded jogger. William King is climbing the hill from the direction of the woodlands, wearing a brown sawtooth parka with binoculars dangling around his neck. I manage to smile at him, though my guard is still up.

"Out for a hike?" I ask casually.

"Bird watching." He indicates the binoculars with a derisive roll of his eyes. "I know, what a geriatric hobby, right? But I've been bird watching since I was a kid, so I figure why stop now?" He peers toward the cliff. "I could never get Jeremy interested in it, though. He preferred shooting birds with his BB gun instead of studying them. Look, there's a black guillemot. Have a look."

He takes off the binoculars and hands them to me. I look through the lenses at a glossy black bird with white patches on its wings.

"Pretty." I return the binoculars and step back.

"You come out here often?" He squints at another couple of birds pecking at the shoreline grasses.

"Sometimes." A wave crashes against the rocks, sending a damp chill through the air. "Just for a run."

"Find anything new about that artist you were looking for?" He lifts the binoculars to his eyes. "I think that's a red-throated loon."

"I'm still looking." I take another step away, disliking my lingering wariness.

"Jeremy tells me you're an art historian." William lowers the binoculars and looks at me again. "Impressive. Allegra and I have been fortunate to see major museums all over the world. Everyone raves about the Louvre, but frankly I prefer the Prado. Hard to beat all those Picassos. Do you have a favorite museum?"

"Not really, but I like the Met." I point my thumb toward the lighthouse. "I'm going to head home. It was nice seeing you again. Good luck with the birding."

He nods, tilting his head back to peer at a V of birds cresting over the sky. I hurry back up the hill toward the lighthouse. The tower windows are dark.

Disappointment flickers in me. I almost wish I could knock on the door, see if Flynn wants to have dinner or to…sit at the kitchen table without talking. Just being around him right now would be soothing.

Strange how I know nothing about him, and yet of all the people I've met, he's the one with whom I'm becoming the most comfortable.

I shake off my uneasy feelings and head home, glad to see

Ghost waiting for me on the porch. After feeding him, I take a shower and go to the library to finish revising my Maria Wood paper before sending a copy to Graham.

Despite my lack of concrete information, the analysis and speculation about the *Red Riding Hood* drawing flies from my fingertips. It's been so long since I've written anything scholarly that it's as if a dam has broken open in my brain.

I describe and analyze the drawing, compare it to the works of other fairy tale artists, discuss the social and historical context. The writing brings me back to the reason I love my field of study —because art is such a fascinating lens through which to examine history, societies, culture.

And in the case of Maria Wood, to bring to light an exceptional and shocking artist who used her creativity to subvert the constraints imposed upon women. To exact revenge against those who had hurt her and likely others.

Whoever Maria Wood was, she's my new hero.

My nerves are jittery and tense when I arrive at the lighthouse on Tuesday morning. The boundaries between me and Flynn are loosening, but our last encounter ended in anger and a slammed door. Instigated by both David's call and a hot kiss.

For the first time, Flynn isn't in the workroom to greet me. Dread pools in my stomach. I push open the unlocked door and set my satchel on the desk. Right next to the computer, there's a large, red stainless steel thermos, so shiny and brand-new that light reflects off the surface.

Before I can process the meaning of it, the cottage door opens. Flynn enters, dressed in a clean but wrinkled T-shirt and worn jeans, his hair damp.

My body reacts instantly to the sight of him—pulse racing, heat filling my chest. It's even more intense now that I remember the possessive crush of his mouth, the glide of his sloped muscles under my palm...

"Good morning." He stops in front of the desk and clears his throat. A warm, soapy scent drifts from him. "Sorry I'm late."

"No problem."

Our gazes touch. He was in the shower. A drop of water slips from his hair down the side of his neck. I want to lick it away.

Desire flashes in my blood. A damp patch colors part of his T-shirt, as if he didn't dry himself off completely before dressing. As if he were in a hurry.

And...

Oh my. His gray eyes are dark with satiation, his muscles more relaxed than I've ever seen them. I recognize the look of self-administered carnal satisfaction all too well. Bringing myself to orgasm is how I get myself to sleep every night.

Did he just masturbate in the shower? And was he thinking about me while he did?

My thighs clench. Even if I'm letting my imagination get the better of me, the *idea* of it is enough to spiral me with lust. I can see it too—a vivid picture as explicitly detailed as my own nocturnal fantasies.

Flynn standing in the shower, water cascading over his naked body, rivulets following the slopes and lines of his chest. Strong, powerful legs planted apart, hair plastered to his forehead, muscles tense with urgency. His cock sticking straight out, thick and so long he could bury it deep inside me and reach places I don't even know exist.

I see him grasping the shaft, working his hips back and forth. Fucking his own fist. A fantasy flashing behind his closed eyelids —me lying naked in front of him, my trembling legs spread wide apart as he slides into me, slow and firm. Our breath rasping through the air, our eyes locking with unspoken messages.

Mine: *Yes, oh please, fill me...*

His: *So tight, so good...*

Then our words dissolve into groans and sighs as he sinks fully into me and starts to fuck. Plunging deep...so deep, my hot pleas filling his ears, my body bouncing under the increasing force of his thrusts.

He envisions it all, everything stripped raw as the hot shower pours onto him and he strokes his pulsing shaft. And I see him—his body infused with mounting urgency, the swollen head of his cock appearing and disappearing within the vise of his fist, his muscles straining and tensing before...oh, *fuck*, an orgasm explodes through him, a deep, heavy groan rumbling from his chest.

"...for original tales versus retellings," he says.

Er...what now?

With effort, I pull myself reluctantly out of the fantasy. My skin is hot, my nerves tingling.

He heaves in a breath and rests one hand against the wall, lowering his head to let the hot water pound against his neck.

Eve, focus!

I busy myself opening my organizer and taking out a pen, hoping my face isn't too flushed. "Excuse me, I didn't catch that?"

"The database. How do I know if a book is an original tale or a retelling?"

"I can show you." I turn on the computer and bring up the database.

He slips his gaze over me. Again it's his *look*—the hot appraising one that brings heat to his eyes. But this time, it's not like he's thinking about kissing or touching me. He's *remembering*.

"You see, I cataloged each title in a three-level system."

I type *Briar Rose* into the title field. He moves around the desk to stand beside me, and his proximity floods my senses with all the good things—the warmth of his body heat, his strong, protective presence. If he were to stand at my side forever, I'd feel like I could do anything.

I pull my attention away from that thought and point to the

search results. "The first level is the original work or a translation, with the author as the primary access point. You'll also find collections there. The second level is adaptations and retellings, and the third is spin-offs involving the same characters."

His breath stirs my hair. I overslept this morning and hadn't had time to slather on the apple-lavender body lotion. *Can he tell?*

"Does that make sense?" I glance at him.

"Yeah." He steps back. "Any questions?"

I gesture to the thermos. "Is that yours?"

"It's for you." He starts toward the door, his posture straightening into the *closed off* demeanor I've come to know so well. "Figured you could use a new one when you're out somewhere."

I pick up the thermos, running my hand over the glossy surface. *He bought me a thermos. He remembered mine is too old to keep my tea hot for very long.*

For me, it's a better gift than flowers and sparkly jewelry.

"Thank you. That's very thoughtful of you."

He shrugs off my gratitude and leaves the room.

Probably no other woman in the world would be so ridiculously pleased by the gift of a stainless steel canister, but I'm the only one who knows Flynn. I'm the one who's developing possessive, intense feelings for him. I'm the one who recognizes this as an effort to make amends.

At least...I *think* I'm the only woman. God knows I've been deceived before.

I set the thermos down and shake that doubt out of my head. Even after David's threatening call, I won't let him ruin my attraction to Flynn.

I work through the morning, pausing once when my phone pings with a text from Graham:

Eve, your paper is phenomenal. I'm attaching it with my notes. Truly excellent work. Wish I'd discovered Maria Wood!

The message floods me with pride. Much as I've lost recently, I've always had my scholarly talent. I've also always had Graham.

My phone buzzes again, this time with a call from an unknown number. My stomach knots. 408 area code, both Graham and my mother's location but not either of their numbers.

Warily, I answer the call. "Hello?"

Silence.

Apprehension slithers into my blood. I sense someone on the other end. David's horrid, crude words fire into my head. *Destroy you...tits and cunt...passable fuck.*

"Hello?"

More silence. The line goes dead.

Shaking, I end the call and block the number. Tossing the phone aside, I turn back to the computer. Not until tears fall onto the keyboard do I realize I'm crying.

CHAPTER 18

He has no reason to hurt me. He's already done everything he can do. Maybe that wasn't even him. Maybe it was a prank Halloween call, someone trying to spook me.

If that's the case, it certainly worked.

For the next two days, I adhere to a strict routine to maintain my sense of normalcy. After work, I run farther and farther on the trail to expend my fears and frustrations. Though my morning interactions with Flynn remain cordially businesslike, he fails to join me for teatime. His absence leaves a hole in my day, and I increasingly long for his secure, unwavering presence.

On Friday at two, I head into the kitchen and stop in the doorway. Flynn is looking out the window, his hands in his pockets. I let my gaze roam over the breadth of his shoulders and back, his dark hair brushing his collar, the fit of his jeans. Just the sight of him loosens the tension in my spine.

He turns to face me. I take a tentative step into the kitchen.

"I didn't know you'd be here," I admit.

"You promised me a tea tasting."

I blink. "You still want to do that?"

"Did you bring the stuff?"

"Yes, I brought it on Monday. It's all still in the trunk of my car."

"I'll go get it."

He heads outside. Pleased, I put the kettle on to boil and set up the pot and cups we've been using. I open a bag of masala chai I'd brought yesterday and spoon leaves into the pot. As I close the bag, the rubber band snaps.

I search through a few drawers for a new one. A junk drawer is packed with local brochures, menus, paperclips, a stapler, stamps, and pens. Rummaging around, I see an old photograph slip from between the brochures.

Curious, I pull it out. Creased and faded, it shows a dark-haired young boy holding up a fish on a line. A wide grin spreads over his face. Beside him stands a smiling older man with a white beard and wearing a tattered Vikings cap. His hand is on the boy's shoulder. Both of them radiate happiness and pride.

"Where'd you get that?" Flynn's voice startles me.

I turn, my heart suddenly racing. He's standing right behind me, a frown darkening his face and his shoulders stiff.

"I…I was just looking for a rubber band." I extend the photo. "I'm sorry. I wasn't prying."

He shoves the photo into his back pocket. "It was a long time ago."

"Looks like you were having fun."

"Yeah. My grandfather used to—" He cuts himself off and indicates the wicker basket and two full bags he'd brought in from the car. "Just how many people are you expecting for this tea tasting?"

He had a grandfather who used to take him fishing.

Like his mention of the school *Peter Pan* play, that little piece of information both assuages my curiosity and incites a thousand more questions. *Is your grandfather still alive? Why don't you want to talk about him? Where are your parents?*

He's watching me. Wariness brews in his eyes, as if he senses all the questions bubbling beneath my surface. But I won't ruin our fragile accord by asking any of them.

"A tasting is serious business." Setting myself to the task at hand, I open the basket and take out several cups. "You need different pots and cups for all the different teas. It'll take me a few minutes to get it organized."

"I can wait." He leans back against the counter with his arms folded, a model of patience as I prepare the pots and brew several varieties of tea.

"Did you bring scones?" he asks. "I've heard of people having scones with tea."

"There's a British tradition of afternoon tea with scones." I focus on putting the leaves into the filter so he won't notice how pleased I am that he remembered our plan. "But for a tea tasting, you shouldn't eat anything too sweet or savory. It could interfere with the flavor of the tea."

He makes a noise that could be either interest or disdain.

"I have to brew them in cups since I don't have enough pots." I lift the filters from the cups. "And we want them to all be properly steeped. Sit down."

Rather to my surprise—considering how often he issues orders—he obeys. I set the cups on a tray and bring it to the table.

"I have six varieties." I point to the cups one by one. "Green, white, black, pu-erh, and oolong. This one is chai, a spiced Indian tea. Black is usually my favorite. It's the most heavily oxidized of all the teas, which is why it has a stronger flavor. White is the most delicate and unprocessed, and oolong is partially oxidized. Green tea leaves are usually either steamed or heated in a pan."

"So what am I looking for?" He lifts the green tea and sniffs.

"Among connoisseurs, of which I am not one, the brewed tea is called liquor. It's really similar to a wine or beer tasting, except you slurp the tea to spread it across your tongue. Then focus on smell, mouth feel, what kind of flavors you taste. Tea tasting has a language of its own. Earthy, fruity, floral, sweet.

But there's no right or wrong answer. It's all about your own experience."

Though Flynn looks far from convinced, he takes a generous slurp of the green tea, then furrows his brow. "Grassy?"

"Agreed. Salty too, don't you think? A little like the ocean. Full-bodied. Fresh vegetables."

He eyes me dubiously over the rim of the cup. "Sure."

My mouth curves. I indicate the white tea. "Try that one. It's called dragon pearl jasmine. The leaves are hand-rolled."

He picks up the cup. "Why dragon pearl?"

"The rolled tea leaves look like little pearls, but I've also heard the name is derived from a Chinese folktale. One winter, a girl sought help from a mystical dragon to cure her sick brother. The dragon had a pearl on his chest, and when he soared into the sky, a drop of water fell from the pearl. A tea plant grew on the spot, and the dragon told the girl that the tea would cure her brother. And so it did."

We both sip the tea. Flowers, cream, sunshine.

"You should see the tea pearls during infusion," I say. "Come here, I'll show you."

I return to the stove and put the kettle back on, then add the fragrant tea to a clean pot. Flynn stops beside me. Beneath the aroma of jasmine, I again catch his delicious scent of salt and spice, one that warms me from the inside out.

"Watch when I add the hot water." I take the kettle from the stove and pour water into the glass teapot.

The tea pearls dance and swirl, rising to the surface of the pot and unfurling like flowers blooming before descending gracefully to the bottom. We watch until the last little tea leaf sinks to join the others.

"It's quite beautiful." I smile.

"Yes, it is."

I lift my gaze. He's looking at me, not the teapot. Pleasure fills my veins.

"The process is called *the agony of the leaves*." My pulse increases. The steam from the pot floats between us, aromatic and sweet. "I've always found it symbolic in a way. Even when infused with boiling water, the dragon pearls dance and float. And in the end, they create something entirely new."

He doesn't respond. I flush and reach for the filter. No need to get all fanciful.

"Your uncle said the same thing about fairy tales."

Sudden hope surges beneath my heart. "Uncle Max talked to you about fairy tales?"

A smile tugs at Flynn's mouth. "Didn't he talk to everyone about them? He told me that was why they're so universal and powerful. The characters all have to undergo trials, some of them pretty intense, before they can have a new life."

A happy ending. Guaranteed in so many stories, but not so much in reality.

Deflecting a stab of sorrow, I pour two fresh cups of dragon pearl tea and bring them back to the table. We sit and sip, though neither of us remarks on the flavors we detect. The steam from all the tea fogs the window, obscuring the grass-covered plateau sweeping to the woodlands.

"I didn't know David Landry was married." Not until the confession is out do I realize how much I want Flynn to believe me. No one else did. I even doubted myself. *What kind of idiot doesn't read the signs from her married lover?*

I look at the window. My solemn, blurred reflection stares back at me. The story bubbles up inside me, the truth I suddenly need this man to know.

"We were together for a couple of months," I continue, old shame still cutting deep. "It happened right when Max stopped chemo. I was in a bad place, not that that's an excuse. I fell pretty hard for David. Never saw a sign that he was married. He even had an apartment in Westwood, a standard bachelor pad. I figured out later that was probably where he brought all his fuck dolls."

"Don't call yourself that." Flynn's tone hardens.

I shrug. "That was probably how he saw me. It wasn't as if we were having deep conversations about artistic theory and venture capitalism. But after Max died, I just wanted to be close to someone, to have someone be there. For the most part, he was...at least, until it all went to hell.

"One afternoon I was on campus, giving a lecture to almost four hundred undergrads. Halfway through an analysis of Delacroix's *Liberty Leading the People*, the door burst open. A woman charged up to the stage and grabbed the microphone from me. I was scared. I thought she was going to attack me or something.

"The whole lecture hall was shocked into silence. She started ranting about how all the students had a whore for a professor. She told them I was fucking her husband, business professor David Landry, and that I was a homewrecker who didn't care he had a wife and two children. She had..."

My breath hitches, horrific shame rising to choke my throat. I swallow and force myself to keep going, to get it all out.

"She had printed some photos of me that David had taken. N-naked photos. *God.*" I close my eyes, press my hands to my hot face. "I never...I never posed for them, I swear. I was stupid, but not that stupid. He was on his phone so often, he'd taken them without me noticing. In bed, at the bathroom sink, wherever.

"His wife had printed them out, and she threw them at me in the lecture hall while she was ranting. I couldn't get the micro-phone away from her. Two guys from the front row came onstage to help me, and she ran out.

"You'd never believe the silence that fell after she was gone. All I could hear was my heart hammering, the panic building. I managed to dismiss the class and get back to my office, but by then it was far too late for any damage control. I called David, but of course he didn't respond. Word of the incident spread over campus like wildfire. Next thing I knew I was being summoned in front of the academic board.

"For some reason, I kept thinking there had been some horrible mistake. That it wasn't David they were talking about... or *me*. It didn't make sense, didn't fit with anything I knew or had even suspected.

"Then the police contacted me. David had requested a restraining order against me. He'd said I'd been stalking him for weeks, that I'd sent him the naked pictures of me, and he was concerned for the safety of his family."

Flynn has a white-knuckle grip on his cup. Tension spikes his whole body. I brush my fingers over his in an indication that he should loosen his grip or risk breaking the cup.

"What happened then?" he asks.

I take a sip of tea and rub my finger over a crack in the hardwood table.

"I never stood a chance. I hired a lawyer, but David knew what he was doing. Obviously he'd done it before. I had no record of texts or emails from him. I figured out later he'd used a burner phone to contact me, so there were no records from his cell company either. Ultimately the only defense I had was to say it had been a consensual affair and I hadn't known he was married. I'd never have gotten involved with him if I'd known.

"No one believed me. Not the police, the board, the provost, the students, the other professors. Not my mother. The naked photos of me showed up in news articles on the internet. Uncensored on other sites.

"You wouldn't think a salacious affair involving an assistant professor would be a big deal, but David is famous in his field. He made it newsworthy. When it became clear the story wasn't just going to blow over, the board of regents fired me."

Flynn's expression is like stone. His gray eyes glitter with anger. "On what grounds?"

"*Personal conduct that impaired the fulfillment of my academic duties,*" I recite with a shrug. "That was it. If Uncle Max hadn't left me his house, I don't know where I would have gone. And if you hadn't given me a job, I don't know what I would have done. David took almost everything from me."

"Was he the one who called?"

"Yes. To tell me to keep my mouth shut." I give a hollow laugh. "As if I'd ever want to rehash that whole humiliating mess."

"If he calls you again, I want to know."

I shift my gaze to him. Inexplicably, the hard, possessive note in his voice soothes the prickling fear and pain elicited by David's call. While part of me realizes Flynn could never put a stop to anything David does, it feels incredibly good to have someone on my side. To have *him* on my side.

"Does he know where you live?" Flynn asks.

"No. I mean, I don't think so." I look down at my tea. "I purposely didn't tell anyone where I was moving, but of course it's not difficult to find people these days. My PhD advisor and my mother are the only ones who have my address. But as long as I keep quiet, I don't think David cares where I am."

"And if he does?"

I don't know. I couldn't do anything against him then. What can I do now?

"I lost a lot." I swallow past the constriction in my throat. "My career, my home, my friends, my self-respect, my voice. Honestly, there's not much more he can take from me."

"He'd better not try." Anger, a hard promise, edges Flynn's voice.

Again my heart warms at the thought that he's more than just my tea companion and the subject of my hottest sex fantasies. He's also becoming my ally. And in a strange way, my friend.

We fall silent again, the pattering of the rain the only sound echoing through the kitchen.

"Max showed me a photo of you," Flynn says.

I look up. "He did?"

"He talked about you a lot. He was really proud of you. He had this photo of you in his wallet...said he'd taken it during a trip you and he took to the California redwoods. You were probably twenty, standing there in this forest of huge trees with your copper hair and green jacket. Like an elf or a wood sprite."

"You remember that picture?"

"I never forgot it." He pushes his teacup aside and shoves to his feet. He starts toward the door, then turns back to me, his expression tense.

"That bastard can't destroy you, Eve. No one can. And that girl in the forest? She still believes in fairy tales."

He leaves the kitchen, the door clicking shut. Shock descends over me like a slow chill.

Oh my God.

He knows my secret.

CHAPTER 19

Run. Run. Run...shit.

I slow to a walk on the coastal trail, my lungs bursting and my chest heaving. Pain shoots through my leg muscles. I rest my hands on my thighs and bend over to catch my breath. The fucking boulder looks like it's a thousand miles away.

I turn and walk slowly back up the hill to the lighthouse. Today, I left the workroom later than usual, needing to catch up on cataloging after my afternoon with Flynn got away from me in more ways than one.

The granite secrets wall climbs alongside the cliff's edge like a prehistoric snake. Bits of wet paper cling between the rocks.

My thoughts tumble and crash. I'd given Flynn the full truth of what had transpired with David, only to discover yet another weird-guy quirk that I have no idea what to do with. Of all the things I've imagined Flynn to be (*undercover FBI, lord of a sex dungeon, international spy*), a secret thief is not one of them.

Did he steal my secret after he saw me hide it in the wall? Does he steal everyone's secrets or was it just mine? And *why?*

I reach the terrace, my breathing still fast, and look up at the tower. He's not there, and the smoky glass is smooth and empty.

Even if I did barge back into the lighthouse and demand answers, they might not be ones I want to hear.

I pause at the wall. A Forestry Department sign is printed with a history of the wall, as well as the statement that the wall is maintained to prevent the paper from damaging the environment. The implication, of course, is the lighthouse keeper clears the secrets out of the wall on a regular basis.

But there's nothing stating he steals them. Reads them.

I no longer believe in fairy tales.

The only secret I had left...which is now no longer a secret.

I still love fairy tales, but as fictional stories to be enjoyed. I don't believe they exist in reality. Certainly they don't for me. In my story, the villain already won. Flynn knows that too.

The more I think about it, the more it burns. This is just one other thing he knows about me, while I still know almost nothing about him. Hot sexy stuff aside, that particular dynamic in our relationship is starting to tick me off.

I shake my head and stride back to my car. This weekend, I need to regroup. I'm getting too caught up in him and his mysteries. Losing focus with all our intimate little teas and that intense way he *looks* at me, and the heated kiss I still feel imprinted on my lips.

Enough of that. I need to do what Juliette has been pressuring me to do—find an art history job somewhere *else*.

I need to distance myself from Flynn. In addition to being a locked door, he's a thief. And I've had enough stolen from me.

Saturday morning dawns gray and drizzly, casting a pall over the old house. From the basement, the heater makes a rumbling noise like some great hibernating beast. It's past time for me to call an HVAC pro in to check the heater, but I dread the possibility that he'll tell me I need a whole new system.

I let Ghost in the back door. He nudges his head against my leg before heading for his food dish. I've made a vet appointment for him next week—another expense that I hadn't expected but am actually happy to make.

Though the dog and I aren't BFFs, he's increasingly affectionate, and I like having him around. I see him patrolling the area around the house every day, and his presence makes me feel safer out here by myself.

Especially after David's horrible call.

Leaving Ghost to his breakfast, I head upstairs to dress in yoga pants and a knit sweater. I drive downtown and park off Lantern Street. The main road is closed to accommodate the farmer's market, which is held every Saturday through November.

At the library, I search for updated job listings.

Visiting professor, Indiana University. Adjunct professor, Spelman College. Instructor, Colorado State. Professor, University of Alaska. Assistant professor, Albright College, Professor, Santa Clara University.

I apply to six more openings, personalizing my letter of introduction, pasting in a statement about my teaching philosophy, and attaching both my CV and the Maria Wood paper.

Good. Another step toward rebuilding my career. Another step away from my growing entanglement with the lighthouse keeper and his unfolding of all my secrets.

As I head back outside, I turn onto Lantern Street to visit the farmer's market. Shop windows display remnants of Halloween decorations. Under covered booths, vendors have set up displays of fall vegetables, maple syrup, jam, and fresh-baked bread. Customers stroll along the street with cloth bags slung over their arms.

A male voice calls my name. Jeremy waves at me from a coffee-stand, where he's standing with his father.

Side-by-side the two men look strikingly similar. Though William is taller and bigger, he and Jeremy share the same noble features.

"Hello, both of you." I approach, pleased to see familiar faces. "When did you get back from your trip?"

"Last night. I was planning to give you a call." Jeremy leans in to brush his lips across my cheek. "You look great, but that's obviously a theme with you."

"Thank you." I turn to greet William with a handshake and a smile. "Good to see you again."

"You too." William slants an inquisitive glance toward his son. "I'll leave you two alone, huh?"

"Oh, that's not necessary," I reply hastily. "I'm just going to get a few more things and head home."

"Jeremy will show you around," William says firmly, glancing at his gold Rolex. "I was glad to hear you let him take you on another date. Jeremy doesn't go out nearly enough, and you seem quite suitable."

"Okay, Dad." Jeremy nudges his father in the side and shakes his head at me in amusement. "He's just here to pick up some lemon cake for my mother. Her appetite isn't great, but she'll eat the lemon cake made by one of the local bakeries."

"It must be delicious then," I remark. "I'll have to pick some up as well."

"Lemon cake is served in *The Great Gatsby*." William looks down his narrow nose at me. "By Sinclair Lewis."

"F. Scott Fitzgerald, but who cares who wrote it if lemon cakes are involved?"

He makes a harrumph of either amusement or indignation. Jeremy rolls his eyes and grabs his father's sleeve, giving him a "go away, Dad" look. I can't help grinning.

"I've been ousted, Miss Perrin." William gives me a nod of

farewell. "Enjoy the morning. Jeremy, buy her a coffee and behave yourself."

Jeremy groans as his father strides off. "Sorry, Eve. You can imagine how embarrassing he was when I was in high school. I cringed whenever he met my dates."

"I think he's charming." I experience an old, almost forgotten longing for my father. Though I always had Uncle Max, he'd lived across the country for much of my childhood and wasn't a daily presence the way a father should be. The way it sounds like William still is for Jeremy.

"Okay if I walk with you?" Jeremy turns from the coffee vendor and hands me a lidded paper cup. "I can show you some of the best stuff to buy."

"Sure. Thanks." I accept the coffee and fall into step beside him as we start toward the market booths. "How was your trip to New York?"

"Not great." With a grimace, he lifts his coffee cup to his mouth. "We're close to closing an acquisition deal, but now the other company wants to renegotiate. My father wasn't happy with how I handled it. Especially considering that King Financial has taken a downturn along with the rest of the town's economy."

"I'm sorry to hear that."

"Just means I have to work harder." He shrugs and smiles. "How about you? Did you have a good week?"

I nod, realizing I can't tell him much of anything about my week. *I'm working for the lighthouse keeper. I wrote a paper about a strangely beautiful drawing I found in my uncle's collection. Flynn warned me away from you. Flynn kissed me until the world spun. We have tea together almost every afternoon at two.*

"I did some reading and research. Got a few more repairs done on the house. It was a banner week on the excitement front."

Jeremy chuckles. "You still haven't found anything about that artist?"

"Not yet. I'll have to keep digging."

We stop at a couple of booths and sample the food—crackers with jam, pretzels and mustard. Our conversation shifts to Castille, and it becomes clear to me that the town and its environs mean a great deal to Jeremy.

"It's a fantastic place to grow up," he says. "Which makes it even harder to see everything in decline. Used to be that we'd have a ton of tourists for the fall foliage season, but now we get maybe half the crowd we once did, if that."

"When will you find out about the sale of the lighthouse?" I ask.

"When the Forestry Department's lease expires at the end of the year. But first, the city council will vote on a change to the zoning law. To get that passed, we still have to convince the residents the sale is a good idea." He puts his hand on my arm. "Excuse me a minute, Eve. One of my clients is over there, and I need to remind him to get me some signed papers by Monday."

"Sure, go ahead."

Promising to be right back, Jeremy hurries over to a gentleman studying the root vegetable offerings at another stand. I walk half a block, passing a bulky, bald resident whom I swear I've seen before. But where? His head is down, his fingers working at his phone.

Pulling my coat more closely around me, I continue looking at the other wares. I splurge on a ten-dollar jug of locally made maple syrup.

As I slip it into my bag, I catch sight of a tall man standing in front of a bakery stall. Worn jeans, black jacket, scruffy dark hair.

Flynn. My heart thumps, my blood lighting up. I start to turn away, not wanting him to see me. He lifts his head suddenly, his gaze darting toward me like a laser homing in on a target. Electricity fires through the damp air, pinning me to the spot.

You're a thief.

The rational part of my brain knows well enough not to

confront him right now in a public place, but...God in heaven, the man is an enigma. One minute he has me hot as a firecracker, the next minute I'm feeling all warm and cozy as we drink Darjeeling tea, and the third minute I think I'm falling into a trap, tumbling down a rabbit hole without knowing what's at the bottom.

I trusted a man once, and his secrets destroyed me. *By trusting Flynn, am I walking into the same kind of nightmare?*

No. I still won't believe my instincts about him or Max's trust in him are misplaced. Though that belief doesn't change the fact that I'm still mad at him.

Flynn turns his attention back to the display of breads, muffins, pastries, and rolls. The vendor plucks four scones from a tray and puts them in a white paper bag. He hands her cash and waves away the change she tries to give him. He looks at me again and indicates the bag.

I smother a surge of pleasure. *Oh, no, Flynn Alverton. You don't get to be all adorable buying scones for our teatime.*

"All set?" Jeremy stops beside me.

Everything inside me tenses, like an overstretched violin string.

Flynn's gaze snaps to Jeremy and ices over, his gray eyes suddenly arctic. Jeremy puts his hand on my back.

"He bothering you?" He jerks his head toward Flynn.

"No." I muster some resolve and turn away.

We walk half a block away to another vegetable stand. I glance back over my shoulder at the bakery vendor. Flynn is gone.

"He's bad news." Jeremy's voice is tight. "I know people think it's all romantic and mysterious, this weird guy living in the lighthouse, but whatever he's hiding, it's not good."

I bristle inwardly. "How do you know he's hiding something?"

"Because no one knows anything about him. Rumors abound, of course. He's in witness protection, he's grieving the loss of a dead wife, he's an escaped convict. All bullshit, if you ask me. But people don't act the way he does if they're not hiding something. And I'm going to find out what it is."

"Why?"

"Because he's trying to stop me from selling the lighthouse."

Surprise ripples through me. It makes sense, of course, that Flynn would want to save his home from destruction, but there hasn't been any indication that he's publicly opposing Jeremy's plan.

"He doesn't own the lighthouse," I say. "I assume it's not his right to say what should be done with it."

"No, but that's not stopping him." Jeremy slips his hand around my arm as we walk to another booth. "He signed a contract with my mother…I don't know, fourteen, fifteen years ago? My father opposed it, but the lighthouse was in a trust belonging to my mother, so she could do what she wanted. I don't think my father even knew the terms. Alverton pays rent on time, usually early, and he has a certain number of tenant's rights, but he has no say in whether or not we sell it."

"So how is he trying to stop you?"

Jeremy gives a derisive snort. "He wrote a letter to the *Castille Times*, some eco-friendly crap about the coastline and environment. He was also supposedly trying to get the lighthouse and lands into protected status, but there's not much else he can do. He can't rally the residents to his cause, that's for sure. They like that he's the local recluse, but no one around here is stupid enough to trust him."

That remark twists inside me like a knife-point. Juliette's voice echoes through my head. *"I suppose people believe that a woman who chooses to have an affair with a married man is stupid enough to repeat her mistakes."*

"Hey, I'm sorry." Jeremy turns to me. "I didn't mean to go off like that. Obviously I don't like the guy, and I really don't like the way he was looking at you. Let's go grab some lunch and talk about something more pleasant."

Regret cracks through me. No matter how much I think dating Jeremy would be a good step on the road to rebuilding my life, I can't do it. The animosity between Jeremy and Flynn runs deeper than I realized. It's way too messy. I didn't get out of one mess only to get right back into another.

Asserting my autonomy is one thing. Getting in the middle of a deep-seated rivalry while being hot for one man and trying to date the other...yeah, that's something else entirely.

"Jeremy, I'm going to head back home."

He presses his lips together. "That doesn't sound good."

"I really like you," I say honestly. "And I'd like to stay friends. But I've had a rough time of it recently, and being new in town with a reputation that preceded me...well, I need to keep a low profile for a while."

He regards me for a long minute, then nods shortly. "If that's what you want, I guess I have to live with it, right?"

"I need more time to settle in," I explain. "I've only been here for a month, and it was unfair of me to think I was ready to date again."

"All right, Eve." His tone is cool, his shoulders stiff. "Let me know when you are ready, okay?"

Before I can respond, he walks away, disappearing into the crowd.

Did I just make another mistake? One that will come back to haunt me?

*a*fter leaving the farmer's market, I drive to the lighthouse, my fingers clenched on the steering wheel. Winter is in the air, the crisp red and gold leaves strewn like a carpet over the road.

Tension grips my entire body. Only Flynn's truck is parked in the lot, the gray cold keeping everyone away from the coast. I hurry up the path to the workroom door, rapping my knuckles against the weathered wood.

Flynn opens the door, a book of Hans Christian Andersen tales in his hand. No expression shows behind his stoic mask, which angers me all the more. I push past him. The accusation bubbles into my throat like lava.

"You stole my secret."

He closes the door and turns to face me. "I told you not to see King again."

"He has nothing to do with this!"

"Why were you with him?" A muscle ticks in his jaw.

"Because I *thought* he'd be a good person to casually date." A faint dizziness washes over me, like I'm standing on the deck of a rolling ship. "I wanted to get my bearings again. And because I'm tired of other people, *you included*, dictating what I can or can't do. I signed your stupid contract because I want and need this job desperately, but I never agreed to do whatever you dictate outside the bounds of work. *That's* why I was with him."

I can almost see him processing that revelation.

"What if I *ask* you not to see him again?" he finally says.

"Well, you might have tried that tactic the first time around." I sigh, pressing a hand to my temple. "But it doesn't matter because I've already decided I'm not going to see him again."

"What made you decide that?"

I have nothing to give him but the truth.

"Because you bought scones for our tea. And because I can't pretend I ever had any interest in him when I can't stop thinking about *you*."

His eyes darken, a crack in his stoicism. Silence falls between us, heavy and thick. Frustration roils inside me like a tsunami.

"Why did you take my secret?" I ask.

"Part of my job is to clean and maintain the wall."

"But you knew which secret was mine! You saw me put it in the wall."

"I knew it was yours." He regards me with detached gravity. "But first, I knew it was *you*."

I pull in a breath past the tightness in my chest. "What does that mean?"

"That day…when you looked at the lighthouse, I saw your face." He turns away, his hands flexing. "Hit me like a ton of bricks. Max's Eve, suddenly right in front of me. Almost couldn't believe it. And when you left, I had to know what kind of secret you could possibly have."

"Why…" I swallow hard. "Why didn't you tell me earlier?"

"It's not a secret if other people know about it."

"Do you steal other people's secrets too?"

He doesn't respond.

I grip the handle of my satchel. "What do you do with them?"

Again he doesn't answer. Outlandish theories pop into my head. *Blackmail, subversion, witness protection, informant.*

Fresh anger surges in my blood. I stalk across the room and give him a hard shove. The impact doesn't move him an inch, but his eyes widen slightly.

"Goddamn you, Flynn Alverton." My body suddenly burns with all relentless emotions and curiosity I've been struggling to contain. "What is *with* you? You hide up here like the freaking Phantom of the Opera, and no one seems to know anything about you, much less what you do up here all by yourself. You act like you're locking me out of the lighthouse, but frankly it feels more to me like you're locking yourself *in*. You won't tell me anything about Max or how you knew him, you make me sign some kind of non-disclosure contract, and now I find out you're doing God knows what with the town's secrets…"

I pace to the windows and back, my heart hammering.

"I mean, this is all fine and dandy if you're the hero in a nine-teenth-century Gothic novel," I snap, "but you like my *tea*, for heaven's sake, and sometimes you look at me like you want to rip off my clothes right then and there, and then you *kiss* me like you're freaking *starving*…and it probably comes as no surprise that I haven't had good sex in far too long, so *yes*, okay? You make me crazy hot…so hot I fantasized about you *at work* last week, which is so completely unprofessional, and if you only knew what I do every night alone in bed while thinking about you, you'd—"

The book he's holding hits the ground with a thud. My breath lodges in my throat. He stalks toward me, his eyes darkening to charcoal.

He stops a foot away, his chest heaving and hands clenching. The air crackles and sparks with electricity, the only sound the rasping of our breath.

We lunge toward each other at the same time. Closing the distance. Desire breaking, splintering, shattering. He opens his arms. I drop my satchel and fly into them, crashing against his chest, wrapping my legs around his waist. Our bodies collide and fuse. He closes his arms around me, holding me against him, our eyes level. His heart beats against my breasts. Hunger fires the air.

"Fuck if I can stay away from you." He brings one hand to the back of my neck, pulling my head closer.

He crushes his mouth down on mine, our lips meeting in a kiss of hot frenzy. Everything else falls away—the unanswered questions, the suspicions, the town gossip, his reticence. Only one thing matters. I'm finally in his arms, his body solid and secure against mine, his arms locked around me and his kiss spinning me into a whirlwind.

I drive my hands into his hair, reveling in the sensation of the thick strands sliding through my fingers, so much better than I've ever imagined. He urges my lips apart and delves his tongue into my mouth, licking and biting. He's tense, hard, his muscles straining with self-restraint.

"Hurry," I whisper against his mouth, tightening my legs around his waist. "Don't be gentle. I can take it. I've dreamed about you so much and want you so badly…"

His groan echoes inside me, his eyes brimming with lust. But just when I expect him to set me down and start ripping off my clothes, he adjusts me in his arms, one hand curving under my knees and the other around my back. He holds me like I weigh no more than a feather.

"What…" I tighten my fingers on his shoulder. "What are you doing?"

He smiles at me. My eyes widen, my heart almost exploding into a song-and-dance because…*oh my God*. He's gorgeous all stern and unforgiving, but his perfect white smile transforms him into downright beautiful. His eyes crinkle at the corners, a dimple pops into his left cheek, and his face transforms from *hot forbidden fantasy* to *sexy, warm, tangible man*.

"I'm taking you to my bedroom." He shoves open the cottage door and crosses to the kitchen.

"Your…" I'm so surprised I barely have the brain power to look around as he carries me through to a dining room, a living room, and up a narrow staircase to a hallway lined with doors.

He kicks one open and brings me inside, lowering me onto a large bed covered with a rumpled navy comforter. Eyes glimmering with desire, he climbs over me, engulfing me in his heat, his hands on either side of my head. He lowers his mouth to mine again.

"I can't stop thinking about you." He strokes his hand up the front of my sweater, cupping my breast. "You cast a fucking spell over me."

Rather than unnerving me, his confession fits right up against my own obsessed thoughts, the lust-drenched visions that have the smoky, blistered quality of a dream.

But now, he's anything but a dream—his solid, strong body pinning me to the mattress, his arms trapping me, his kiss spiraling through me. Stifled by the weight of my clothes, I'm burning up. I wiggle beneath him so I can yank my sweater over my head.

"Perfect," he mutters hoarsely, lowering his head to press a trail of kisses over my throat and shoulders, down to the curves of my breasts.

"Wait," I whisper, need rising in me like steam from a boiling pot. "Let me…"

I tug futilely at my yoga pants. He grasps the waistband, pulling them off me and dropping them to the floor. Cooler air prickles my skin, but our carnal heat is ratcheting up with every passing second.

He lifts his head to stare at me, his eyes hot on my breasts, my stiff nipples pressing against my bra, the cotton panties hugging my hips. He twists the straps of my bra, pulling it off my shoulders and down.

I shiver, acutely aware that I'm mostly naked and he's still fully clothed—and while, yes, I have imagined this exact scenario more than once, I'm never shy in my imagination. Just the opposite, in fact.

"Goddamn, Eve." His throat works with a swallow as he stares at my naked breasts. Never in my life has a man looked at me with such aching *need*.

His breath escapes the instant before his mouth covers mine again. He palms my breasts, his long fingers pinching my nipples gently. Electric currents travel down to my core, melting my self-consciousness into pleasure. He slides his mouth across my cheek, down to my neck where my pulse beats. He flicks his tongue out to lick the throbbing vein and closes his teeth around my collarbone.

I can hardly pull in another breath. I spread my hands over his chest. His body heat burns through his gray cotton T-shirt. Slipping my hands underneath it, I moan at the sensation of his rigid abdomen and smooth, hard muscles.

"I've thought about this so much." He lowers his head to press his lips against my breasts. "Tasting you. Touching you. Hearing your moans. Sinking my cock into you…"

He curves his hand over my inner thigh. Easing one finger under the elastic of my panties, he groans when he discovers how wet I already am. I'm trembling with excitement, every part of my body sensitized.

He kisses me as if he wants to devour me. God knows I want him to. I want him to invade me, fill me up, turn me inside out. I want him to fuck me, force me, make me come so hard I forget my own name.

Time slips away. Rain patters against the windows. A crashing sound echoes in my head, but I can't tell if it's the ocean or my heartbeat. He kisses my cheeks, my neck, my breasts, before moving back to my lips. He tastes like everything delicious—

peppermint, allspice, amaretto. He lifts himself away from me only long enough to pull my panties off.

"You're like a nymph." He slides his hand over my breast to my belly. "A naiad dwelling in the water. All pale skin, red hair, perfect curves."

Images of Victorian painted nymphs appear in my mind, their wild beauty mirroring forests, rivers, oceans, and meadows; their creamy, supine bodies spread decadently alongside riverbanks and sea grottos.

In all my years of studying such images, never once have I felt a kinship with the much-coveted erotic nymphs of mythology. Not until now.

He strokes lower, caressing my hips and thighs before his fingers delve into my sex. I shiver, a nascent flame rising in my blood as I open myself for the seeking penetration of his touch. And, oh dear lord, touch me he does, stroking my labia, sliding his forefinger into my opening. His breath rasps against my neck, hot and heavy.

I fumble for the buttons on his fly. He pushes to his knees and unfastens the buttons, shoving his jeans off. His cock is a heavy weight in his boxer briefs, his thighs corded with muscle. I swallow and slowly pull the briefs over his hips, breathing out at the sight of his thick erection. God in heaven, he's beautiful.

"Flynn. Hurry."

He moves away from me only long enough to retrieve a condom packet from the bedside table. He sheathes his erection and turns back to me, his expression filled with both lust and something else…a touch of disbelief, wonder…*awe.*

Desire snaps between us, like a piece of stained glass breaking in half. Then he's hauling me toward him at the exact instant I pull him down to me, our bodies colliding and lips crashing together.

He braces one hand beside my head and positions himself between my legs. Dizzy with longing, I expect him to plunge into me with one hard thrust, but he eases into me slowly, his muscles taut.

My heart beats wildly, my blood spilling like molten lava through my veins. I bite down on my lower lip, arching my hips. He sinks fully inside me and strokes back and forth, a delicious, rhythmic cadence. Heat uncoils through every part of me.

I unclench my fingers from the bedcovers and brush my hand over his chest, awed by the strength of him, the power he's kept leashed. He's such an extraordinary specimen of *man* with his sweat-damp chest and burning gaze, his messy black hair glowing in the late-morning light, his muscles bunched with urgency.

I never want it to end, the rocking and thrusting of our bodies, never want to emerge from the drenching haze of lust. I match his thrusts as arousal spreads through my belly, urging me toward the blissful peak.

Colors burst through me, a kaleidoscope shattering. I cry out. He murmurs low in my ear, still sliding in and out of me as the sensations slowly ebb. Then a deep groan rumbles from his chest the instant before his body flexes and clenches with erotic release.

He collapses beside me and hauls me against him. Our breathing is heavy, sated. He threads a hand through my hair, twisting a few strands around his fingers. Fatigue washes over me. I close my eyes.

He whispers a word, something poetic and musical that floats into my encroaching sleep. I reach for the word, but it's gone, vanished, as if I tried to grasp a fistful of light.

I wake to the scent of Darjeeling tea. An early-afternoon sunlight has broken through the clouds and slants through the window. I must have been asleep for at least an hour.

I roll over and open my eyes. Flynn is slouched in a chair beside the bed, wearing a pair of drawstring pajama pants, his gorgeous chest bare. His foot is planted on the edge of the bed, and he's watching me with an intent, pensive expression in his gray eyes. The way a person looks at a painting or a sculpture.

I push to my elbow, holding the sheet to my breasts. Our eyes meet. Hot and tender.

"You look like *Flaming June*." He skims his gaze over my body. "A lovely dreaming woman draped in rippling folds."

"That's the most poetic thing you've ever said to me."

"It's not the most poetic thing I've thought about you."

"Really?" I finger-comb my hair away from my forehead. "And here I thought you were so busy slamming doors on me you couldn't be bothered to think much about me at all."

"I've thought about you, Eve." His voice roughens with desire, sparking heat in my blood. "I've been thinking about you for a very long time."

Consternation flickers in his expression, as if he'd just said too much. He turns to a tea tray on a nearby table and pours two cups from a pot. After adding milk and sugar to them both, he hands one to me.

"You made this?" I accept the cup, then shift to sit and face him on the edge of the bed, adjusting the sheet around my body.

"Warmed the pot and everything."

He settles back into the chair. The sun streams through the window and falls over him, spiking his hair with gold and caressing his muscled chest. For the first time ever, I'm jealous of the sun.

"So…a long time?" Given how much I've been dreaming about him, I'm not about to let that comment pass by unremarked.

"Since Max showed me that picture of you in the forest." Flynn shrugs. "Aside from being the most beautiful woman I'd ever seen, you looked so…I don't know. Happy. Content, like you belonged there. Guess I envied you."

My heart warms. "So why have you been trying so hard to lock me out? When I first started working for you. If you and Uncle Max were friends, why didn't you want to be *my* friend?"

Flynn looks at the mug. "I knew I couldn't just be friends with you. And getting involved with me is the worst thing you can do. You don't need people talking about you more than they already are."

Rebelliousness stiffens my spine. "I don't care what people say anymore."

"Yes, you do."

You have to. The statement snaps through my head in Juliette's sharp voice. But even if I didn't hear her, I'd know the truth. If I want to restore both my career and reputation, of course I have to care what people say.

What people said had destroyed my life once, and *what people will say* can help rebuild it, unless I make another terrible mistake.

Flynn is not that mistake.

"I've already done the *worst* thing." I set my cup on the night-stand. "And I paid the price. Now, for the first time in a long time, I trust myself. I won't let anyone take that from me again. Not even you."

He gazes at me for a long minute, emotion shifting behind the darkness in his eyes. "I can't offer you anything else."

"I'm not asking for anything else."

"You deserve something *else*, Eve. As much as I appreciate this town, it's not the place for you."

"Flynn." I lean forward and put my hands on his thighs. "First you try and shut me out with your *I'm-a-brick-wall* act, and now you're trying to keep me at a distance like you're afraid I don't know what I'm getting into…well, stop it. I've been burned so badly the roots of my hair are still scorching, and it's taken me a long time to put myself back together.

"However, you have made me hot as fuck since the day I ran

into you outside the bookstore. I love that you bought Uncle Max's collection, that you were friends with him, that you remembered a picture of me, and that you couldn't stay away from my two o'clock teatime. I think you're adorable for reading books about the Firebird and buying scones. I just *like you*.

"I like being with you, looking at you, talking to you, and God knows I love touching you...all because you're the most compelling man I've ever met, and more importantly because you make me like *myself* again. So shut up with the excuses and the futile efforts to push me away because they won't work. The only thing I want from you, Flynn Alverton, is *you*."

Tension coils through him. He flexes his hands, as if he's waging some kind of internal battle. For one heart-stopping instant, I think he's going to be vintage Lighthouse Guy and walk out of the room, closing the door behind him.

Instead he sets his cup down and pulls me onto his lap, settling me against his warm muscled chest. He twists a few strands of my hair around his fingers and brings them in front of me.

"Look." He rubs my reddish locks. "In the light, your hair is a thousand different shades of red and gold. It was the first thing I noticed about you when I saw you at the wall. But then I realized it's not just your hair. It's *you*. You're crimson, gold, scarlet. You're a sunrise."

I stare at him. My throat closes over. When has anyone ever called me a *sunrise*?

"I changed my mind." I swallow hard. "*That* was the most poetic thing you've ever said to me."

He smiles faintly and runs his hand over my cheek. "I lost track of how many times I had to stop myself from touching your hair. From touching *you*. And when I did, there was no turning back. I've never met someone with your honesty and strength. You've already changed my world."

More broken pieces slide back into place, seamless and smooth. If I let him, he could make me whole.

"Kiss me," I whisper.

He covers my lips with his, bringing both arms around me, locking me against him. His strong, eternal heart beats in rhythm with mine. His body is a wall of strength, his arms a protective circle I never want to leave. He lowers me onto the bed, his hands stroking, reawakening the desire simmering just beneath the surface of my skin.

I surrender all over again, enfolding him with my arms and legs, our lips locked, endlessly seeking. There's not an instant when we're apart. Our skin slides together, our limbs tangle, his cock eases into me again and again.

We fall into the sweet hot crush of urgency before spiraling and cresting upward. His groan echoes my cry of pleasure, like a timeless call of promise.

Afterward, I curl up against his side as we absorb the feeling of warm satisfaction. He caresses my shoulder with slow, lazy circles.

"I figured it out." I run my hand over his abdomen, tracing the ridges with my fingers. "Your favorite fairy tale is *The Emperor's New Clothes*. I, for one, would be happy to see you walk naked through town."

He pats my hip. "If you were the only one watching, I would."

"But it's not your favorite?"

"No."

"Hmm." Pursing my lips, I lift my head to study him. "What about a story about a mischievous, magical imp, like *Rumpelstilt-skin*? He could spin straw into gold, after all, even if he does tear himself into two at the end."

Darkness and something else I can't quite read—Shock? Trepidation? Fear?—flash over his features, quick as a comet.

I suddenly feel like I said something wrong, though I have no idea what. To deflect the cloud, I trail my fingers across his upper arm. "Considering you like my hair, maybe it's *Rapunzel?*"

He shakes his head and tugs at a lock of my hair.

"I don't think it's an animal fairy tale," I muse, mentally reviewing a list of popular stories. "Max always liked *Puss in Boots*. He said trickster characters are always hard to pin down. They can be heroes or villains, geniuses or fools. And trickster animals have been around for ages. The origins of *Puss in Boots* can be traced all the way to the fifth century and a Sanskrit text called *Panchatantra*, a collection of animal fables that included a conniving cat. Uncle Max said fictional tricksters are more like real people than most human characters are."

"Max also talked a lot," Flynn observes, his voice drowsy. "Must be an inherited trait."

I lift an eyebrow and give his thigh a little pinch. He squeezes my ass in response.

"You like to order people around," I remark peevishly. "So maybe your favorite is a more obscure story, like Andersen's *The Evil King*. An arrogant king wants to conquer all the countries of the world until he's defeated by a tiny mosquito."

"I have zero interest in conquering the world." He closes his eyes, circling his hand slowly over my rear. "I wouldn't get enough sleep."

"Ah, is it *Sleeping Beauty?*" I nuzzle his shoulder.

"No. But I do wish I could stop time for a hundred years."

"Why?"

He tightens his arm around me. "So everything would stay exactly the way it is now."

CHAPTER 21

*P*ulling myself from another light sleep, I peer at the bedside clock. Four p.m. A pale gray seam lights the horizon, the place where the sea meets the sky. Rain falls again in a gloomy drizzle, drops gliding down the panes of the two large bedroom windows. A peaceful feeling spreads through me like hot syrup, sweet and thick.

I turn, reaching toward Flynn's side of the bed. It's empty, but the sheets are rumpled and still warm from his body.

I push the covers back and get to my feet. His gray T-shirt lies crumpled on the floor. I pick it up and put it on, letting the soft worn cotton envelop me. Orange spice and autumn leaves.

Brushing my hair away from my face, I glance around. Like the kitchen, the bedroom is small but recently renovated with smooth hardwood floors and cream-colored paint. The bed is made of warm, honey maple, large enough to take up half the room. Aside from a dresser and narrow desk, the room is otherwise empty, as if not to detract from the windows with the striking view of the rocky cliff sweeping toward the ocean.

I go in search of a bathroom, finding one right next door. After using the toilet, I splash water on my face. I peer at my reflection in the smudged mirror over the sink. In a sharp contrast to the rigid way I've been looking, now my hair is a tousled mess, my lips reddened, my skin still flushed. I look like a woman who has been well and thoroughly loved. A woman who wants it again.

A shiver rattles through me. I almost can't believe my fantasy came to life—the start of everything I've craved since the day we ran into each other outside the bookstore.

The day he warned me away.

"Flynn?" I pause at the top of the stairs. Everything is silent, only the distant sound of the waves filtering through the stone walls.

I start down the stairs, then hesitate. I was contract-bound not to enter the cottage or lighthouse, but I didn't cross the threshold alone. Flynn brought me, *carried me*, here. The rules no longer apply.

Barefoot, I walk down the staircase. It opens onto the front sitting room with a leather sofa and chairs seated around a stone fireplace. Warm tones of royal blue and gray dominate the space, making it both masculine and aligned with the lighthouse's natural surroundings.

I peer into the dining room—rough-hewn farmhouse table, earth-toned hues, black-and-white historical photos of the light-house lining the walls. I cross to the kitchen, but aside from a pot of coffee brewing, there's no evidence of him.

"Flynn?" I check the workroom, which is also empty, and return to the dining room.

Next to it is another room that could serve as a study, but contains a forest-green sofa and chairs, a second stone fireplace, and a wide-screen TV. On the opposite wall is the entrance to a narrow staircase spiraling upward to the lighthouse tower.

I stop. My heart knocks against my chest. All of the living quarters are in the cottage. So what's in the tower?

There's always a forbidden room. A place you shouldn't go.

It's where Mr. Rochester's wife is hidden away, where Bluebeard hangs the bodies of his dead wives, where Sleeping Beauty pricks her finger on the spindle.

It's the dark part of the forest where witches lure children with candy, then lock them into cages. It's the basement in a horror movie, the dragon's gold-filled cave.

We shouldn't enter...but we do. No matter the consequences, the known is better than the unknown. We need to see it to know the truth.

I cross the room and start to climb the staircase. My breathing grows shallow. The stone wall hugs the steps on one side. The other side is bordered by an iron railing. Smooth crevices are worn into the stairs from countless people climbing and descending.

I reach the lantern room. My heart beats relentlessly, like a billowing tide. There's a small landing edged by the iron railing. A curved wooden door, scuffed with age, a keyhole without a key. A crack around the doorframe, gray light shining through.

"Flynn?"

No answer.

Cautiously, I step forward and rest my hand against the door. "Flynn, are you in here?"

No answer.

Nerves tighten in my stomach. I wrap one arm around my middle, gripping a fistful of his T-shirt. I nudge the door open slightly, catching sight of the glass surrounding the tower, the magnificent, sweeping view of the ocean and metal-gray sky.

Gathering a breath of courage, I push the door open and step inside.

A drafting table, littered with paper and pencils, sits on one side of the room beside a large rolling corkboard studded with drawings and images.

There's a bookshelf haphazardly stuffed with books and boxes of supplies, a big cushy blue chair and sofa, a large cabinet cluttered with items, and a coffee-table piled with notebooks and a chess set. Crumpled balls of paper surround the area around the trash can, which is topped with a small basketball hoop.

An office. A messy, disorganized one clearly belonging to a *guy*.

No dragon's gold or secret horrors. Amusement curves my mouth. So much for letting my imagination run away with me.

I glance at the cabinet, which contains dozens of items— seashells, coins, rocks, wooden puzzles. I walk toward the desk and bulletin board. A chaos of drawings and sketches covers the cork matting. A woman standing on the side of a cliff wearing a suede coat and boots, her reddish hair—

Oh my God.

I stare at the drawing. It was the day I put my secret in the wall.

They're *all* drawings of me, or of females with my face. A woman in a black cloak, eyes big and haunted, a naked nymph stretched out languidly beside a pond, a winged fairy, a sorceress rising from a nest of fire. A girl in an embroidered tunic, a basket looped around her arm as she approaches the edge of a dark forest. Another naked woman with elaborate bird wings.

All of them wear my face—oval-shaped with green eyes, arched eyebrows, narrow nose. Red hair falling just past the shoulders, sometimes caught in a ponytail or knot. Expressions of power, fear, pleasure.

I tear the bird-woman off the board. Bare breasts, curved hips, a triangle of hair between her legs.

Betrayal, thick and bitter, floods my throat. Some scholarly part of my brain recognizes the artistry and beauty of the drawings, but all I can see are the grainy, vulgar cell-phone photos of me smeared over the internet, black bars slashed across my breasts on the news sites, but exposed everywhere else.

My face, my body. Stolen and used against me.

Ice freezes my blood. I sink to my knees and press my hands

to the floor, unable to remain standing. My breath comes fast and shallow.

I'm not Alice in Wonderland, falling and tumbling. I've hit the ground and splintered all over again.

"Eve."

Flynn's voice stabs me, deep as a puncture wound. He closes his hands around my shoulders, hauling me to a sitting position. Confusion darkens his eyes in the instant before he sees the picture crumpled in my hand.

"Don't touch me." Cringing, I scramble away, acutely aware of my naked body under the T-shirt. Fear and shame descend like a thunderstorm. "You shithead, you're doing exactly what *he* did!"

"No." He falls to his knees in front of me, his hands up. "God, Eve. *No.*"

Through my blurred vision, I register the despair etched on his face, the plea in his eyes, but I can't understand it, can't fathom any other reason he would have so many images of me. A horrific thought strikes.

"Did you...did you take pictures of me?" I gulp down a wrenching sob. "Do you have video cameras? Oh my God, do you have pictures of me...when we...we..."

"No." He edges closer, his hands still up like he wants to prove he won't try and touch me. "Please, Eve. Listen. I swear, I never took pictures of you. There are no video cameras anywhere in the lighthouse. What...what can I do to make you believe me?"

I don't know. I don't know. I don't know.

I scramble away from him until my back hits the wall. I pull my knees up to my chest, covering my legs with the shirt, hugging my arms around them. Humiliation scorches me from the inside out.

"Eve."

"Go away." I crumple the picture into a ball and rest my head on my knees. "Just go away."

Silence. All I hear is the sound of my sharp breaths, the thump of my panicked heart. I squeeze my eyes shut, trying to block out the ugly images burned into my brain. The pictures that will haunt me forever. My mother's voice, shrill and accusing, pierces me.

Stupid girl. Idiot. Slut.

Nausea roils in the pit of my stomach. Slowly I lift my head. Flynn is still on his knees in front of me, his features lined with deep grooves of pain and regret.

"I'm so sorry, Eve. I didn't know anything about the photos until you told me. I swear to you I wasn't doing what that fucker did."

I clench my jaw. "Drawing naked pictures of me without my knowledge is *the same thing*. You used me, just like he did."

He pushes to his feet, his shoulders slumping. He grabs a cardboard box from the corner of the room. Pulling the drawings off the corkboard, he puts them in the box. Images in colored pencil, ink, charcoal, watercolors, pastels. The stack grows bigger. I don't move, everything inside me broken, brittle like a crushed leaf.

Flynn tears the last picture from the corkboard and takes more from the desk. He piles them all in the box, puts a lid over it, and puts the box beside me.

"Take them," he says. "I don't have a computer, so nothing is scanned. They're all here, but you can search the house if you want to."

I shift my gaze to him warily. Shadows edge the hollows of his cheekbones. For all his impassivity and stoicism, I've never seen him look...defeated.

I don't know whether or not to believe him, but what choice do I have? Once again, I'm subjected to someone else's control.

"Eve." He crouches in front of me, resting his elbows on his knees. "I'm not...I don't have much of a life up here by myself. I wanted it that way. I chose it. I do maintenance for the Forestry Department, take care of the grounds, and work. I exercise—

hiking, jogging, or I go to a gym over in Benton, but other than that I don't go anywhere or do much of anything else. It's pretty boring. But I've been okay with that. Then…"

He pauses and clears his throat. "I saw you down by the wall. You…you lit something inside me. Like you were a flame. I wanted…I tried to keep you out because you deserve more than someone like me, but you broke my self-control like no one else ever has. You make me want more. All it took was tea, crossword puzzles, and you."

He reaches out to brush a lock of hair from my forehead, then stops when I flinch at his touch.

"You're so…you're so fucking beautiful." He rises to his feet, his voice hoarse. "Everything about you, not just the way you look. You said those bastards destroyed you, took everything from you, but they didn't. No one can take your strength, your goodness, your intelligence, your fire. No one can take *you*."

He steps back, his dark gaze burning into me like metal flaring.

"I wanted what you have," he says urgently. "I *need* it. But I've been trying to stay away from you so you could have what *you* want. So you could focus on finding another professorship, rebuilding your life, everything you deserve. I failed badly. I'm so sorry."

He turns and leaves. His footsteps echo on the spiral staircase. For a long time, I sit there and breathe, trying to calm the racing of my heart, to suppress the shameful memories.

I straighten my legs out. My elbow bumps against the box. Wary, I tug off the lid and peer at the drawing on top of the stack. My face cloaked by a red hood, locks of hair windblown against my neck. My eyes looking back at me—hard, suspicious, strong.

With a shaking hand, I leaf through the first few drawings. Again I notice the expertise and technique, clearly the work of an immensely talented artist. On another page, I'm inside an intricate garden maze laden with open flowers and cascading vines, the pathways winding through cultivated hedges and sculptures.

Recognition prickles the back of my mind. I've seen images like this before, in Renaissance etchings and engravings of pleasure gardens, in the chaotic wildness of Hieronymus Bosch paintings, in the beauty and terror of Leonardo's *The Last Judgment*. In...

Like when I first saw the Maria Wood drawing, I can't link my recognition to a specific source.

I pick up another drawing. I'm standing in another maze formed within a jungle, huge palm leaves and thick trees cascading over a dark, coursing river. Animals—bright toucans, coiling snakes, agile monkeys—creep around the foliage along with numerous, intricately detailed insects.

Another close-up sketch of my face—brow furrowed, mouth tense, a fearful glimmer in my eyes. A striking resemblance to the way I'd felt when my world teetered on the edge of collapse.

I drop the drawings back into the box and get to my feet. The tower has a 360 degree view of the coast, stretching from the ocean around to the grassy fields and woodlands in the distance. No wonder he locks himself away up here all the time. Who wouldn't want to be surrounded by such beauty?

I stare at the spot by the wall where I'd stood, imagining him looking down at me from this angle, seeing me put my secret between the rocks.

After turning back, I pause beside the bookshelf. Stuffed among sci-fi novels and history books, seven picture books sit upright like a row of soldiers, their spines facing outward.

I touch the spines. A vague memory pushes forth. This was where I'd seen a similar aesthetic—in a picture book. I take the first book off the shelf and look at the author name.

The truth crashes through me on a wave of pure shock.

CHAPTER 22

"You're Riley Flynn." I stop in the kitchen doorway.

Flynn's jaw tightens, almost as if he's not accustomed to being called that. A strange sense of unreality descends over me.

His gaze goes to the stack of hardcover picture books I'm holding. I open the first book, touching the glossy pages, the elaborate drawings of underground tunnels, seascapes, a cluttered toy room, the pyramids at Giza—all imagined as complex mazes concealing hidden clues to solving the mystery of a lost reflection.

A dark-haired boy named Westley, distinctive in his green T-shirt and accompanied by a loyal black dog named Tugg, is the reader's guide and companion through all seven books as he searches for the missing image of himself.

I turn to the back cover flap. There's no picture of Flynn, only a short author biography: *Riley Flynn has been drawing and studying the art of mazes since he learned the story of Theseus and the Minotaur when he was a boy. He lives on the coast in the Northeast.*

Riley Flynn is also an author/artist who lives at the top of the bestseller lists with his *Mirror Mirror* books. He's acclaimed for his intense attention to realistic detail and authenticity. His books are beautiful, elaborate puzzles, enigmas, question marks.

Not unlike their author.

"Why..." I lift my eyes to his again. "Why didn't you tell me?"

He sighs heavily. "If I could have told anyone, it would have been you. But I couldn't."

"Why not?"

"Anonymity." He stares out the window, his tone bitter. "Privacy. Once something gets out about you, even if it's not true, it's all over."

Don't I know it. And how does he know it too? What happened to him?

"No one in town knows who you are?" I ask.

He shakes his head.

"I never forgot that photo of you in the redwoods." He shifts his gaze back to me warily. "Thought about it every time I drew a forest scene. And I've...I haven't written a book in three years."

"I remember reading an article about that in an entertainment magazine." I close the book, tightening my fingers on the stack. "There was all this hype about your new series, but then it was never published."

A short laugh breaks from him. "Yeah, because I never wrote it. After I finished Westley and Tugg's seventh book, I couldn't come up with any ideas. That was okay for a while since I didn't need the money. But fans kept writing to me, and a lot of them were disappointed, so that sucked. And later it turned out I did need the money, so I tried to get back to it, but everything fell flat. Figured I was done.

"Then I was at the window one morning. I looked down and saw you standing by the wall. That was it. An idea sprouted wings and flew right into my head. I've been working on it ever since. That's why I did all those drawings. Maybe I was using you. I don't know. I just knew I couldn't stop."

I swallow past the constriction in my throat. "You could have *asked* me."

"No." He rubs his scruffy jaw. "I was trying too damned hard to stay away from you. And if I'd asked and you'd said no...I was scared I'd never pick up a pencil again."

He approaches me. "But Christ in heaven, Eve, if I'd thought for one second that my drawings of you were *anything* like what that bastard did, I never would have done the first sketch. Never. I'm so fucking sorry. I haven't shown them to anyone, uploaded them anywhere, nothing. And you have them all now, every single one. Please believe me."

"I don't know what to believe anymore."

"Throw them away, if you want to. Tear them up, burn them. I don't care. I want..." He steps closer. "I *need* to make this right for you."

I grip the books and stare at the top cover, the picture of Westley gazing into a pond and seeing only the ripples on the surface.

"How did you know my uncle?" I ask.

"He was the one who told me to submit my work for publication."

I look up. "Really?"

Flynn nods, the lines of his face softening a bit. "When I first came to Castille, I went to a talk and book signing he gave at the library. *Fairy Tales and Magic*. After it was over, I was sitting there drawing, and next thing I knew Max was standing next to me. He saw the sketch I was working on...a troll in a forest. He said it looked like an illustration from a Norwegian folktale."

"Was it?"

"Nah. More like a self-portrait." He lets out a humorless laugh and drags a hand through his hair. "I didn't want to talk to him. Sure as hell didn't want him to see my drawings. But he was a persistent old cuss. For whatever reason, he decided we were going to be friends. So we were."

Tenderness nudges through the ice in my chest. "Did you take any of his classes at Ford's?"

"No. I was just in Castille doing odd jobs, renting a room month to month. Hadn't planned to stay in the area long. Max and I would get together to play chess or go for a hike. He was a good guy. Talked a lot, but never asked a bunch of questions.

"He liked my work and kept pushing me to write a fully illustrated story and send it to his publisher. Even told his editor to expect it. Finally I did, mostly to get him off my back. But the publisher came back with an offer, and the *Mirror Mirror* books got their start. Wouldn't have happened without Max."

Because Max saw something in Flynn no one else had.

"He talked a lot about you." Flynn gives me a faint, gentle smile. "There was no one he loved more."

In fairy tales, the thing that is of the highest good is often bathed in a golden, metallic light. For a brief moment, my heart pulses with such a light, glimmering and warm.

"It was the same for me." My throat tightens again. "Did you keep in touch with him when he left Castille?"

"Yes, but when the *Mirror Mirror* books started taking off, he knew I didn't want anyone to know. So he kept the secret."

Maybe that was why Max had never mentioned Flynn—at least, not to me.

"Why did you buy his collection?" I ask softly.

The light in his eyes dims. He stares out the window. Remoteness descends over him, like he's in some other time.

"I...when I was a kid, I was into stories about dragons and monsters. Mazes. Used to draw a lot, but stopped when I was a teenager. It wasn't until I left Minnesota in my early twenties that I took it up again. I was on the road for about three years.

"And when I came back to Castille, it was just chance that I saw the flyer about Max's talk at the library. I learned a lot about fairy tales from him. Started incorporating the themes into my work. I guess I thought he wouldn't like it if his collection ended up in Europe or something. He'd have wanted it back in Castille. I hope."

"Yes. That's exactly what he'd have wanted."

His words roll through my mind, coming up against all the questions I've had about him, instigating more.

A drawing of a troll was a *self-portrait*? He came back to Castille? That means he was here before. Why did he stop drawing when he was a teenager? Why was he on the road for three years?

An ache pushes at my head. Too many questions. Not enough answers.

I indicate the Riley Flynn books. "Can I borrow these?"

"You can keep them."

I clasp the books against my chest. "I'm going to go now."

"Okay." He rubs the back of his neck, the distress on his face aging him ten years. "Eve, I'm sorry. Whatever I can do to make it up to you, I will."

"I just need to be alone for a while."

"Do you remember that note Max gave me?" He spreads his hands out in a plea. "The Hans Christian Andersen quote from *The Butterfly*. 'To live, you must have sunshine and freedom, and a little flower to love.' I've spent a lot of years with none of those things. I've been okay with that. Deserved it, even. But you...you make me *want* them. Even believe I could have them. You make anything seem possible."

A sound echoes inside me. *Is it my heart breaking?*

Still holding the books, I return to the bedroom and change back into my wrinkled clothes. After collecting the rest of my belongings, I drive home. I manage to make it into the house before the tears start. I sink to the floor and cry.

CHAPTER 23

*T*he next morning, I change into my running clothes and hit the trails crisscrossing the woods. I sprint around the trees, my sneakers slamming on the dirt-covered surface.

Icy air blasts against my face. The crisp smell of pine fills my nose. My breath is fast, my lungs and muscles aching, my heart pounding. I keep going, letting the exertion of my body take over my thoughts.

But fragments float through my mind like pieces of broken glass.

Max... mazes... Riley Flynn... trolls... a little flower to love... my body... my face... I can't offer you anything else... you make me like myself again...

I cross a two-lane road cutting through the woods and turn onto a new path. Dried leaves carpeting the forest floor crunch under my shoes. The trees are almost all bare. Winter will be here soon.

I circle around and head back home, keeping my pace rhythmic and strong. I reach the road again and jog along the side to get to the path leading back to Uncle Max's house. A couple of cars slow and edge into the other lane to pass me.

Shortening my stride, I look over my shoulder to see if the road is clear to cross. A pick-up truck turns the corner and comes toward me. I ease farther off the road to give the truck room to pass safely before I cross to the trail.

The driver revs the engine. A gasp sticks in my throat. This is a country road with clearly marked pedestrian and bike lanes, not a—

Shit!

The truck careens past me, tires skidding. The rush of air shoves me off the asphalt. I stumble into a shallow ditch beside the road and come to a shaky halt. The speeding truck disappears around a bend.

What the fuck?

My heartbeat pounds in my head. I rest my hands on my knees and gulp in air. Part of my brain struggles to attribute the close call to drunk driving or reckless teenagers, but another part prickles with terror.

He knows where I am.

I straighten and run across the road, not feeling safe again until I'm deep in the forest.

I let Ghost into the kitchen, then lock the door behind him. I'll keep him inside today as another layer of protection. I crack open a bottle of water, still trying to calm my racing heart.

Why would David come after me now? Doesn't he know he scared me enough with his phone call? I'm half-tempted to try and reach him to tell him exactly that, but the restraining order is still in place. I'm certainly not about to violate it.

I ensure all the doors and windows are locked, then feed

Ghost and go upstairs to take a shower. For the first time, the creaking of the house is eerie rather than comforting.

When I go downstairs again, Ghost is lying in front of the door, like he's guarding it. I smile and scratch his ears. "Thanks, boy. You're a good friend."

Maybe my only friend.

An unwelcome image of Flynn emerges. My chest aches. The stack of Riley Flynn books and the box of drawings he'd given me yesterday are still on the coffee-table where I'd left them.

Though the shock of discovery has worn off, I'm wary of everything the box contains. All images of me.

I sit down and open a Riley Flynn book, *Sea Storm*. The elaborate, detailed pictures almost leap off the pages into living, breathing life.

His secret is *art*.

The illustrations and mazes of the books are already familiar to me. I'd purchased the first book in the series when it was published at least thirteen years ago, enthralled by the vibrant colors and expertly concealed clues of keys, stamps, puzzle pieces, and rings.

I've bought the books as gifts for friends and their children, to give as graduation presents, for school libraries. I'm a *fan* of Westley and Tugg's adventures. And I understand Flynn's desire for anonymity much more now than I would have a year ago.

I set the books aside and pull the lid off the box. What had he said—I'd inspired an idea that broke through three years of writer's block?

I take out a stack of drawings and study them. Yesterday, the naked pictures had eclipsed everything else, but there are only two of them. In the others, Flynn has reimagined me in numerous guises—a sorceress, a witch surrounded by radiance, a fairy nestled in a tulip like Thumbelina. A woman cloaked in red, standing before a full white moon. A warrior clad in armor, a powerful elf pulling an arrow into a bow.

All of them are intricate and aesthetically beautiful, sketched with a deft, talented hand.

I take a worn notebook from the box and open it. Written in a distinctive black scrawl is the title:

Fiamma
A Fairy Tale

Fiamma. That was the word he'd whispered right before I fell asleep yesterday. The Italian word for *flame.* *"You lit something inside me. Like you were a flame."*

The knot in my chest loosens a bit. I turn the page.

Once upon a time there lived a cobbler's son who loved a wood-cutter's daughter. The girl's name was Anne, and she lived with her father in a village that nestled like an egg at the base of a mountain.

Though the father was poor, he always said his life was filled with gold and silver, for that was how he saw his daughter. Her soul was the gold of the sun, and her beauty the silver of the moon. With his sun and moon, his gold and silver, the wood-cutter wanted for nothing.

And the cobbler's son? Jack's life would have been darkness were it not for the light of Anne. He had loved her since childhood, but never had the courage to tell her. He showed her in small ways—repairing her father's shoes, helping with chores, bringing them fresh bread. For a long time, he thought that might be enough, that one day she would look up and realize she loved him too.

Then the cold came. Sheets of winter blew down from the mountains and through the forest that had protected the town for countless generations. In the span of a week, the cold had killed all the crops—apples, potatoes, wheat, corn. Anne's father grew sick, his cough worsening like rocks rattling in a tin can.

The townspeople murmured it would warm up soon, but another week passed, then another, until they were looking back at a month of cold. Then two months. Three.

Now the cold will stop, the villagers whispered.

It did not stop.

It's a curse, they whispered.

And their eyes landed on Anne, sinking into her like the talons of a predatory bird. For it was not that long ago when a stranger had ridden into town, a man with a pale, narrow face and glittering green eyes. Those eyes chipped away at Anne like an ice pick, leaving her cold and trembling.

He'd pointed a long finger at her. "You are the one I will have."

Though Anne didn't consider herself brave, her mind filled with an image of her father and Jack. The two people she loved most in the world.

"No." The word was weak but firm.

The stranger's features sharpened like a blade. He turned, the horse's hooves stirring up a whirlwind of dirt as he rode off in the direction from which he'd come.

Then the cold began and did not stop. The food supply shrank. Animals starved. The villagers weakened, even as they continued to blame Anne for the curse.

One night after Jack helped Anne with the chores, they sat by the dwindling fire, trying to keep warm and drinking cups of hot water flavored with tea. He set his cup down and knelt by her side. The firelight cast a warm glow over her, like an embrace. All light loved Anne.

"I'm going into the forest." Jack's voice was so low, Anne leaned forward to hear.

"What?"

"I'll hunt for food. I'll find something. Enough to last us through winter, I hope."

Anne shook her head. "No one goes into the forest."

The massive trees and thick foliage protected the village on three sides—or had until the cold invaded—but it was vast, dangerous, spreading over the foothills, the mountains, no one knew how far.

Generations ago, those who had tried to navigate or map the terrain never returned. Even the village dogs and cats didn't go near the tree-line.

But for Anne, Jack would enter the forest.

I stop and leaf through the rest of the notebook. Flynn's black-ink penmanship covers the recto side of the pages, the scrawl giving a sense of urgency. And on every reverse side, there's a detailed sketch in colored pencil and ink. Anne, a young woman with my features, clad in an embroidered tunic and wool skirt, her eyes bright and inquisitive.

Jack, a dark-haired young man looking back over his shoulder, his hands fisted. A little brown sparrow in a forest. A black-cloaked man with a narrow, pale face and brilliant green eyes. A womanly figure rising from a nest of fire, multicolored wings outstretched.

I turn back to the beginning and continue reading, unwillingly captivated by the story.

When Jack fails to return from the forest, Anne summons her courage and goes after him. She searches for hours, befriending a helpful sparrow, before she's captured by an evil sorcerer, Koldun, who cast the cold spell as punishment for her rejection. He is also holding Jack hostage, lashed to a tree with invisible bonds.

To free him, Anne must solve twelve mazes before the clock strikes twelve. She works her way through the complex puzzles— an undersea maze with walls made of bright, twisted coral and seashells. A star maze composed of bright constellations, a flower maze where thorned roses stick out at every turn. A maze constructed of ancient ruins, an Amazon jungle maze with vines slithering around every corner.

I envision the story as a finished book, each maze captured on the page with painstaking detail, the story sending the reader on the same journey as the heroine.

Though Anne solves every maze, the sorcerer fails to keep his promise. But Anne refuses to give up. She has a vision of a golden egg, and with Sparrow's help she realizes she needs to break it.

Using a slingshot, she battles Koldun and finds the egg hidden deep in the forest. She fires a stone at the golden egg.

Koldun screamed in outrage. The egg shattered, releasing a foul-smelling black liquid. Gray smoke spiraled upward like snakes. The egg shrieked—a high-pitched noise that made Anne's head spin. She grabbed another stone and launched it at Koldun.

It hit him square in the chest. His cloak began turning to smoke, his eyes dimming. Even as she watched him change, she was changing too. Her arms took the shape of wings, her body grew brilliant red-gold feathers, her eyes grew glassy and bead-like. A word appeared in her mind, whispered in a woman's milk-smooth tones.

Fiamma. Flame.

She understood. The egg had contained the wizard's dark soul, and the one to break it would destroy him and absorb his power, shaping it anew. She rose into the air, flooded with strength.

She swooped toward the wizard, lashing out with her wings. Fire shot from the tips of her feathers, striking Koldun down. With every flash, he grew colorless and lifeless, his face twisted with agony. Finally he faded completely, sinking into the forest floor.

The firebird flew to Jack, sending shafts of light to break the invisible bonds lashing him to the tree. He fell. She caught him in her multicolored wings and carried him safely back to the ground. Her wings folded into a circle around them both.

Light shimmered. She became Anne again, and it was her arms embracing Jack, and his face pressed to her hair, and neither needed to speak. Though they had entered the impenetrable forest alone, they would walk out of it together.

By the time I close the notebook, my heart is pounding with both trepidation and a slowly brewing hope. I gaze at a drawing of the heroine in battle.

Is this how Flynn sees me? As a loyal, clever girl, a powerful woman, a creature strong enough to defeat evil?

The answer is here, in every stroke and line of his pencil. He saw me at the secrets wall and thought of a flame. A Firebird. His inspiration.

I pile everything back into the box and close the lid. Ghost pads over to me from the foyer, butting his head against my leg. I rest my hand on his back.

Somewhere deep inside me, in a corner of my soul I've forgotten about, a change is taking place. Maybe it started a long time ago. It feels scary and exhilarating, even painful. A seed breaking open, an oak tree shedding brittle leaves, a wound knitting into a scar.

It's the realization that I wasn't destroyed or defeated after all, not in the most secret part of my heart.

No one ever had that kind of power over me.

CHAPTER 24

I arrive at the lighthouse just before eight on Monday morning, carrying the box of drawings and my usual work supplies. Flynn opens the door before I knock, his posture tense and guarded.

He's a mess. Dark shadows ring his eyes, his jaw is scruffier than usual, and deep grooves bracket his mouth. He's wearing the same clothes as yesterday, his hockey sweatshirt rumpled and fraying at the edges.

"May I come in?" I finally manage to ask.

He blinks, as if coming out of a trance. "Yeah, sure. I mean…of course. Come in."

I pass him and set the box on the desk. He steps back, shoving his hands into his pockets.

"What are you doing here?" he asks.

"It's Monday. A workday."

He scratches his head. "You…uh, you still want to work?"

"I want to finish cataloging the collection, yes." I place my hand on the box. "I spent most of yesterday looking at your drawings. I read the story too."

He looks away. "I'm sorry."

"You don't have to apologize anymore."

"I should have told you." His breath expels on a heavy sigh. "It didn't even occur to me that you'd see similarities between my work and what that bastard did to you. I didn't think you—"

"Flynn." I hold up my hand. "Stop."

He meets my gaze, still wary. I dig deep to find the courage that has been so stifled. It's still there, pushing through the dirt like a little green shoot. Seeking light and air.

"For a long time…" My throat closes over. I swallow hard. "I didn't think I would feel anything again except fear and shame. I was so devastated by everything that happened. So humiliated. I stopped talking to people, especially men. I hated knowing they'd seen the pictures of me, that they were probably imagining the things I'd done…*everyone* was…"

Flynn tightens his hands into fists. "Eve, you don't have to—"

"Wait. Let me finish." I take a breath and keep going. "When I moved here, I hoped it would finally be a new start. A smaller life, one in which my past could at least stay in the past. But I discovered quickly that my reputation had preceded me. And if you hadn't come after me that day at the museum, I don't know what I would have done.

"Working here and reconnecting with Uncle Max's collection, finding an artist to study, running alongside the ocean, even learning how to repair things at the house…it's all been more healing than I could have imagined. And *you*…"

Tears blur my vision. Flynn steps toward me, then stops as if he's uncertain how I'll react to his nearness.

"You gave me something else to think about and focus on. I spent so much time wondering about you. And even though you didn't know it at first, you helped me…um, relearn how to like my body. To appreciate feeling attractive and desired again. Even you *looking* at me felt good because I knew you weren't seeing the horrible pictures or speculating about what I'd done."

"All I ever saw was you." His voice is rough, like rusted metal, his gray eyes burning.

"I know." I press a hand to my chest. "It was just one of the reasons I trusted you even though I knew so little about you. That and knowing you'd been friends with Uncle Max. He could sense a black-hearted person a mile away. He'd never have befriended you if you'd been anything less than honorable."

His expression hardens. He looks past me to the window. "I'm not honorable, Eve. I steal secrets. Keep them."

"I think you do that because it feeds whatever is inside you. Whatever makes you create art. It's why you stole my secret, isn't it? Why you didn't tell me who you really are, why you're so guarded and protective of yourself. Your secrecy gives you freedom."

"I wish it were that pretty." He shakes his head, his jaw tightening. "It's not. I'm a selfish coward who thinks it's easier to hide than deal with the world. If people think I'm strange and even dangerous, they stay away."

"I don't want to stay away."

He jerks his gaze back to me. Our eyes collide with sudden heat.

"You…" He rubs a hand over his hair. "You need to stay away, Eve. I'm not good."

My insides clench. "Don't say that."

"It's the truth."

"No one who creates such beauty is anything less than extraordinary."

A hoarse laugh breaks from him. "Right. I'm so extraordinary I used you without your consent, just like *he* did."

Pain stabs me. "That's what I thought at first, yes. But I've looked at every drawing, every sketch. I read your story of *Fiamma*. You didn't manipulate and exploit me. You didn't attack, ruin, or threaten me. You didn't think I was worthless. A nobody. You saw me as a woman strong enough to defeat evil. As fire."

"That's not how I saw you." His eyes glitter. "That's how you *are*."

The rich golden light encircles my heart again. I nudge the box in his direction.

"Take these back. I want you to have them again."

"No." He stills, his shoulders slumping. "I don't give a damn about the book anymore."

"I want you to write it."

"After what I did to you?" He shakes his head. "No."

"Flynn." The courage inside me has broken through the dirt and is spiraling upward, spreading through my veins. I will give him everything he sees, everything he believes me to be. Everything I am. "I feel more for you than I've ever felt for anyone."

His head jerks up. I cross to where he's standing and rest my trembling hand on his chest. His heart hammers against my palm. He stares at me like he's seeing me for the first time.

"I'm not telling you because I expect you to say the same thing to me," I say softly.

"Eve, I…" His voice cracks.

"I'm telling you because I haven't felt something so powerfully good in a very long time. And you're the reason for it. I want to be the loyal girl who braves the unknown forest, who solves mazes, who dares to look a villain in the eye even though her knees are shaking. I want to win battles and walk out of the darkness. I want to be the woman who will do all of that for love."

A rapid pulse beats in the hollow of his throat. He lifts a hand and touches my hair.

"You're killing me, Eve," he mutters.

"You're bringing me back to life."

A groan breaks from him. As if he can't do anything else, he slides his hand to the back of my neck and brings his mouth down on mine. I curl my hand into his shirt and open my mouth to let him inside. My confession opened a box inside me, freeing whatever inhibitions I might still have had.

He brings his hands to either side of my neck, tilting my head to just the right angle, and presses his lips to mine. For the first time in my life, with him, I know what it means to be kissed right to your soul, to feel a kiss in every inch of your body.

He urges my lips apart with his. Our tongues meet. My veins surge with light, like a million flickering fireflies. I slip my arms around his waist, pressing our bodies together, loving the sensation of his heat flowing through my skirt and blouse.

He murmurs something low in his throat, caressing the arch of my back and down to my hips. I nestle closer, rubbing my breasts against his chest. He unzips my skirt, letting it puddle onto the floor. I ease away only long enough to unfasten my blouse and push it off my shoulders. Flynn's eyes darken as he rakes his gaze over my navy lace bra and panties.

He cups my breasts, his thumbs flicking over my hardening nipples. I lift my face to his again, desperate for more of his intoxicating kisses, and then he tucks his arm beneath my legs and lifts me against him. He takes a few strides to the sofa and lowers me onto it.

Bracing himself over me, he kisses me again and again. The weight of his body combined with the deliciousness of *him* fills me with light and pleasure. I run my hands over his back and part my legs so he can settle between them. His erection presses against my thigh, the sensation eliciting a new wave of lust.

Tension rolls through his body. He unfastens my bra and drops it to the floor. A rumble of appreciation echoes in his throat as he presses his mouth against the swells of my breasts.

"Touch me," I whisper. "Please…"

He mumbles a response against my skin and slides his hand down my belly, into my panties.

"Ah, fuck, Eve…" His breath is hot against my neck. "I need you…"

The words reverberate inside me, like a violin string plucked and vibrating.

He eases two fingers into my body. Desperate need floods me, sweeping me into the pleasure of his heated kisses, his muscular body pressed against mine. An explosion of heat and light bursts through me, wrenching a cry from my throat.

He pulls at my panties, tugging them down my legs and off. He lowers his head, and then he's kissing my breasts, trailing his lips down to my belly, his tongue circling my navel as his hands glide over the curves of my waist and hips.

An ocean rolls and pitches inside me, whitecaps licking at my blood, riptides surging beneath my skin. I tangle one hand into his hair, brushing it back from his forehead as he moves to press kisses against my thighs, my hips, over my arms and shoulders. By the time he reaches my lips again, I'm tingling all over with fresh desire. I open my mouth under his for another slow, hot kiss.

"I want to touch you now," I whisper, easing myself to a sitting position.

We adjust our bodies so he's lying on the sofa. I straddle his thighs and pull off both his sweatshirt and T-shirt. My heart races at the sight of him—the slopes of his hard pecs, the ridges of his abdomen, the trail of hair disappearing beneath the waistband of his jeans.

His gray eyes lock to me as he watches me spread my hands over his chest. I run my finger down the line bisecting his pecs, trace the flat circles of his areolae, skim my palms over his hips and thighs. He's so much *more* than anything even my vivid imagination could dream up.

I move back on his thighs to unfasten his jeans, releasing his thick, erect cock. I close my hand around his smooth shaft and run my fingers over the pulsing veins.

With a groan, Flynn grasps my wrist. "Can't take much more."

He eases me onto my back again. Our bodies press together, his body heat warming me to the center of my being.

"I need you," I gasp, sweat trickling between my breasts as he glides his fingers into me again. "Do you have a—"

He fumbles to get his wallet from his jeans and take out a condom. I roll it onto him before he moves between my legs to align our bodies. He slides into me. Our eyes meet, his glittering with heat and passion.

An emotion floods my heart, something I can't name, but that feels like all the good and wonderful things in the world wrapped into one. Trust, power, hope. Happiness. Truth.

In that instant, Flynn lifts a hand to my face, cupping my cheek as if I'm precious to him. Our breath puffs between us, our eyes linked by a bright silver thread.

"Okay?" he whispers.

"Oh, yes."

He lowers his mouth to mine. Our lips crash together in a collision of urgency, our bodies tensing and flexing. He slips his hands beneath my thighs, opening me wider, and thrusts again and again. My world distills to the sound of our moans and gasps, the friction of our skin.

I come first, crying out his name. His body tenses, pressure uncoiling as he increases his thrusts and drives into me with a deep, heavy groan.

"Christ, you're incredible." He rolls off me and pulls me against him, his breath hot on my forehead. "I can't believe you came back."

"Believe it." I run my hand down his damp chest. "Because I'm here."

He brushes his lips against my forehead. "Don't leave."

"No."

I close my eyes, listening to the sound of his heartbeat and cadence of his breath.

Come with me, Eve.

Since the day I followed him here, we've been creating a place that belongs only to us. A place of slow-building trust, comfortable silences, hot looks, and fairy tales.

And, as it turns out, a place where our imaginations transform and envelop each other. Maybe even a place where dreams come true.

CHAPTER 25

*T*he rest of the morning is hazy and soft-edged like a mirage but infinitely real. Fog condensing on the windowpanes. The aroma of Assam tea, steam scented with raspberry, scones slathered with creamy butter.

Flynn, his body so achingly touchable I spend lengthy amounts of time running my hands over all the slopes of his chest and shoulders, endlessly fascinated by his sheer strength, the tactility of his muscles.

I'm rediscovering my own body as well, finding such exquisite pleasure in everything he does to me, everything I do with him, that all my past experiences fade into nothing. Our bouts of love-making are broken by physical explorations as I discover he's ticklish right near his hipbones, and he finds the birthmark on the back of my thigh.

I still have questions, but I don't ask and he doesn't offer anything beyond what he already has.

Does he have any family? How did he become an artist? Why has he hidden away from the world for so long? And what the heck does he do with all those secrets from the wall?

Maybe I'll have answers one day. But for now, I'm content to leave things as they are between us, intimate and private. I've never known a man like him before, one who can turn me inside out, twist me open, take me apart, and then put me back together. One who sees such magnificence in me.

I spend the night with him, which is both weird and pleasant. I'm not accustomed to spending the night with a lover. Though I had with David, those hours are now ugly, stained memories that can no longer be classified as "nights with a lover."

But this? Flynn sleeps deeply, his powerful chest rising and falling with his breath, his body deliciously strong beside mine. Even in sleep, he's possessive—his leg lies heavily over my thighs, and his arm cradles me close to his chest. Whenever I shift a little to change position, he tightens his grip like he doesn't want me to escape. I silently assure him he doesn't have to worry because I don't want to leave.

When the gray morning light of the seaside wakes us, he slides his hand over my back and kisses my shoulder.

"I need to do the rounds," he says.

I roll over to peer at him, my heart softening at the sight of his warm gray eyes and stubbly jaw. "What kind of rounds?"

"Twice a day I drive through the public trails, see if any maintenance needs to be done, check things out. Come with me. I want to show you something."

I glance at the clock, startled to discover it's almost nine. "I should get home and feed my dog."

He lifts his eyebrows. "You have a dog?"

"He's a stray but I think I've adopted him. Or he's adopted me." I push back the covers. "And I don't have any extra clothes either."

"We'll stop at your house before we go."

We dress and head outside. The sun is rising on the horizon, a pale circle of light burning through the gray sky and throwing shimmers on the ocean.

We drive in Flynn's pick-up to Sparrow Lane. Ghost is

waiting on the front porch, his ears and tail rising to alert when he sees the unfamiliar truck. He barks.

"It's okay, boy." I jump out of the truck and start toward him as Flynn descends from the driver's side.

Ghost takes a few tentative steps off the porch, then directs his attention to Flynn and bares his teeth. Flynn stops, his hands going up. I settle my hand on the dog's head. He sits on his haunches, lowering his bark in volume.

"Come inside," I tell Flynn.

He climbs the steps, rattling the old wooden boards. Ghost growls. Flynn stops to look at the dog, eyes narrow. For an instant, they stare each other down. Then Ghost retreats, still growling low in his throat.

I murmur a few soothing words to the dog before feeding him. To assure him this is still his territory, I leave the front door open. Flynn steps into the foyer. He pauses and extends a hand to me.

"Careful." He prods the floorboards with his boot. "You have a loose board here."

"It's on my list of things to repair." I follow him into the foyer, stepping around the board. "Which is at least two miles long. Come on, I'll give you a tour."

As we walk through the upstairs rooms, I wonder what Max would think if he knew Flynn and I are "together." Would he be pleased? Some deep part of me whispers, *"Yes."*

"This is a great place." Flynn looks at the view of the woods from the bedroom window. "How much work have you done so far?"

"Not much, unfortunately, but at least it's habitable."

Now that I have an income stream to take care of more house repairs, I've started to notice the architectural beauty of Ramshackle Manor. Scarred wood paneling lines the staircase and lower part of the walls, and a lovely carved mantel surrounds the stone fireplace. Delicately engraved crown molding borders the ceilings and the pilasters on either side of the doors.

If the house were ever restored to its former glory, it would be beautiful.

I lead Flynn back downstairs, deflecting a pang of regret. Even if I wanted to *consider* renovating Uncle Max's house, I have neither the time nor the resources. I can afford to do smaller repairs, but certainly not any major renovation work. And as generous as Flynn's pay is, the job won't last forever. It'll end either when I finish the work or when I find another job and leave Castille.

But I don't want to think about that right now.

Ghost is in the foyer, his ears up and alert, his suspicious gaze on Flynn.

"If Max didn't intend to come back to Castille, why didn't he sell the house?" Flynn studies the books on the living room shelves.

I run my hand soothingly over Ghost's head. "Maybe he thought he *would* come back one day."

"For Allegra?"

Surprised, I glance at him. "I was wondering if Max had talked to you about her."

"He told me she'd always be the one who got away."

"That's what he told me." A bittersweet feeling swirls through me. "Did he tell you anything else?"

"No."

"They met during his second year as a literature professor at Ford's." I scratch Ghost behind the ears. "She was his student. He was about ten years older than her, but they had a romance and fell in love. Then Max received a grant to teach in Germany for a year. Allegra didn't want him to go, but he knew it might be his only chance, so he left."

Ghost licks my hand and trots into the kitchen. I cross the living room to where Flynn is standing.

"When Max returned from Germany," I continue, "he found out that Allegra was engaged to William King, the man her father had always wanted for her. Max tried to get her back, but it was too late. She married William. Max returned to his position at Ford's, and they both lived in Castille for over twenty-five years until he moved to San Francisco."

I look out the window at the weed-covered backyard. "Honestly, I don't know why he chose to stay in Castille after all that. It must have been torture to see Allegra and William everywhere, the golden couple. The woman he loved who married another man."

"That's probably why he stayed." Flynn wraps his arms around me from behind, hugging me against his broad chest. "Penance."

"Maybe." I shrug and turn to face him. "Or they were having an affair, though I hate thinking Uncle Max would have been capable of that. But people are capable of all kinds of things, I've learned."

A shadow passes across his face, like a crow darting in front of the sun. He tugs a lock of my hair. "You want to change, and we'll head out?"

Taking my cue from what he's wearing, I dress in jeans and a cable-knit sweater, grabbing my parka before following him to the pick-up. He drives over the trails cutting through the woodlands, making note of a rotted tree that needs to be cleared. As he turns onto the road where I'd had the scary close-call with the truck, a shudder rattles through me.

Should I tell him about that? Why? What could he do about it anyway?

Nothing. The answer settles like a block of ice in my gut.

Making an effort to push the incident from my mind, I focus on the trees standing like rows of stalwart soldiers, the thickets of undergrowth where gnomes and fairies live.

After finishing the rounds, Flynn drives toward the coastline.

He parks off the side of the road beside a plateau of rocks jetting into the ocean.

We get out of the truck and walk down a slight incline. A cold wind lashes through my hair and plasters my coat against my body. The ocean batters the coastline, waves splashing and spraying a freezing mist.

"Careful." He extends a hand, and I take it.

His strong fingers closing around mine spread warmth through my veins. I have the sudden sense he won't let go, not unless he has to, not unless I pull away first. Like he's anchoring me.

"You know, when you said you wanted to *show me something...*" I pick my way carefully across the rocks behind him, "...I was thinking more along the lines of a nice warm café or museum."

"This is a kind of museum. It's also one of my favorite spots. The intertidal zone."

He spreads his arm out to indicate the jutting rocks, the surface pocketed by thousands of tide pools. A distance away, the lighthouse perches on the cliff, hazy in the fog.

"Why is this your favorite spot?"

"It's a really intense habitat, even though you wouldn't necessarily know that by looking at it." He crouches beside a tide pool. "But then you see how many species live out here, and you realize that for them, it's a daily struggle to survive."

I pause beside him and peer into the water, which teems with fish, sea stars, anemones, algae, snails and dozens of other creatures. Flynn reaches into the water and plucks out a tiny crab, extending it so I can see the little claws waving around.

"These creatures are flooded twice a day, then left out in the sometimes blazing sun." He sets the crab gently back into the pool. "Some of them have adapted to cling to the rocks so they won't be swept away by the waves, and others need the ability to seek shelter. There are constant predators, temperature extremes, lack of food. It's all about survival. And at the same time, it's beautiful. Each tide pool is like a living painting or a collage."

"A living painting." I gaze at the morass of plants and algae floating and dancing in the freezing water. "I've never thought of them like that, but you're right. So many different textures and colors."

"They're entire ecosystems all by themselves." He points to a huge crab with a mottled shell. "That's a rock crab. You can see the barnacles clinging to its shell."

"Do you come out here often?"

"Yeah, a few times a week." He squints out at the ocean where the whitecaps are picking up speed. "This section of the coast is reasonably well-protected from the waves, so there's a lot revealed during low tide. I was out here a couple times a day when I was working on the third *Mirror Mirror* book."

"*Sea Storm.*" Realization hits me, and I see an elaborate maze winding through the tentacles of a sea anemone, the shells of dog whelks and periwinkles, the intricacies of a starfish. "Of course. Some of the mazes were underwater sea adventures. Did you actually come out here and do the sketches?"

He nods. "I do preliminary pencil drawings from nature, then incorporate them into my own illustrations."

"That's why you're known for such realistic detail." I shake my head with awe. "Do you do it all with colored pencils?"

"Pencils and ink. Sometimes watercolors."

"You're amazing. I love *Sea Storm*. I love all your books."

He shoots me an abashed smile. "You're good for my ego."

"I'm just telling you the truth." I crouch at another tide pool. "How do you come up with your ideas?"

"I don't know." He turns a smooth, rust-colored rock over in his palm. "That's why I've had such trouble writing a new series. If I knew how I got my ideas, I'd just do the same thing over again. But I haven't come up with anything in years...well, until you."

"I'm starting to feel like your muse."

"You are." Flynn puts the rock gently back into the water.

I smile. "Now *that* is the most poetic thing you've ever said to me."

We make our way around the rocks, Flynn pointing out different fish and sea creatures. He knows the map of the coastal landscape, every step secure and certain, like this is his second home.

"I still don't think *The Little Mermaid* is your favorite fairy tale." I cross the terrain carefully. "But is it an ocean tale, like *The Sea Maiden* or *The Great Sea Serpent?*"

"No."

"What about the trickster tales Uncle Max liked?"

A smile edges his mouth. "You think I have the essence of a trickster?"

"Riddles and puzzles are your thing, right? Or Riley Flynn's, at least."

The sea wind ebbs and flows past us. I feel his gaze on my face, and a sudden chill washes through me. I turn my attention back to the tide pools.

"So did you grow up on the coast?" I ask.

"Minnesota, not far from the Twin Cities." He bends and studies a sea snail. "Max told me you grew up near San Francisco."

"A town called Richmond. My mother worked at a hospital there before she became a professor at Stanford, and we moved to Palo Alto."

"She's a neurosurgeon, right?"

"One of the best." I crouch beside a tide pool and gently poke an anemone to watch its tentacles flutter closed. "She wasn't around a lot when I was growing up, and my father died when I was four. I was so lucky to have Max. He visited us at least three or four times a year, and I was thrilled when he was finally able to move to San Francisco. I honestly can't remember a time when he wasn't there for me. I'd have been a very different person if it hadn't been for him."

"Me too."

A wave crashes against the rocks, spraying us with cold mist.

"Tide's coming in." He reaches for my hand.

We walk back to the shore. He doesn't let go of my hand until we reach the truck. We're both quiet on the way back to the house, but like our teatimes, it's a comfortable, easy silence that makes me feel as if I've found something peaceful in the noise of the world. The eye of the hurricane, a pearl in an oyster, cream swirling through coffee.

A faint warning flashes in the back of my mind—*don't let yourself fall too hard, Eve*—but for the first time in a long time, I'm not scared. Not of Flynn, not of my growing feelings for him, not even of what *could* happen with us. After shipwrecking and splintering on the rocks, I'm finding solid ground again.

Flynn guides his truck back along the two-lane road heading toward town, then turns onto Sparrow Lane. There's a black BMW parked in the drive.

My stomach tenses. The car belongs to Jeremy King.

CHAPTER 26

Flynn pulls to a stop beside the car and parks. Jeremy is on the front porch, holding the screen door open. He turns to face us and lets the door close. Even from a distance, I can see the tense set of his shoulders.

"What's he doing here?" Flynn's eyes narrow, like he's looking through a target sight.

"I don't know. Let me talk to him." I grab my bag and climb out of the truck.

"Jeremy." I approach the front porch.

Behind me, Flynn's booted feet land heavily on the leaf-strewn dirt road. The driver's side door slams shut.

"Hello, Eve." Jeremy descends the steps, his attention darting suspiciously to Flynn before returning to me. "I texted you but didn't get a response, so I drove out here. You mentioned you were doing repairs on the house, so I thought I could help." He gestures to a shiny toolbox on the porch. "I brought some supplies."

"That's very kind of you, but I thought I made things clear the other day."

His responding smile is tight. "You also said you were good

with being friends, so I figured you'd be okay with me helping you out. But it looks like you got yourself another friend, huh?"

"Watch it, man." Flynn steps in front of me, his broad shoulders blocking me from Jeremy's view. Tension leashes his muscles. "Stay away from her."

Jeremy's eyes darken. "You don't get to decide that."

"She's with me."

He gives a short laugh. "One in a line of many, right?"

Flynn starts forward, his hands fisting.

"Wait a second." I grab his sleeve and yank him to a halt. "Stop it. Both of you. Jeremy, I appreciate your help, but I meant what I said."

A low, rough bark echoes through the air. Ghost bounds around the side of the house. Flynn turns, darting between me and the advancing dog.

"What the…" Jeremy steps back.

"Ghost!" I run toward the dog and hold up my hands. "It's okay, boy. Stop."

He skids to a halt, panting, eyes like slits. I put my hand on his head.

"So you have a guard dog." Jeremy straightens his shoulders. "Good. You'll need one if you're hooking up with *him*."

He jerks his thumb toward Flynn. Ghost growls.

"This is none of your business, Jeremy." I tighten my fingers in the dog's fur. His muscles vibrate with wariness.

"Seems to be *your* business though." A dark scowl twists Jeremy's face.

"Fucker." Flynn spits out the insult like a bullet, then lunges past me to grab Jeremy by the shirt.

I flinch and keep my hand on Ghost. "Flynn!"

"Go ahead and clock me, asshole," Jeremy snaps. "I'll have you slammed with an assault charge so fast your head will spin. I would fucking *love* to see you arrested. Maybe then we'll find out what the hell you've been hiding all these years."

Flynn's whole body tenses with fury and restraint. He shoves Jeremy hard enough to make the other man stumble and almost fall. Jeremy lets out a laugh, grabs his toolbox, and strides to his car, giving both me and Ghost a wide berth as he gets into the driver's seat.

A second later, his car roars out of the driveway, spewing dust and dead leaves.

Flynn looks at me, his features hard. "You okay?"

"What in the love of God is with you two?" I stalk into the house. "Is this all because Jeremy wants to sell the lighthouse?"

"And because he's an entitled, controlling dickhead who thinks he owns this town." Flynn slams the door behind him.

Shock flashes through me. "That's pretty harsh."

"It's the truth." He paces to the windows and back. "He grew up privileged, and he wants everyone to see him as Castille's golden boy. He's nothing but a vulture. When he started working for King Financial, he pushed out low-income housing in Benton for complexes built by a company that had financed his father's political career. He likes to pretend he's all for Castille, but he's done jack shit around here. His efforts to buy up land and housing haven't gone through, likely because of his mother. But last year he somehow got ahold of the lighthouse property, or said he did. Now he wants to push his own agenda and no doubt make a hefty profit with total disregard for the consequences."

I stare at him, stunned by the tense anger and contempt in his voice. "How do you know that?"

"Because Allegra would never have willingly given him or her husband control of her holdings, not even when she was sick."

"Wait a second." I hold up my hands in confusion. "You actually know her?"

"I used to." A muscle ticks in his tight jaw. "I haven't seen her in a few years. When I first came to Castille, I got a job doing some landscaping work for her and William. She had heart surgery a few months ago and ended up with severe complications that kept her in the hospital. That was when Jeremy and his father took over. And why he now wants to sell the lighthouse."

I frown. "He made it sound like the development would improve the town's economy."

"Sure, that's what it sounds like." Flynn rubs the back of his neck. "That's what he wants everyone to think. That's why he's trying to shove the approval through with his charm instead of giving the residents a chance to review it fully.

"If the zoning codes are broken, the coast and woodlands are in danger, and the residents get slammed with a tax burden. If the experiment isn't a complete disaster, housing prices shoot up and the people who have lived here for years could be forced out. Not to mention all the things that go along with unreviewed developments—fiscal policy changes, pollution, traffic issues, hits to local businesses. I'm all for economic growth, but not the scorched-earth way King wants to do it. And giving him more power? Fucking disaster."

"What about his father?"

"He's letting Jeremy take the reins, but he agrees with it. Apparently he's been showing up at city council meetings as a show of support."

"And you're trying to stop him."

"I was..." He slants his gaze to the window, like he's half-expecting Jeremy's car to come roaring back. "I was trying to. That was why I needed to come up with another book idea. I was in breach of contract with my publisher because I hadn't produced anything in years. I wanted the rest of the advance so I could make a case for buying the lighthouse and registering it for historical protection. But there's no way I can match what the development company is offering. I can use the money as a preservation fund, but only if the zoning change is voted down."

"Have you ever gone to the city council meetings?"

"No."

"Have you told anyone this?" I spread my arms out. "Jeremy

said you're trying to stop him from selling the lighthouse, but are you fighting for it? Do any of Castille's residents know what you just told me?"

"Yeah, I've told them." He paces back to the foyer. "As you can imagine, no one much cares what the strange guy in the lighthouse has to say about anything."

"Only because they don't know you," I remind him. "If you've isolated yourself up there for fifteen years without getting involved in local politics, can you blame people for not listening to you now?"

He clenches his hands. "No, I can't blame them. And that's the fucking worst part."

I study him for a moment. All the urgency and conviction he's kept stifled is clear in his stiff shoulders and the burning light in his eyes. An idea sparks in my mind.

"Flynn, I heard there's another meeting at the end of the month. A final discussion before the city council votes on whether or not to allow the zoning change. We could attend the meeting together. You could give a counter-argument. And why don't you tell people you're Riley Flynn? I understand your hesitation, but people would definitely listen to a famous author resident."

"No." The word is sharp, driven like a nail.

"Why not? You could use your name for good. To advocate for a cause."

He shakes his head.

"But—"

"Eve." His eyes turn cold. "No."

A chill ripples through my blood.

"You can't complain about changes people want to make if you're not willing to fight for what you believe in." I harden my tone to make my point. "I mean, you *can*, but it's not exactly productive. Do you think it was easy for me to publicly tell people about my relationship with David? To admit I was such a hot mess I couldn't even read any signals that my lover was *married*? Then to try and convince them I wasn't a stalker?

"You wouldn't believe the emails and voicemails I got from people, everything from hate mail to hook-up propositions. But I did it because I couldn't let him get away with spreading lies. And even though I ended up crushed by the shitstorm, I'd still do it all over again because if only a handful of people believed what I had to say, then David didn't completely win. My truth made a difference. But only because I spoke up."

Silence descends. My heart beats faster, my muscles tensing as my body recalls the anxiety and panic attacks I'd experienced during those months.

Flynn is watching me, his eyes hooded and his shoulders stiff. Irritated, I pace to the windows. I can accept that he has reasons for wanting to be alone, for staying on the outskirts of things, but clearly he's passionate about what happens to both this town and the environment. And if he's not speaking up because he's afraid of Jeremy King—

No. Just like I couldn't believe Flynn was a creep, I can't believe he's a coward either.

"Eve." He approaches, but doesn't reach out to touch me. "You're the bravest person I know."

Tears sting my eyes. "I never felt brave. I just knew I wouldn't be able to live with myself if I didn't try. But I ended up running away to Castille to hide, so that's not very brave at all."

"You didn't let any of it stop you, though. And sometimes that's the only way out. The only way to survive."

He puts his hand on the side of my neck.

"I hate what you went through." A rough undercurrent edges his voice. "I hate that it caused problems for you here. And I really fucking hate that I could make them worse."

I blink. "What are you talking about?"

"Jeremy King knows you're with me, which pisses him off.

And now he could make things worse for you than they've already been."

A humorless laugh breaks out of me. "I've been through the *worst* already. And really, if people are so interested in what you and I are doing, then why don't we just own it? I can respect the fact that you don't want to tell people you're Riley Flynn, but you still have a voice as a resident of this town. We can go to the meeting together, argue against the zoning change, make a point. I have no idea whether or not it will do any good, but at least it's something. At least we can try."

He rubs his thumb against my neck. I sense a reluctant surrendering in him, the twist of a key.

"Besides…" I place my hand on his chest. The heavy, strong beat of his heart thumps beneath my palm. "Being with you could never make things *worse*. Ever since I met you, my life has only gotten better."

He shakes his head, disbelief mixing with the warmth in his eyes. "You're unbelievable. I'm still not sure you're real."

As if to prove I am, I thread my fingers through his dark hair and press my lips to his. He yields instantly, grasping my hips and pulling me against him.

We fall together into the hot, spiraling pleasure, shedding our clothes and dropping them to the floor like falling leaves. Stripping each other bare. Even as I touch the slopes of his chest, spread my legs for his penetration, an understanding rouses in my mind.

When I first came to Castille, I'd thought I was running away. But now, my body and soul reawakened, my intellect inspired, my heart open…maybe all along, I was running toward him.

CHAPTER 27

*L*ike Sleeping Beauty's castle awakening, everything in the lighthouse is the same and yet completely changed. The atmosphere is brighter, the cobwebs swept out of the dark corners. For the next few days, I continue cataloging the books, and Flynn works in the tower, but the doors all remain open. Elvis's liquid, deep tones filter through the heating vents.

I venture into town a couple of times for groceries and to go to the library, but no one asks me about Flynn or even looks at me askance. It's probably too much to hope that the gossip mill won't spring into action as soon as people find out about our relationship, but for now all remains quiet.

Every day, Flynn shows up in the kitchen for lunch, and we work on a crossword puzzle before returning to our tasks. I organize the collection with a renewed enthusiasm borne of knowing that he shared not only a friendship with my uncle, but a love for fairy tales. I reread all the *Mirror Mirror* books both with my art historian's eye and with my newfound knowledge about Flynn.

He's there, a part of all the books—in the boy Westley's dark hair and eyes, the complexity of the mazes and puzzles, the hidden pictures only divined through careful searching. Myths and fairy tales thread through Westley and Tugg's adventures—encounters with ogres and monsters, slippages of time, treks through fantastical lands, magic spells and curses.

This afternoon, he comes to the kitchen for tea, but we bring our cups back up to his tower office. We sit on the sofa, encircled by the sweeping view of sea and earth, watching the waves break over the cliff.

"I need to go out of town for a few days, so I'll give you a key." Flynn tugs my legs onto his lap and strokes my bare feet. "I'll leave on Monday. My agent and editor want to talk to me about *Fiamma*. They love it so far."

"I'm not surprised." I place my cup on a side table and settle back against the cushions, letting my eyes drift closed. "It's weird to think of you meeting with people, much less an agent and editor. I'm used to thinking of you just…here."

"*Here* is where I'd rather be." He closes his hands around my foot and rubs gently, sending warmth through my leg. "But considering I haven't written anything in years, I owe them a meeting."

"When is the next *Mirror Mirror* book coming out?"

"There is no next one. The series is finished."

I open one eye to look at him. "Really?"

"Yeah. The story's over."

"But…" I open the other eye, my forehead knitting. "Westley never finds his reflection."

Faint tension threads his body. "He and Tugg return home again. That's the end of the story."

I frown and tap my fingers on the sofa cushion. "But how can he not find his reflection after everything he and Tugg went through? Shouldn't he find what he was looking for?"

He shrugs. "Not all of us do."

"What about a happy ending?"

"The homecoming is the happy ending."

He sounds so detached, almost as if the story were an intellectual exercise rather than something personal to him. Which makes no sense—*Flynn* vibrates through every page. His love of art, detail, puzzles, the sea, the imagination, is evident in every single line and curve of the pictures.

"I don't get it," I finally say. "You said you were influenced by fairy tales. I see them in all the books, but the point of a fairy tale is that the characters get what they were looking for."

"Maybe Westley wasn't looking for his reflection after all." He strokes his fingers over the soles of my feet. "Maybe he was just trying to get home."

"Whoa." I press my hands to my temples. "Now you're messing with my mind, Riley."

He stops massaging my foot. "It's not that intellectual, Eve. It's just a story about a boy and his dog."

"Right, like *Fiamma* is just a story about a girl and a bird." I eye him pointedly.

He chuckles, exasperated affection smoothing the tension in his features.

"This is my penance for getting involved with a brilliant, stunning art historian." He grabs my arm and pulls me across the sofa and into his lap. "Sometimes a story is just a story."

"Mmm, like a cigar is just a cigar?" I let myself fall against him, wrapping my arm around his shoulders.

Warmth softens the gray in his eyes. He slips his hand under my chin and lifts my face to his. "And a kiss is just a kiss...unless I'm kissing you. Then it's so much more."

The world shifts the instant our lips touch. I curl my fingers into the back of his shirt and open my mouth under his. It's so damned easy now, like slipping between folds of silk, like spinning effortlessly into the stars. He cups his hands on either side of my face and deepens the kiss, sweeping his tongue into my mouth in his unspoken message of claiming.

Oh, how the man can *kiss*. Gentle pressure alternating with the tantalizing graze of his teeth and stroke of his tongue. The way he holds my face like I'm precious to him, the way he tilts my head to just the right angle. He tastes like spices and sugar. Our breath increases, a swirl of heat. He slides his hands down to grip my hips and shifts us both so I'm lying underneath him.

I wrap my legs around him, urging him closer. Little fireworks pop and crackle in my blood. My breasts press against his chest. Just the light contact stiffens my nipples, sending shivers over my skin, eliciting a delicious pulsing in my core.

I pull away for an instant. "It's the middle of the workday."

"I'm giving you the day off." He tweaks my nose. Amusement mixes with the increasing lust in his eyes.

"Are you sure?" I frown and tighten my legs around him. "There's nothing in the *contract* about days off."

"I'm the boss." He unfastens the top button of my blouse and gives me a stern look. "I make the rules. Rule number one is that you have to obey my orders."

"Okay," I breathe.

He unfastens another button. A thickening heat presses against the air. We both watch as he slowly unfastens button after button of my silk blouse, revealing the valley of my cleavage beneath my white bra and clinging slip. He pushes the shirt off me, then works the zipper on the back of my skirt and helps me wiggle out of it.

My hard nipples poke against the thin fabric of my lingerie, and Flynn's gaze locks to the clear evidence of my growing arousal. He strokes my bare arms and shoulders, moving slowly down to cup my breasts. I love the way his big, ink-stained hands slide with such assurance over my body, as if he's touched me a thousand times before. As if he never wants to stop.

Our lips meet again. He twists the straps of my slip, pulling them down my shoulders. I fully expect him to take my bra right off me, but instead he keeps moving lower...lower...dragging his lips over my breasts, sucking my nipple through the silk of my

bra, running his hands over my thighs before pulling my slip up
and finding the waistband of my stockings. He rolls them off me,
pressing little kisses to my legs before going down on his knees
beside the sofa…

"Flynn!"

He looks up at me, his eyes smoky. "Spread your beautiful
legs."

Hesitation ripples through me. He presses his hands to my
inner thighs and parts them. I wiggle to the edge of the sofa. He
slides his finger under my panties. A growl sounds low in his
throat.

Shudders rock me. I force my muscles to relax, to let him in. I
expect him to take my panties off, but instead he eases the elastic
to the side and leans forward. The first touch of his tongue
explodes me with heat.

"Oh my God, *Flynn*…"

He clasps my hip with his other hand, steadying me. He licks
up one side of my sex and down the other. Part of my mind is
hazy with disbelief that I'm actually doing this. Just weeks ago I
was frozen inside, and now I'm spread out naked on a sofa, quivering with heat at the touch of this man's tongue.

I can't believe he's doing this either—the mysterious, reclusive
lighthouse keeper who was so intent on keeping me at a distance,
now worshipping my body with such expertise that an earth-
quake begins to tremble in my blood.

"Flynn, I'm already…" I fist one hand in his hair.

He makes a muffled noise. "Do it."

I squeeze my eyes shut. Need unspools. He licks, sucks,
thrusts…and the world shatters into bright, blinding colors. I cry
out, trembling and shaking as he works the final sensations from
my body.

He rises to standing, his eyes gleaming with satisfaction.
Tingling all over, I run my hands up his abdomen, reveling in the

heat of his chest, the strain lacing his muscles. I press my palm to his groin and trace the thick ridge of his erection.

His breath expels on a rush of need. I unfasten his jeans and tug them down along with his boxers. He digs his fingers into my scalp.

"Turn around," he whispers. "On your knees."

I ease away from him and turn, bracing my hands against the back of the sofa. A sudden intense vulnerability washes over me. As if sensing it, Flynn strokes his hand over my ass, rubbing it with gentle circles.

I glance at him over my shoulder. My breath catches at the hot, possessive, *needy* look in his eyes. He grabs the back collar of his T-shirt and yanks it over his head, giving me a breathtaking view of his naked chest.

He makes a gesture with his forefinger. I turn back around, lowering my head to my folded arms. My whole body slackens and yields. He slips his finger into my damp folds, probing and gentle. Then there's a rustling noise, the opening of a condom packet, and his sheathed cock rubs against me.

My blood flames. I bite my lip on a moan. He reaches beneath me, splaying his fingers over my clit as he presses forward. He takes his time fondling me, the slow massage easing my trepidation. I rock my hips backward.

With a grunt, he eases into me. Every nerve ending flares to life as my body opens to take his thick cock, each millimeter an excruciatingly delicious invasion.

Flynn pauses. His breath saws through the air. "You okay?"

I nod, pulling in a heavy gasp. Slowly, I thrust my hips back a little, and he sinks into me farther.

"Fuck." He groans, grabbing my hips to stop me from moving. "Keep doing that and I'll come before I even get all the way inside you."

I drag in a breath, wiping a trickle of perspiration from my forehead. I arch my back and shift again, opening my legs wider. He slides in like a key fitting into a well-oiled lock, filling me.

"Okay?" Strain laces his voice.

"Yes," I gasp, bracing my hands on the sofa arm. "Fuck me."

He draws back and pushes forward, the intense friction driving my need higher with every stroke. I let him set the rhythm before I start pushing back to meet him. Twinges of pain shoot through me at first as my body struggles to accept the new position, but the discomfort soon melts into a fog of pure sensation.

A strange disbelief floods my mind, the razor-sharp edge between reality and my explicit imagination. *Am I actually here? Is this happening? Is he real?*

Everything about him certainly *feels* real, especially the deep plunge of his shaft, stimulating me in all the right places. He fists one hand in my hair, easing my head up, arching my back to deepen the penetration.

Arousal clenches my lower body. He slides his hand under me again, expertly working me. A whirlpool of excitement builds.

"God…" I squeeze my eyes shut. He fills me again and again, pushing me ever closer to the edge. "So deep. Flynn, I'm going to…*oh!*"

Bliss crashes through me, sending me into a frenzy of quivering sensation. He groans, gripping my ass and thrusting into me so hard the world seems to tilt on its axis.

I choke out a cry, clenching around his shaft the instant before he pulls out of me. Behind my closed eyelids I see him stroking his cock, his muscular, sweaty chest heaving, his face flushed with pleasure. A string of curses rips from his throat the instant before he comes, the thick spray shooting all the way up my back.

Gasping for breath, I fall back onto the sofa, every muscle limp. A shadow darkens the air. I open my eyes.

Flynn is above me, his corded arms caging me in, his hands

planted on either side of the cushions as he holds his weight off me. His gray eyes are still hot, his angular features damp with sweat.

He kisses my forehead and shifts to wrap me in his arms. I press my face to his heaving chest. His heart hammers, the sound filling my blood, my soul, every part of me.

He lowers his lips to my ear and brushes my hair away from my face.

"If I could love anyone," he whispers, "it would be you."

My breath catches. I lift my head to look at him. "You can love anyone you want."

A faint smile curves his mouth, but his eyes darken. "I wish it were that easy."

An ache squeezes my heart. I want to tell him it is that easy, but we both know it's not. Love can be hard, painful, dangerous. And yet we'll brave enchanted forests, search for elusive golden eggs, confront dragons…all for the privilege of both loving and being loved in return. It's just that extraordinary.

So why doesn't he want it as much as I do?

CHAPTER 28

*F*lynn leaves for New York after the weekend. I fill my time with enough work and preparation for the city council meeting that I don't spend too much time missing him.

It doesn't feel right to be at the lighthouse without him, so I stick to my schedule of eight to four, then head out for my increasingly cold coastal jog. Brief snow flurries whip through the air. The mid-November sunlight is already long gone by the time I return to Ramshackle Manor.

Two days into Flynn's absence, I set a pile of Italian fairy tale books on the shelf and dust off my hands. I've unpacked almost all the boxes, and the shelves are now filled with books—anthologies, criticisms, picture books, compilations, monographs.

While I still have a number of paintings to catalog, the sight of the near-empty workroom is both satisfying and a bit unsettling. Once I finish organizing the collection…the job is finished. *What happens then?*

I push that thought out of my mind and focus on the database. I'll cross that bridge later and hope there are no trolls living under it.

My phone buzzes with an unfamiliar number. Instinctive fear

grips me. The last number I hadn't recognized had been David. Then there was the odd silent call, which was also a 408 area code. I'd blocked both of those numbers, but…

No. I will not be afraid anymore.

I answer the call. "Hello?"

"Is this Eve Perrin?" I don't recognize the male voice.

"Yes."

"Ah, Dr. Perrin, I'm glad to reach you. I've been having some trouble with your number. This is Dr. Andrew Gregory, the chair of the Department of Art and Art History at Santa Clara University."

"Oh, hello." Relief eases my anxiety. "Have you called before?"

"Last week, but something went wrong with the signal. Do you have a moment to talk?"

"Yes." I expel a silent breath, my shoulders relaxing. "What can I do for you, Dr. Gregory?"

"Andy, please. We received your application for our interim professor position next spring, along with your paper about the artist Maria Wood. We were impressed by both your research and credentials."

"Thank you." My heart starts beating faster, though from excitement rather than fear.

"Are you available to come out for an interview?" Andy asks. "Mid-December before our winter break, if at all possible. We'd like for you to see the campus and meet the rest of the faculty. Ideally we'll also arrange for you to give a lecture on a topic of your choosing so you can interact with the students."

I press a hand to my chest. My heart is racing now, flooding me with both hope and a sudden, strange anxiety.

"Dr. Perrin?"

"Yes. Yes, I'm here. Thank you so much. I'd love to come out for an interview."

"And you're available the week of December twelfth?"

"Yes. Any time."

"Great. I'll have our admin give you a call to set up the details, if that's all right? Once we firm up a date, I'll get the lecture organized. If you could speak about the Maria Wood drawing, our students will be enthralled."

"I'd love to. Thank you so much for your interest."

"Thank you for yours. We'll look forward to seeing you soon."

I end the call and sit in shock for a minute. All the time I've spend applying for positions and working on my paper, I've been hoping for *this exact call.*

Excitement bolts through me. I pick up my phone to call my mother, then hammer out a quick email instead. I don't want to talk to her or subject myself to whatever cutting remark she'll make.

A job interview. Across the country again, back in California. What will Flynn say?

I stand and run my trembling hands over my skirt. I wish he were here, but he won't be back from New York until tomorrow. He'd left me his hotel information and his agent's cell phone if I need to reach him, but I'll wait to tell him in person.

Instead I call Graham. His wife Mary picks up.

"Eve, he's gone to the office and forgotten his phone." She laughs, and I can almost see her shaking her head. "Is there something I can help you with?"

"I just wanted to tell him I have a job interview offer. Santa Clara University."

"Really? How wonderful. You'll be back in our neck of the woods."

"Yes. As soon as I have the dates settled, I'll let you know. I'd love to see you both again. Maybe I can take you out to dinner?"

"That would be lovely. I'll let Graham know, if he doesn't already."

I blink. "How would he...oh, he didn't call them on my behalf, did he?"

"I don't know, Eve. He's always going on about you, so I wouldn't be surprised if he reached out."

Though I don't love the idea of Graham interceding after he's already done so much for me, it would be just like him to try and help me.

"Could you ask him to call me, please?" I tell Mary.

"Certainly. Have a good evening, and congratulations."

I end the call, hoping I've actually garnered interest for my credentials rather than Graham's intervention.

I start back toward the bookshelves when a movement out the window catches my eye. With the weather changing to a mixture of rain and early snow, the number of people coming to the lighthouse has dwindled, but a woman is walking up the pathway from the parking lot. A black umbrella shelters her from the flurries, and she's wearing a black flared coat.

Normally I wouldn't pay much attention, but there's something oddly familiar about her. Have I seen her in town or—

Allegra King.

I back away from the window, but not before she looks up and sees me through the glass. We gaze at each other for an instant. She starts toward the front door. The bell rings. Having no choice, I hurry through the kitchen to answer it.

"Eve?" She peers at me from underneath the umbrella.

"Yes." I'm unaccountably nervous. "I'm sorry, Flynn isn't here at the moment."

"Too bad." Disappointment etches her face for an instant before shifting to resolve. "But never mind. I'm here to see you. I stopped at your house, but you weren't home. Given what I've heard from my son, I suspected you might be here."

"Oh." Fighting a blush, I step aside, holding the door open. "Please come in. Would you like to sit down?"

"I would."

I take her coat and umbrella. She crosses to sit on the wingbacked chair in the front room and sets her large Chanel handbag down. She's an incredibly lovely woman in her mid-fifties with silver-streaked dark hair cut in a wavy sweep past her ears. Her beauty is evident in the elegant lines of her face, her bright blue eyes, her graceful hands.

"It's a pleasure to finally meet you, Mrs. King."

"Call me Allegra." She encloses my hand in both of hers. "And likewise."

"Can I offer you a cup of tea?"

"*Tea?*" She arches an elegant eyebrow. "I'm not an eighty-year-old British dowager, for heaven's sake. Neither are you, by the look of things. Don't you have anything stronger?"

"Flynn has a bottle of Glenlivet in the cabinet. I'm sure he won't mind if we have a glass."

"That's more like it." She waves an imperious hand.

I hurry to pour the scotch, then hand one glass to Allegra and sit on the sofa with mine. Shadows smudge the area beneath her eyes, and the lines of weariness around her mouth are more evident now that I'm closer to her. Recalling her health issues, my heart clenches. My memories of Max's illness are still vivid.

"Where is Flynn?" she asks.

"He had to go out of town. He'll be back tomorrow evening."

Regret compresses her lips. "I haven't seen him in years."

"I'm sure he'll be sorry he missed you."

She eyes me shrewdly. "You're his lover."

The blunt comment causes a heated flush to spread over my face. I take a swallow of scotch to avoid having to respond.

"I've always been fond of him." Allegra's lips curve into a slight, musing smile. "Bit of an oddball, but that's what makes him so appealing. And he's the one person in this town who's always been good about minding his own business."

Does she know about Flynn's conflict with her son? It's not my place to ask. She doesn't appear to hold anything against Flynn, in any case.

"He speaks highly of you," I say. "I've heard so much about you."

"And I you." She settles back in the chair and glances at her watch. "I can't stay long. I'd have paid you a visit sooner, but getting away from my fussing husband and son isn't easy these days. They both went off this afternoon to work on some sort of acquisition deal, so I took the opportunity to escape."

Though the word *escape* rings strangely in my ears, I nod. "I heard you were ill recently. I hope things are improving?"

"More or less." She gestures to her chest. "Previously undiagnosed heart issue. Ever since I had three stents put in, William and Jeremy have had a tendency to treat me like an *old lady*. As if I need constant care and don't know better. I swear they expect me to take up crocheting. It's a bit annoying."

I smile faintly. "I can imagine."

She sets her glass on a table and reaches for her handbag. "My son told me you'd stopped by the house recently to find out about a certain Victorian artist."

"Maria Wood, yes."

"I'm sorry I didn't have a chance to talk with you then." She opens the bag and takes out an old, leather-bound book. "But I hope you'll find this useful."

My heart shifts, sudden anticipation striking me. She hands me the book. Despite the worn edges and loose pages, the cover has a strikingly intricate design, a black background embellished with crisscrossing red curves coming together in the center like a drop of blood.

Hands shaking, I turn to the first page: *The Book of Fairy Tales, compiled and illustrated by Maria Wood. Lyons and Steele, San Francisco, 1868.*

I turn to the first illustration, a detailed drawing of a prince, a demonesque twist on his face, approaching a supposedly sleeping woman whose hand conceals a knife. On the reverse side, the prince lies crumpled on the floor while the princess, only her hand visible at the frame, strides from the room.

I leaf through the pages. All of the tales are illustrated in a similar fashion, graphically depicting sexual violence with a vengeful aftermath. I look at Allegra.

"The Maria Wood book." My voice trembles.

"Your uncle gave it to me as a parting gift before he left Castille. It was special to him, unlike any of the other books." She picks up the scotch and takes a sip. "I want you to have it now."

Fresh shock ripples through me. "I can't—"

"Oh, stop it." She waves a hand impatiently. "Of course you can. It's been sitting in a drawer for the past fourteen years, so heaven knows it could use some light and air. I would love for you to show it to the world and give this Maria Wood the credit she deserves. I imagine she was quite the woman to be reckoned with. And according to Max, you'd do well to look into your own ancestry to find out who she really was."

I stare at her. "Did he know?"

"I believe he had an inkling, but never found out for sure. That's one reason the book was so important to him. And why it legitimately belongs to you."

"I...I don't know what to say." *Could it be possible I'm somehow related to Maria Wood?*

"Say you'll take the book and do something worthwhile with it," Allegra replies. "Examine, analyze, connect it to social norms and culture, all that sort of thing you historians do. Give Max yet another reason to be proud of you."

"Thank you. I promise I will."

She nods, her expression softening. "What has he told you about me?"

"That..." I run my hand over the book's leather surface. If there's anything I've learned, it's that one of the few things I truly own is the truth. "That you were the love of his life."

She sighs, a mixture of regret and pleasure.

"I was twenty years old." She twists the gold chain at her neck. "I walked into that classroom expecting to see a doddering old professor. Instead there was Max, big and blond…handsome as a Greek god. All the girls were just enraptured with him. And then the fairy tales…well, he was just a romantic fantasy come to life."

I smile. "He once told me he'd come up with excuses to stop by your desk just so he could be close to you."

"And I came up with excuses just to go to his office hours. It's astonishing how often I *forgot* the assignment or needed him to check my thesis statement." She chuckles and takes another sip of scotch. "I don't mind telling you I never stopped loving him. If that makes me disloyal to my husband, so be it. Life isn't always quite so black and white, is it?"

"No. Max never stopped loving you either."

Warmth brightens her eyes. "We didn't speak much over the years. Once when he asked me to rent the lighthouse to Flynn, then again when he left to take the job in San Francisco. Avoiding temptation, I suppose. We were never lovers, rather to my regret." She sets her glass down, still toying with her necklace. "How is he, Eve?"

I blink, startled. How *is* he?

"You don't know?" I ask.

She skids her gaze to mine. A heartbeat passes, thickening with tension and wariness.

"Max…" I swallow hard. Old grief shifts in my chest. "Allegra, Max died over a year ago. He had cancer."

All the color drains from her face, the light in her eyes dimming.

How could she not have known? The logical part of me knows the answer. There was no reason she could or should have known. She and Max were long estranged, and she didn't know his friends or family. There was no one to tell her.

Still, it's shocking to discover that Max's lifelong love hadn't known of his death.

I lean forward, putting my hand over hers. Her skin is cold.

"I'm sorry." I don't know what else to say. "He battled as hard as he could. And he had so many friends, colleagues, students. He was happy in life, Allegra. I promise."

"I can't believe it." Her eyes fill with tears. She takes a tissue out of her handbag. "A world without Max is a much darker place."

"Yes, it is."

She dabs at her eyes, lost for a minute in private grief. Her gaze moves to me again. A spark of realization dawns through her sorrow. I release her hand and sit back.

"I need to go." She looks at her gold watch and loops her bag over her arm. "I apologize for rushing out, but as I said I don't have much time."

I rise to get her coat. "I'll walk you to your car."

"No, no." She waves me away and slips into her coat. "I have enough fussing at home."

"All right. Thank you for coming to see me and for the book. It means a great deal."

"I know." She buttons her coat and opens the door. Just before she steps out, she takes hold of my arm. Her fingers tighten. "He was a good man, Eve. The best."

My throat closes over. "I know."

She nods, her eyes misting again. She opens the umbrella and hurries toward the parking lot, her coat billowing behind her like a witch's cape.

CHAPTER 29

*H*e's back! At the end of Sparrow Lane, the headlights of Flynn's truck glow through the evening darkness. My heart does a happy cartwheel.

I hurry from the front window to the porch, mindful of Ghost creeping around the house. His ears flatten back as he watches Flynn park the truck and descend from the driver's side.

He looks wonderful. He's travel-rumpled, but strikingly gorgeous in a navy suit and tie beneath his black coat. Smiling, he holds out his arms.

I hurry across the driveway, leaping right up against him with the certain knowledge that he'll catch me. And he does, closing his arms tightly around me. Our lips meet in a warm kiss of promise and homecoming.

Oh, what would it be like to feel *this* all the time? Butterflies, flowers blooming, stars sparkling in your blood.

For the first time ever, I find a degree of understanding in all the darkness through which I was forced to walk. If I hadn't experienced the bleakest despair, I wouldn't know now that happiness is such an extraordinary gift.

"Welcome back." I ease away to look into his warm gray eyes

and tug at the knot of his tie. "Pretty fancy duds, Lighthouse Guy."

"I clean up pretty good, huh?"

"You also get dirty pretty good."

He grins and lowers me to my feet. A low growl sounds from nearby. We part and turn to find Ghost near the front of the truck, body tense and teeth bared in warning.

"I got this." Flynn reaches into his truck and emerges with a thick beef bone.

Ghost's growl lessens in volume. Flynn crouches and extends the bone. I ease forward to intervene in the event Ghost attacks. He stares at Flynn, eyes narrowed. Flynn doesn't say anything. Ghost takes a few tentative steps forward, then lunges to grab the bone.

He trots back to the porch and settles down to gnaw at the peace offering. Flynn and I pass him without incident to enter the house.

It's a start.

Less than three minutes later, we're in the bedroom, tugging at each other's clothes and seeking out the naked skin beneath. Pent-up lust fires between us. I'm already ready for him, and he buries himself inside me with one swift thrust.

Everything about him, about us, is already so familiar—his grip on my hips as he pulls halfway out of me before plunging back in, his breath hot against my neck, his low rumbling grunts. The flex and pull of his muscles, the response of my own body, quivering and tense.

We're both so eager that neither of us is willing to prolong the moment, driving each other quickly toward the breaking point. He comes first, a deep heavy thrust that sparks my own shattering release.

"Christ, I missed you." He plants his hands on either side of my head and presses kisses over my face—my forehead, my cheeks, my lips, the tip of my nose. "It's insane. I've lived alone for years, and then *you* show up and…"

His voice breaks off abruptly. He rolls off me and onto his back, his breathing still hard and chest damp.

I lift to one elbow to look at him. "And what?"

"Nothing." He drags a hand down his face. "Just strange how fast I got used to having you around."

"Really?" I nudge my knee against his thigh. "That's what I say about the dog. I've gotten *used to having him around.*"

"Okay, sorry." He slides one hand around my neck, his eyes creasing with amusement. "I have an extremely intense, heart-warming crush on you, Eve Perrin, and if your uncle knew all the raunchy things I want to do to you, he'd kick my ass."

"Not true. Uncle Max wanted me to be happy." I lower my head and kiss him, sliding my hand over his chest. "And even with all your bad-tempered glowering and door slamming, you make me happy."

Tenderness softens his expression. "Likewise."

"And now that my physical urges are satisfied," I remark, "how was your trip?"

He gives me a summary of the meetings with his editor and agent.

"They're planning a big publicity push for *Fiamma*." He twists a few locks of my hair around his fingers. "The return of Riley Flynn, that kind of thing."

Pride fills me. "As well they should. Do your editor and agent know your real identity?"

"Yeah." His eyes cloud over. "For payments and stuff. Lawyers too. They've never much cared. With the first *Mirror Mirror* book, my publisher tried to get me to go on a tour, do interviews. They stopped asking after I threatened to go to another publisher. Now they all figure I'm just a strange eccentric living up here by myself."

"You are," I remind him.

"Yeah." He narrows his gaze. "Good thing you have a fetish for strange eccentrics."

"I have a fetish for *you*." I kiss his shoulder. "And apparently I can't hide it either because Allegra King knows we're together."

"Allegra?"

"She came to visit me." I curl against his side. "We drank your Glenlivet, and she gave me the Maria Wood book I'd been looking for. She didn't know Max had died. I still can't believe that."

"How would she have known?"

"I guess she couldn't have. Her husband hadn't told her, maybe because he didn't know how close they'd once been or didn't want to know. I just thought it was sad. They loved each other, and she hadn't known he died."

Jeremy hadn't told Allegra either...but did *he* know? Had I told him?

"Did you tell her about the collection?" Flynn asks.

I arch an eyebrow at him. "And break the *contract*? Heavens no."

He grins. My heart lights up. The sight of his smile never fails to spark me with pleasure and warmth.

"I think we can officially declare the contract null and void. Except for the clause about you being required to wear apple-lavender body lotion."

"Done."

I press my lips to his again, revived passion swirling through me. Then my stomach growls, effectively putting a halt to thoughts of a second sex romp.

Since my pantry only contains canned soup and tea, I suggest going downtown for dinner. We shower and dress before walking back to Flynn's truck. Ghost, still working diligently on the beef bone, doesn't look up when we pass.

"People will notice we're together." Flynn glances at me as we pull on our seat belts.

I shrug. "So? They'll know when we show up at the city council meeting next week. We might as well forewarn them, so to speak. Besides, I'm proud to be with you."

Disbelief flashes in his eyes for just an instant. He starts the truck. His shoulders are still tense as he drives to Lantern Street. It's close to six, and most of the retail shops have closed for the night. Light flurries of snow fall.

We decide on a diner that has finished with the dinner crowd and sit at the counter to eat club sandwiches and fries. If anyone glances at us sideways or wonders about us being together, I neither notice nor care.

It's a strangely freeing sensation, *not caring*. Knowing that people might gossip about me or think badly of me, but that there's nothing I can do about *people*. All I can do is tell the truth that I know is real and live the way my heart desires.

And my heart desires Flynn Alverton.

The waitress sets slices of apple pie in front of us with a cheery, "Here you go."

As we indulge in the dessert, I muster the courage to tell Flynn about the job interview offer from Santa Clara University.

"That's great, but no surprise to me." He shoots me a quick, approving smile. "You're damn good at what you do. It's about time people remember that. When's the interview?"

"We don't have a date settled yet. Middle of December." I hesitate and brush my fingers over his sleeve. "Maybe you can come with me. I'd like for you to meet Graham and his wife."

A shield comes down over his expression. He shakes his head. "Aside from the rare trip to New York, I don't go places."

"Ever?"

"I'm not one for traveling."

I pull my hand back. "You mean you haven't gone anywhere in the past fifteen years?"

His lack of response is enough of an answer. I shouldn't be surprised—the most people know about Flynn is that he's lived in the lighthouse all these years—but it hadn't occurred to me he's never left the boundaries of Castille.

"Told you my life is boring." He reaches for his wallet and takes out a few bills. "I did a lot of traveling once. Well, more like I wandered aimlessly before landing in Castille."

"And you've never left?"

"No reason to."

"What about your family?"

"I don't talk about my family." His voice is flat.

Not even to me?

I manage to swallow the question. Most of us have an unpleasant family story to tell—wicked queen mothers, troubled siblings, abusive fathers—but I don't imagine many people lock themselves away in a lighthouse in an effort to...escape? Hide? Run away?

He follows me out to the sidewalk, shrugging into his coat. Tension threads the air between us. His eyes darken to charcoal with sorrow and regret.

"Eve, I'm sorry. This is who I am. I can't change. Not even..."

For you.

He doesn't have to say it. An ache pushes at my chest. I don't get it. He has so much talent, so much to offer, so much to give. I know all too well that men can and do use their power for evil. So why doesn't Flynn use his power for good?

"Flynn, I—"

Excuse me." A woman's inquisitive voice breaks off my words. "Eve Perrin?"

I turn to find a tall, blond woman approaching, her heels clicking purposefully on the concrete, her sharp gaze pinned on me. A bulky man follows her, carrying a large object concealed by the shadows.

Unease roils through me. Flynn steps forward, putting his body between me and the woman.

"I'm sorry." She stops and smiles. Not a friendly smile. More of a baring-one's-teeth smile. "I didn't mean to startle you. You are Eve Perrin, correct?"

"Who wants to know?" Flynn straightens his shoulders, his muscles tensing.

"My name is Rebecca Forester." The woman's gaze slips to him before sliding back to me. "I'm a reporter with KCBN news. I've been following the recent accusations against UCLA professor David Landry and would like to ask for your comment."

Before I can break through my shock, a microphone is shoved in front of me. The unblinking bright light of a camera blasts onto my face.

Panic floods me. I stumble back. Flynn closes his hand on my arm.

"Get away from her!" he snaps at the reporter.

"Ms. Perrin." Rebecca Forester, still smiling, steps into my line of vision. "I'm sure you've heard about the sexual harassment allegations against Professor Landry, and the most recent charge by an undergraduate student of alleged rape—"

The world tips, a black pit opening beneath me. The only thing keeping me from falling is Flynn's grip, the harsh sound of his voice. He pushes me behind him, blocking me from the camera's eye. I catch sight of his truck half a block away and start toward it. My heart races.

"Ms. Perrin, if you'd care to comment on your own involvement with Professor Landry?" Rebecca Forester's tone grows shrill, her heels clicking faster.

She's running to catch me. I'm being chased.

"Is it true that you stalked him and sent him naked pictures of yourself? You claimed to have had an affair with him, but according to him, you..."

"Shut the *fuck* up!" Flynn's bellow is like a thunderstorm crashing over the sky. He yanks open the passenger side door of his truck and shoves me inside.

The reporter and cameraman skid to a halt, still shouting questions, still filming through the smudged windshield. His face a mask of rage, Flynn slams a hand over the camera lens. A small crowd has gathered outside the diner, peering toward the commotion.

"Back off, man." The cameraman snarls and forces his way toward the truck.

Flynn blocks him. They struggle for two seconds. Flynn shoves hard. The cameraman hits the ground. His camera crashes to the sidewalk.

Spitting another curse, Flynn climbs into the driver's seat and starts the engine. He rams the truck into drive. The tires squeal. He swerves into a U-turn and guides the truck on the road out of town.

I'm shaking so hard my teeth rattle. Wrapping my arms around myself, I huddle against the truck door and try to contain the panic. Flynn yanks the car to a sudden stop. He reaches across the seat and hauls me into his lap, locking his arms around me. My breath clogs my throat, sticky and hot.

"Breathe." He presses my head to his chest. His heart hammers. "They're gone. You're safe now."

I struggle to drag air into my lungs. Leafy shadows flicker over the windshield. He's stopped somewhere in the forest.

Anger tenses his whole body, but his voice is calm and measured as he murmurs words of comfort. His arms are protective steel bands around me. I squeeze my eyes shut. His deep voice slides into me, echoing through my blood, my heart.

An eternity passes before we're both breathing steadily again. I lift my head slowly from his chest. Though his expression is controlled, a storm still rages in his eyes.

"Are you okay?" he asks.

"I will be." I shudder and lean against him. "You?"

"Same." He rubs his hand over my arms. "Let's get you home."

Home. God. What if the reporter is waiting for me there? I

have no doubt she knows where I live. As if sensing my thoughts, Flynn eases me back over to the passenger seat. "We'll go to the lighthouse."

He starts the truck and maneuvers back to the road. I'm cold all over. The reporter's words assail me like ice pellets. *Alleged rape...rape.*

God in heaven. Had I been with a man capable of that? Could I have done something more to challenge him? To prevent him from hurting another woman? Nausea curdles in my stomach.

Flynn pulls into the lighthouse parking lot. It's not until we're inside that a sudden, shocking thought hits me.

He closes and locks the front door behind him, turning to face me.

"Flynn, they..." My panic sparks to life again. "They probably have you on camera."

"Good." His expression darkens. "They'll get the message they have to go through me to get to you."

"But what if they try and find out who you are? What if they start harassing you?"

The idea that *I* could be responsible for the destruction of his privacy is almost more than I can bear.

"Eve." He grasps my shoulders and lowers his head to look at me, his eyes weighted with conviction. "That is the last thing you need to worry about."

"But...what if the cameraman comes after you with some sort of assault charge? What if they find out you're Riley Flynn?"

"Eve." Urgency threads his voice. "I can take care of myself. The only thing that matters is that you're safe. Has that reporter contacted you before?"

I shake my head. "No one from the press has, not since I was fired. I...she said something about a rape charge..."

With a shudder of revulsion, I grab my phone out of my bag. Rather than try to scour the internet for information, I call Graham.

"I didn't want to tell you." He lets out a long sigh. "But I figured you'd find out sooner or later. It's ugly. An undergrad says she'd made an appointment to talk to him about a paper. She went to his office. He made insinuations about improving her grade, then touched her inappropriately. She tried to leave, he locked the door…and forced her on his desk. He's on suspension while the university investigates."

My nausea intensifies. Flynn rests a comforting hand on the back of my neck.

"Has anyone asked you about it?" Graham says.

"A reporter, yes. I made no comment, obviously."

"Good call. Mary told me about your job interview. Sounds like it's come at a perfect time, if the press knows you're in Castille now."

That's certainly true. Getting out of town for a few days might be a blessing.

"Speaking of which, I'll have you know I've made no calls on your behalf," Graham continues. "Not since you asked me not to. Any offers you get are solely based on your credentials."

The compliment eases my tension a bit. "Thank you."

"That's not to say I won't give you a glowing recommendation when they ask for one. Good luck, Eve."

I thank him again and end the call. Fatigue hits me hard. My shoulders slump.

"I don't get it," I tell Flynn. "What do they *want* with me? I have nothing more to give them, nothing more to say. I thought it was over."

Sorrow and regret fill his eyes. He runs his hand over my hair, rubbing a few strands between his fingers.

"I know." His voice is heavy. "That's the tough thing about life. Some things are never over."

❄

A light snow drifts past the lantern room windows, collecting on the edges like salt. In Andersen's fairy tale, Kay's grandmother called snowflakes "white bees."

The Snow Queen is the queen bee, who flies where the swarm is the thickest. When winter arrives full-force, the glass windows will be etched with beautiful, icy patterns left by the Snow Queen on her midnight flight.

A shiver skates down my spine. I sit back on the sofa, pulling Flynn's gray sweatshirt tighter around me. The Snow Queen is never defeated. Before Gerda arrives at the palace to rescue Kay, the queen flies away to cast her cold spell over other parts of the world.

I've always wondered if she knew Gerda was coming. If she feared the little girl's power.

At one point in Gerda's quest, she takes shelter with a woman from Lapland. A reindeer asks the woman to give Gerda a potion to increase her strength.

The Lapp woman replies, "I can give her no more power than what she has already. Don't you see how great it is?"

Gerda doesn't feel strong or great. But still she struggles forward, battling exhaustion and cold. In the end, she finds both her beloved best friend and a rose-filled summer. She returns home to her family. She has new friends, animal companions, the wisdom of experience.

Her bright, colorful life is her triumph over evil.

CHAPTER 30

Flynn won't leave my side in the few days following our encounter with the reporter. Inwardly, I question our plan to attend the city council meeting about the potential zoning change that could allow for the hotel development, but then I remember the day I felt as if I could do anything if he were beside me. Now he is.

I place *The Green Fairy Book* on a shelf, turning to look at the workroom. All of the boxes are gone. Books and manuscripts fill the shelves. Any bare space on the walls is covered with framed illustrations and paintings of fairy tale scenes—historical works by Rackham, Dulac, Harbour, Goble, and Nielsen alongside contemporary artists with their own unique twist on the stories.

Flynn's drawings belong among them, these wildly imaginative pictures of poisoned apples, hidden doorways, straw spinning into gold.

What has he done with all the original artwork he created for the *Mirror Mirror* books? I can't imagine—or bear—the thought that he'd have thrown it all away.

I still have stacks of books to shelve and paintings to display, but there's no more room. Either Flynn will have to store them somewhere else or find a place for them in the lighthouse.

My work here is almost done. Uncle Max's collection is cataloged and searchable through a robust database. I've finalized the details for my job interview.

What happens then?

That's the thing about fairy tales. We start reading them already knowing what will happen at the end. We know the witch will be defeated, the prince will marry the princess, the curse will be lifted.

That's why the tales have endured for generations, why storytellers wrote them down for posterity, why they've been retold again and again. We know there will be a happy ending. We all need the assurance that it's not only possible, but *inevitable*.

Because life itself can be so painfully different.

"You look as if you're thinking very hard."

I glance up as Flynn enters the workroom, all rumpled male beauty in jeans and a flannel shirt that stretches beautifully over his broad shoulders. Though I love the sight of him in a suit, I much prefer the warm masculinity of his everyday look.

"I'm an academic. Thinking hard is what I do."

"And you do it so well." He slips his hand under my chin and gives me a kiss that spins pleasure through me, light and airy like cotton candy.

We indulge in each other for a few moments before he lifts his head and runs his hand over my cheek. "I need to get the rounds done before the meeting tonight. You want to come with me?"

"I can't." I glance at my watch. "I need to get home to feed Ghost and pick up all our notes about the zoning laws. I should also shower and change. Why don't we meet downtown?"

"No, I'll come pick you up. If you'll take my suit with you, I can change at your place."

He tucks a lock of my hair behind my ear before stepping

back. To my enjoyment, he touches me a lot, as if now that he finally *can*, he's not about to pass up any opportunity to do so.

"This place looks great." He sweeps his gaze over the shelves and walls. "You've done a phenomenal job. I might have to give you a bonus."

"I'm pretty sure you already did. Oh, no wait. You gave me your *boner*."

He chuckles, sliding his arms around my waist and pulling me against him. "I'd give it to you again right now, except we'd be late."

"Are you nervous?"

"No." His expression darkens a little. "Just not all that convinced it will make much difference. The majority of the residents are against the zoning change, but that doesn't mean the council won't vote in favor of it. Especially when that much money is involved."

I squeeze him around the waist in reassurance, even though I have the same concern. It's a lot for two people to go up against.

"Go get your suit and I'll take it with me." I stand on tiptoe to kiss his chin. "Then after the meeting, I'll take it off you."

"Deal." He pats me on the rear and heads out of the workroom.

After packing up my things and collecting his suit, I return home. Darkness cloaks the sky, and snow flurries whirl through the cold air. An almost full moon peers out from behind the clouds.

Ghost trots around the side of the house to greet me, tail wagging and ears perked. I walk around to the back door to pick up his food and water dishes from the porch where I leave them during the day. I open the door and refill both dishes, setting them down in the kitchen.

I head upstairs to the bedroom and check my phone for messages. The council meeting is scheduled for eight, which gives us an hour to get ready and be there early to distribute the handouts we've compiled.

After showering, I dress in a navy pleated skirt and white blouse. Next to Flynn in his charcoal suit and gray-and-blue striped tie, we'll hopefully serve as a subconscious reminder of the coastal landscape. I add silver earrings and slip my feet into navy heeled pumps before returning downstairs.

A chill washes through the living room. Ghost is gone, and the back door is wide open. Had I left it open for him? I close and lock it.

Turning my attention to the notes for Flynn's statement, I ensure they're all in order. A knock sounds at the door.

I hurry to let Flynn in. Then hesitation shivers down my spine. The reporter hasn't tried to contact me since the other day, but given all the weirdness happening, I can't be too careful.

I peer through the smudged peephole, catching sight of a man's shoulder in a black coat. Not entirely certain it's Flynn, I open the door a crack.

William King is on the front porch, wearing an impeccable dark brown suit beneath his coat. Though relief flickers through me that he's at least familiar, I can't grasp a reason why he'd be here.

"Hello, Eve. May I come in?"

"Actually, I'm just getting ready to—"

"I won't be long." He edges his foot into the door and lays one hand flat against it, pushing it open. My heel catches on the loose floorboard, tipping me briefly off-balance.

"Whoops." William catches my elbow. "Sorry about that. Are you all right?"

"Yes." I ease my arm away from him, sharply aware that he's now blocking the doorway. "What are you doing here?"

"I wanted to talk to you before the city council meeting." He closes the door behind him. Slides the deadbolt into place. "I understand you and Mr. Alverton are on the agenda to give a statement about the potential lighthouse development."

"That's correct." I back toward the living room.

William remains in the foyer, his hands in his coat pockets, and his eyebrows drawn together in curiosity.

"My son tells me you and Mr. Alverton are now a couple, so to speak."

"Our personal lives have nothing to do with what happens to the lighthouse." My voice hardens.

"Sorry." William lifts his hands in a placating gesture. "I just hate to see a nice girl like you getting involved with a man like him."

I've lost track of the number of times I've second guessed myself over the past year. The times I thought I might be misremembering, misunderstanding, going crazy.

Then I trusted myself about Flynn. I believed my instincts about him were sound and true. I knew in the deepest part of my soul that he was good.

I was right. And that knowledge makes me trust myself again now. Something sinister radiates from William King. I need to get away from it. From him.

"I need to ask you to leave." I eye the front door. I have to get around him in order to get to it. "Flynn will be here any second."

"Eve, I realize you have little reason to trust me," William says. "But I must warn you about your lover. Given his recent opposition to the development plans, I was forced to hire a private investigator to conduct research on Mr. Alverton. I'm sorry to tell you his findings were quite grim."

"What are you talking about?"

He smiles, his eyes softening with sympathy. "He didn't tell you, did he? He hasn't told anyone."

"Told me *what*?"

He eases his cuff aside to look at his watch. "Time is running short. Why don't we drive to the council meeting together, and I'll explain everything?"

I shake my head. Nothing will make me get into this man's car.

What the fuck is he talking about? And why is he here? If he wants to scare me away from the council meeting, he's had plenty of opportunity in the past week to—

Oh shit. He's the one who tried to run me off the road.

But that happened before Flynn and I even thought about attending the meeting. Long before we were put on the agenda.

So what the hell is going on?

My heart hammers. I step toward the kitchen. I left my phone in my bedroom. I can't get to it. There's no way to escape from upstairs.

I edge closer to the kitchen. My car keys are on the counter. Near the back door. William's keen gaze follows me. He doesn't move.

"As I said, I'm expecting Flynn." I try to keep the tremble from my voice. "You need to leave."

"I realize this is upsetting to you." He steps toward the opposite entrance to the kitchen, the one facing the back door. "Given your experience with your last…gentleman, I'm sure it's painful to hear that your current lover has been keeping such unpleasant secrets from you."

I clench my jaw. From the corner of my eye, I spot my car keys.

"I don't know what you're talking about."

"Come with me, Eve." He stops in the doorway and regards me across the expanse of the kitchen. "I'll tell you everything you don't know about your lighthouse lover."

Grab the keys. Get out the back door. Run for the car.

"Eve." William takes a step toward me. "Mr. Alverton is—"

I lunge for the keys, closing my fist around them. Swerve toward the door. Snap the lock. Behind me, William curses.

I yank the door open.

Run.

I rush down the porch steps and toward the front driveway. My heels sink into the soft dirt, slowing my pace. I pray for Ghost to attack William. I round the corner of the house and head toward my car...closer...almost there...

A force slams into me from behind, knocking all the breath from my lungs. The keys fly out of my hand. I hit the ground. Pain cracks through me. He pins me down, one big hand closing around my hair and yanking my head back. I gasp, tears springing to my eyes.

"Goddammit," he snaps. "Why didn't you just come with me, you stupid bitch?"

Anger swells, firing my blood. I lash out, twisting to throw him off. He tightens his hand on my hair. For an instant, the pressure of his body lessens. I thrust my elbow back, connecting with his rib cage. He grunts. I pull my hair from his fist and turn, kicking his kneecap. A flash of silver glints.

Panting, I sweep the ground for my keys, but it's too dark to see. Panic spurs me forward. I reach the edge of the woods and start to run.

Icy snowflakes stings my face. My body goes on autopilot. Never before have I been so grateful for my coastal jogs. I sprint into the brush. My heeled pumps stick into the ground. He's behind me, the leaves crushing beneath his shoes.

Oh God...oh God...

Tremors race over my skin. My foot slips out of my right pump. I stumble, yank my other shoe off, and keep running, running, deeper into the forest. Trying to throw him off, I zigzag, darting right and left through the labyrinth of trees and brush.

Multicolored wings striking out. Fire lashing from every feather. Strength. Courage. A flame.

The harsh sound of my breath fills my ears, and my heartbeat throbs in my throat. Stones rip the soles of my feet. A branch claws at my face.

The safety of the forest is gone. Menacing shadows lurk and crawl in the underbrush. Trees grab me with skeletal arms.

I trip over an exposed root and fall, catching myself on my hands. Jarring pain shoots up my arms. My chest heaves. No sound comes from behind me, only the rustle of wind.

Did I outrun him?

Not willing to risk stopping, I haul myself upright and keep going. Tears blind me. My pulse thunders through my head, my blood. I've lost all sense of direction, but it doesn't matter. I just need to keep running, to lose myself in the forest, as far as I can—

He hits me from the side, leaping from the moonlit darkness like a wolf. Fear explodes. A scream lodges in my throat. I fall, struggling to resist his weight and strength.

"You thought I couldn't find you?" His breath is hot against my face, his eyes glinting through the black. "I grew up in these woods. I know every fucking tree and path. I know exactly how to make sure you're never found again."

Get away from him. The order flashes through my panicked brain. I lash out with my hand, seeking any vulnerable spot I can reach—his eyes, his throat. A sharp, fiery pain lances through my arm. I gasp, falling back.

He pins me to the ground, his body heavy over mine. Cold anger masks his features. Blood swells from my arm.

"Why…" I drag a breath into my aching lungs. "Why are you doing this?"

"I can't have you messing up my plans." He wraps one hand around my throat. "You should've just minded your own business."

He's choking me. My breath grows shallow. The glint of silver appears again. The chopping knife from my kitchen.

Terror floods me. He tightens his grip on my throat and brings the knife up. My vision blurs. I grab his wrist, trying to loosen his hold. The knife tip slips into the hollow of my throat. Black seeps into my consciousness, my—

His weight lifts off me with a sudden, sharp jerk. Flung to the side, he crashes against a tree with a grunt.

Flynn.

Relief billows in my chest. He casts a quick assessing glance over me. Gasping, I struggle to sit up.

"He has a...a knife," I rasp.

In the distance, a dog barks. Ghost.

William straightens, the knife still clutched in his hand. Moonlight flashes off the blade. Flynn circles him warily, his body lined with tension.

"Eve, run," he orders.

I won't run. Not again. I back toward a copse of trees, clutching my wounded arm.

Flynn lunges forward, tackling William around the waist. A shout. They both go down, slamming hard against the ground. The knife falls from William's hand. I rush forward to grab the knife just as William rolls over it. Flynn pulls back a fist, landing blows on the other man's face. Grunts fill the air.

"Sonuva..."

William brings a knee up and catches Flynn in the groin, bucking him off. Flynn doubles over. An eerie shock crushes me at the sight of him in physical pain—this man who has never seemed anything less than invulnerable.

I start toward him. William staggers to his feet, his breath heavy and eyes murderous.

Oh, shit.

The knife.

William and I spot it at the same time. I lunge for it, panting and scrambling past a briar bush. If I don't get the knife before he does—

Thorns rip my blouse, scrape the open wound on my arm.

William closes his hand around the knife. Horrified, I recoil and stumble back. He grabs my wrist, halting my retreat.

"Stop." He yanks me against him and presses the knife to my throat.

I drag air into my aching lungs. Every part of me hurts. His heavy body pushes against me from behind, chest heaving, his arm locked around my waist. The knife blade digs into my throat. Hot tears of panic spill down my cheeks.

Flynn straightens, holding his hands up, his eyes darkened to black. Our gazes meet, but there's no comfort to be found, no unspoken reassurance. We both know the bad guy sometimes wins.

"You should have listened to me." William's breath rasps against my ear. He jerks his head toward Flynn. "This fucker has been lying to all of us."

A noise rustles through the leaves. An animal or—

The moon emerges from behind a cloud. Ghost charges into the clearing, barks echoing deep into the forest.

"Ghost!" Hope swells past my fear.

The dog lunges at William, snapping and growling. William kicks him hard in the side. With a yelp, Ghost flies backward and hits the ground.

"No…" I struggle forward. The blade cuts a thin line in my skin. I stop.

Flynn advances again, eyes burning. "Let her go."

"I'll let her go," William replies coldly. "In fact, I'm walking out of here with her. Or everyone will know you murdered your twin brother."

The earth tilts.

Flynn freezes. He darts his pitch-black eyes to me.

William forces me a few steps backward. The knife digs into my throat. Cold panic ices my blood.

Murder? Twin brother?

Ghost gets to his feet and stalks William from behind Flynn.

Growls rip from his throat. William drags me backward again. My bare feet skid on dead branches and rocks.

The forest whispers and stirs. In a part of my brain that isn't dark with terror, my internal compass sharpens.

He's going deeper into the woods. He's not walking out of here with me at all.

"Eve!"

Flynn's shout reverberates through me. The sound shocks me into action. I drive my elbow into William's gut, loosening his grip for an instant. Long enough for Flynn to tackle him again shoving him away from me. He brings the other man down. They struggle.

Ghost races around them, snarling and snapping, trying to get at William.

Does he still have the knife? Muffled shouts fly from both men. Flynn gains the upper hand and slams William's head against a tree root.

William collapses. His body goes limp.

Flynn pushes to his feet, chest heaving. He staggers.

"Flynn."

I reach him the instant he slumps against a tree trunk. His face is pale and ghostly, his breath growing shallow.

"Are you…" He winces and claws at his chest.

"Flynn, what…" I put my hand on his abdomen. My palm comes away wet. "Oh my God…"

Blood spreads over his shirt. He sinks to the ground, his back against the tree.

I struggle against a fresh wave of terror. He closes his eyes. He's losing too much blood. He's going into shock. I don't know what to do.

Ghost barks, breaking me from my paralysis. Without thinking, I strip out of my skirt, wad it into a ball, and press it to the wound. His blood smears on the slip I'm still wearing.

"Flynn!" Putting my hand under his chin, I force his head up. He peels his eyes open and looks into mine. Blurry. Dim.

"Listen to me." My heart jackhammers. "I'm going for help. Keep a steady pressure against the wound, okay? Don't let up."

He nods and holds the makeshift bandage. Ghost nudges my arm.

"Stay here." I run my hand over the dog's tense body and point to William. "Guard him and watch over Flynn."

Taking a deep breath, I start through the woods again.

Trust yourself. Trust your instincts. Trust the forest.

I focus my concentration on finding my way back home. The snowfall is getting heavier, flakes collecting on the ground. My feet ache, scraped raw and bloody from pebbles and brush. I keep going, turning right, left, right again. Straight. The cold penetrates my skin.

Don't think. Don't panic. Just run.

I skid to a halt, my chest heaving. Trees and brush tangle in front of me, unpassable. A dead end. I whirl around and run back.

Ghost barks. The distant echo orients me to his location. I need to go in the opposite direction.

Wiping my eyes on my sleeve, I start running again. Right. Right. Left. My lungs burn. The moon slips out from behind a cloud again.

Old tales whisper through my fear—the princess who seeks help from the four winds to rescue her prince in the castle that lies east of the sun and west of the moon. Uncle Max weaving his stories, almost forgotten lore about the moon lifting into the sky.

It's still early evening. And if the moon rises more or less in the east…

I turn right and race toward the moon. Clamber over a fallen tree trunk, force my way through the prickly brush.

Pinpoints of light appear in the distance. The porch lamps of

Ramshackle Manor. Relief engulfs me. Tears spill down my cheeks.

I sprint the rest of the way and fling open the door. My cell phone is on the bedside table where I'd left it. I call 911 and quickly pull on a pair of jeans and sneakers.

I hurry back downstairs. By the time I reach the porch, sirens resound in the distance. When the police and paramedics arrive, I lead them back to Flynn.

Gerda's love melts the ice in Kay's heart. Beauty's devotion lifts the Beast's curse. The water of life brings Ivan back from the dead. A dragon's tea plant cures an ill child. Rapunzel's tears heal the prince's blindness. A single Firebird feather illuminates the dark.

If only.

CHAPTER 31

*T*he fluorescent lights of the emergency room cast a greenish-yellow glow, the color of an illness. Exhaustion and fear battle for supremacy inside me.

Flynn is taken into immediate surgery. An ER doctor bandages my arm and feet, and tends to my various cuts and scrapes. I give a statement to the police and answer their barrage of questions. William regains consciousness and is kept in a guarded room.

An attendant asks me to fill out a form for Flynn, but I don't know any of the information except for his name. I'm not even sure I know that anymore. Is *Flynn Alverton* his real name? Has he been lying about everything?

Murder? Twin brother?

I'm not about to believe the truth of the accusation, especially coming from William King, but part of my brain burns with recognition.

The boy Westley and his lost reflection. Flynn and "someone else" exchanging roles as Captain Hook in a school production of *Peter Pan*. His reaction to my remark about *Rumpelstiltskin*, who tears himself into two pieces at the end of the story. The photo of his grandfather and a boy who might or might not have been Flynn.

He's a twin. He *lost* his twin.

A deep, dark pain spreads through my heart.

After a three-hour surgery, he's brought into the ICU. I'm allowed to see him after he comes out of the anesthesia. Though I've been numb for hours, the instant I walk into the room, everything inside me crumples.

Flynn.

It's impossible for me to believe this is *him*. My impenetrable, stern lighthouse keeper. My mysterious crush. My hot fantasy. My beloved lover. My secret thief.

I approach the bed and brush my fingers over his arm. An oxygen mask covers his face. Tubes snake from his body to various machines. His eyes are bloodshot and heavy, his breathing still shallow.

"The doctor said you'll be okay. They're going to watch you closely for the next few days, but the knife missed any major organs. Now you need to heal."

He shifts, frustration rising to his eyes. I lift the oxygen mask covering his mouth.

"You…?" His voice is barely audible.

"I'm fine. They have William in a guarded room, and the police will get your statement when you're able to talk."

He closes his eyes. A breath escapes him, like a sigh of defeat.

The next day passes in a blur. William is taken into custody, and the knife is recovered as evidence. Flynn had found me after arriving at the house and seeing the back door open. He'd followed the tracks into the forest, where my discarded shoes had marked the path.

The city council meeting was cancelled due to "extenuating

circumstances" and will be rescheduled at a later date. My phone buzzes with calls and texts. I ignore them. I spend the day keeping vigil at Flynn's bedside before returning home to feed Ghost and try to sleep.

At night, I sit in bed with a stack of Riley Flynn books, re-reading and studying them with near obsession. I pick out the clues and riddles, make my way through the mazes as if somehow they'll lead me through the path of Flynn's heart. Through all his untold secrets.

It's all there, woven into the story and illustrations. The complicated mazes with their twists and turns, the narrow passageways and dead-ends. The single exit. The boy who never finds his reflection. The undersea worlds and icy landscapes. The mirror images.

I run my hand over the glossy picture of an underwater castle, laden with sea plants and coral. I trace the exterior of a seashell attached to the castle door. The spirals and whorls decorating the shell are so delicate and thin they might have been painted with a brush composed of a single bristle. I follow a shape that looks like the letter A.

I stop. Peer more closely at the shell. The A is attached to another swirl-like shape resembling an L.

My heart thumps. I sit back and stare at the picture. It's entirely possible I'm seeing something that isn't there. But no. That's definitely the letter L.

I fumble in the nightstand for an old magnifying glass. I turn the open pages to the light and peer at the shell through the glass.

I...am...afraid...

My breath catches. I trace the letters all the way to the tip of the shell.

I will...always be...alone.

I straighten, suddenly feeling as if I'm poised on the edge of a momentous discovery. I run the magnifying glass over the page, my eye catching lines, loops, and coils that only take the shape of letters upon very close scrutiny.

I wish I fit in.

I liked being a bully.

What I did was so wrong.

Secrets from the wall, concealed in the elaborate, whimsical illustrations of Riley Flynn's books.

When I return to the hospital in the morning, Flynn is awake. Dark circles ring his eyes, and heavy stubble coats his jaw. I stop beside the bed and touch his arm.

"Hi, Sleeping Handsome."

A faint smile twitches his mouth. He lifts a hand to take off the oxygen mask.

"How do you feel?" I ask. "Do you need a nurse?"

He shakes his head and struggles to sit up. I adjust the pillows behind him and pour him a cup of water.

"You're still here," he whispers.

"I'm still here."

His expression darkens. "Eve, I…"

"Tell me later."

"No, I…"

"Flynn." I squeeze his hand. "Later."

Though I'm delaying the inevitable, part of me doesn't want to know what he's going to say.

CHAPTER 32

*O*ver the next two days, Flynn regains his strength. One morning I enter his room to find him sitting beside the window. He turns to look at me.

A sense of foreboding crackles between us, like barbed wire slowly unrolling. Fatigue and sorrow etch his face, the lines around his eyes aging him.

My heart thumps. I close the door, pull up a chair, and sit in front of him. Our knees touch.

"His name was Riley." He swallows, his voice raspy. "He died the winter before our twenty-first birthday."

I clasp my hands together. Chills slither through my blood. "What...what happened?"

"My real name is Flynn Donovan." He slides his gaze to the wall. Tension laces his shoulders. "My father used to own the Donovan's chain of sporting goods stores. They went bankrupt a while ago. But when Riley and I were kids, the business was great. Our father was tough on us, but we had everything we wanted.

"And we were close. Inseparable. We liked the same things— Legos, astronomy, sports. The only thing I liked that he didn't was drawing and making up stories. For a while, it seemed like that was our only difference.

"We were so identical we used to pretend to be each other. Sometimes it was a joke. Sometimes we took tests for each other or just did it to trick the teacher, even our parents. The only person we couldn't fool was our grandfather. He always knew who was who. Remember that photo you found in the kitchen?"

I nod. The picture of that smiling, dark-haired boy is etched in my mind forever.

"That was Riley and our grandfather." His throat works with a swallow. "I took the picture. *If I'm you, then you're me.* He and I said that to each other all the time. Then things started to change."

"Why?"

"It was clear pretty early on that Riley was superior in a lot of ways." He stares at his hands, flexing his fingers. "He was the first born. According to our mother, he did everything first—walked, talked, read. I'd watch him and then do whatever he did. Throughout school I was stronger academically but he was more popular, athletic, outgoing, got away with stuff. Girls liked him better. Teachers liked him better. I was okay with that for a long time because he was my twin. We had the same DNA. Maybe I thought some of his magic would rub off on me.

"We both played a lot of sports and had been skating since we were five, but when we were nine, our father wanted us to focus on hockey. Riley wasn't just more talented than me—he was a natural on the ice. Amazing speed and instincts. Coaches took notice and were soon grooming him for amateurs and possibly even the pros. My father couldn't believe his luck. He'd always been a huge hockey fan, and now here was his prodigy son like a future Gretzky."

"Didn't you play too?"

"Yeah, but only because he did. I liked hockey okay, but it was more about sticking close to my brother. Not wanting part of me to go off in some other direction. I couldn't stop it, though. Neither could he. He once told me he felt like he was on a roller coaster, unable to get off or slow it down even though it was making him sick.

"Our father pushed him hard. He was up at five for weight training, on-ice practice. I went with him at first, then our father and his coach said he needed to focus on his own. He had a military-like regimen. We didn't even see much of each other anymore. When we did, he didn't want to talk to me.

"I knew he wasn't happy, that he didn't know how to handle everything. No way could he tell our father to let up either. I had no idea how to make it easier on him. For the first time, I couldn't take his place.

"That was when I stopped drawing." He spreads his hands out and studies his fingers. "I guess I felt like if my twin had to be miserable, to give up part of his life, I should too.

"I didn't make any of the youth hockey teams. Riley was the center and team captain. Our father hired a former NHL player to be his personal trainer. Agents and pro recruiters came calling. He got a lot of praise, accolades, scholarship offers. The Canadian *Globe and Mail* did a series of reports about him. He could've entered the NHL draft, but our father wanted him to go to college before turning pro. Riley and I had gone to the same schools our whole lives, so we both ended up at the University of Minnesota, my father's alma mater—Riley because of hockey, me because of my GPA.

"We lived in the same dorm room, but we had different lives. He had hockey, tons of friends, girls, fame. I studied. We argued a lot. Did stupid things. He hit on a girl I had a crush on and started dating her. I didn't remind him about homework and tests. We stopped looking out for each other.

"I did go to his games. People knew I was his twin, obviously. I connected with some guys who were into sports betting. I guess I somehow thought I could finally get some of Riley's glory. I fucking hated that I was jealous of him. But what if I could make money off him?

"I gambled a lot. Lost a crap ton of my trust fund money. Then one night, he came home drunk. He told me he was having a rough semester. His grades were terrible. If he didn't do well on his finals, he'd get suspended from the team. He begged me to take his finals for him."

Silence falls, heavy with the weight of regret and sorrow. I grip my hands together so tightly my knuckles burn white.

"Did you?" I ask quietly.

Flynn stares out the window.

"I'd placed a wager on the opposing team for his next Big Ten game. One I couldn't afford to pay off. I was already in too deep. I told Riley I'd take his finals for him if he threw the game.

"He couldn't believe what I was asking. Either way, he couldn't win. He throws the game, and they lose, or he flunks his finals and gets kicked off the team. I'd trapped him. And the worst part…" He stops, his throat working with a swallow. "The worst part was that it felt good. Finally I was the one with some power."

My breath is shallow, a strange panic brewing. "What…what did he do?"

"He played the best game of his life." A short laugh breaks from him. "Like he was a chess master, knowing exactly where everyone else on the ice would go before they even moved. They won, four to one. Riley was the hero. I was in a shitload of trouble. I paid the bookie what I could, but I had to come up with the rest of the money. Fast.

"The game had been right before the holidays, so we went back to our parents' house. They had a party to celebrate the win. I couldn't ask my father for the money. *Wouldn't* ask my grandfather. Riley didn't talk to me at all. I knew I should apologize, but he still had everything. I had less than nothing. It was my own fucking fault.

"One night I asked him to come out with me to the lake where we used to practice. Thought maybe I could talk to him there, if it was just the two of us again."

His eyes darken to burned-out charcoal. "Wooded area on the edge of town. There's a lake that people use for hockey practice and ice-skating. It was a full moon, clear sky. We walked out there, got our skates on, hit the puck around.

"We had a good time. Like we were kids again. He started going farther out on the ice and challenged me to a race. I skated to where he was, and next thing I knew, he was on me. Fists flying. Furious that I'd wanted him to throw a game, refused to take his finals, didn't care that he was flunking out. I fought back, enraged that he'd always been so much better, that he'd forgotten about me, that hockey had taken over his life.

"He was stronger. In better shape. I got in some punches, but I knew I'd never beat him, not in anything. I managed to get away from him, grabbed my stick, and skated off the ice.

"When I was taking my skates off, he started yelling. Saying he hated his life, hated school, that he'd never wanted to play pro hockey. He was sick of all the work and training, never had a chance to be normal like I was.

"And he hated me for that, hated that he couldn't have the life I'd had, one where no one paid attention to him. But he'd never had a choice, could never go against our father. Had no idea how to get off the roller coaster. He wished he was dead."

Flynn falls silent again, his gaze unfocused. The air twists, changes, pressure collecting with the force of an exploding star.

"I didn't go back. Thought he was blowing off steam, that he didn't really believe that. He had everything. I had nothing, not even him anymore. But I thought he'd come after me. I really thought…"

He pauses and clears his throat. "I thought he'd get off the ice."

A slow, black pool of dread begins to expand in my gut.

"What happened?" I whisper.

"I went home." He clenches his jaw. "My mother woke me up the next morning, asking where Riley had gone. He'd never returned. Even without knowing...I knew. I just...*knew*."

Unshed tears glitter in his eyes. "The rescuers found him a few hours later. It had been an unusually mild winter. He'd skated out to the center of the lake where the ice was thinnest. Broke through. They calculated he'd been dead for at least eight or so hours. Which meant he'd gone under not long after I'd left."

I press my hands to my chest, sorrow cracking through my bones, my heart.

"In that instant, I knew nothing worse could happen to me." Flynn wipes his eyes on his sleeve. "I'd lost half of myself. My parents were devastated. There was a massive outpouring of grief for Riley, both in Pembroke and the university.

"Because the coroner had found bruises on Riley, and I'd also taken a beating, the police launched an investigation. News reports speculated about whether I'd killed him. It was a lurid, sensational story. *Hockey phenom murdered by his jealous twin.*

"I was terrified something would come out about my betting, so I told my father. He paid off my debt and said I was the one who should have died. My mother locked herself in the house and drank.

"My grandfather told me it wasn't my fault, but I couldn't even talk to him. It *was* my fault. Every part of it. He wouldn't have died if it hadn't been for me."

Pain slices through me. "What did you tell the police?"

"A version of the truth. I said we had a fight because I'd always been jealous of his success, but I walked away. I repeated that same story over and over again. Everyone had an opinion about what had happened, but there were no witnesses, no evidence. The investigation came to a dead-end. But the speculation never stopped. Our family was destroyed."

He rises slowly to his feet and goes to the window. "My mother had a breakdown. My father lost investors, shareholders.

I knew I had to leave. So after the investigation closed, I did two things. I legally changed my last name so the internet wouldn't shadow me.

"And I left home, took off traveling. I was on the road for close to three years. Hitchhiked across the country, worked on a fishing boat, in warehouses and factories, whatever I could find. Thought about Riley all the time. I had nightmares about being stuck in a maze, unable to find my way out.

"That was when I started the first *Mirror Mirror* book, only I didn't have the idea of a book in mind. It wasn't until I met Max that I even considered publishing. But writing about Westley and Tugg became a kind of catharsis, I guess. At first I hated profiting from it, but I was able to channel the money into some good things. A hockey scholarship in his name, funding local leagues, helping my parents. Not that any of that made up for what I did. Or didn't do."

He continues looking outside, his shoulders slumped. Silence fills the room, thick and heavy with pain. The puzzle of Flynn snaps together in my mind, a picture of a man with sharp missing pieces and an irreparably shattered heart.

I stand and walk to him, resting my hands on his arms. I press my forehead between his shoulder blades. Cold infuses my bones, settles in my throat, my soul.

I'm so sorry.

I don't say the words, afraid they'll sound insipid and useless. There is nothing I can say to change anything or make it easier for him to bear. He hasn't isolated himself in the lighthouse for all these years just to work. He's been punishing himself for having challenged and then walked away from his own brother. Not having been there to save him. Rehashing everything he should have done differently.

"Did you ever go back?" I ask.

"A couple of times. Once when my grandfather got sick and passed away. Then later because I felt like I owed it to my parents. They didn't much care. My father ended up filing for bankruptcy. At least I've been able to help them financially. But everything was destroyed long before that."

Because I made a mistake. Because I walked away.

He doesn't say that last part, but he doesn't have to. I know all about making mistakes.

He turns, reaching out to touch my hair, his mouth tightening with regret. "I'm sorry, Eve. I wish I could have stayed away from you."

My throat aches. "I have my own mind and heart. It wasn't just you. And you did warn me away, remember? I chose not to listen."

"I should…" He swallows, his voice cracking. "I shouldn't have come after you that day. But you…it's so stupid, but you were like a dream come to living, breathing life. I *couldn't* stay away from you. I'd been thinking about you ever since Max showed me that picture of you in the forest. Maybe I even fell in love with you then."

A tight, painful longing wraps around my heart. "Why…why didn't you tell me?"

He brings his hands to the sides of my face. Tears dampen his eyes, turning his eyelashes black and spiky, but tenderness gleams beneath his despair.

"I meant it when I said I have nothing to offer you. I've kept Riley a secret all this time because I don't want it all to come to the surface again. And if people found out that Riley Flynn the author is the same Flynn Donovan who was investigated in the death of his brother…I can't imagine the shitstorm that would follow. I don't know how much William King knows or how he found out, but I didn't ever want to risk people digging into the story again. I don't want Riley Flynn stained by Flynn Donovan."

"You're not…" My breath hitches painfully. "You're not a stain, Flynn. You're not a troll, like that picture you drew. You don't need to hide away from the world anymore. You've punished yourself enough."

He slides his hand over my cheek.

"I love you, Eve," he says roughly. "You're everything I'm not. Remember that quote Max gave me from *The Butterfly*? Being with you has already given me everything I need to *live*. Sunshine. Freedom." He strokes his thumb across my lower lip, the light in his eyes softening. "And you're my little flower to love."

My tears spill over. "I love you too. I think I've loved you since the day you said my name. Certainly since the day you smelled my hair."

A faint smile tugs at his mouth but doesn't reach his eyes. He drops his hand away from me.

"How can you love me knowing I was keeping secrets from you all this time?" he asks. "That I did what I did to my own brother? That I was lying?"

"You weren't lying. I was with a man who lied, cheated, deceived, manipulated. I *know* what that's like. His secrets were evil and destructive. Yours are not. There's a world of difference between keeping secrets to hurt people and keeping secrets to protect them. You only ever wanted to protect. Your parents, Riley, your grandfather. Yourself. Me. Even the town of Castille. But your secret is the *truth*."

He twists his mouth. "No one wants that kind of truth. Do you know the ending of *The Butterfly*? The butterfly ends up pinned to a mounting board."

"He also wants to marry a flower who's dainty, delicate, and useful in the kitchen, so I think we can take what we want out of that story."

A hoarse chuckle breaks out of him. He scrubs his sleeve over his eyes.

I rest my palm on his chest. His heart beats weaker now owing to his physical trauma, but still as steady as ever.

"It's at the end when the butterfly realizes what it means to live," I remind him. "But by then it's too late. He regrets missing his chance. And it's time for you to stop punishing yourself. To live, you also need to be out in the world. You need to let people in."

He moves back to the chair, his shoulders hunched. "I don't know how."

"Yes, you do. You've done it with me. And you've proven it through the *Mirror Mirror* books, through Westley and Tugg's adventures. Their determination, courage, love for each other. The friends they make and battles they fight. The things they lose and find again. Their homecoming."

I sit in front of him again, my heart pounding and my soul filling with what I now know is destiny. I didn't run away to Castille. I wasn't exiled. I was meant to come here, drawn by the lantern glow at the top of the lighthouse. The light that pulled me home.

"Flynn." I rest my hands on his thighs and lean forward. "We can do this together. I've made terrible mistakes too. Everyone knows about them, but I'm still here. More capable of loving you than ever because I've been through enough darkness to recognize true light. And whatever William King knows or doesn't know…it's up to you to tell the truth. *Your* truth. And when you do, I'll be there with you."

"God, Eve." He chokes out another laugh and covers my hands with his. "You're more than I could have imagined *Fiamma* to be. I love you so damned much."

"Then prove it. Don't deny me *you*."

He gazes at me for a moment. "I can't deny you anything. I don't want to." He smiles faintly. "See? I'm telling you all my secrets now."

"What about the secrets in the Riley Flynn books?" I turn my palms face up so I can link my fingers with his. "I found them hidden in the mazes and illustrations. Are they all from the wall?"

"Yeah." He shrugs, slightly abashed. "I don't know why I started doing that. The Forestry Department told me to clean the wall regularly and discard the secrets, but part of me felt like that was wrong. I guess putting them in my books was my way of keeping everyone else's secrets. Reminding myself that we all have them hidden away."

"Not you and me." I press my forehead against his. "Not anymore. No matter what happens next."

And neither of us has any idea what that will be.

CHAPTER 33

"*E*xcuse me."

Flynn and I look up from the crossword puzzle we're working on. Jeremy King stands at the hospital room door, his hands shoved into his pockets and his posture lined with wariness.

Beside me, Flynn tenses. In the three days he's been in the hospital, he's received well wishes from several residents, including Allegra King, but Jeremy is his first visitor.

I rest my hand on Flynn's arm, mindful of the fact that he still has a long way to go in his recovery.

"What do you want, Jeremy?" I ask.

"Just to talk to you." He steps into the room, putting his hands up. "I swear. And to apologize for...well, you know."

I nod toward a seat at the table. "Sit down."

He pulls out a chair, glancing at Flynn. "How're you feeling?"

"I'll be fine."

"Good." Jeremy clears his throat, a sudden nervousness radiating from him. "So I wanted you both to know I had nothing to do with...uh, what my father did. King Financial has been struggling badly in the past few years, and he's lost a lot of money.

"I'd asked him a while back if I could spearhead the lighthouse sale… figured it would be good for my own career…and he agreed. When you…" he nods at Flynn, "…started making noise about preventing the sale, Dad hired an investigator to find out what you were hiding."

"Wait a minute." I hold up a hand. William had told me about the investigator when he'd come to my house, and now a thought strikes me. "Was this investigator a heavy-set guy? Bald, about six feet tall?"

"Uh, I think so," Jeremy says. "Why?"

Disgust rises to my throat. So I wasn't being paranoid when I saw that man several times in town. My instincts were right yet again.

"And this investigator dredged up my past." Flynn's voice is flat and cold.

"Quite a story too," Jeremy remarks. "Obviously my father intended to use the information to get you to change your mind."

"You mean blackmail him," I correct sharply.

"Okay, whatever." Jeremy fidgets, twisting his fingers together. "The point is that the PI found out about the suspicious death of your brother. It's pretty clear you've wanted to keep that a secret. Fine. That's why I've come to make you an offer."

Flynn narrows his eyes. "What kind of offer?"

"You know my father has done a lot for this town," Jeremy says. "He's always been well-respected around here. You can imagine that both my mother and I really don't want to see his legacy ruined over this."

Anger lances through Flynn's body. "*This* was the fact that he tried to kill Eve. I could give a shit about his fucking legacy."

"Look, I get it, okay?" Jeremy shifts his gaze to me, a plea darkening his eyes. "But something happened to drive him to it. I found out he's a shareholder in the Oracle Corporation, which is why he was pushing their agenda. He could've made fortune if they'd signed the development contract. But risking it by attacking you? I don't get it. Maybe he's having some kind of mental breakdown."

"And that's an excuse?" I glare at him.

"I'm not here to argue about why he did what he did," Jeremy says. "I'm here to ask if we could work together on this."

"On *what?*" Flynn asks.

"Look, you don't want anyone to know about what happened to your brother, right?" Jeremy spreads his hands out, tension stiffening his shoulders. "And I'd rather this stuff about my father be kept on the down low as much as possible. So how about we make a deal? I'll do what I can to bury the information the PI dug up, if you'll agree to issue a statement about this whole incident being a mutual fight, or even a simple assault charge. We can spin the story so it looks like a difference of opinion that took a wrong turn."

Stunned, I don't know whether to laugh or call security to have him escorted out. "Are you kidding me?"

"It's beneficial to all of us," Jeremy insists. "King Financial isn't completely wrecked, our family reputation stays more or less intact, and Alverton's *murder* investigation stays a secret. Honestly, what choice do you have?"

Flynn and I exchange glances. Understanding passes between us like the current beneath a river's surface, steady and strong.

"King." Flynn points at the door. "Get the hell out of my room."

Jeremy blinks. "You're serious? You think people around here are going to leave you alone when they find out what you've been hiding?"

Flynn rises to his feet, his height and breadth dominating the other man. "I said, *get out.*"

"Okay, okay." Jeremy pushes his chair back. "But if you know what's good for you, you'll think about it. Hard."

He stalks out of the room. Flynn sits back down, still tense with suppressed anger. I nudge his attention back to the crossword, not wanting any additional stress to impact his recovery. Though we return to the puzzle, unease simmers like a cloud in the wake of Jeremy's visit.

It still doesn't make complete sense, either to me and Flynn or the police. William had apparently been digging into Flynn's history for ammunition to block him from opposing the lighthouse sale. His interest in the Oracle Corporation is certainly a strong motive. As of now, William is only speaking through his lawyer and hasn't yet revealed anything else.

But if Flynn was the one he wanted to stop, why did he come after me?

"I cannot believe this." My mother's shrill voice pierces me from clear across the country.

I stare out the front windshield of my car. The hospital parking lot is filled with vehicles, and the sky is the color of metal.

I'd called Juliette right after the attack in the forest to assure her I was all right before she heard the news reports. She'd been both shaken and relieved. But now that she's had a few days to process the events, she's back on the warpath.

So am I.

"What is wrong with you, Eve?" she snaps.

"Nothing." I grip my cell phone and take a deep breath. "In fact, everything is very *right* with me. Probably for the first time in my life."

"Oh my God. I read the reports. It's that man from the lighthouse, isn't it? You've gotten yourself involved with another scumbag who's using and manipulating you. He's the one who made you cancel your Santa Clara interview. Can you really be that stupid? Have you learned nothing?"

"I've learned everything," I reply, my voice cool though I'm trying not to shake. "And Flynn had nothing to do with my interview cancellation. I've decided to take time off and work on independent study projects before looking for a permanent position. There are some other local colleges in towns around Castille where I might teach interim classes, but I have a new focus now."

"Spreading your legs?" Juliette snaps. "He's making you do this, isn't he? And you're stupid enough to let him."

"He's not *making* me do anything. It's my decision."

"How do you expect to earn a living? To rebuild your career?"

"I'll find a way."

"You are as foolish and impractical as your uncle was. I should never have let you associate with him."

She goes on, her voice hard. I stop listening. I peer through the windshield at the hospital, counting up to the fifth floor windows. Though I can't see him, I know Flynn is standing at the third window from the right. Watching me. Waiting.

"...this kind of idiocy, and if you think—"

"Mother," I interrupt. "It's time for you to fuck the hell off."

I end the call. Though I'm still shaking, a sudden laugh breaks out of me. I picture her standing there, holding the phone, her eyes wide with shock and her mouth agape.

Just let her try and contact me again. If she does so with graciousness and the effort to make amends—not likely, but also not impossible—then I'll meet her halfway. If not, I have my life to live.

And my love to love.

Dropping my phone into my purse, I walk into the hospital and take the elevator to Flynn's room. He turns from the window to smile at me, his eyes crinkling at the corners. Though he's still pale and somewhat weak, the light inside him is stronger than ever. My heart fills to bursting.

"Hi," he says.

"Look at you, Lighthouse Guy." I slide my gaze admiringly

over his charcoal-gray trousers and navy shirt. "I thought you'd wear the jeans and ratty old T-shirt I packed for you."

"And miss the chance to impress the woman I love?" He shakes his head and holds out his arms. "No way."

I step right into them, mindful of the bandage still covering his wound. We exchange a kiss that deepens in intensity before a loud *"Ahem"* breaks us apart.

"You can just wait until later for that," the nurse says cheerfully, pushing a wheelchair into the room. "You ready to go home, Mr. Alverton?"

"Actually, it's Donovan." Flynn squeezes my hand. "Flynn Donovan. And yes. I'm ready."

CHAPTER 34

Two days after Flynn's return from the hospital, he and I sit in his truck across the street from city hall. Snowflakes swirl through the air and collect on the windshield. The building's windows glow with light in the darkness of evening. Dozens of people walk up the steps to the atrium.

Tense silence fills the space between us. His hands are fisted on the steering wheel. My chest is a tangle of nerves. I feel his gaze on my profile, potent as a touch.

Turning, I meet his eyes. Beneath the hard set of his features, tenderness gleams. A tenderness reserved for me alone.

"I like the way you smell." His voice is a deep, warm rumble.

I manage to smile. "I figured that out a while ago when you ordered me to wear my apple-lavender body lotion to work." I lean across the seat and kiss him. "But thanks for finally admitting it."

He wraps his big hand around my nape, holding me against him. The kiss strengthens my courage. I rest my palm on his chest. His heart beats strong and steady, the vibration echoing into my blood. Never will I tire of feeling and listening to his heart.

I remember the day I felt like I could do anything if he were at my side. Now I know I can.

We get out of the truck and walk toward the city hall. Though we're not even touching each other, people glance our way as we approach the steps. Thanks to both Jeremy and the news reports, everyone has heard about Flynn Donovan and his twin.

A crowd circulates in the atrium, people slowly heading through the open doors of the council chambers. Rows of chairs are set up in front of the dais, where the twelve councilmembers sit. Most of the seats are already taken, and people stand alongside the walls.

I catch sight of Carol from Jabberwocky, seated beside her son Alex and a tall, lanky man who must be her husband. Jeremy King is in the front row, his blond head bent as he listens to something the woman beside him is saying.

Flynn and I stop behind the last row of seats. A palpable curiosity goes through the room. Some residents twist around to look at us. I grasp Flynn's hand and curl my fingers around his.

There are a thousand reasons for so much curiosity and interest. The mystery of Flynn and revelation about his past, the endless gossip and stories about me, the lighthouse conflict, the fight, the Kings.

The townspeople now know Flynn's true story. The question is—*will they forgive him for it?*

A gavel thumps. The chatter dies down. People turn to face the dais.

"While we're here to discuss the issue of the lighthouse development and zoning laws," Mayor Richards, a thin man with a bird-like face, leans toward his microphone, "we know you're all interested in hearing what certain speakers have to say. So we'll get to them first. Mr. Jeremy King."

The crowd shifts with eager anticipation. As Jeremy approaches the microphone, an odd understanding rises in me. I know what it's like to want to desperately please a parent and have them fail you. And though my mother is now estranged from me in a different way than William is from Jeremy, we've both effectively lost a parent.

"As I struggle to process recent events…" Jeremy stands at the microphone and unfolds a sheet of paper, "I would like to remind the residents of Castille of the public service my father has done for this town in his three terms as mayor. His reelections speak to his popularity and dedication to the well-being of Castille."

He pauses and clears his throat. "His efforts to build a development on the acres of land where the Castille Lighthouse sits were, in fact, instigated by a desire to improve Castille's failing economy. To that end, he set me to the task of fulfilling the project, which I, too, believed in. Unfortunately, I was unaware of my father's connections to the Oracle Development Corporation as a major shareholder. Had I known, I never would have advocated on Oracle's behalf. And I sincerely apologize for any part I have played in my father's deception.

"But this doesn't change the fact that I still believe a coastal development is the best thing we can do for our town. While I recognize my need to step back from the situation and regroup, I would like to ask the residents not to discount the idea for the future."

Most of the audience applauds, though there's a smattering of boos. The mayor silences them with a slam of his gavel.

"Thank you, Mr. King." He peers at the agenda. "Mr. Flynn Alverton."

Chatter, edged with excitement, rises. People turn and crane their necks to look at us.

My stomach tightens. Our plan is that Flynn will speak first before I join him and we advocate for the lighthouse preservation together.

He squeezes my hand, then walks to the front of the room. Whispers follow in his wake—people staring at him as if they've never seen him before, women lifting their eyebrows in admiration, curiosity thick in the air.

Flynn stops at the microphone and faces the crowd. And just like that, my nervousness slips away, replaced by a pride so great it swells in my chest like a balloon.

Confronting your secrets is one thing. *Owning* them in front of an entire town is something else altogether.

He takes hold of the mic. He looks magnificent in a charcoal-gray tailored suit with a blue-and-gray striped tie, his thick dark hair shining under the lights.

"Thank you for giving me the chance to speak," he says into the mic. "All of you know me as Flynn Alverton. Or more accurately, the weird guy up at the lighthouse."

A few chuckles spread over the crowd.

"I owe this town and residents more than I can express," Flynn continues. "More than anyone knows. You've allowed me to live here, despite the fact that no one knew much about me. You allowed me privacy and isolation. The Forestry Department gave me a job. You treated me with respect, and if you gossiped about me behind my back, I did nothing to counteract the rumors. I could certainly understand the reasons for them.

"But I haven't lived in the lighthouse all these years because I *wanted* to be the local recluse. The fact is, I felt like I had to be. I didn't deserve to live in the same world as everyone else. Because I never stopped thinking my brother's death was my fault. I never will stop thinking that."

He pauses. Silence fills the room. My heart pounds.

"I'll tell you the facts as I recall them," he says. "Given all that's happened, I owe it to you. This will be my final statement about what happened."

His voice breaks a few times as he recounts the events—his brother's hockey success, he and Riley alone on an isolated lake, the fight, the investigation, the police reports, the public scrutiny leading to the bankruptcy of the family business.

When he's finished, not a rustle breaks the thick silence.

Grief mixes with my pride in him. Every day, he must wonder what his life would be like if his twin had lived.

"When Riley and I were kids…" his voice cracks again, "…every summer for a month, our grandfather would bring us to a picturesque little town on the coast of Maine."

I blink. Surprised murmurs spread through the crowd.

"The town was called Castille." Flynn stops for a second, his eyes glittering. "We had the greatest time of our lives here. And we were best friends, my brother and I. Pop…that was our grandfather…took us fishing, boating, swimming. We explored tide pools and went lobstering. We rented a cottage at the Watercress Inn and had ice cream every day at Peddler's over on Dandelion Street. We saw exhibits at the museum and went to story-time at the library. We biked through the woods and roasted marshmallows over campfires. We spent countless hours at the lighthouse. Put dozens of secrets in the wall, along the lines of *Riley has a crush on Maggie McGinty* and *My brother is a boogerhead*."

Laughter ripples over the audience. My vision blurs with tears.

"Pop took us traveling up and down the coast a few times, but we always came back to Castille," Flynn continues. "And after…"

He stops again and pulls in a heavy breath.

"After Riley died and the investigation was over, I…I guess I ran away. Tried to escape. I traveled aimlessly for about three years, hitchhiking, working odd jobs. Then one day I found myself back in Castille. Figured I'd stay for a week or two and then move on.

"But this…this town had a hold on me. Like a spell. The more time passed, the less I wanted to leave. Then I met a man named Max Dearborne who proved to me that fairy godfathers really do exist."

Well, that does it. My tears spill over. I fumble in my purse for the handkerchief Flynn had given me a lifetime ago. I wipe my eyes, not sure my heart can contain so many emotions.

"And *you* all..." Flynn spreads out a hand to encompass the entire town. "No matter how weird you thought I was or what you suspected I was hiding, you never made me feel like I was unwanted here. Instead you let me live quietly in the one place where I was closest to my brother. For that, I thank you."

A second of silence is broken by a sudden rolling wave of applause that catches Flynn off guard. He steps back, his gaze searching.

Across the expanse of the audience, our eyes meet. A warm current flows between us, one of strength, promise, and love.

"Quiet, please." The mayor raps the gavel. "Continue please, Mr. Alverton."

"Thank you. I swear I'm almost finished." He approaches the mic again. "It's past time for me to give something back to Castille. In addition to working for the Forestry Department, I have a second career as an author and illustrator. I've written several picture books under the name Riley Flynn."

Another heartbeat of silence. Then an uproar—voices rising, gasps of shock, a few shouts, people getting to their feet.

Alarm flickers through me. Flynn and I had both expected a reaction, even one of potential anger that he's been hiding his author identity, but I suddenly can't tell if the residents are upset or just surprised.

"Quiet!" The mayor hammers the gavel again. "Please, everyone, sit *down*."

"Why would you hide that from us?" calls a woman from a middle row.

"It wasn't our business!" Alex responds, shooting her a mild glower.

Flynn holds up his hands. "There's a reason I'm telling you now. I know the economy has been on a downslide, and that the

lighthouse development agenda is still very much on the table.
So I—"

The chamber doors open. A cold wind sweeps through the
room. Papers flutter. People turn to scowl at whomever is interrupting.

Allegra King enters, followed by two men in suits carrying
leather briefcases. Imperious as a queen in a fitted navy dress
and pearls, she stops and casts her assessing gaze over the
crowd.

When her eyes meet mine, she winks.

What in the...

Allegra strides down the center aisle to where Flynn is standing. Every eye in the room locks onto her. Jeremy stands, trying
to catch her attention. She ignores him and extends both hands
to Flynn.

He takes them, as surprised as everyone else to see the conva-
lescing first lady of Castille not only here, but looking as strong
and lovely as she does.

She gives Flynn a warm smile of affection and says something
the mic doesn't pick up. He responds and leans in to brush his
lips across her cheek. Then Allegra turns and takes hold of the
microphone. The two men stand off to the side, holding their
briefcases like shields.

"Good evening, everyone," Allegra says. "I am Allegra King. I
apologize for having been away from town for so long. I assure
you that changes now."

A number of people applaud. A man in the back row whistles.

"Thank you." She sweeps her gaze over the room again. "I'm
here to address this ridiculous talk about selling the lighthouse
property, which is held within a trust I created long ago. While I
appreciate my son's efforts on behalf of Castille, I assure you all
there will be no development...certainly not a hotel or golf
course...anywhere on the coastal land currently leased by the
Forestry Department."

The audience responds with a mixture of loud applause and a few boos. Allegra holds up her hand for quiet.

"In 1973, the Castille Lighthouse was taken out of commission," she explains, "and purchased by my family. For many years, the lighthouse and fifteen acres of land were owned outright by my father. Then I married William King. While I do not wish to discuss the personal details of our marriage, I will say we had our ups and downs."

She clears her throat. "Clearly, my husband and I are currently in the midst of a *down*. Or rather, an *end* as the case may be."

People rustle with discomfort and wariness.

"Through our marriage," Allegra continues, "William and I shared common ground in our love for Castille and public service. However, I was always aware of his money-hungry streak.

"And I've known for years he's had his eye on profiting from the lighthouse. I also knew he would convince my son to do the same. Therefore, I had the lighthouse and land protected by the creation of a very specific trust, the terms of which William discovered only recently. Neither my husband nor my son are beneficiaries of this trust."

Murmurs rise, people turning to each other and whispering. Jeremy gets to his feet.

"It's really quite simple," Allegra says. "Jeremy, sit down. The trustee was a person who I knew would keep the land and lighthouse as they are...an untouched testament to the beauty of this town. Jeremy, *sit down*."

"So who will get the lighthouse?" asks the mayor.

"It's not who *will* get it, Tom." Allegra extends her hand to one of the men who'd arrived with her. He steps forward and hands her a sheaf of papers. "It's who *owns* it now. The lighthouse and land are held within the Max Dearborne Trust, of which Max Dearborne was the sole trustee."

Disbelief falls over me. Another ripple of shock courses through the room.

"Mr. Dearborne was a dear friend of mine," Allegra continues, riffling through the papers. "I trusted him implicitly to protect the trust assets, as he did until his death. To my regret, and owing to my own health struggles as well as the rather...overprotective actions of my husband and son"—she eyes Jeremy pointedly —"I've only just become aware of Mr. Dearborne's untimely demise. And I would like to formally announce that the Max Dearborne Trust had one beneficiary, who is now legally entitled to the entire property."

She pauses, as if for effect. The crowd shifts impatiently. Tension and curiosity flare. My nerves tighten like overstrung wires.

"That beneficiary..." Across the room, Allegra's gaze locks on to mine, "...is Ms. Eve Perrin."

$\mathcal{T}$he door to the mayor's private office closes, blocking out the commotion in the council chambers. I sink into a chair in front of the desk, my knees shaking.

A whooshing noise fills my ears, but I can't tell if it's from the noise outside or the shock wave still ricocheting through me. Flynn stands at my side, his hand secure on my shoulder.

"Please give me a moment alone with Eve and Flynn." Allegra turns to the two lawyers and the mayor, who have followed her into the office. "Everything will be explained in due course."

The three men return to the chambers. Allegra sits in the chair beside me and touches my arm. "I'm sorry to have shocked you, but I needed to make the announcement publicly so everyone would know. That's why the lawyers are here as well. I assure you it's all legally sound."

"So your husband and son didn't know?" Flynn tightens his hand on my shoulder.

"Jeremy had no idea." She shakes her head, regret shining in her eyes. "He's always been so under his father's thumb, so anxious to please him. If he'd been more independent-minded, I might have explained the situation to him years ago. And of course I hadn't told my husband. He'd have been furious, not to mention he was always jealous of Max.

"William had known the lighthouse belonged to my family, but he didn't have anything to do with it because of the long-term lease agreement we had with the Forestry Department. He started asking more about it when King Financial got into trouble. Bad investments and a stock market crash…well, he lost more than I even realized. And the lease renewal date was approaching, so it was a perfect time for William to push for development.

"He was conveniently having an affair with an assistant at the law office, which is how he got a hold of the Max Dearborne Trust. This was all during the time I was in the hospital." Her expression dims. "At one point, I was ill enough that he obtained power of attorney over my estate. He'd wanted to use it to sell the property. Even after I recovered, he did an excellent job putting up a wall between me and the world. I'd thought at the time he was being overprotective, but now I realize he wanted to keep me ignorant."

"Of what he was doing?" Flynn asks.

"Yes. And the fact that he'd found the Dearborne Trust. One clause states that in the event of Eve's death, the lighthouse goes to her heirs…with the exclusion of one Juliette Perrin. And in the absence of heirs, the property reverts to the King family."

Silence falls. The pieces of the puzzle turn and fit slowly into place. If I were out of the picture, William would have complete control of the lighthouse. And he'd intended to use Flynn's history to get to both of us.

I feel Allegra's somber gaze on me.

"Do you understand?" she asks. "I'd have told you sooner, but I didn't know Max had died. Neither did William, not until you came to Castille. As for his extreme actions…once he discovered Max was gone, you were the only person standing in his way."

I close my eyes, pinching the bridge of my nose. The only

thing keeping me steady is the weight of Flynn's hand on my shoulder.

"Why didn't Max ever tell me?" I ask.

"He never wanted to be trustee," Allegra explains. "But he was the one person I knew would keep the assets safe and secure. He did exactly that. As I know you will as well."

I open my eyes. She's watching me with warmth and a hint of concern.

"I didn't tell you when I visited you at the lighthouse because after William's attempted takeover of my estate, I needed to ensure the legalities were still in place," she explains. "And they are. The lighthouse belongs to you."

"I can't…I can't accept this," I stammer.

"Of course you can." She pats my arm. "As the settlor of the trust, I also have the power to revoke it. I intend to use that power. Aside from wanting the land protected, I've no interest in it. I don't believe Jeremy will do anything good with it either.

"So enough of this nonsense. You can choose to renew the Forestry Department's lease, or you can find a way to have it all put on one of those national registries. I also suggest you create your own trust to ensure its protection for future heirs."

She glances meaningfully from me to Flynn and rises to her feet.

"Now for heaven's sake, let's bring this meeting to an end and get ourselves a good stiff drink. Flynn, you can buy the first round."

Over the next few days, the frenzy of excitement and shock rises, then lessens to rippling waves. The lighthouse terrace bustles with people eager to get a glimpse of Castille's most famous resident. Reporters show up with cameras to try and get a statement from Flynn, but they leave after he gives his only interview to the local high-school newspaper—thereby ending the hope of a national scoop.

I come to the realization that my ownership of the lighthouse property is a way to keep things as they are. The Forestry Department can continue to lease the land, preserving it for public enjoyment and conservation, and I make plans to submit it for national registry protection.

A week after the meeting, I stand at the glass of the lighthouse tower, peering down at the tourists roaming the terrace and the secrets wall. Waves break and crash against the rocks at the base of the cliffs.

"It's time to leave."

I turn as Flynn enters, unbearably beautiful in faded jeans and a flannel shirt that stretches over his broad chest. Though he still moves with care, he's well on the road to a full recovery.

"Leave for where?" I ask.

"Leave here."

He indicates the lighthouse and approaches, filling the space in front of me, the breadth of his shoulders blocking my vision of everything except him. He slides his arms around my waist. His delicious scent tickles my nose. A spell washes over me, lulling me into a place of warmth and safety.

"I've been here long enough," he says. "I don't want to go from being the strange guy in the lighthouse to the strange famous author in the lighthouse."

"So where do you want to go?" I settle my lower body against his, my blood heating.

"I heard there's a rundown old house over on Sparrow Lane." He twists a lock of my hair around his finger, his gaze tender. "A place where a guy might earn his keep by doing some much-needed renovation work."

"Really?" My heart begins lifting upward into the clouds. "You want to come live with me?"

"Live with you." Flynn kisses my cheek. "Love with you." He kisses my other cheek. "If you'll have me."

"Of course." I smile, happiness tumbling through me. "That's a wonderful plan. But what will we do with the lighthouse?"

"We'll think of something together."

He eases away from me and goes to his cluttered desk, the corkboard beside it covered with drawings of mazes, elaborate landscapes, and sketches of me, of *Fiamma*, in dozens of different guises. He shuffles through the drawings. A crease appears between his eyebrows.

"When Riley died, I lost half of myself," he says. "I thought I'd never get it back. That's why Westley never finds his reflection. I'd never find mine again either."

"I know."

"Then a woman named Eve walked into my life." He picks up a drawing and approaches me again. "And I discovered that she was a mirror, one who reflected everything good in the world, who forced me to confront the person I was and the person I should be. A woman who eased her way right into my heart and filled the empty half of me. The *whole* of me."

He holds up the drawing. It's a self-portrait, a profile of his strong features and black hair, his gray eyes concentrated on a round mirror. On the other side of the glass is a drawing of me—not Fiamma, not a firebird, not a nymph.

Just me, wearing yoga pants and a sweater, seated cross-legged amidst stacks of fairy tale books, my reddish hair loose around my shoulders. And in the sky above me, the air around me…flowers bursting into life, flourishing plants, whirling stars like Van Gogh's *Starry Night*. Whimsical teapots, a dog named Ghost, Ramshackle Manor lit up in the woods like a fairy castle.

"I don't see emptiness in the mirror anymore," Flynn says. "Because I know you're right there, waiting for me on the other side."

"Oh my God." With my sleeve, I wipe the tears spilling from

my eyes. "I'm losing track of all the poetic things you've said to me."

"I never thought I'd have a happy ending, Eve." He sets the drawing down and rests his palm against the side of my neck, a sense of wonder rising to his eyes. "Never believed in them. But you...you make everything possible. I love you."

"I love you, Flynn." I press my hand to his cheek. "Because of you, I believe in fairy tales again."

He smiles his beautiful smile, his gray eyes glowing from within. A powerful, sweet energy courses between us, like a dozen tiny comets. He puts his hand under my chin, angling my face. A thousand heartbeats pass in the instant before he lowers his mouth to mine.

Sensations explode inside me, fireworks streaming colors through my veins. He strokes his lips gently over mine at first, then with increasing pressure, urging me to open my mouth. I curl my hands around his arms, part my lips, let him inside.

The kiss softens me like cotton candy, marshmallows, melting candlewax. I wrap my arms around his shoulders, drinking in the taste and feel of him. He urges me closer, grasping my hips, fitting my body against his. All the parts of the world begin turning smoothly in place like clockwork.

We fall into each other so easily, like a slippage of time. I'm flooded with gratitude and hope—for him, for us, for all that is to come. Even if he doesn't see it yet, he's already done an immense amount of good with his stories. He still has so much to give.

The world needs more proof that we can escape complicated mazes, reach the other side of an impenetrable forest, defeat monsters and ogres. We need to know that puzzles can be solved, hidden things can be found, and that riddles have answers.

We need the courage and faith of a ten-year-old child, the unbreakable bond between old friends, the belief in fairy godparents. We need to find our way home, even when *home* is not where we expected it to be. We need to be reminded that a loyal dog will stay by your side through the most difficult of journeys. We need more admissions of love.

And we need to know that a happy ending is more than a kiss, an embrace, a promise. It's loving the person who will struggle through the darkness with you, who believes in your strength, who sees the light you thought had been extinguished. It's conquering fears, making sacrifices, finding both peace and wild storms in your togetherness.

If you have all of that, there is no ending after all. Only an infinite thread of happy beginnings.

EPILOGUE

Six months later

The frozen Maine winter quiets the storm. Flynn and I move out of the lighthouse and into Ramshackle Manor, where Ghost commandeers both a chair in front of the fireplace and much of Flynn's attention. We make plans for repairs and an eventual renovation that will honor both the architecture and heritage of the house.

The Forestry Department renews their property lease, allocating a greater budget for care and maintenance. William King is sentenced to ten years in prison, though the town's disgust with him does not transfer to either Allegra or Jeremy. Nevertheless, Jeremy leaves Castille for the first time in his life, taking a job with a Philadelphia finance company.

The Jabberwocky Bookstore hosts Riley Flynn's first-ever book signing, which lasts all day with throngs of people flocking in from neighboring towns to meet the famous, once-reclusive author. Flynn's agent calls with news about movie rights offers for both the *Mirror Mirror* books and the upcoming *Fiamma*, scheduled for publication next fall.

We visit Allegra King regularly—or at least, when she's available given her busy schedule. Several months ago, she accepted the chairperson position of the new Castille Arts Center committee.

She's taken full charge of the development of the center, which will be built on the site of an abandoned paper mill factory just outside of town. With plans for two theaters as well as art galleries, studios, classrooms, and rehearsal space, the Arts Center is intended to both showcase and inspire creativity in all forms.

Only Allegra knows the founding money for the Castille Arts Center is coming from the sale of Riley Flynn's original artwork, which I've been marketing through both New York galleries and online sites. Though we still need to do a great deal of fundraising before the Arts Center can come to life, Flynn's drawings and paintings are selling for more than either of us expected. With the profits, the Arts Center planning is already ahead of schedule.

I stay in touch with Graham, who informs me that David Landry was terminated from UCLA and is scheduled for trial to face the sexual harassment and rape charges. The news is gratifying and carries the hope that justice will be served, though I find no pleasure in the destruction he left in his wake or in my invisible bond with the other women he'd violated.

I receive a letter from several members of the UC board of regents—not exactly an apology, but a concession that perhaps the "series of events" leading to my termination could have been more thoroughly investigated.

Flynn hires a team of IT experts and lawyers to scour the internet and send take-down notices for any sites still displaying the explicit pictures of me. While I know they likely won't be eradicated, the effort significantly decreases their visibility. The search results for my name now display articles about the Castille

Lighthouse, the Riley Flynn artwork, and my recent art history research.

I spend most of winter and spring working on my Maria Wood book, exchanging information with Graham and several other professors who have expressed interest in my findings. I've been invited to give two guest lectures—at Dartmouth and the University of Pennsylvania—and two graduate students have contacted me to ask if I'd be interested in serving as an adjunct advisor on their theses.

I'm still searching for Maria Wood's true identity, which Allegra insinuated has something to do with my own ancestry. When I consider I might be related through Max—and even through brilliant Juliette Perrin, crusher of glass ceilings—to a powerful, provocative artist who subverted convention and created a whole new aesthetic…how can I not hope that her wild, creative energy runs through my blood?

It's now my first spring in Maine. Fresh leaves pop from tree branches, flowers burst into colorful bloom, and the woodlands hum with birdsong.

After parking my car, I walk up the winding pathway. The lighthouse sits atop the cliff as sedate and calm as ever, a guardian of the sea. We'd closed it up for the winter, and the curtains and shutters are all drawn.

I cross the terrace and stand at the top of the trail sloping down to border the ocean. In the distance, the massive boulder is silhouetted against the gray, late-afternoon sky.

Lifting my arms, I stretch upward. My whole body fills with fresh air and determination.

Go!

I run down the hill. My sneakers thump on the hardened soil. My lungs expand. The trail is deserted, leaving me alone with the sky, the ocean, the pale circle of sun burning through the fog.

I keep running. My leg muscles start to ache, protesting the impact of the earth after several months on a treadmill. Salty air courses through my blood. My breath puffs out faster, harder. I squint at the boulder. Still far, but closer than it was.

The mechanics of my body take over. All thought disappears. My chest burns. My heart hammers. My thighs strain with protest.

I don't stop. *Won't.* I run and run and…

…fly past the three-mile boulder with a resounding *"whoop!"* of victory.

I slow to a heaving, gasping halt, bending to catch my breath. *I did it.* When my heartbeat calms, I straighten and do a little victory dance before starting back over the trail.

Next goal? Five miles. I am unstoppable now.

Digging a key out of my track pants pocket, I climb up the hill and unlock the lighthouse door. Memories wash over me the instant I step inside.

The air is musty, though I detect the faint scents of Assam and Darjeeling tea. Uncle Max's collection lines the walls of the workroom, the books shelved and cataloged, the paintings on display. All the fairy tales waiting to be retold.

The workroom isn't big enough to house the entire collection, and a number of books and artwork are still awaiting their final place. We have plans for all of it, Flynn and I.

When he returns from his editorial meeting in New York—any minute now, thankfully—we'll start planning the creation of the Max Dearborne Fairy Tale Library, an international resource for students, writers, scholars, artists, and anyone who wants to learn more about the rich heritage of enchantment woven through fairy tales.

Each room in the lighthouse will contain books, paintings, illustrations, and resources devoted to specific countries, with plenty of tables and comfortable chairs so people can research or simply sit and read.

In addition to the library, we plan to build an addition to the kitchen so we can open *The Mad Hatter Tea Shop*, a fairy-tale themed café serving pastries and, of course, a variety of teas. Flynn and I will be the establishment's co-owners, and when the library opens—hopefully in the fall to coincide with the publication of *Fiamma*—I'll start my official position as chief curator.

I leave the workroom and walk up the spiral staircase to the tower. I turn the light on. Flynn's desk, cabinets, and corkboard are all back in his office at Ramshackle Manor, so the tower is empty aside from the expansive view streaming in through the windows.

We haven't yet decided what role the tower will serve in the fairy-tale library. Flynn has suggested we keep a specific collection of fairy tale books here—Hans Christian Andersen, maybe—or use it as a reading and study space.

I have my own ideas for a Riley Flynn Room, a place to display the artwork he doesn't want to part with, and also for other local authors to give readings and lectures. We could even have small-scale art classes and children's programs here. The tower is too special not to share with everyone.

I look down at the ocean, the waves breaking along the cliff, the secrets wall bordering the plateau. A figure appears in the distance from the direction of the parking lot. Dressed in jeans and a black coat, his stride long and certain, his dark hair rumpled from the wind...he's unquestionably the man I love.

My heart spins, wild and happy. The past four days without him has felt like four weeks. Funny how I've gotten so *used to having him around.*

I start to turn, anxious to run and meet him, but he passes the front door and continues toward the hill. As if drawn by the light, like I have been so many times, he glances up at the tower. He keeps walking.

He stops by the secrets wall and takes something out of his pocket. After pushing it into the crevice of two rocks, he ambles to a bench, sits down, and...waits?

I hurry downstairs and open the front door. Our gazes meet

with a warm, sparking current as I pass him on my way to the wall. I kneel and reach between the cold, damp stones. His secret is the only one here.

I stand and unfold the crumpled paper. Written in his distinctive black scrawl is one sentence.

You are my favorite fairy tale.

A breath catches in my throat. I turn toward Flynn. With a smile, he stands.

My soul fills with a love so powerful it could make the sun rise. I cross the terrace and fly right into my husband's arms.

ABOUT THE AUTHOR

New York Times & USA Today bestselling author Nina Lane
writes hot, sexy romances about professors, bad boys, candy
makers, and protective alpha males who find themselves
consumed with love for one woman alone. Originally from
California, Nina holds a PhD in Art History and an MA in
Library and Information Studies, which means she loves both
research and organization. She also enjoys traveling and thinks
St. Petersburg, Russia is a city everyone should visit at least once.
Although Nina would go back to college for another degree
because she's that much of a bookworm and a perpetual student,
she now lives the happy life of a full-time writer.

www.ninalane.com

ACKNOWLEDGMENTS

As much as I love words, there aren't enough in any language to express my gratitude to the following people for their extraordinary help bringing Flynn and Eve's story to life.

Stacy Jerger, your insights, knowledge, and ridiculously sharp brain are treasures, and I love that I get to reap the benefits of them all. I can't thank you enough for the time and care you've invested in this book. Jessa Slade, your ideas never fail to get both me and my characters out of a rut and to take my stories to a whole new level. Cathy Yardley, I never want to write a book without you.

Lea Ann Schafer, how you perceptively pick up on things I can't see at all is a mystery for which I am so grateful. Corinne DeMaagd, thank you for pushing my ideas both in the right directions and outside of the box. Thank you, Lori Devoti, for your incredible knowledge of story structure, and Jennifer Bray-Weber for your insightful ideas. Kelley Heckart, your eagle-eyed copyediting is always a perfect polish to my books.

Danielle Sanchez of InkSlinger PR, thank you so much for your energy, support, and efforts on my behalf. I'm so thankful to have you in my corner.

Thank you infinitely, Letitia Hasser of RBA Designs, for working so hard on the beautiful cover; Paul Salvette of BB eBooks for the rock-solid formatting, and Wander Aguiar for the cover photo. An extra big hug to Andrey Bahia for getting the job done with such professionalism and speed.

Victoria Colotta, if I weren't so happy to have you as a friend, I'd be jealous of how multi-talented you are. From book and website design to art, writing, and editing—I don't know anyone else who can do it all so well. Thank you so much for bringing your A-game every single time.

Special thanks to my amazing friends and readers MJ Fryer, Rachel B., and Maria D. Your support and love leaves me speechless, and I still can't wait for the day when I get to hug you all in person. Warning: I will cry.

I owe an immeasurable debt of gratitude to the storytellers, folklorists, collectors, artists, and writers who have preserved fairy tales for countless generations. Though not a complete list, I relied heavily on the following resources.

The Original Folk and Fairy Tales of the Brothers Grimm, ed. Jack Zipes; *The Twelve Fairy Books,* ed. Andrew Lang; *From the Beast to the Blond: On Fairy Tales and their Tellers*, by Marina Warner; *The Hard Facts of the Grimms' Fairy Tales*, by Maria Tater.

Hans Christian Andersen, *The Snow Queen*, (1845): hca.gilead. org.il/snow_que.html

Hans Christian Andersen, *The Snow Queen*, Lit2Go edition, (1845): http://etc.usf.edu/lit2go/198/the-snow-queen

The Little Red Riding Hood Project: media.usm.edu/english/fairy-tales/lrrh/lrrhhome.htm, ed. Michael N. Salda, University of Southern Mississippi.

SurLaLune Fairy Tales: www.surlalunefairytales.com ©Heidi Anne Heiner

Folklore and Mythology E-Texts: www.pitt.edu/~dash/folktexts.html, ©DL Ashliman

Mapping the Fairy-Tale Heroine's Journey: theodoragoss.com/2017/04/03/mapping-the-fairy-tale-heroines-journey/ ©Theodora Goss

My ideas for Flynn's books and Maria Wood's art were inspired by the following artists:

Graeme Base: graemebase.com
Natalie Frank: www.natalie-frank.com
Hieronymus Bosch: www.hieronymus-bosch.org
Hiro Kamigaki, author of the *Pierre the Maze Detective* series
Chris van Allsburg: www.chrisvanallsburg.com

THE SPIRAL OF BLISS SERIES

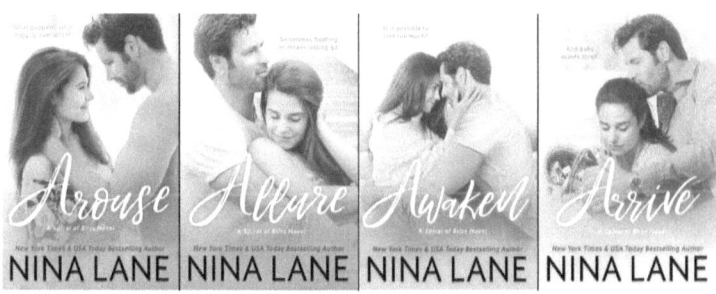

"Give me a kiss, beauty."

From an exhilarating crush to the intensities of marriage, Liv and Dean West embark on a passionate lifelong journey together. As the medieval history professor and his beloved wife face both personal challenges and painful battles, they never lose sight of the hope, humor, and devotion that belong only to them.

Liv and Dean's everlasting romance will melt your heart, turn you on, and enchant you with the power of a love to end all loves.

First we fell in love. Then we fell apart.

Shattered by tragedy a decade ago, two lovers fight the secrets that could destroy them.

"This book is a work of art."

A woman fleeing scandal. A town's mysterious recluse.

Lust and secrets collide in this provocative romance.

THE SUGAR RUSH SERIES

Taste the sweetness of life.

From the Stone family patriarch down to the youngest bad boy, follow the lives and loves of the Sugar Rush men in Nina's sexy, compelling series.